A former au pair, bookseller, marketing manager and seafront trader, **Jessica Gilmore** now works for an environmental charity in York, England. Married with one daughter, one fluffy dog and two dog-loathing cats, she spends her time avoiding housework and can usually be found with her nose in a book. fessional emotional romance with a hint of b............... and a great deal of de............... heroes!

USA TODAY bestselling and RITA® Award-winning author **Marie Ferrarella** has written more than two hundred and fifty books for Mills & Boon, some under the name Marie Nicole. Her romances are beloved by fans worldwide. Visit her website, marieferrarella.com

WINNING BACK HIS RUNAWAY BRIDE

JESSICA GILMORE

AN UNEXPECTED FATHER

MARIE FERRARELLA

MILLS & BOON

First Published in Great Britain 2021
by Mills & Boon, an imprint of HarperCollins*Publishers* Ltd,
1 London Bridge Street, London, SE1 9GF

www.harpercollins.co.uk

HarperCollins*Publishers*
1st Floor, Watermarque Building,
Ringsend Road, Dublin 4, Ireland

Winning Back His Runaway Bride © 2021 Jessica Gilmore
An Unexpected Father © 2021 Harlequin Books S.A.

Special thanks and acknowledgement are given to Marie Ferrarella for her contribution to the *The Fortunes of Texas: The Hotel Fortune* series.

ISBN: 978-0-263-29922-9

0221

MIX
Paper from
responsible sources
FSC C007454

This book is produced from independently certified FSC™ paper to ensure responsible forest management.

For more information visit: www.harpercollins.co.uk/green

Printed and bound in Spain
by CPI, Barcelona

WINNING BACK HIS
RUNAWAY BRIDE

JESSICA GILMORE

For Jess, Amelia, Mike and Kaia.

CHAPTER ONE

'Who was it, Charlie?'

'Just the postman.' Charlotte Samuels looked down at the heavy manila envelope she'd just signed for and hoped the wobble in her voice wasn't too obvious.

'Oh, is that my new dress? I didn't think it was going to get here in time.' Phoebe skidded into the hallway and stopped, throwing Charlie a concerned look. 'Is everything okay?'

'Everything's fine.' Charlie was aware her voice was too bright, too loud, too high, and she forced a smile as she turned to look at her cousin, best friend and house-mate, a three-in-one petite but forceful package. 'It's just the papers.'

'Papers?'

'The divorce papers.' She was trying for nonchalant and failing badly.

Phoebe shot a quick glance at the envelope. 'Already? It's only a few weeks since you and Matteo…' She tailed off and Charlie rushed to fill the awkward silence. If she kept talking, maybe she could convince herself as well as Phoebe that everything was completely fine. Never look back, that was her motto. Now more than ever.

'Yes, well, you know Matteo. There's nothing he can't achieve when he sets his mind to it!' Including, it seemed, helping her achieve a quick divorce. Almost as quick as their marriage.

'That's good though. Right? You can head off on your travels a free woman.' Now it was time for Phoebe to offer an unconvincing smile, worry clouding her grey eyes.

'Ye-es.' She could and she would. Maybe these very official papers would convince her stupid heart to catch up with her head and accept her brief, foolish marriage was well and truly over. 'Yes. At least, I'm on the way to being free. This is the notification that the judge is happy for us to divorce. Matteo has accepted the unreasonable behaviour cited so I—or my lawyer—need to go back in six weeks to take care of the rest. But if the lawyers act as quickly as they did with this…' she held up the envelope '…by the time I get back it will be as if my marriage never was.'

And then she could really move on. Because although she was a no regrets kind of girl, walking away from a marriage after less than a year was pretty monumental even by her standards. But she also knew that, no matter what anyone else might think, divorcing Matteo wasn't one of her crazy, impulsive moves; it was the best, the only thing she could have done.

Phoebe took another swift glance at the envelope. 'I've got a good idea. Let's make your leaving party a divorce party!'

'A divorce party?' Charlie wrinkled her nose. 'Isn't that a little bit tacky?' To say nothing of the fact that for once in her life she didn't *want* to party. She wanted to slink out of the country and hope that by the time she returned her failed marriage would no longer be the number one item on the village grapevine and she could go to the village shop without everyone staring at her as if she were some latter-day Miss Havisham, wandering the aisles in her wedding dress.

'Not at all,' Phoebe said staunchly. 'You deserve to get something out of this marriage after all, even if it's only a party. I still think you should have taken the settlement.'

Charlie sighed. She knew Phoebe wasn't alone in thinking she was an idiot to walk out of her marriage with nothing but the handful of things she had taken into it. After all, Matteo had more than enough money to keep *numerous* ex-wives, just as his father had—and did. But she hadn't married Matteo for money; she had married him for love. Maybe in the end love hadn't been enough but that didn't mean she wanted to profit from her shattered dreams.

'I couldn't, Pheebs. It would have felt like I'd been bought off. I want him to know that some things and some people are not for sale.'

'I hope your principles keep you warm at night,' Phoebe said and Charlie laughed at her cousin's disapproving tone.

'It's not like I'm destitute and starving. Thanks to Gran I have a home...' even if still living with her grandmother at twenty-eight might seem a little pathetic '...and there's always supply teaching if I can't find something permanent for the start of term. I don't need millions. I never did. I didn't really feel like me in that lavish life. I guess that was part of the problem.'

Not the whole problem. Matteo's continual absences, his workaholic tendencies, his habit of throwing money at each and every bump in the road had in the end been too much for her. But Charlie was self-aware enough to admit that her own discomfort in his gilded world hadn't helped. Too many people she'd met had seemed superior and superficial; she'd never settled in Matteo's expensively and sparsely designed Kensington mansion, never been comfortable spending the equivalent of a week's salary on clothes. Reverse snobbery, Matteo had called it. Maybe he'd been right.

'Just a small party,' Phoebe wheedled. 'A few friends and some drinks and nibbles to see you on your way and celebrate the start of your new life.'

'I don't know.' A divorce party was probably the kind of response most people would expect from her, but Charlie had always preferred the unexpected. 'Let me think about it.' She scooped up the rest of the post and took it through to the bright, welcoming kitchen which ran across the back of the cottage. She'd always loved this sunshiny room with its bright yellow walls, the wooden cabinets a soft green, the tiles a riotous rainbow of colour matched by the curtains and cushions. She couldn't imagine a greater contrast to the sleek silver and grey kitchen she'd left behind her in Kensington. She had still been discovering mysterious gadgets and cleverly disguised drawers the week before she'd left.

Charlie sank into a battered but supremely comfortable armchair, her grandmother's ginger cat immediately joining her, turning round and round on her lap before settling. Charlie stroked it absently as she grimaced at her cousin.

'"Marry in haste…"' Gran said, you said, everyone said. I need some leisure to repent. Maybe when I get back from travelling, when the divorce has been finalised, I might be ready to have some kind of gathering. But for now I just want to slink off to Vietnam, join Lexi and her friends, and try and forget the last year ever happened.'

The cat butted her hand, demanding more attention, but Charlie's focus returned to the envelope. She should be—she was—glad that, thanks to Matteo's contacts and willingness to be cited as the guilty party, the divorce looked as if it might be almost as speedy as their whirlwind wedding. But although she knew most people thought her wedding another of her madcap schemes, when Charlie had looked into Matteo's eyes and promised to love and honour him she'd meant it. She'd hoped to spend the rest of her life with him, hoped to start a family with him. But it took two to make a marriage work and so here she was, barely a year on from the day she'd first set eyes on Matteo Harrington, starting to figure out how to begin her life all over again.

A buzzing from the kitchen table alerted her to a call and she reached out for her phone, squinting at the unknown number. 'Yes?'

'Is that Charlotte Samuels?'

'I…yes. Who is this?' Dread stole into her chest at the grave official tone. 'What is it?'

'I'm afraid there's been an accident…'

'Matteo Harrington?' Charlie gasped at the reception desk and turned, wild-eyed, as the receptionist motioned to a doctor standing behind her. 'Doctor? Matteo Harrington? How is he?'

'Charlotte Samuels? Hello, I'm Dr Lewis. We have Mr Harrington in a private room through here. He is very lucky; he's got a severe concussion and a couple of broken ribs but it could have been a lot worse. Here, sit down.' And the doctor guided the suddenly dizzy Charlie to a chair.

'Thank you, but I'm fine.' Now. She hadn't realised how tense, how overwrought she had been until she heard the words *very lucky*. 'But I don't understand. Why is Matteo here? I thought he was in London. What happened?'

'The police will be able to tell you more, but I understand he swerved on a bend, maybe to avoid something.'

'He's a very good driver; he wouldn't speed,' she said mechanically. 'Can I see him?'

'Of course. Don't worry, he looks worse than he is, but he needs to be kept quiet, no sudden upsets or noise. But he'll be pleased you're here. He's asking for you.'

He is? She managed not to voice the question. Under the circumstances she thought she might be the last person Matteo would want to see. 'Yes, of course. Thank you.'

A nurse led her through the long corridor with its distinctive hospital aroma of disinfectant and boiled food until she reached a closed door and nodded at it. 'In there.'

'Thank you.' Charlie took a moment to collect herself before turning the handle and walking in. The room was dim, the blinds half closed, lit up by the lights on several machines clustered around the hospital bed, the silence punctuated by a reassuringly constant beep. She took a step closer to the bed and stifled a half gasp, half sob as she saw Matteo, propped up on pillows, eyes closed. It was very unfair. Even unusually pale, his forehead bandaged, Matteo managed to look absurdly handsome, the sharp lines of his jaw accentuated by dark shadow, his hair, for once, allowed to fall naturally, tousled over his brow. Charlie swallowed, aware of her own heart beating in time with the beep of the monitor.

Cautiously she approached the bed. Matteo looked so peaceful, all the stress and strain wiped as if it had never been, more like the man she had married than the one she had left. She nudged a chair a little closer and slipped into it, watching his chest rise and fall and doing her best not to think about how it would have been, how she would have felt, if he hadn't been very lucky.

'Hey.'

She startled at the rasp of his voice, turning her gaze to his face to find his eyes half open, a small smile playing about his sensuous mouth and, despite everything, her heart missed a beat, her treacherous pulse responding to him like it always did.

'Hey yourself. I just spoke to the doctor and she said you are going to be just fine.' She stopped, wanting to rush on and tell him that she was still his next of kin, for the next six weeks at least, that of course she had come, they were still friends, weren't they? But the doctor had said to keep him quiet and a rush of excuses didn't seem like the best way to do that. 'But you gave us quite a fright.'

'I'm sorry.' Slowly but determinedly he moved his

arm, taking Charlie's hand in his. His touch shuddered through her, familiar and yet forbidden. 'I don't know what happened. A rabbit maybe, or a bird.' He frowned. 'I can't remember.'

'What were you doing?' There was no reason for him to journey down to Kent, not any more. Not that she knew of anyway. Already there were things, places, people in his life she didn't know; she was no longer part of his present or his future.

She was his past, but it was her he'd asked for, her number he'd given to the doctors. Charlie tightened her grip on his hand.

'I missed you, Carlotta.' Her stomach tightened at the pet name only he used, a nod to his Italian DNA. 'I know it's bad luck to see the bride before the wedding, but...'

Wait? What? 'Wedding?' she whispered and his face twisted in confusion.

'How long have I been here? We didn't have to cancel, did we?'

'But Matteo, the wedding was nearly a year ago. We're already married!' And about to get divorced, she nearly added, but stopped as she saw the shock on his face. 'Don't you remember?'

Matteo Harrington scowled at the determinedly pleasant doctor. 'I know who the Prime Minister is and I can count to ten. There's nothing wrong with me. I am just missing a few memories, that's all.'

A few crucial memories. Like getting married. Like *being* married. How could it be June already? Over a year since he had swept Charlie off her feet. He'd known the moment he'd first laid eyes on her. *They'd* known. Even though the vivacious girl in her bright clothes and the rainbow stripes in her hair was completely unlike his usual type, she'd felt like coming home, warming him with her smile and enthusiasm for life, and by some miracle she felt the same way. Matteo had never believed in fate before.

But he couldn't remember a thing about their marriage. Not how Charlie had looked as she'd walked down the aisle, about the small, intimate reception at her local pub, attended by just a few close friends and her grandmother and cousin. Not the honeymoon…

A man should remember his honeymoon!

'What happens now?' Charlie asked, her face white, lips bloodless no matter how much she worried her usually lush bottom lip. 'Will he get his memories back?'

The doctor sighed. 'Amnesia is a lot rarer than the soaps would have you believe and every case is individual. In time, yes, most localised amnesia like this does resolve itself and I see no reason why this won't—but there are no guarantees.'

'So he may never remember?' Charlie whispered, even paler if such a thing was possible.

'It's unlikely but can't be discounted. More worryingly, Mr Harrington has suffered a severe concussion, no doubt a contributory factor, and the combination of the two means he needs to be kept quiet and allowed time to recover. No work, no sudden shocks. Peace and quiet is my prescription. Let his memory return in its own time.'

'No sudden shocks…' Charlie repeated, her voice pensive, but Matteo didn't have time to dwell on why that particular instruction had struck her; instead he homed in on the most important part.

'No work? Impossible. I'm the deputy CEO of Harrington Industries, Dr Lewis, I can't just rest and leave it to look after itself.'

'You want to get better? Then no emails, no work calls, no contracts. I suggest seclusion and no distractions until the concussion is healed. Longer. Give those memories a chance to come back on their own. My very strong recommendation is that you go on holiday. Take it easy. Or you might make things a lot worse.'

'Impossible,' he said flatly. 'I will, of course, try and cut down, but...'

He stopped as Charlie took his hand in hers, her fingers sliding through his. 'Matteo, you nearly *died*.' He could hear the wobble in her voice and hated that he was responsible for it. 'If the knock had been just an inch, less than an inch...' She paused and swallowed. 'Please,' she said. 'Listen, for once. There are things more important than work. You are more important.'

The echo of her 'for once' reverberated around his aching head, as if he had heard those words before. He shot a keen look at his wife. There was so much about her, about his marriage, he didn't know and the enormity of that struck him. He was always in control, always knew exactly what he wanted, when and how. This accident hadn't just physically weakened him; the loss of his memory had put him on the back foot, an intolerable situation. Returning to work, to order, would help him regain that control.

But then Matteo saw the tears brimming in Charlie's eyes and his conscience stirred. He looked up at the doctor. 'How long?'

'For you to stay quiet? At least two weeks. Allow your body, your brain some rest, Mr Harrington. Switch off and your memory will most likely return quite naturally. But push yourself too hard too soon?' She shook her head. 'My strong advice is don't.'

He sighed. 'Okay. You win. I'll do my best to rest.'

He felt Charlie relax beside him, heard her gasp of relief. 'Really?'

'Will it make you happy, *cara*?'

'Yes.'

'Then let me discharge myself and we will head home. I think we've trespassed on the good doctor's time long enough, don't you?' He started to pull himself to his feet, trying to hide his wince of pain as his broken ribs protested and his head swam.

'I would prefer you to stay in overnight for observation,' the doctor said and Charlie nodded.

'Besides, Matteo, we need to figure out where is the best place for you to recover. I don't think you should return to London. Far too tempting for you to start browsing the internet or watching the news and before you'd know it you'd be back at work.'

'True,' he conceded. 'Your house—I mean, your grandmother's?' Because, of course, Charlie would long have left the quirky cottage to move in with him. To his surprise she firmly shook her head, her expression unreadable.

'Too noisy. There's building work going on.' She chewed her lip again and then turned to the doctor. 'Can he fly?'

'It's not advised, but a short distance should be fine. No reading, no looking at screens, no bright lights and if you can lie flat then that would be best.'

'Then how about Italy? Matteo owns a villa overlooking Amalfi. Would that work?'

'Amalfi?' The doctor smiled. 'I honeymooned on the Amalfi coast. I can't imagine anywhere nicer to recuperate. As long as you take the journey slowly and steadily, you should be fine. But when you are there, rest.' She gave Charlie a stern look. 'Don't let him even read an email, keep him away from all news and try not to prompt him. Just live in the moment for a couple of weeks and let his memory try and come back naturally. No stress, no shocks, no over-exertion physically or mentally and he should be just fine. Just try and relax and enjoy yourselves.'

Amalfi. Italy. Home. For all he had been born and brought up in London, sent to school in the home counties, for part of him, Italy would always be home. Matteo half closed his eyes. He could feel the warmth of the sun, smell the all-pervasive scent of lemons mixed with the salt of the sea, see the vibrant blues and greens of that God-blessed coastline. 'We honeymooned there too.' He smiled at Charlie. He might not remember the honeymoon but he remembered the planning. 'Paris, then the Orient Express to Venice because the book is one of your favourites...' But at the shuttered look on Charlie's face he paused, uncertain, hating the holes in his memory. 'Have I got it wrong?'

'No, that was the plan, but we didn't get any further than Paris.' She looked away, her cheeks pink. 'A business deal gone wrong. We postponed the rest.'

'I'm sorry,' he said futilely. What had he been thinking? They had planned the honeymoon together and she had been so excited.

Charlie waved a dismissive hand. 'I understood. It's ancient history. I mean...' She stopped, a stricken look on her face. 'I am so sorry. Ancient history to me, but the future to you.'

'No, don't apologise.' This was ridiculous. They were married, in love, and yet they were dancing around each other like guarded strangers. 'I should apologise, for not having taken you to Amalfi yet. It shouldn't take an accident and memory loss to prompt me. But let me make it up to you. This can be a second honeymoon.'

He smiled but, to his surprise, Charlie avoided his gaze. Dread curled around his gut. Something was wrong. Very wrong.

'Yes,' she said. 'Lovely.'

CHAPTER TWO

'YOU'RE DOING WHAT?' Phoebe froze in her chair, her wine glass held up to her half-open mouth. 'Are you insane?'

Charlie plonked her bag onto the kitchen table and sank wearily into the opposite seat, pulling the wine bottle and spare glass waiting next to it to her. She had no idea how to truthfully answer that question. 'It would look weird if I didn't go with him, and the doctor said very clearly that Matteo wasn't to get any shocks. He knows we're married; there's no good reason why I *wouldn't* go.' Besides, she couldn't help replaying the moment she'd first seen him, lying so still, hooked up to all those machines, the doctor's words echoing in her head. *He is very lucky.* She had to make sure he was on the road to recovery before walking away. Again.

Phoebe looked over at their grandmother for backup. 'Can you hear this, Gran? No good reason? There's *plenty* of good reasons, Charlie. Number one, you're getting divorced. Number two, you're supposed to be flying out to Vietnam on Friday. What is Lexi going to say?'

Charlie poured a generous glug of the wine into

her glass and gratefully accepted the bowl of soup her grandmother held out to her, helping herself to bread from the plate in the middle of the table. 'This smells incredible, Gran, thank you. I don't think I've had a chance to eat since breakfast; there's something about hospitals that makes you lose all sense of time and appetite.' She took a bite of her gran's home-made bread, still warm from the oven, and immediately felt a little better.

'Pheebs, you know that Lexi has fallen in love—or lust—with some rugby-playing New Zealand backpacker. From what I can tell, she's at the smitten, can't-spend-a-second-away-from-him phase. Honestly? I think she'll be relieved if I don't turn up to be an awkward spare wheel on her holiday romance. And as for your number one, that's kind of the problem. Matteo doesn't know about the divorce, Phoebe. He doesn't even remember getting married. As far as Matteo is concerned it's last year. The day before our wedding.'

'But it's not. A lot has happened since then and you have wasted enough of your life on him. You don't owe him anything, Charlie.'

'No, but we *are* still married and I *am* still his next of kin, for the next six weeks anyway. It's my responsibility to get him safely to the villa and keep an eye on him until his concussion heals. Then, I just need to think of a good excuse to come home and by the time my absence looks suspicious hopefully he'll have remembered.' It wasn't much of a plan, but it was all she had. 'I did promise "in sickness and in health" after all.'

'Oh, Charlie. You promised for ever and ever, through good times and bad. And they are lovely sentiments, but that's all they are.'

'Phoebe!' her grandmother scolded, and her cousin looked shamefaced.

'I'm sorry, Charlie, but you have to admit, even by your standards this is a terrible idea.'

Charlie rubbed her eyes. All the adrenaline that had fuelled her through the long afternoon of tests and doctors had faded away, leaving her as worn-out as her grandmother's ancient tea towels. 'Phoebe, I know you're just trying to help, that you're looking out for me and I appreciate it, I really do. But I *have* to do this.' She hesitated, trying to find the right words. 'This isn't me doing something crazy because someone told me not to or because it looks like fun. This is me trying to do the right thing. I hate that we failed, Matteo and I. I hate what happened to us. That in the end I couldn't make it work.' She took a large gulp of her wine, looking for the courage to say the next words. 'You don't know how many nights I've lain awake and gone through every argument, every disagreement, every moment we just didn't connect and wondered if there's a way I could have played it better, if there's a way we could have fixed it.'

'Are you thinking that this might get you back together?' Phoebe couldn't have sounded more incredulous if Charlie had announced she was heading off to Mars. 'That because he's gone back to being the Matteo from before the wedding it's like a reset? Charlie, I know you love him but...'

'No.' She wasn't that naïve, not any more. Although how she wished she was, that this could be exactly what Matteo had suggested: a second honeymoon. Her cheeks heated as she remembered the touch of Matteo's hand on hers and the way her body had leapt to attention, just as it always had. Her mind knew that it was over, but her heart and body clearly had some catching up to do. 'No,' she said again, more strongly this time. 'It's too late. But something beautiful turned so bitter, so sad, it hurts me here.' She touched her heart. 'If I help now, if I do the right thing, maybe I'll finally manage some closure, whatever that is.'

'But…'

'That's enough, Phoebe,' their grandmother said from her usual chair by the big range cooker. 'Charlie's made up her mind and you need to respect that. For what it's worth, I think she's right. I just hope you're careful, darling. You've been through enough.'

'Nothing I didn't bring upon myself.' Charlie smiled wryly. 'Thank you for never saying it, Gran.'

'For not saying what?'

'That you told me so. And for giving me a place to come back to.'

'What else would I do? This is your home, Charlie. It will always be, as long as you need it.' Her home and her sanctuary. Charlie looked around the vibrant, warm kitchen with affection.

Both she and Phoebe had spent their teenage years here in this cottage. Phoebe's parents were in the RAF and often stationed all over the world, whilst Charlie's mother was an increasingly high-ranking diplomat, moving from posting to posting every few years. Charlie had hated the stifling restrictions of diplomatic life and when her grandmother had announced that Phoebe would be coming to live with her for her secondary education Charlie had insisted on doing the same, despite her parents' protestations.

'What's the plan?' Gran asked. 'Are you taking Matteo back to London before heading to Italy?'

Plan seemed like a very grand name for a hurried series of spur-of-the-moment decisions. 'Going back to London for a night would probably have made the most sense,' Charlie said. 'But the problem with deceiving is the tangled web I'm weaving. None of my things are back at the London house. I mean, all those fancy dresses and the jewellery might be, I don't know what Matteo did with it all, but none of my own belongings. My photos, my own clothes, books, the picture Mum and Dad gave me, I brought them all back here. He'd be bound to notice I had nothing personal there.'

'So you're heading straight to Italy tomorrow?'

Charlie nodded. 'As soon as he gets released. I called Jo—you remember Jo, his PA? I got in touch with her while he was in X-ray. It was more than a little awkward, because obviously she's been doing the paperwork for the divorce. But when I explained what had happened and what the doctor said, she was really helpful and agreed that this is the best course of action.' Jo's instant acceptance of the situation had removed some of the doubt from Charlie's mind. 'She's going to arrange for a driver to meet me at the hospital tomorrow, and from there we'll head straight to London City Airport, where the Harrington plane will be waiting for us.' She took another gulp of wine. 'Turns out there are some advantages to being married to an obscenely rich man.'

'And then what?' Phoebe motioned to Charlie to pass her the bottle of wine and poured herself a healthy second helping. 'Matteo is surgically attached to his phone and his tablet and his laptop, usually all three at the same time. How on earth are you planning to stop him checking his email and seeing a nice communication from his solicitor telling him the divorce is on track? Oh, I can see why you think this is the right course, Charlie, but there's no way it's going to work.'

'It's all taken care of.' Charlie wasn't exactly comfortable with the subterfuge, but Phoebe was right. It wasn't just the possibility of Matteo realising the truth about their marriage that worried her; it was his inability to switch off. There was no way he'd follow the doctor's orders if he had access to the outside world. The only solution seemed to be to up the deceit levels. 'The hospital handed everything that had been in the car to me. So I *might* have told him that everything was destroyed in the crash and Jo will sort out a new phone and courier it over.'

'Kidnapping him and cutting off all contact to the outside world? Nice work.' Phoebe grinned as she swiped the last piece of bread.

'I'm not kidnapping him!' Charlie's protest was half-hearted even to her own ears. She felt on pretty shaky moral ground, no matter how good her intentions. 'He owns the house in Italy and agreed, wanted to go there. And I have his stuff in my bag—when he gets his memory back, everything will be there waiting for him. But for the next couple of weeks, until he's outside the rest period the doctor prescribed, all contact comes through me. Luckily, Jo agrees; I am not sure how I would manage without her. Chauffeured limousines and private jets are making this whole situation easier.'

'I wouldn't know.' Phoebe stared dreamily into the

distance. 'Private jets have never been in my existence. But I'd love the chance to find out.'

'Take it from me,' Charlie said bleakly, 'there are worse things than flying economy.'

'Tell me that again when you finally reach Vietnam. Several hours crushed up against the person next to you while your seat is constantly kicked by the person behind and you'll be begging for the luxury of a private jet again.' She looked meaningfully at Charlie's left hand, where the paler skin showed clearly where her rings had been. 'Good thing you didn't sell your rings yet. It will be strange wearing them again, I guess.'

Charlie's stomach swooped and she automatically covered her left hand with her right. Taking the rings off had felt like such a huge step; she didn't want to wear them again, perfect as they were. Because they were perfect. 'I'll tell him they are being resized. I've lost some weight over the last few months.'

'You seem to have thought of everything. Okay, Charlie. If this is really what you feel you have to do then I'll support you in any way you need me to. Just let me know if you need anything at all. Especially onsite support. It'd be a sacrifice for me to spend a few days in a villa in Italy but anything for you.'

'Thank you. I can't tell you how much better I feel with you onside.' Another wave of weariness hit Charlie and she yawned. 'I'd better head up; it's been a long day and tomorrow won't be any easier.' She gave her cousin a quick hug and kissed her grandmother. 'I'll be gone very early tomorrow, but I'll call from Amalfi. Love you.'

She made her way to the door and paused, doubt filling her. Was pretending that their marriage was still okay the right thing to do, or would this deception just lead to more heartbreak in the future? But the doctor had been very clear; Matteo needed quiet and stability. Once he was well, he'd understand. And if he didn't? Well, what could he do to her now? His power to hurt her was over.

Or so she hoped.

'I can't believe Jo didn't have a phone ready for me; she is normally so competent.' Matteo sat back in the car, his hands idle. It felt wrong to be doing nothing; he was always holding something, a phone, a laptop, a steering wheel. He couldn't remember the last time he'd just sat with his hands heavy in his lap. He flexed them and scowled down as the bruises on his arms twinged, a reminder that this was no pleasure trip. The physical pain didn't bother him as much as what it signified: weakness. The loss of his memory, the instructions to rest, the ceding of control all ate away at him. He shifted again, ignoring the protest in his ribs.

'Competent doesn't begin to describe Jo,' Charlie said. 'She managed to pack our suitcases, organise the plane, the car from the hospital, this car to take us to the villa, all in less than twenty-four hours. She has also made sure that the villa has been aired and stocked with everything that we need, *and* she offered to tell your grandfather that you need two weeks' peace and quiet. I think you can let her off not replacing a phone within twenty-four hours. Not to mention the small fact that the doctor explicitly said no phones, remember?'

'Okay,' Matteo conceded. 'You may have a point.'

He sat back and tried to concentrate on the scenery, which got even more stunning as they left Naples and its environs behind them and headed south along the famous Amalfi coastal road. But he couldn't relax, something Charlie had said niggling away at him. 'Didn't you speak to my grandfather yourself?'

Charlie reached for her bag and avoided meeting his gaze, her blue eyes clouding momentarily. With a chill, the sense of wrongness Matteo had felt yesterday returned. 'I didn't get a chance. I'll call him when we get to the villa.'

The sense intensified. After all, a whole year was gone from his memories, wiped away as if it had never been. Anything could have happened in that time—and, God knew, his grandfather hadn't exactly been in the best of health last year. He'd been so angry with Matteo over his decision to marry as well, although whether it was the swiftness of the courtship or the fact that Charlie was a primary school teacher and not a tycoon or heiress, Matteo didn't know. But he could remember all too well the choler on the old man's face as he had shouted that Matteo was no better than his father, led by his emotions and not by his brain.

He pushed the memory away, wishing for a moment that his amnesia could have wiped that particular scene out as well. 'Charlie, don't hide things from me. Is there something I should know? Is he okay?'

She looked up quickly. 'Matteo, don't worry. He's fine, honestly.'

'But?' There was more here; he'd stake his life on it.

She bit down on her lip. 'Look, he did have a mild stroke last year, but it was very mild. That's the reason why we left Paris early and didn't go on our honeymoon, not a business deal like I said. But he made a full recovery and he's back at work as belligerent and difficult and demanding as ever. Honestly, the only reason I didn't speak to him yesterday was because by the time I'd left the hospital and made all the arrangements for today it was getting really late. And I was back on the road before breakfast. Besides…' she grimaced '…you should know that I am still not his favourite person. He thinks you could have done a lot better than me. He likes Jo. She handles him better than I do.'

But Matteo could barely focus on the reassuring words, her first sentence reverberating around his aching head. 'A slight stroke? In that case there's no way I should take this time off; he's going to need me more than ever. We should head back.'

'No.' Charlie put a hand on his arm and with a jolt Matteo realised how little she'd touched him all day. 'I promise you he's fine. Fighting fit. It's you who needs to take things easy now, and it's his turn to give you the time and the space to do that. That's what I'll be telling him later; it might be a little bit easier now he's had a night to sleep on it. The only thing I'm keeping from you is that I'm a complete coward who is secretly relieved that Jo was the one who broke the news to him. But I'll take my medicine later and call him, and you can take yours and stop worrying. Deal?'

Matteo paused, the familial duty instilled in him by his grandfather making it hard for him to respond. How could he relax when his grandfather, the business needed him?

'Look, Matteo,' Charlie said softly, 'we are all hoping

you get your memory back sooner rather than later but, even if you don't, at some point you'll return to work. And if your memory doesn't come back then you'll need an entire year's worth of decisions and plans explaining to you so you can get up to speed on any changes. It'll take you time to get to full effectiveness quickly, even without the tiny fact of a severe concussion. I know how hard it is for you to rest, I know you see relaxation as a dirty word, but if you really want to be back at full capacity then you need to recover properly. The last thing anyone needs is for you to have some kind of terrible relapse and be out for even longer just because you didn't do the right thing now.'

Matteo frowned but he couldn't deny the sense in her words. 'Okay.'

'Okay?' Her mouth curved into a teasing smile. 'Does that mean you'll do as you're told?'

'I'm not sure I'll go that far, but I will try to relax and not worry about what's going on back at the office.'

'I guess that's as much as any of us can ask for.'

Charlie lapsed into silence again, her focus on her own phone, which had barely left her hands since she had picked him up from the hospital that morning. Matteo leaned back and studied his wife.

Some things were familiar. The mint-green three-quarter-length trousers had a distinct fifties vibe, especially teamed with a pink flowery twinset, a matching scarf twisted in her hair, but there were changes too. Charlie seemed a little thinner and had deep shadows under her eyes that he devoutly hoped were a result of the last twenty-four hours and not something more permanent. The last time he remembered seeing her—just two days ago to him—she'd had platinum blonde hair, the tips a bright pink, replacing the sky-blue streaks she'd previously sported. Her hair was still blonde, but shorter, just past her shoulders and a darker honey shade, with strands of copper and bronze running through it. A little more sophisticated maybe, but he missed the pink.

'When did you change your hair?'

She put a hand up and self-consciously pulled on a lock of the shoulder-length waves. 'A few months ago. The way I usually wore it was okay for a primary school teacher, but I looked a little bit out of place at some of the dinners and events I attended with you.'

'That's a shame. I love never quite knowing what colour your hair will be, how you will wear it.'

'I...' She paused, still pulling the silky strand through her fingers. 'All that bleach takes a toll. I decided to give it a rest and a chance to restore. You know me. I'll be ready for something new sooner rather than later. Maybe I'll be a redhead for a bit.'

'Sounds fun.' But as the car continued purring along the twisty narrow roads Matteo realised that in many ways he didn't know his wife at all.

His wife. He'd always known he'd marry one day—there was the title and the company after all. A baronet needed an heir and there had been a Harrington at the head of Harrington Industries for over two centuries. Matteo had known his duty. But he'd assumed he would pick one of the perfectly nice women from his wider circle at some point and they'd spend a perfectly pleasant life together. Nothing exciting, nothing dramatic, just like his previous perfectly pleasant relationships.

And that was what he'd thought he'd wanted—after all, he'd grown up seeing all the fireworks and the subsequent messy fallout passion brought. He didn't need anything like that in his life.

But then he'd met Charlie and everything he'd thought he'd wanted, thought he'd known, had been swept away. A whirlwind romance, the papers had said, and now he understood what that meant because it had felt as if he had been taken over by uncontrollable forces from the moment he'd walked through the elegantly austere lobby of Harrington Industries to see a vivacious young woman doing her best to disarm their fierce receptionist. Charlie had been wearing a bright paisley shift dress straight out of the nineteen-seventies in lurid swirls of purple and green, her blonde hair sporting matching purple highlights.

'Can I help?' he'd asked, only to see the brightest smile he had ever witnessed light up vivid features as Charlie explained that she was trying to hand-deliver a box of brownies along with her application to the charitable trust Harrington Industries ran as part of their corporate responsibility programme.

'I promise you, it's not a bribe,' she'd said, the bluest eyes he'd ever seen fastened earnestly on him. 'I just want to show the trustees what's possible with the kitchen we have now so you can imagine just what we could do with bigger premises.'

Charmed, he'd offered to take her out for dinner to hear more and found himself captivated by her tales of village life and the small community centre that desperately needed renovating, where she held dance classes and helped her grandmother to organise cooking classes for lonely rural people.

'The brownies I brought were baked by a local farmer who had never cooked as much as pasta in his life. And now he's turning out the most amazing baking there's a good chance he's going to win all the prizes at this year's village show. Come and see for yourself. Please?' She'd raised imploring eyes up to him and he was helpless to say no.

Two days later they'd fallen into bed, a breathless tangle of desire and kisses; a week later he'd known he was falling in love. Less than two months later he'd proposed and they'd planned their wedding for three weeks' time. The earliest they could manage it. 'Why wait?' she'd laughed. It was the end of the school year, the perfect time to hand in her notice; her cousin could take over her dance classes. He could see no reason to delay.

It was as if colour had come whirling into his life, lighting up every dark corner and warming him through, and for once he didn't care about his grandfather's warnings, or the slightly amused expressions on his friends' faces as Charlie swept into the room in yet another gaudy vintage outfit, her hair barely the same colour or style twice, with no knowledge of social protocols. No, that wasn't true; she was a diplomat's daughter. She knew the rules perfectly well. She just didn't care and that, to Matteo, was one of the most attractive things of all. To him image and responsibility were everything. She showed him another way and it was intoxicating, living for the moment.

It was still hard to get his head around the knowledge that he was actually married to Charlie, that they'd been living together for a year. What was it like, waking up next to her every day? Had they settled into little routines? The problem with a whirlwind romance and a three-week engagement was that it gave him no benchmark. He had never spent more than a night at a time with her, not experienced normal life. It was supposed to be all to come.

For him it *was* all to come—he pushed the unwanted doubts to one side. He was married to the woman of his dreams and he couldn't wait to find out just what that meant.

CHAPTER THREE

SHE MIGHT HAVE spent years studying dance and drama but Charlie realised that, embarrassingly, she was terrible at improvisation, at least when it really mattered. Every time Matteo made a comment or asked her an innocuous question she prickled with defensiveness, as if he were trying to catch her out, not show genuine interest about his missing months. Interest in her. The kind of interest she'd stopped hoping for months ago.

To be fair, her hair *was* a sore subject. After all, he was the one who had asked her to look more grown-up and professional and not so much like a children's TV presenter. The words still hurt. Yet here was the proof that she hadn't imagined it; he had loved her hair, once. She tugged at a strand, inwardly wincing at the expensively, subtly blended colours. She'd meant to change it back weeks ago, had bought the dye and yet somehow had kept putting it off, hating the unwanted doubt he'd planted in her mind.

No, she reminded herself, thinking this way was unfair; her feelings were not the issue. Matteo had no clue about the last year, about all that had gone wrong, and so if she was going to be here she needed to act as if she was equally clueless.

Turning and looking out of the window, Charlie felt some of the tension ease from her tired body. The scenery was utterly glorious, the car smoothly negotiating hairpin bends above an impossibly blue sea stretching out to the sun-filled horizon, picturesque villages clinging to the cliffside below. She inhaled, taking it all in properly for the first time. She was going to be spending at least the next few days in this beautiful place so why not enjoy it? After all, it was only for a finite time. Once Matteo had the all-clear his memory would return—or she'd have to find a way to tell him the truth. Either way, she'd be heading back home. Who knew if she'd get the chance to travel here again? She needed to chill a little, be her normal live-for-the-moment self, not this uncharacteristically nervy person.

Mind made up, Charlie slipped her phone back into her bag and turned to Matteo, her smile genuine, not plastered on. 'How gorgeous is this? I can't wait to explore. Your maternal grandfather left you the villa, have I got that right?'

Matteo nodded, also visibly relaxing as he took in her enthusiasm. 'Yes, it's been in the family for generations. A bolthole and retreat long before this area became so fashionable.'

'It must be old then; wasn't this an upmarket Roman destination?' she teased and he laughed.

'It was. We must take a trip to Pompeii so you can see that for yourself. Maybe not *that* old, but we have owned land here for generations. To be honest, I was surprised when he left the villa to me and not one of my half-siblings or cousins; we weren't close. Maybe it was a way of binding me to here. My Italian grandparents, especially my grandfather, always felt that I was too English.'

'In what way?' She shifted round to look fully at him and, despite herself, she couldn't help hungrily taking in every inch of him. He was still uncharacteristically pale, the olive skin sallow, not glowing, his hair tousled, not ruthlessly tamed, shadows accenting his hazel eyes. All she wanted to do was reach out and hold him, run her hands through his hair, along the sharp defined lines of his jaw, touch her mouth to the pulse in his neck. She pressed her nails into her palm, the sharp pressure helping reinforce the barriers she needed to uphold for both their sakes.

'He was never comfortable with the fact that I was not just born and raised in England but stayed there even after my mother returned to Italy.'

'But didn't she leave you when you were still a child? You didn't have any choice in the matter.' She had never even spoken to his mother, let alone met her, and they hadn't invited her to their wedding—although, to be fair, they hadn't invited any of his family. Her parents weren't able to make it on such short notice so they had decided to keep the ceremony very small and hold a big celebratory party at a later date—but somehow they hadn't been able to find a date Matteo could commit to and the party had never happened. It was probably for the best. 'Wasn't she unfit to look after you? I thought your paternal grandfather had custody?'

'Not quite. My father had legal custody but he left me with my paternal grandfather; a small kid would have just been in the way of his lifestyle. But when my mother remarried I was old enough to choose, and I chose England.' He half shrugged. 'So my Italian grandfather had a point, I guess.'

'You didn't want to live with your mother?' How had they never discussed this before? She knew Matteo had been raised by his grandfather—if you called boarding school at seven and a series of nannies raised—and was pretty much estranged from his parents, but not that he'd had the chance to live with his mother and turned it down. With so much left unsaid no wonder they hadn't managed to build the foundations a successful marriage needed.

'Feelings didn't come into it. It was clear by then that my father would never be fit to take over Harrington Industries, that I was the heir. It was clear back when my parents first divorced. I can see why my grandfather wanted to make sure he brought me up in the right way.'

By sending you to boarding school before you could even tie your own shoelaces? Charlie managed to bite back the words. It had felt like a meaningful coincidence when they'd discovered they had both been mainly raised by grandparents while their parents lived abroad. But she had soon realised that her own cosy, comfortable upbringing with frequent contact with her loving parents could not have been more different from Matteo's cold reality: boarding school, his mother busy with a new family, an ageing playboy for a father and a stern, demanding grandfather he spent his life trying to make proud. She'd wanted to give him the family he'd never had, the unconditional love he needed and she'd failed. His scars were too deep for her to heal.

'I hope they knew that, no matter what choices were made for you when you were still a child, you are proud of your Italian heritage.'

'Proud? Of course I'm proud. But I've not visited the country much, not since my teens. And I barely use the villa, which I do feel bad about. As you'll see, it's far too nice to just be left empty, but as it's entailed I can't give it away or sell it. Truth is my mother uses it far more than I do.' He reached over and squeezed her hand and once again her whole body responded, a sweet, almost painful ache of memory. 'It will be good to spend some time there. Even if it did take concussion to make it possible.'

'We need to talk about your skewed priorities,' Charlie couldn't help but tell him, even as every part of her focused on the casual touch of his fingers round hers, tightening her own grip, despite herself. She'd missed the feel of him like a deep breath of fresh air. 'Whatever else comes out of all this, promise me that it won't take nearly dying for you to take a holiday again.'

Matteo returned the pressure, his hand wrapping round hers. 'As long as you promise to be there next to me.'

'I...' Charlie was saved from having to find an answer as the car took a sharp left and began to make its way up a vertiginously steep road. 'Oh, look, Matteo.' The world fell away beneath them, and as she twisted to look behind her she saw a beautiful small town at the foot of the cliff with whitewashed buildings clustered around the picturesque harbour.

'That's Amalfi,' Matteo told her. 'I can't wait to show you around. You'll never eat seafood anywhere else in the world to compare. And as for the *gelato*...'

'I've been dreaming of the *gelato* for the last twenty-four hours,' she said, transfixed by the scenery as the car kept climbing until they finally reached the small hillside town of Ravello, Matteo pointing out the sights as they went. He sat bolt upright, clearly delighted to be back.

'That's the Villa Rufolo,' Matteo said as they passed a spectacular building poised on the edge of the cliff, surrounded by beautiful gardens. 'Every year the village holds an arts festival—music, ballet, film—over three months, much of it centred there. World-famous performers take part. We should see what's on; it will start while we're here.'

'That would be lovely, if you're recovered that is. No loud noise or bright lights, remember?'

'I remember. But I was thinking, concussion isn't going to make this much of a second honeymoon, is it? And it sounds like the first one was cut way too short. So let's spend some real time here, a week or so for me to recover and then a couple of weeks of proper holiday. What do you say?'

What could she say but, 'That sounds lovely'? And it *did*, painfully so. Because this was how she had imagined her marriage to be—not the holidays or the private jets or the chauffeured cars, but the spending time together, the making plans, the spontaneity. After all, that had been their courtship—short, full of spur-of-the-moment plans and so very sweet. But their actual marriage had been so very different once real life had intruded into their idyll. Now here they were, back in time. Was there a chance this Matteo would choose a different path or was he doomed to make the same choices, the way she'd come to realise he'd been programmed to do?

Ravello was as charming as Matteo had promised with its red-roofed whitewashed buildings and village squares full of cafés and restaurants. The car drove through the village and a little further up the steep hill before pulling in at a wrought-iron gate which swung silently open at their approach.

The curving driveway was surrounded by flowers, bright pink bougainvillea and many others she couldn't name in vivid hues of pink, red and purple contrasting with the gleaming white of the villa ahead. Charlie tumbled out of the car as soon as it drew to a stop, forgetting for one blissful, flower-scent-filled moment why she was here, almost drunk on the beauty of the scene before her. A large courtyard filled with lemon trees led to the front of the imposing old villa with its arched balustrades and balconies overlooking the gardens and spectacular views of the sea. In a daze, Charlie followed the path round to a shaded terrace, also heady with the scent of lemons and spring flowers, wandering down stone cut steps to a sunbathing terrace on the very edge of the cliff, leading to a magnificent old swimming pool with marble steps descending into its blue depths, classical statues at every corner. This was no sleek modern home but a place rooted in history, from the greenery covering the villa to the twisted trees on the cliff edge.

The ache she'd carried inside her for months now

seemed to swell under all this beauty. She could have been so happy here. They could have been so happy.

She sensed rather than felt Matteo come up behind her, his arms slipping around her waist in a hold so natural it almost undid her. 'So, what do you think?'

'I think it's the loveliest place I've ever been.'

'Then it's the fitting setting for you,' he murmured against her neck and her stomach tightened, every nerve straining towards the faint touch of his lips, the whisper of his breath, and she wanted this moment to be real with every fibre of her being.

They could have been so happy—and maybe they still could. She had told Phoebe this was no start over, that she would leave as soon as she possibly could, but why not take this unexpected time and see if there was any way of trying a different path, searching for a different outcome? She was no fool. Matteo would hopefully regain his memory soon, and if not then she would have to tell him the truth. But if they were in a stronger place when she did so, then maybe things would seem different. The failure of her marriage had eaten away at her, but if she could honestly say she had given this unexpected second chance all she had then would she be able to achieve the closure she so desperately needed?

All she knew was that fate had intervened and given her an opportunity to step back in time and reshape her marriage. She could throw this chance away or she could adopt some of those old techniques from her drama classes. Not *pretend* that things were okay between them but to live as if they *were* okay. To become the character, not act the character. It would be easier for them both.

But she had to keep a guard on her heart. Because she'd nearly been broken once. She couldn't let it happen again.

Matteo inhaled, the scent of lemons and flowers tinged with salt taking him instantly back to childhood, to roaming free with his cousins, long lazy days by the pool or out at sea, the warmth of summer evenings as the grown-ups drank wine and talked, the children playing out till late like puppies, left to tumble until they slept where they fell. A bigger contrast to the confines of boarding school with its strict lights out and every moment timetabled it was hard to imagine. And yet in the end he was the one to turn his back on the villa and family, spending his summer in his grandfather's office instead, thinking the suit and tie made him an adult. Responsible. The man he had to be.

Long, sun-drenched days were for his dissolute father, his fun-seeking mother. Not for real Harringtons. Or so he'd believed. Still believed, much as he wanted to do otherwise. But he yearned for colour. That was what had first drawn him to Charlie, with her sunshine disposition and rainbow clothes. With her spontaneity and joy.

And she was his. Now he could make new memories. Memories with his wife. He tightened his hold on Charlie, burrowing his face in her hair. How could he have forgotten their wedding, the few days of honeymoon they'd managed, their life together? It seemed impossible that today wasn't their wedding day. Still, it was their honeymoon…

'Come on, let me show you around.'

Charlie turned to face him. 'I have a better idea. I'll have an explore while you rest.'

'Rest?' he scoffed, refusing to acknowledge the persistent pulse in his temples, the soreness in his ribs, the stiffness of his neck and shoulders. 'I don't need to rest after a short journey like that. This sun and the view is all I need.'

'Not according to the doctor's instructions,' Charlie said sweetly, pulling a typewritten list from her pocket.

Matteo groaned. He was already heartily sick of that list. Thanks to it he'd been forced to spend the whole flight reclining back, no film or book to occupy him, and wear sunglasses through the airport like some attention-seeking pop star. 'I'll show you around then sit on the terrace for an hour,' he countered, but his obstinate wife shook her head.

'You'll lie down and have a nap.'

'A nap? I am not having a nap.' But he *was* drained, the early-afternoon sun hot on his aching head, the light painfully bright despite the dark glasses, and secretly he couldn't help thinking that a darkened room sounded rather enticing.

'A siesta then. Does that make it sound more respectable?'

'A sun lounger on the terrace.' But Matteo knew when he was fighting a losing battle and accompanied Charlie back to the villa door with only the minimum of face-saving grumbling.

The villa door was wide open, Maria, the housekeeper, waiting for them, and Matteo subjected himself to her shocked outcry as she fussed over his cuts and bruises and scolded him for his carelessness, pausing only to embrace Charlie in loud, voluble Italian that his wife clearly couldn't understand before switching to her excellent English. 'Signor Matteo, welcome home. And to bring the beautiful *signora* with you. But you must rest. Your bags are in your room. Come, come.'

He clearly was going to have to assert his authority soon. Otherwise, between Charlie and Maria, he would find himself wrapped in a blanket and forbidden to move. '*Grazie*, Maria, it's good to be home. I don't suppose you have any of your excellent lemonade and those delicious biscuits of yours ready, do you?'

'But of course, I will bring them to you,' Maria said. '*Signora*, would you like yours on the terrace?'

'Please. And do call me Charlie.' Charlie grinned up at him as Maria bustled away. 'Don't tell me; she knew you when you were a baby?'

'Practically. She's worked here all her life—she is supposed to be retired now, just make sure that the villa is aired and organise cleaners every now and then, hire staff for when my mother is here, but whenever I manage to get here she insists on looking after me herself. She lives in the village with her family though. You don't mind not having twenty-four-hour staff?'

'A year of marriage hasn't left me unable to make my own cup of tea or pick up my own clothes,' Charlie assured him as they ascended the sweeping curved staircase that led from the large hallway to the upper floor. Since inheriting the villa Matteo usually took the corner suite with its sea views, sizeable en suite bathroom and dressing room and, sure enough, his small suitcase was already lying open in the dressing room; he hadn't asked Charlie to pack much, he kept a wardrobe here for the too rare occasions he visited. The windows were flung open to let in the warm sea air but shuttered against the sun, the bed freshly made up.

'Hang on, where's your bag?' He could only see his suitcase, already half unpacked, his washbag in the en suite bathroom.

'I asked for a separate room to be made up for me,' Charlie said and held up a hand as he tried to protest. 'Rest, Matteo. Fluids and plenty of rest; that's what the doctor said and that's what you are going to get. Right now this isn't a holiday and it definitely isn't a honeymoon; it's a place for you to get better. And that will take at least a week or two of early nights, late mornings and siestas.'

'And what will you be doing while I'm re-enacting *Sleeping Beauty*?' It struck him that he had no idea what Charlie did nowadays. Was she teaching? Doing something else? His wife was a mystery—one he was desperate to unravel. But not now, not while the pressure in his head began to tighten to vice-like proportions and his ribs ached.

'Me? I'm planning to go dancing in the village, flirt with dark-eyed Italian men and drink Prosecco. That's okay, isn't it?'

'Only if you wait for me.' But the pain was intensifying and it was harder and harder to sound nonchalant. Matteo slipped his shoes off and gratefully lay down on the cool bed, closing his eyes as Charlie sat lightly next to him, stroking his hair with soft, soothing fingers.

'Do you want me to go?' she half whispered and he reached up to hold her hand in his.

'No. Don't leave me, Charlie. Promise you won't leave,' he managed as fatigue crashed down and carried him away. But as he fell into a deep sleep he could have sworn he heard his wife swallowing back a sob, and felt a tear fall onto his brow.

CHAPTER FOUR

'Every morning I promise myself that I'm only going to have fresh fruit and some of this delicious yoghurt for breakfast.' Charlie sat back, smothering a groan. 'And yet every morning I somehow manage to not only heap my plate with bread and cheese and these little pastries, but I always finish off with lemon cake as well. Lemon cake! For breakfast! You're going to have to roll me onto the plane to get me home if I carry on like this.'

It wasn't just the breakfast. Lunches and dinners were ostensibly healthy, thanks to the concussion-friendly diet sheet the doctor had provided, involving lots of salad, fish and olive oil. But the meals also came with slices of warm home-made bread and meltingly delicious garlic-fried potatoes and were always followed by creamy tiramisu or delicate little sponge cakes served with lemon cream—and Charlie usually managed seconds of everything.

'Maria's lemon cake is the stuff of legend.' Matteo reached for another sizeable slice with a grin. 'You might as well make the most of it while you're here because, I promise you, you'll be dreaming about it for months.'

'I can believe it. In fact, I'll be dreaming about this whole place every night, wishing I was sitting here, eating my bodyweight in cake. Can you tell me again why we live in London when we could be living here?'

'Right now, I'm not entirely sure,' Matteo admitted. 'But if this was normal life, would it feel this special or would you just gulp down a coffee and not even notice the view?'

'I'm up for testing that theory.' Charlie tilted her face up to the already hot morning sun and closed her eyes, letting the warmth permeate through to her bones. It had, in some ways, been an almost idyllic week despite the oddity of her situation. Her initial worries over Matteo's health had quickly disappeared, along with his headaches and the fading of his bruises. A local doctor had come out to see him the day before and suggested he continue to take it easy for another few days to be on the safe side, but assured them both that he was well on the road to recovery. As long as there were no more headaches, double vision or any of the other symptoms in the leaflet she still carried in her bag everywhere she went, he should be safe to resume normal life by the end of the week.

Normal life. The words which filled Matteo with such pleasure caused nothing but dread to Charlie, and it had been hard to match his delighted smile. Normal life meant that he wouldn't be able to resist checking in with his office and then what? Once work intruded he'd lose the relaxed, playful air she had missed so much, his responsibilities once more weighing him down and taking centre stage.

Normal life would mean the return of his phone and

contact with other people, with his grandfather, who was champing at the bit to speak to Matteo. After an extremely awkward conversation and some initial resistance she'd persuaded his grandfather that Matteo needed this holiday, reiterating the doctor's instructions that Matteo stayed quiet and received no sudden shocks. But she still didn't trust the old man not to let something slip about the divorce; she knew full well he was no fan of hers.

She took another thoughtful sip of her coffee, her gaze lingering on Matteo. He had tanned even in the short week they'd been here, his skin no longer sallow but a deep olive, setting off the dark fuzz that covered his jaw. The casual short-sleeved shirt highlighted the breadth of his shoulders, the undone top buttons showing the hollow of his throat, the vee of his chest. Her stomach tumbled, tightening with a desire that had never, not even in the worst of times, gone away. It felt like such an illicit pleasure, sitting looking at her husband, allowing her gaze to linger on every plane and hard muscled edge.

It was an illicit pleasure because he was no longer hers to enjoy. And that was increasingly becoming a problem. Normal life didn't just mean access to phones and emails. Normal life meant Matteo would be expecting them to be the still practically newlyweds he thought they were, the passionate-about-each-other, head-over-heels couple he remembered. He was already making it more than plain that he would prefer Charlie to be sharing his room, his bed, and every night it was harder and harder for her to resist his playful entreaties.

It was harder and harder for her not to throw cau-

tion to the wind and react when he touched her waist in
passing or took her hand as they walked around the gardens. Not to turn and kiss him when he slipped his arms
around her waist and held her, when he kissed the exact
place on her neck he knew always sent her weak with
desire. Not to allow a quick affectionate kiss to develop
into a longer embrace. Easy, intimate gestures, each one
an exquisite torture. More than once she'd allowed the
moment to go on a few seconds longer than was wise,
unable to break the embrace with an easy laugh and a
reminder that he needed to take it easy, just revelling
in the feel and the touch of him. But in the end she always stepped away. Anything physical would only be
a lie for them both. However much she wanted to she
couldn't ignore the envelope of not-yet-posted divorce
papers packed in the bottom of her suitcase—nor the
reasons they existed.

'What shall we do today?' Matteo finally pushed his
plate away and picked up his coffee, wincing theatri-
cally. Charlie was still enforcing the no caffeine rule,
much to his loudly voiced disgust.

'Why don't we, oh, I don't know. How about we
swim and sunbathe or we could sunbathe and swim?
Or go crazy and do both?'

Matteo peered over the top of his sunglasses to give
her a mock stern look. 'Nice try, Charlie, but the doctor said I was quite okay to leave the villa.'

'Well, yes, but he did stipulate that you still needed
plenty of rest and plenty of fluids and to take things
easy and not to rush anything…'

'Noted, but I don't think a walk in the village is going
to tax me too much, do you? They even have establish-

ments that sell beverages to keep up those fluid levels. Come on, Charlie, you must be going stir-crazy. We've been here a week and you haven't left the villa once.'

'That's what you think, but I've been out, drinking Prosecco and dancing with dark-eyed Italian men every time you've been snoozing, so don't you worry about me.'

But although his mouth curved into an appreciative smile the expression in his hazel eyes was still firm. The truth was that although Matteo had repeatedly suggested that she go and explore, walk around the village, take a taxi or a local bus down to Amalfi or even along the winding road back to Sorrento with its designer shops and fancy restaurants, she had yet to leave the luxurious confines of the villa. She knew that Maria was more than capable of keeping a close eye on Matteo, but Charlie still didn't like the idea of leaving him on his own. She told herself it was because she was there solely to make sure he was on the road to recovery, but the truth was she was loving the long lazy days with nothing to do but read, swim, play cards and enjoy each other's company. This was how she had imagined their marriage to be, companionship not loneliness.

The only awkward moments came when Matteo asked questions about their life together. Not wanting to lie to him any more than she already was, Charlie had put off answering for now, reminding him that the doctor said it would be best to see if his memory came back by itself before trying to prompt it in any way. But, much like their sleeping arrangements, she knew she could only put him off for so long.

Matteo pushed his chair back and got to his feet in

one lithe graceful movement. 'Come on. Up you get. Let's go.'

'You have to give me time to get changed,' she protested. 'I'm not wearing any make-up and this dress is barely fit for lounging round the pool, let alone being seen in public.'

'You look beautiful,' he said. 'You always do.'

'Even so. Give me five minutes.' She touched his arm lightly as she passed him, wanting more than anything to hold on tight and let him anchor her, to hear him tell her again that she was beautiful. To see appreciation in his heated gaze, not cool impatience as he suggested she might be more comfortable in something less like fancy dress.

What would happen if his memory never returned? This time would he always tell her she was beautiful, like the colours she chose for her hair, appreciate the bright vintage styles she preferred? Or would he once again come to find her too much for his moneyed, sophisticated world and seek to tame her, to suggest chartreuse and olive and slate dresses in draping fabrics, diamond studs and subtle make-up?

Almost defiantly, Charlie pulled out a red polka dot halterneck dress with a full circle skirt and wide white belt, teaming it with huge hoops and a string of false pearls, each the size of a baby's fist. She carefully outlined her lips in deepest red, filling in the colour before layering on the mascara. She added a jaunty hat and a pair of cat's-eye sunglasses and gazed at herself in the mirror. It was months since she had been so very much her. This was the Charlie Matteo had fallen in love with, and this was the Charlie who didn't fit into his world.

If she was going to survive the rest of this trip with what was left of her heart intact, then she needed to be herself more than ever. Armour, weaponry and retreat wrapped into one red-lipsticked package.

Charlie looked good enough to eat. Lightly tanned to the colour of the milkiest coffee, she was like a delicious chocolate enticingly hidden in a polka dot wrapper, and all Matteo wanted to do was unwrap her.

In fact, all he'd wanted to do for a whole week was unwrap her as she lay on a sunbed next to him, encased in a series of vintage-style bikinis, all ruffles and straps and tempting shades of pink and yellow and turquoise. But Charlie was adamant. He was meant to be resting and that, in her book, seemed to mean celibacy. Separate beds, separate rooms and barely a peck on the cheek at night. It was enough to make a man ill, not cure him.

'Come on, wife.' The word was still new to him, strange yet exotic, with all its connotations of belonging. He tapped a foot mock-impatiently as she emptied half the contents of one bag into another. He'd been cooped up for too long and, nice as it had been to be so uncharacteristically indulgently lazy, his body was now primed for movement, for exercise, to walk off some of this ache in his body.

An ache that intensified as Charlie slowly and deliberately settled her outrageously huge sunglasses over her eyes and adjusted her hat to an even more jaunty angle, every curve exaggerated by the halterneck of her dress.

How had he got so lucky?

She gave herself one more long look then nodded. 'Okay. Ready.'

'Then let's go.' He held out his arm with exaggerated courtesy and, after a brief hesitation he couldn't help but note, she took it. Her light touch on his arm was like a balm, soothing some of the ache inside him.

It wasn't just the physical distance between them that preyed on his mind. There was an emotional distance too that Charlie was trying very hard to hide, but he could sense all the same. She was clearly watching what she said to him, stopping or backtracking or changing the subject with an airiness belied by the anxiety in her expression, her eyes sometimes so haunted with sadness it hurt him to see. She'd assured him that both of their families were safe and well, that Harrington Industries was thriving, but something was responsible for those shadows. If it wasn't their families, his business, then was it him? Was it *them*? Was their marriage less than perfect after less than a year?

He could, maybe should, demand answers even though she'd made it plain she wouldn't answer any questions, not yet. But in the end he'd decided not to notice her sudden pauses or abrupt subject swerves and didn't press too hard with any questions, not sure if he wanted the answers after all. He'd never considered himself a coward before but forcing the truth out of Charlie was a step he just couldn't face yet. Not when there were times when the shadows ebbed away and her smile tilted those provocative lips and he could tell himself he was imagining things.

It took them less than fifteen minutes to reach the village square, the sun beating down relentlessly as they walked down the steep footpath leading from the villa gate to the village, a handy shortcut bypassing the windy road. The season was in full swing and every restaurant had tables and chairs spilling out onto the square, each filled with a mixture of tourists and locals.

'It's so busy,' Charlie said in surprise. 'I thought this was a sleepy hillside village.'

'Once maybe, but not for many years—Ravello is filled with boutique hotels, exclusive villas, expensive shops and people prepared to pay outrageous prices to enjoy the views—although not as outrageous as Capri. I'll take you over there one day soon. Prepare to be amazed at just how much a coffee can cost if you sit in the main square there. But it's an experience not to be missed.'

'Sounds fun.'

Matteo took Charlie on a circuitous route through Ravello. He wanted to show her everything. It had been several years since he'd spent more than a couple of days here, but with every step he felt more and more as if he had come home. Every alleyway, every ancient villa, every peep of a courtyard garden, every hidden restaurant and café was as familiar to him as his Kensington square. He exclaimed over several changes of ownership as they walked past shops and restaurants, insisting on buying Charlie *gelato* from his favourite ice-cream maker, even though she protested that she was too full from breakfast to manage more than a few bites.

'The cathedral is definitely worth taking a look at,' he told her as they wandered down another alleyway. 'And there's a little museum with some rare Roman finds in it as well, but the main attraction in Ravello is the villa and the botanical gardens. They're on every Amalfi coast must-see tour.'

'It all sounds amazing,' she said, taking another lick of the ice cream she managed to almost finish despite her earlier protestations. 'Ravello may be small, but it's definitely not sleepy.'

'That's its charm,' he said. 'Being here feels like living in the perfect Italian hillside village, only you get spectacular views, five-star food, concerts with world-renowned artists and high-end shops as well. But, of course, there's so much to do all round here; you can get a boat from Amalfi over to Ischia and Capri, travel up the coast to Positano or to Sorrento, further afield to Naples or Pompeii or Herculaneum...'

'You've missed your calling as a tourism expert.' Charlie grinned up at him. 'If you ever get bored of being a business tycoon you could turn the villa into a B&B and take people all over the coast. I'd sign up. Hang on.' She looked down at her hands in surprise. 'Where did that ice cream go? I could have sworn I wasn't going to manage more than a couple of bites.'

Matteo laughed, taking her hand in his, and her fingers closed round his as they fell into step together. He'd been an idiot, seeing things that weren't there. Those concerns, the imagined silences were just because she was worried about his concussion. Everything was perfect between them, just as it should be. As he had known it would be. His grandfather had told him he was a fool to marry a girl he hardly knew, a girl with no connections, without a family name to use or a business to utilise. But Matteo had known what he wanted, what he needed. And, for once, his views weren't the same

as his grandfather's. He owed the old man a lot, everything. The only stability he'd ever known for a start.
But that didn't mean he could dictate who Matteo fell
in love with.

They continued wandering along, looking in the shop
windows and reading the menus of every café and restaurant they passed, planning what they'd have in each
one until, turning a corner, Matteo heard his name
called and, stopping, saw a slim dark-haired woman
pushing a buggy, with children either side, hurrying
towards him, her face wreathed in smiles.

'Lucia, how lovely to see you. What are you doing
here?'

'Matteo, I wondered when I'd see you. Maria told me
you were in town. This must be your beautiful wife…'
She held out a hand to Charlie and, when Charlie took
it, embraced her with a quick triple kiss. 'I am Lucia,
Matteo's cousin, not that you'd know it, for all the communication I have with him.'

'Hi, Lucia, I'm Charlie,' Charlie said, smiling back,
although her smile seemed a little forced. 'It's lovely
to see you. I've not met any of Matteo's Italian family
so far. In fact Maria is the only person I've met since
I've been here.'

'In all the ways that count, Maria is family. We were
all terrified of crossing her when we were younger but
we wouldn't be without her now. I moved here several
years ago, Matteo. Giuseppe, my husband, is a wine
merchant and specialises in the region. And these…' she
waved her hand at the buggy and the children standing
by it '…these are my children, not that you probably
remember them.'

'I do,' he protested and she grinned.

'Go on, name them.'

Matteo held up his hands in surrender. 'I wouldn't want to deprive you of the pleasure of introducing your children.' He knew he'd sent gifts for each birth—or, rather, Jo had; gifts for christenings and Christmas and all his cousins' children's birthdays were programmed into his work calendar so Jo could send a generous cheque in their direction, but that was as far as his knowledge of the younger generation went. His lack of engagement didn't bother him, usually. But today he felt a slight inkling of something that felt a little like guilt, and possibly an acknowledgement that in some ways he had missed out. They had all been so close as children and he hadn't even attended a single wedding or birthday party, hadn't contacted them when he was over on a duty visit to his mother. If he and Charlie had children, this would be their family. He would want them to grow up as surrounded by love and laughter as he had—during the summer holidays at least. Not the lonely austerity of the rest of his childhood, the many months he'd spent in England at school or rattling alone around his grandfather's country estate or the cold, forbidding house on Richmond Hill.

'This is Elena.' Lucia indicated the small girl sleeping in the pushchair. 'Lorenzo.' She laid a hand on the head of a boy of around six. 'And this is my Rosa.' She put an arm around an older girl of eight or nine who had red-rimmed eyes and a sulky look on her face, then gave Matteo a hard stare. 'Your goddaughter, Matteo.'

Charlie shot him a quick glance. 'You have a goddaughter?' She sounded surprised and Matteo shifted slightly uncomfortably.

'Haven't I mentioned it? Her, I mean.'

'No.'

He shifted again, searching for the kind of diplomatic words that might get him out of this awkward situation, only to grin a little sheepishly as Lucia and Charlie looked at each other, identically pursed mouths before laughing.

'Completely useless,' his cousin said, nudging him affectionately and Charlie nodded.

'He is. I am so sorry. I wish I'd known; I've always wanted to be an aunt. I am an only child so am already planning to spoil any children my cousin has as much as possible. You will have to let me take you out for ice cream or something when I'm here, Rosa. If that's okay, of course.' She clapped a hand over her mouth, looking embarrassed. 'I forgot, of course, she doesn't speak English. She must think I'm a right idiot, babbling away to her in a foreign language.'

At that Rosa's mouth twitched into something close to a smile. 'Oh, she speaks a little,' Lucia said. 'She's just not speaking very much at all right now. She is very disappointed, and I can't do anything to fix it.'

'Oh?' Charlie took off her sunglasses and looked sympathetically down at the small girl, her smile understanding. 'Is there anything I can do to help cheer you up? I am sure Matteo owes you at least eight years' worth of treats; do you want to claim one today?'

Matteo had never really seen Charlie around children. He knew, of course, that not only was she a primary school teacher but that she also worked some evenings in a local dance school. It stood to reason that she would like children, be interested in them. But seeing her display such empathy warmed him. His own parents had been so disinterested in him, and he himself knew very little about children. But he couldn't help a vision of him and Charlie walking down a street, surrounded by their own sons and daughters, just as his cousin was—and for the first time such a thought didn't terrify or bore him. It excited him.

'She's a good person to tell problems to, Rosa,' he said. 'And she has a point about those treats.'

Rosa slowly shook her head, tears welling up and spilling over, splashing down onto her thin cheeks, and Lucia sighed. 'There's no point crying, Rosa,' she said. 'There's nothing to be done and you just have to accept it.' She looked up at Matteo and Charlie and shrugged. 'Rosa here is a very keen ballet dancer and she is very lucky to learn with a wonderful teacher. They have been working towards a gala in two weeks' time, to raise money, you see, for the refugee children who live in the region. It is a good cause. And Rosa was to have a solo. But, unfortunately, her teacher's mother has just been taken into hospital and so Signora Natalia has had to go back to Roma. So no gala, no solo for Rosa, and right now it feels like the end of the world.'

'It's not just a solo,' Rosa ventured in a little voice still thick with tears. 'It is because of Violeta…' Her voice wavered again and then broke. Matteo quickly translated so Charlie could understand and Charlie crouched down to look into Rosa's woebegone face.

'Violeta?'

Lucia nodded. 'Yes, Violeta Costa, the ballet dancer?

She is the prima ballerina at La Scala and she and her partner are coming to Ravello to give a gala performance at one of the concerts. Rosa's teacher was at school with her when they were younger and so Violeta agreed to do a solo at the gala and to be guest of honour.'

Charlie took Rosa's hand and squeezed it. 'Violeta Costa? No wonder you're disappointed; what an opportunity. And nobody else can take over? You're so close, just two weeks to go, surely you must know your roles by now? You only need a rehearsal director.'

Lucia shook her head. 'There's no one suitable in the whole area, not to the standard needed. No, we must postpone until next year and try not to be too sad, hey, Rosa?'

Matteo grinned. 'And you said I am a useless godfather? I might just be able to help you out, Rosa.'

Charlie froze as Lucia laughed. 'You? Don't tell me that you're qualified to teach ballet, Matteo?'

'Hardly, but Charlie is. She can help you get ready, can't you, Charlie?'

CHAPTER FIVE

CHARLIE FOLLOWED MATTEO into the villa's hallway and slipped off her sandals before heading into the deliciously cool sitting room, glad of the chill of the tiled floor against her hot, bare feet. Matteo looked at her, eyebrows raised quizzically.

'Okay. You've been quiet all the way home and not just because it's a steep climb back. What's wrong?'

'Nothing's wrong.' She paused. That wasn't exactly true. 'I just wish you had checked with me first before telling Rosa I'd take on the ballet gala.'

'I guess I should have done. I'm sorry.' Matteo leaned against the door, his smile contrite, like a kid caught stealing biscuits, knowing he was in trouble but sure he would be swiftly forgiven. 'I was just so pleased we could help—you can help. I know the language barrier is a slight issue...'

'Just a small one!'

'But I can translate. I'd like to be involved. Is that what was worrying you? After all, you're a qualified ballet teacher.'

'Not to that standard! Rosa's ballet teacher trained at one of Italy's top ballet schools. It's not the same.'

'Charlie, they are kids, not professionals. They'll just be happy someone can make this happen. And it's for a really good cause.'

Charlie flopped onto the sofa, taking her hat off and shaking her hair out. 'Oh, yes, the cause is really important and I'd like to support them. But Matteo, think about it. You have volunteered me to prepare fifty children I don't know and who speak a different language to me for a gala in front of their proud parents and one of the world's top dancers. In just two weeks! That's a big ask.'

It was a big ask, huge in fact, but normally it was the kind of challenge she loved, language barriers and all. And she understood why he'd jumped in with the offer, which was why she hadn't said anything while they were with his cousin. How could she have crushed the fledgling hope on Rosa's wan little face?

'Besides, we might not be here in two weeks.'

She might not be here. There was no doubt that Matteo was getting better by leaps and bounds; she didn't need a medical degree to see how much more colour he had, how much more energy. Once the doctor gave him a clean bill of health then her promise not to give him any shocks would be at an end and she would be free to tell him the truth. Free and morally obliged. And then what? She could hardly stay here in the same villa as the man she was divorcing.

But if she agreed to take on the dance gala then she would have to stay in Ravello for two more weeks at least. Which, under different circumstances, would be perfection but, as it was, the sooner Matteo knew the truth and she was out of Italy the better. Every day it got harder to remember that none of this was real, to remember that her marriage was over.

'Why wouldn't we be here?' Matteo sounded surprised. 'I promised you a second honeymoon, didn't I? Lovely as the last week has been, it's not exactly been honeymoonish, has it?' He grinned at her, a wolfish gleam in his eyes that sent her pulse racing despite all her attempts to stay calm.

'Matteo…' She couldn't find the right words. She threw up her hands in defeat. 'I just wish you'd checked.'

He gave her a quick keen look, then strode across the room to sit beside her, taking her hands in his. His touch lit her up inside and it was all she could do not to sway towards him. It was too dangerous being here with him. Her heart was too susceptible, her body too unreliable, forgetting all the reasons to keep him at bay.

'I'm sorry, Charlie, I didn't think. I can see that teaching small children ballet on honeymoon isn't exactly the most romantic thing to do. Don't worry, I'll call Lucia and apologise. I should be wining and dining you, planning boat trips to Capri and tours of Pompeii, not expecting you to put fifty small ballerinas through their paces.'

Was that what he thought? That she was the kind of person to take umbrage because she expected champagne and flowers rather than helping out his goddaughter? Of course, he only had a few months' memories of her; he didn't really know her at all.

'No, that's not it. This sort of initiative is exactly the kind of thing I enjoy. In London I was volunteering at a local community centre, teaching dance to some of the borough's most disadvantaged children and we put on our own gala. It was a lot of fun…' She stopped abruptly. The Kensington gala was one event she did *not* want to relive.

'Then what is it?'

She sighed, freeing her hands as she got to her feet and walked over to the large French windows, staring out at the lemon trees framing the sea far below. 'Matteo, look, I know this is difficult for you. The doctor said not to try to prompt your memory, that it is better if it comes back by itself, and so I am really trying to not talk about things from the last year. But I need to tell you that experience has taught me that where keeping promises is concerned, you can't be relied upon.'

He made no sound and when she looked back at him he was sitting statue-still, his eyes fixed on her, his expression unreadable. 'I see.'

She looked down at her hands, hating that she had to say this to him, that reality was intruding on their idyll.

'Your intentions are always good; I do know that. You don't mean to be so…' She searched for the right word, not wanting to say self-absorbed, one of the many words she had thrown at him the day of the gala. The day before she had walked out. 'So hard to pin down,' she said instead. 'But the reality can be so very different. Right now, I'm sure that you are absolutely certain that you will prioritise the rehearsals and the ballet, that of course you will be here in two weeks' time. But at some point you're going to get access to a phone and a laptop and to work emails and that means something will come up and you will need to be in New York or Paris or Berlin. Then where will I be? I don't want to promise anything to Rosa, just to have to let her down. That would be much worse than letting her get over this initial disappointment.'

Charlie looked up and bit her lip as she absorbed the shock in Matteo's hazel eyes. Shock, hurt and dawning knowledge. 'Am I that unpredictable?' he asked, his voice low and even. She swallowed. 'It can't be easy for you. Not trusting me to keep my word.'

'No, it's not always easy.' She couldn't, wouldn't, lie to him, not more than she had to. 'I do my best to understand, but it's not much fun having to always cancel plans or do things on my own. So maybe it's best if you do make our apologies. Safer.'

Matteo rose with easy sinuous grace and was at her side before she had a chance to move away, turning her to look at him, one hand tilting her chin so she had no choice but to meet his determined gaze. 'Charlie, I'm not an idiot. I can see things aren't perfect between us. I can see there are things you are trying desperately not to say. But I also know that I love you, and I know that asking you to marry me felt like the most right thing in my life, that being here with you is exactly where I want to be. Where I need to be. So, trust me on this. Trust me to keep my word. Trust me to make it up to you. All of it.'

She wanted to—how she wanted to. 'I…'

'Carlotta, *cara*,' he said, low and intent. 'Give me a chance?'

She was drowning in the intensity of his gaze and all the reasons, the many good reasons, to stand her ground slipped away as if they had never been. Could things be different? Could she trust him this time?

'Okay,' she said before she could think about it too closely. 'But Matteo, please don't let Rosa down.'

Or me, she wanted to add. Please don't let me down again.

The sun was beating down, hot and fierce. Matteo had forgotten just how intense the early summer sun could be when he was away from the shady arbours of the villa, the sea breeze of the pool and the dark alleyways of the village itself. But he welcomed the heat, he welcomed the prickle on his skin, the tightening band around his head. The discomfort focused him and he forced himself to walk ever faster, ignoring the aching muscles still recovering from the accident just nine days before.

The path he was on was well known and well used. The whole coast was a mecca for ramblers and walkers, especially at this time of year with the early summer flowers blooming in such profusion. But Matteo strode grimly on, following the path as it wound downhill towards Amalfi, barely seeing the colourful displays on all sides or noticing the spectacular views as he rounded yet another curve in the road. Much of the path had steps, and he pounded on, overtaking walkers and botanists as they ambled at a more sedate pace down the steep hillside path, barely nodding at those taking the far more onerous route uphill from Amalfi to Ravello.

Something was wrong, and he couldn't push that knowledge to the back of his mind any longer. His marriage was clearly no idyll and he was even more clearly no perfect husband. Ever since his conversation with Charlie yesterday grey shadows had been gathering at the corners of his mind. Words and hints of scenes, of empty rooms and pained silences, of misunderstandings and chasms and himself imprisoned in pride and isolation. He had no idea if they were real memories or his imagination working overtime with all the things she'd left unsaid.

Okay. Start with the facts. He took a deep breath and forced himself to focus, to face the problem rationally, as if it were a thorny legal problem or a contract issue he needed to resolve. What did he know for sure? He was clearly an absent husband, clearly an unreliable one, at least in Charlie's eyes. But that was it. He had no more, no idea how things could have come to such a pass in so short a time.

It seemed inconceivable to him, right now mentally and emotionally still at the cusp of married life, that in a year's time his wife would tell him that she couldn't rely on him. His work was demanding, time-consuming and international but that didn't mean there was no room for a personal life. His work-life balance was skewed towards work, of course it was, but there had been time for girlfriends and events, to ski or rock climb or sail before.

It was so discombobulating. This difference between who he thought he was and who he actually seemed to be. Worse was the lack of control. He'd known since childhood that a man in his position couldn't show any weakness. Yet not only were his ribs still sore, not only were his bruises protesting at the relentless pace, but his mind, the mind he relied upon to manage a multibillion-pound company, was also letting him down. No wonder he hadn't pressured Charlie to give him a phone or access to the internet, no wonder he had been happy to let her manage his grandfather; he could only imagine what the old man would say to him about this current state of affairs.

Matteo cursed long and low in both English and Italian. He'd spent thirty years proving how strong he was to his grandfather, how fit he was to take on the generations-old family business, to show that he was not just better than his parents but free of all their taints, and yet here he was. Just fallibly human after all. Not just with his memory loss but, it seemed, with his inability to manage a marriage as well. Just like his father, on wife number five, or his mother, who had spent the decade between divorcing Matteo's father and remarrying with a string of famous lovers. He'd wanted the opposite of that. He'd wanted stability. He knew all the best relationships required shared goals and compromise. So why wasn't he compromising in his?

Or was he? Charlie was his only source; she could be an unreliable narrator.

Matteo had planned to take the walk in one go; it was only three kilometres or so after all. But when he reached the pretty and unspoiled seaside village of Atrani he realised that, despite the days of rest and recuperation, his body was still not fully recovered and he thankfully stopped at one of the local *ristorantes* for some much-needed water, the thick black espresso he so missed in London and an almond pastry.

He sat under the shade of the umbrella, looking out at the bustling village square with the tantalising hint of sea between the buildings, but he barely took in the view, barely noticed the conversations babbling around him in several different languages. He was still reliving the last few weeks, trying to figure out what had gone wrong, reaching for those grey shadows in the corner of his mind.

Everything had been perfect up to the day before the wedding. That he knew as if it were yesterday. He smiled wryly. For him it practically was. The only cloud on his otherwise perfect blue-sky horizon had been his grandfather's obvious disapproval of Charlie.

Their first meeting had not been a success; from the moment she'd walked into the ostentatiously formal restaurant in a floral maxi dress teamed with chunky jewellery, her hair silver, it was clear his grandfather was not going to be her biggest fan. He had been slightly mollified when he'd realised that Charlie's mother was a diplomat and her father a reasonably well-known political journalist and biographer, but that approval ebbed when Charlie confided how much she disliked embassy parties and networking.

He'd clearly hoped that Charlie was just a passing phase, so when Matteo had announced their decision to marry as quickly as legally possible it had led to the first and only argument between them. An argument which had ended with his grandfather downright refusing to come anywhere near the ceremony.

The memory of that fallout was still so recent to him he could still feel the twist of shame and guilt at disappointing the man who'd raised him, the man who believed in him, the man who had given him the only family he'd ever really known.

Matteo reached out for a cube of sugar and crumbled it slowly into his coffee cup, his mind racing. But that wasn't true, was it? He had always thought of his grandfather as his only real family, the only person willing to raise him after his parents divorced. But although his mother had been too flighty to take care of him herself, his Italian grandparents had wanted him too, had given him long glorious summers here. And when his mother did finally settle down and remarry, she'd offered him a home. He was the one to refuse, his ties to his grandfather by then too strong.

Besides, he'd secretly gloried in the knowledge that he was the chosen one, the heir to a company with roots hundreds of years old. Harrington Industries had grown and grown over the years, surviving wars and depressions to become the globe-spanning behemoth it was today. Much of that growth had been driven by his grandfather and it was up to Matteo to maintain it, to keep growing it, to know where to invest next, where to pull out of, responsible for the jobs and livelihoods of thousands and thousands of people.

He finished the coffee and pastry, leaving a handful of euros on the table before resuming his walk. What else did he know? His last memory was of the day before the wedding. His mood was excited, anticipating the day, their honeymoon, their life together. He'd had no doubts that this was the right thing to do.

What had changed?

According to the police he'd been on his way to Kent when he'd crashed and Charlie had come to the hospital from her grandmother's cottage, he was sure of it. Why was she in Kent; why had he been on his way there? Had she gone home to her grandmother while he was away; had they moved there? Once more the answers danced around his mind, tantalisingly within reach before darting away again.

Focus. His grandfather had been ill, they'd been on honeymoon, they'd cut it short. And then what? He cursed again. It was time he remembered.

Amalfi was just ahead, busy with tourists and day trippers, coaches swinging down the precipitous narrow roads, small scooters darting here, there and everywhere. Still preoccupied, still trying to *remember, goddammit,* Matteo glanced casually one way then the other, then crossed the busy road leading into the town, only to find himself crashing to the ground as he threw himself out of the way of a scooter speeding along the road. The rider yelled out some profanities, not even slowing, and Matteo lay there for one long second, every bruise and rib yelling its protestations at further ill treatment.

'I'm fine…*bene…grazie,*' he repeated as concerned people tried to help him up, muttering at the lack of care shown by scooter riders. He was barely aware of his surroundings as events and memories began to swirl faster and faster through his dizzied mind. Finally on his feet, he headed, as if in a daze, to another café, where he ordered a grappa, drinking it down in one swift gulp. And slowly, slowly, all the jagged memories slotted back together.

He remembered. Everything.

The wedding. Charlie glowing, his pride and happiness. The three perfect days in Paris, followed by the terrifying worry as he had been summoned home to what he thought was his grandfather's deathbed. Worry— and guilt. Their last words so bitter, his grandfather so angry. Angry at him. His determination to make it up, and with that determination the old single-mindedness. A single-mindedness that meant he barely noticed his new wife's growing unhappiness until it was too late.

All he could do was let her go, expedite the divorce and try and carry on with his life. It had seemed he owed her that much.

Only then he'd got the divorce papers and realised he would never forgive himself if he didn't fight for his marriage. For his happiness—for her happiness. He'd been on his way to Kent to beg Charlie to give him a second chance.

He'd been planning to win his wife back.

That plan hadn't changed. The only thing he needed to figure out was how.

Matteo leaned back in his chair. If he returned to the villa and told her that he remembered everything, would she leave? Knowing Charlie, it was highly likely. But she wasn't indifferent to him; he would swear to it. The way she leaned into him, that secret smile just for him, the way she looked at him sometimes…

No, she wasn't indifferent. If he could just buy himself some time, prove to her that he had changed, remind her of all that had been good in their relationship, then maybe they had a chance.

She had brought spontaneity and joy into his life. Maybe it was time he returned the favour. And he knew exactly how to do it. It would involve a little subterfuge at first, but the cause was good. His mouth curved into a smile. Winning back Charlie wouldn't be easy, but it would be fun.

CHAPTER SIX

CHARLIE LOOKED UP as Matteo walked slowly down the stone steps leading to the swimming pool, then jumped to her feet in alarm. He looked terrible, as if all the rest and recuperation of the last eight days had been for nothing. She could have sworn there were new scrapes and bruises on his arms; his skin had lost some of the recently acquired healthy glow and perspiration shone on his forehead.

'Whatever happened to you?' she exclaimed. 'Are you okay?'

'Nothing's wrong. I'm fine,' he said not altogether convincingly. 'I just decided to do the walk down to Amalfi; I needed to clear my head.'

He'd done *what*? 'Walk down to Amalfi? In this heat? Are you insane? You haven't been given a clean bill of health yet.'

'It's only a few kilometres, three at the most. It's fine. If it hadn't been for an unfortunate encounter with a scooter, you wouldn't have noticed any difference. I'm fighting fit, I promise you.'

Charlie crossed her arms as she looked at him sceptically. 'Please elaborate on what an unfortunate encounter with a scooter means?'

Matteo grinned unrepentantly at her and her heart tumbled as he walked over to her, casually taking her hand in his, a zip of desire running through her veins at his touch. She was a sad case, lusting after the man who'd broken her heart.

'I'd like to say that the scooter came off worst in the encounter, but sadly it rode off unscathed. My fault. I wasn't looking where I was going.'

'Yes, you're clearly fighting fit if you are walking out in front of scooters and think taking a long walk in the midday sun is a sensible idea,' she couldn't help but scold him, trying to sound calm even as she frantically searched his face for any sign that his concussion had returned. 'I'm not sure that any of this will have helped your ribs to mend, to say nothing of your concussion.'

'I'm sorry, I didn't mean to worry you, but I am pretty sure the concussion is gone. You're right about my ribs though; if it's any consolation they are making their feelings about the matter very clear. But, to be honest, I've had worse outcomes from climbing sessions or riding particularly aggressive waves before. Honestly, Charlie. You don't need to worry.'

'It's all very well saying that,' she said, freeing her fingers and returning to her sun lounger, both relieved at the space between them and instantly missing his touch. 'But you're the one doing crazy things. Maybe if you didn't I wouldn't need to worry.' Charlie didn't want to examine her feelings too closely, think about the fear that had quickly filled her when he'd limped in pale and bruised, how her heart had skipped a panicked beat and she'd mentally been reaching for her phone to call the doctor. He was a grown and free man. If he wanted to do stupid things, that was on him. 'How was the walk, heatstroke and nearly getting run over aside? It's on my list of things to do while we are still here. The walk part; you can keep the other two.'

'Absolutely beautiful, but I'd recommend doing it early in the morning or in the evening. Truthfully, it was a little bit too warm to really enjoy it. How about you? How was your morning?'

'Buon giorno,' Charlie said very, very slowly and carefully, pronouncing every syllable. *'Mi chiamo Charlie. Tu com ti chiami?'*

Matteo's eyebrows shot up and she giggled at the surprised look on his face. 'I decided that if I was going to try and teach Italian children ballet I needed to be able to say more than thank you in their language so I finally opened that app I installed when we got married. To be honest I'm no natural linguist; my mother would be so disappointed in me. It's a good job I decided not to follow her into diplomacy.'

'You're starting to learn Italian? Does that mean that you're happy to go ahead?' He looked and sounded pleased, but there was a studied wariness in his expression she couldn't quite read.

'I guess so,' Charlie said slowly. She hadn't been able to think about much else apart from whether to stay and help out at the gala—stay with Matteo—for the last twenty-four hours, reasons for and reasons against tumbling around in her mind. The reasons against were clear: she shouldn't have been in Italy in the first place, no matter how good her motives or how little choice she'd felt she had. Staying any longer meant crossing a line from good intentions to downright deceit as Matteo, scooter accident or not, was clearly getting better every day.

On the other hand, it could be argued that her reasons for staying were noble. She'd be helping out some very disappointed children, and Charlie could never bear to see disappointed children. She'd be saving the day by enabling the planned show to go ahead and that was exactly the kind of activity she thrived upon. Better still, she'd be helping some of the poorest, most desperate people in the region. But she also knew that her reasons for saying yes weren't all altruistic. The last week and a bit had been a little too close to perfect for comfort. She wasn't quite ready to walk away and pick up the tattered remains of her life just yet.

So stay she would, but to do so she had to be honest with Matteo, especially now that he seemed so much better. But with honesty this easy camaraderie, this intimate companionship would collapse. Who could blame her for wanting to hold onto it for just a little longer?

She couldn't. Charlie inhaled a deep steadying breath and turned to Matteo, who had seated himself next to her.

'Matteo…'

Reaching over, he took her hand again, his thumb caressing her wrist in deliciously slow circles, and she half closed her eyes, savouring the sensation for what might be the last time, wanting to hold him, to cling onto him.

'Matteo…' she tried again, but he tightened his hold on her hand and when she looked across at him his expression was serious.

'Charlie, I have to ask you something.'

Dread stole through her heart. 'Anything,' she said as brightly as she could manage.

'Things are beginning to clear a little, especially after our conversation yesterday,' he said. 'I know there are things that you would like to tell me, and that they are things I should probably hear. But can you give me some more time, to allow me to try and recover those memories by myself?'

'Matteo...' she said for a third time. 'It's not that simple.'

His fingers laced through hers. 'I know I'm asking a lot. Just until we leave Italy. If I don't remember everything by then, then tell me everything you need to.'

Charlie swallowed. Matteo was giving her a way to have her cake, eat it and save some for the next week. 'You don't want me to tell you *anything*?'

'If I ask you a question then please be honest, but only if I ask. Is that okay? Can we try and just be the way things are right now for a little longer? Just Charlie and Matteo.'

She gently disentangled her hand from his and hugged her knees into her chest, staring unseeingly at the pool, trying to figure out what the right thing to do was. Acquiesce, even though it would make the reckoning so much harder?

But Matteo now knew that things hadn't been perfect between them, which meant she wouldn't need to pretend quite so much. Maybe this request would make it easier to carve out a new way for them to be. And if she was being painfully honest then she didn't want reality to intrude on this time out she'd been gifted. She turned his request over and over.

'Okay. If that's what you want. But if you change your mind at any time, tell me. There are things you should know and I am honestly unsure whether I'm doing the right thing here.'

'I will. And Charlie, I appreciate everything you've done and are doing more than you can know. I hope to show you how much very soon.'

Blinking back sudden hot tears, Charlie only just managed to nod. 'You don't have to thank me, Matteo. This is what marriage is.'

'Even so. You've gone above and beyond. Which is why I have arranged a little treat for you. Pack your bags. You and I are off to Rome.'

Rome? Charlie stared at Matteo incredulously. Was she hearing things? 'What do you mean we're going to Rome? Why?'

Matteo took her hand again, his grip firm and warm and, oh, so familiar. 'Several reasons,' he said. 'Number one, I know how nervous you are about taking on the gala. I don't think you need to be, but it might put your mind at rest if you speak to the teacher yourself and find out how she planned the next two weeks would go. I dropped in on Lucia earlier and she's arranged for us to see Natalia at her mother's apartment in Rome later today. Secondly, don't think I've forgotten that you and I were supposed to be spending a couple of our honeymoon nights in Rome. I suggested this trip could be our second honeymoon; let's start it in Rome. I know you are still owed a trip on the Orient Express and I can't arrange that yet, but hopefully this is a good start.'

A second honeymoon? Charlie's mouth dried, conflicting emotions shooting through her, mingling hope and desire with panic. Matteo had mentioned a second honeymoon several times but she'd not really allowed herself to think about what that might mean, sure she'd have left Ravello long before the thought became action. Honeymoons were about intimacy, coupledom. They were about making love. Her body began to pulse with desire at the thought, a sweet ache low down in the core of her. It wasn't that she didn't want to sleep with Matteo; on one level she yearned to, more than anything else. But how could she if he didn't know the truth about their relationship? And how could she plunge back into that kind of intimacy when walking away once had been so very, very difficult?

'Matteo, that sounds amazing but…'

He squeezed her fingers. 'And thirdly, I've been thinking a lot about what you said yesterday. About how I've been so distant physically and, I guess, emotionally as well.'

Her nod was wary. What was he getting at? 'That's a fair assumption.'

'I've been going over what that distance says about our marriage. If I'm someone who can't be relied upon for an event in two weeks' time, then I'm guessing I'm also unavailable for any kind of spontaneity. Charlie, there are many reasons I fell in love with you. One was your ability to just be in the moment. I've never experienced anything like it before, at least not in a positive way.' He looked away, his expression inscrutable. 'I don't want to go into some big boring conversation about my parents and the first few years of my life. I'm sure you know there was precious little stability. I never knew where they'd be, left with that week's nanny as they headed off again to Monaco or a house party somewhere. I guess, as a result, I thought that acting spontaneously and living for the moment was something to be disparaged. Something sensible upstanding people didn't do. One of the things I've loved most about the last couple of months…' his mouth quirked wryly '…the last couple of months for me, I mean, is how you've given me the gift of living for the moment.'

It was so bizarre, this living in two different times. The memories so recent and precious to Matteo were older for Charlie. Older and tainted by their conclusion. When had she and Matteo last done anything spur-of-the-moment? 'We didn't do anything so very spontaneous,' she said.

His mouth curved reminiscently. 'Maybe not for you, but for me? It was such a surprise, that Saturday you called me to say that the forecast was so gorgeous you'd packed the tent and I needed to drive down right now as you'd booked a campsite for the night. That was one of the best evenings I have ever had because it was so unexpected, one moment in the office, then just a couple of hours later in a field, sitting on a hay bale with a glass of cider and eating chips. The day you woke me up at six to suggest we jump on a ferry to Calais for a day because you were yearning for a meal abroad and we just went.' He shook his head as if still in disbelief. 'The Eurostar would have been so much quicker, but you told me the journey was part of the point. I still can't believe you made me play bingo on the ferry.'

'I still can't believe how competitive you got,' Charlie couldn't help but chip in and he grinned, boyish and so kissable it hurt to look at him.

'Turning up at my office brandishing last-minute theatre tickets for seats high up in the gods. Not opening night in a corporate box, just a spur-of-the-moment decision because you really wanted to see the play and bought them on a whim. I know none of this sounds radical, but for me it was—it is. So let's go to Rome. Let's be spontaneous. Let's live in the moment.'

Charlie just stared at him for a couple more moments, digesting his words, each one precious, a validation of what they had once been. 'Let me get this straight. You, Matteo Harrington, are happy to just turn up at the train station, grab tickets and arrive in Rome with no booked accommodation or plan?' She reached out and touched his forehead. 'Are you sure the concussion hasn't come back? Did you knock your head when that scooter careered into you?'

'No, no, perfectly clear-headed, thank you very much. Don't be too disappointed in me, but I went to a hotel in Amalfi and booked a room just so I could get in touch with Jo. She's organised everything. A car will be here in an hour to take us to Naples, where we have first-class train tickets booked for the high-speed train; we should be in Rome by four. She's also sorting out hotel reservations for two nights and is emailing all the details to you as I still don't have a phone. I hope having a planned itinerary hasn't lessened your opinion of me.'

Charlie laughed, still a little incredulous. 'I can't really argue with first-class train tickets, can I?'

'So you'll come?' The laughter had dimmed from his

eyes, replaced by an intensity that hit her heart. Matteo wanted this trip but, more, he needed it in ways she couldn't quite calculate. He wasn't the only one. She wanted and needed it too.

Charlie had always understood that they had to call off the honeymoon. How could they have gone ahead with his grandfather in hospital? Especially after the bitter words he and Matteo had exchanged, words about their marriage. She'd understood the pressure Matteo had been under, running the company without his grandfather's advice and input. She knew how capable he was, but he'd shouldered every decision, every meeting, every consideration as if he didn't have a highly experienced board and senior leadership team to do some of that work. The first two months of their marriage had been tough, true, but she had known why, supported Matteo in every way.

It wasn't until his grandfather had started to recuperate and was back at work part-time that Charlie realised that she was in trouble, that their marriage was set in lines she hadn't prepared for and couldn't live with: work first, his grandfather's needs second and her a poor last. She'd tried not to be selfish, not to think less of Matteo for the way he barely seemed to remember her existence, to tell herself to buck up when yet another evening approached bedtime and Matteo still hadn't returned from the office, when another meal was interrupted by a phone call that took over the rest of the evening, when she found herself sitting alone in restaurants and theatres waiting for him to arrive, only to receive a barely apologetic text. Because when it was good it was really good, those all too rare moments when she had him to herself. But as those moments got even rarer she'd had to ask herself what exactly she was staying with him for.

But he was trying to put everything right, without even knowing exactly *what* their problem was, just that something *was* wrong. The hope, the need in his eyes as he waited for her answer gave her a validation she hadn't even known she needed. Validating her decision to marry him in the first place, and validating her feelings that something had been so wrong with her marriage that it was too much for her to fix it alone.

Besides, he was offering to take her to Rome. The Eternal City. She'd travelled all over the world with her parents, seen most of the great cultural icons there were to see: she had walked on the Great Wall of China, visited temples in Cambodia, Mexico and Peru, marvelled at the Botanic Gardens in Singapore, stood on the bridge in Sydney staring at the Opera House. Yet she still had to discover so much of Europe thanks to her mother's postings usually being outside that continent. And she'd never been to Rome. How could she pass up this opportunity?

She smiled. 'Did you say the car will be here in less than an hour? I'd better pack.'

'Will this do?' Matteo could barely conceal his smug smile as Charlie turned slowly, taking in their sumptuous suite, her eyes wide with delight and her mouth a perfectly shaped o.

'Will this do? Oh, my goodness, Matteo. This is beautiful. I can't believe we got it on such short notice.'

'Never underestimate Jo,' he said with a grin. Jo had

indeed done them proud, securing them a corner penthouse suite at a hotel at the top of the Spanish Steps. Bifold doors opened out onto a wraparound terrace with views out over the city, furnished with comfortable sun loungers, a hot tub and a small infinity pool if they decided not to mix with other guests and use the extensive spa facilities. A large sitting room was decorated opulently but tastefully, in creams and soft gold. Both bedrooms contained huge beds with an entire menu of pillow choices and luxurious en suite bathrooms with baths set near windows, so even while relaxing in the bath Rome was spread out before them.

It was no accident that Jo had booked a suite with two bedrooms. Now Matteo had regained his memory he understood Charlie's desire to sleep in a separate room. It wasn't just concern for his health. It was a statement of the state of their marriage. He respected her choice, much as he yearned to change it. How he was to do so when they were both darting around the truth of their situation he wasn't yet sure. He hoped the romance of the ancient city would show him—show them—the way.

'I can't believe I'm actually here,' Charlie said as she wandered out onto the terrace for what must be the twentieth time since they'd arrived. 'I can't wait to explore it all. The Vatican, of course, the Colosseum and the Forum and even the Spanish Steps. I know it's a tourist cliché, but I want to do it all and they are right here. Where shall we begin?'

Matteo had been busy exploring the suite himself, nodding in approval at the fully stocked bar at one end of the sitting room. He selected a bottle of vintage Pro-

secco and opened it smoothly, pouring it into two crystal glasses. He joined Charlie on the terrace and handed
her a glass. 'I've engaged a guide to take us around,' he
said after he'd made a toast and taken a first sip. 'I know
you prefer to do things as one of the crowd, but Rome is
so very full of crowds. You'll appreciate the VIP treatment when you don't have to queue up for hours in the
hot sun to get into the Forum, I promise you.'

'I must appear very ungrateful if you think I'm not
going to appreciate our own personal guide around
Rome,' Charlie said a little ruefully and he touched
her cheek.

'Ungrateful? No, never. I love the way your feet are
so firmly rooted on the ground and how much you appreciate the little things. Tonight's dinner will hopefully
be exactly to your liking.'

'Intriguing.' She raised her eyebrows. 'In what way?'

'You'll have to wait and see. A car will be here
shortly to take us to Natalia's apartment so you can
get all the information you need for the gala. Tomorrow the guide will take us to the Vatican in the morning, then the Forum and Colosseum in the afternoon.
The evening and the following morning are left free
for us just to wander, train back mid-afternoon. How
does that all sound?'

'It sounds blissful. I'll tell you one thing I want to do
and that is have a very long bath at some point. Have
you seen anything more decadent than that tub looking out over Rome? I'll feel like some kind of empress
lying there.'

'Let me know if you need your back scrubbing.' It
was supposed to be a light remark, an offhand com-

ment, but he caught her gaze as he said it. Their eyes held, all the emotion of the last few weeks charging the air as they stood there on the terrace, the city spread out before them.

'I will,' she said a little huskily.

Matteo moved a little closer, just an inch. They still weren't touching but she was so tantalisingly close. He'd told himself to take things slowly. That winning back his wife was a campaign, not a quick endeavour. But she was holding his gaze with her lips parted, her breath coming faster, pink warming her cheeks and all warnings were lost as his blood pounded around his body, his pulse roaring in his ears.

Charlie was his and he hers. Nothing could—should—change that. He'd made mistakes, he knew that, but this was right. *They* were right.

He took her glass from her unresisting hand and placed it along with his on a table. She didn't demur as he put one hand on her waist, tilting her chin with the other, her gaze fearless, filled with a desire that matched his own. 'Oh, Carlotta, *cara*...' he breathed.

He had no idea who made the first move. One moment they were looking at each other as if there was nothing, no one else in the world, the next they were holding each other tightly, wrapped around each other so he had no idea where he ended and Charlie began, his mouth on hers and hers on his, their kiss so incendiary he was surprised they weren't lighting up the city. This had always been good, always been right; even when they'd had no words to communicate with each other their bodies had spoken a private language of their own and every word was coming back to him as Charlie threaded her hands around his neck to tug him closer and he ran one trembling hand down her back, resting it on her hips, pulling her tight against him, groaning at the sweetly painful pressure.

'Matteo,' she half whispered, half sighed and he wasn't sure if she was urging him on or telling him to stop, but as he stilled, pulling back in question, the suite phone shrilled out and she stepped back, laughing shakily.

'Wow, welcome to Rome indeed. Are you going to get that?'

'It'll be Reception telling us our car is here; are you ready?'

'Give me five minutes.' She paused, staring at him, and he could have sworn her heart was in her eyes as she raised one hand to his cheek before whirling round and disappearing into one of the bedrooms, leaving him standing there, alone but hopeful. The first steps had been taken. He could make this right.

CHAPTER SEVEN

ROME WAS AS beautiful and exciting and atmospheric as Charlie had always dreamt it would be. It was a short journey to the residential area near the Vatican where Natalia's mother lived, but she took in every detail of the journey: the groups of tourists obediently following an upheld umbrella or flag, the snappily suited men and fashionable women of all ages, the small children clinging onto their parents' hands—and all around beautiful buildings in golden stone, cafés and restaurants and shops and the ubiquitous coffee bars where men stood to drink their grappa or espressos to avoid the seat fee.

But even as she drank in the sights she was ultra-aware of Matteo next to her, the breadth of his shoulders, the flex of his wrists, the heat radiating from him despite the seat between them. The atmosphere between them had been charged ever since they'd left the hotel suite. Electricity sizzled almost tangibly between them every time they came within touching distance, with every darting glance.

How she'd missed the way she fitted exactly into him as if she had been made for him, the way a light kiss could make her forget her own name, the way he knew exactly how to touch her, the taste of him. Charlie quivered with the memory, as if he were touching her still.

It was a relief when the car pulled up outside the building where Natalia was staying and Charlie could turn her attention to the matter at hand. Natalia's mother's high-ceilinged apartment was elegantly furnished with antiques and Charlie felt out of place at first next to the sophisticated slim woman with hair swept up in an enviably chic chignon. Natalia seemed every inch the ballet teacher from her neat slippers to her wrap cardigan, and Charlie couldn't help feeling gaudy with her own hair held back by a headband that matched her sixties-style pink shift dress. But Natalia soon put her at her ease, clearly delighted that Charlie was willing to take on the gala, and soon Charlie was perched on the narrow sofa with a coffee, discussing all the details.

There was definitely an element of interview about the whole process, on both sides. Charlie needed a clearer understanding of what she was proposing to undertake and was relieved to find out that all the choreography had not only been taught but recorded so she would have videos to help her with the final rehearsals. All the costumes had been ordered and should be with her in plenty of time and the tickets already sold and distributed.

'It really is just a matter of putting them through their paces, making sure they know where they are when on stage and dealing with all last-minute panics and hitches,' Natalia said in her beautifully accented English. 'I very much hope my dear *mamma* will be better in time for me to come and see the performance at least, maybe even be there for the dress rehearsal, but there are no guarantees. She is still in hospital and she needs me here. But it will be much easier for me to manage, knowing that my girls and boys are being looked after.'

In her turn, Charlie was very politely grilled about her training, and found herself revealing that she too had once harboured dreams of being a ballerina. 'I was too tall, and never had the right kind of turnout,' she confessed. 'I did audition for training at sixteen, even though I knew it was a long shot, but didn't get a place. Instead I went to theatre school at eighteen and studied commercial and musical theatre, but soon found that I gravitated towards the teaching side. In the end I didn't even try to perform as a career; instead I converted my degree into a full teaching qualification and never looked back. Now my stage career is confined to putting on school plays and teaching in the local village hall at evenings and weekends. At least it was before I married Matteo.'

Looking over to the other side of the room, she noted Matteo's look of surprise. She'd never confided those early ambitions to him, a little embarrassed by her girlish dreams. He was a man who had always achieved everything he set out to achieve, and her change of direction, the crushing of her childish dreams didn't seem like things that he would understand. Funny, she had never thought of herself as being the one who'd kept secrets in their marriage before. Their gazes caught and held and it was as if he could see through to the very soul of her.

It was so hard to remember that this feeling was just an illusion. That in the end he'd wanted her to change, to fit into his world, that all her differences had become a liability to him, no longer a refreshing change. And the opposite was true as well. She'd known of his ties and loyalty, applauded his steadfastness and commitment, but in the end hadn't she wanted to change him just as much as he'd wanted to change her?

She dragged her attention back to the matter at hand and after an hour they both had everything they needed. Natalia wished her luck as she showed them to the door.

'I'm here for anything you need, anything at all,' she said. 'You have my number. Please do use it. And Charlie, I can't thank you enough. A couple of those girls are really talented and there is one boy for whom I have very high hopes. For them to have an experience like this, to dance with an artist like Violeta, is a once-in-a-lifetime opportunity. It would have broken my heart if the gala hadn't gone ahead. I'm so glad that they are in your hands, with someone who isn't just a teacher but someone who knows what it is to dream.'

Matteo was quiet as they made their way down the steep stone staircase, through the foyer and out into the busy street below. He'd sent the car away, suggesting to Charlie that they walk back to the hotel, picking up dinner on the way. 'Rome is very walkable,' he'd said. 'And, of course, there is the Metro if you do get tired.'

After an afternoon of travelling, Charlie had relished the thought of a walk. Besides, her parents always said that you only ever got to know a city by walking through it. But the silence was so charged she almost wished for a car and the presence of a driver to dispel it.

'We need to cross the Tiber,' Matteo said after they'd walked a block in silence. 'We're heading towards the

Piazza Navona. It's tourist central but the place we're looking for is around there.'

'Great!' she said brightly. He half smiled but said nothing else, his expression hidden by his sunglasses.

'Natalia seems nice,' she said after a while.

'Yes.' He paused. 'I didn't know you wanted to be a ballet dancer.'

'It's all such a long time ago now,' she said. 'To be honest, I only really auditioned because I felt like I should. I knew even then that it's one thing to be the very best in your own dance school, one thing to be good enough to go to elite weekend classes in London, but it's quite another to get a place to train. It's not easy to be so very close but in the end just not good enough. It's not something I like to dwell on so I put it behind me. And I love teaching. I wouldn't change how things worked out if I could.'

'But you're not teaching now?'

She looked at him in surprise and he shrugged. 'It's still term time in the UK, isn't it? And you haven't mentioned having to contact your job so I assume you're not working.'

'No,' she said slowly, trying to figure out how to answer his question without volunteering any extra information about their life together as she had promised 'I meant to, but things were so hectic when we got back from our honeymoon I put it off and ended up volunteering at the local community centre as a stopgap. Soon the centre seemed to take up all my time and of course money wasn't actually an issue. You had more than enough for both of us and didn't mind if I worked for a salary or not.' She paused, trying to find the courage to say the words she'd never actually said to him before. 'What I didn't expect was how much I disliked being dependent on anyone, even someone as generous as you. I think maybe not working was a mistake.' She bit her lip as she realised she was speaking in the past tense, but he didn't seem to notice.

'Do you resent me for it?'

'No, of course not.' It was true that financially at least, Matteo was generous to a fault. He'd presented her with a credit card and her bank account was topped up weekly; she'd had more money than she knew what to do with. But it wasn't hers. And so when she had rushed home triumphantly brandishing a dress from a new designer she'd found in Dalston and he'd suggested she choose something less eccentric for the ball she'd bought it for she'd felt obliged to. After all, he'd paid for it. Just as he'd paid for her hairdressing appointments, the food they ate, her activities. It had become harder and harder to assert her independence when their tastes were so different. But when she had casually suggested looking for a teaching position Matteo had tried to put her off. It was such a demanding, time-consuming job, he had said. It would make it even harder for them to spend time together, he needed her to help him entertain business contacts too.

And, blinded by love and wanting their marriage to be a success, she had agreed. She should have known better than to go against her instincts like that. 'No,' she repeated. 'But it was the wrong choice for me, for now at least. I love my job; it's part of who I am.'

'Then,' he said, taking her hand, 'when we get home let's find you the perfect job.'

'When we get home. Yes.' But where was her home? Not in London and she couldn't stay with her grandmother for ever. She'd planned to visit her parents in Malaysia as part of her trip but, much as they would welcome her, she wouldn't want to stay with them for more than a few weeks. She'd lived all over the globe and yet still didn't have a home of her own. She'd thought it would be wherever Matteo was. How she wished that was true.

Matteo was unsure why Charlie's confession of her youthful wish to be a dancer had struck him so hard. Of course it was impossible to know everything about a person, especially after just a year of actually knowing each other, but he had told her more about himself than he had told any other living person and had thought the opposite was true. She knew how hard it had been when his grandfather had insisted he spent his summer working and not at the villa in Ravello with his Italian family. He'd told her about a boyhood dream to be a pilot, and the lessons he had taken, but how he had never had the time to get in the hours of flying needed to get his licence. He'd even told her about his university band days, although he hadn't inflicted any of their music on her. She had kept something that was clearly very important to her from him, not on purpose, but it still stung.

For so much of his life he had been the lonely outsider looking in, although he had hidden it well with a veneer of confidence polished by his boarding school and his grandfather's expectations. Charlie had made him feel alive, really, truly alive, for the first time in his entire life. It was shaming how quickly he had taken that for granted, to remember that when she'd left he had told himself that they were too different after all, that for her living in his world was like imprisoning some beautiful wild bird in a cage, a gilded luxurious cage but a cage nonetheless.

He shook himself impatiently. One comment, one surprise from her past and he was immediately dwelling on all the things that had gone wrong, all the things he'd done wrong, all his fears. This trip to Rome was about making new memories, about reminding her how good it could be between them, about starting the process of winning her back, and that wasn't going to happen while he strode along brooding as if he should be on a windswept Yorkshire moor instead of on the streets of one of the world's most enticing—and romantic—cities.

He squeezed her hand. 'Are you hungry? Do you want to head straight for dinner or get a drink first?'

Charlie bit her lip thoughtfully. 'I am hungry,' she said. 'But I wouldn't mind walking around for a little bit first. Maybe we could have a wander, stop for a drink and maybe some olives and then go and eat?'

'Excellent idea,' he said as they reached the bridge that took them over the Tiber River. It was early evening now and, although the city was still busy, it was less hurried, with a relaxed meandering air as people headed out for an evening of pleasure, not the buzzing busyness of work or tourists ticking another thing off their must-see list.

The route Matteo chose took them to the busy, bustling Piazza Navona and onto Campo di Fiori, where all the market traders had packed away, their colourful wares sold out long before. Now the graceful old square was filled with tables and chairs and so they stopped for beers and delicious bread dipped in fresh olive oil, watching the world wander by.

'Show me the sights,' Charlie said and so he did, taking her to the Pantheon and then the Trevi Fountain, where she insisted on throwing in a coin to ensure her return. Rome was as beguiling as ever. One moment they were on a wide paved street full of designer shops, the next in a twisting alleyway emerging into a square filled with people, full of cafés and *gelaterias* and shops selling everything from one-euro souvenirs to handbags costing thousands.

He'd planned a circuitous route, so they ended up back near the Piazza Navona again. This time Matteo led them through the bustling square to a side street where a group of people were queueing to get through the door of a small, unpretentious café.

'What's this?' Charlie asked, and he smiled.

'Dinner.'

'Here?' She looked through the window at the long oilcloth-covered tables in surprise.

'This is one of the most famous pizzerias in Rome,' he told her. 'A real local hotspot, as well as a destination for thousands of tourists in the know. But most will pass it by, not knowing that inside this very unassuming place is the best pizza in Rome. So good that there is nearly always a queue.'

It wasn't too long before they reached the front and were soon sitting at one of the long tables alongside other patrons to enjoy the most delicious pizza Rome had to offer. It was the kind of place Matteo would never usually choose for a romantic date, wanting to impress with an expensive, exclusive restaurant, all hushed voices and fine dining, but he knew Charlie would be charmed with this slice of Roman life and he was right. She quickly struck up a conversation with the family next to them, and then when the Americans left did her best to practice her new Italian phrases on the young fashionable couple who took their places.

'That was amazing,' she said, practically skipping as they left the restaurant. 'I've never eaten anything so perfect in all my life. I'm spoilt for all other pizza now for ever.'

Pizza was followed by *gelato* from one of Rome's oldest and most celebrated ice-cream shops and they wandered through the streets, eating the deliciously cold dessert. 'I love Rome,' Charlie said, her eyes filled with dreams and stars. 'I always knew I would. Have we got time to visit the cat sanctuary? Oh, and Shelley's grave?'

'If we don't then we'll come back.'

'Promise?'

'Yes.' The words felt like a renewal, a promise of a future. Matteo looked down at Charlie and his heart beat painfully as he saw the hope written all over her face, mirroring his own hope, love and desire for this vibrant, beautiful, caring girl.

The past wasn't a prophecy for the future. He had messed up, he knew that, but things could be different, they *would* be different, he vowed. Taking her hand, he drew her to him, slipping one arm around her waist and tilting her chin up to look down into the beloved heart-shaped face he knew better than his own, drinking in

every detail from the smattering of freckles on her nose
to the fullness of her mouth before losing himself in
the blue of her long-lashed eyes. Matteo forgot where he
was, who he thought he had to be, all the events of the
last year. All he knew was her. And what could he do
but bend his head and kiss her, a sweet, lingering kiss?

There was no hesitation as Charlie kissed him back,
her own hands resting on the nape of his neck, holding
him tight as if she didn't want to let go. All the sounds
faded away and all he knew was them, just two lovers
in the Eternal City. Matteo lost track of time, lost in
the feel of her, the taste of her, this kiss and this moment. They could have been there for seconds, minutes or hours until the sounds of a large group walking
past made them both jump and they drew apart a little
shakily.

'Come on,' Matteo said unsteadily. 'Let's go back.'

Charlie didn't demur, her fingers laced in his as they
swiftly walked the half mile or so back to the Spanish
Steps and their hotel. They didn't stop for selfies or to
admire the view as they walked up the famous steps,
darting around groups of teenagers and families enjoying the warm summer evening, climbing in silence.

It seemed to take an eternity to reach the top, walk
through the lobby of their hotel and take the lift to the
top floor but finally they were back in the penthouse
suite and Matteo drew Charlie out to the terrace. For a
long moment they stood looking out over the city, her
hand still in his as she leaned against him, her head on
his shoulder.

'This has been a wonderful day, thank you.'

'It's not over yet...' he teased and kissed her once

again. Her response was no less immediate, no less passionate than it had been on the street, but she drew away much more quickly this time and looked up at him, framing his face with her hands.

'Matteo, it's not that I don't want to. I do, but I just can't.'

Matteo inhaled, taking in a long deep breath, steadying his nerves, his hopes and his desires. 'Charlie, you don't have to do anything you don't want to. I hope you know that.'

She laughed then, soft and low and a little shaky. 'I do want to, I want to more than anything. But it's not that simple.'

'You don't have to explain.'

'You see, I know you want your memories to return in their own time and I respect that. But there are things you don't know, important things, and sleeping with you, making love with you, when we...' She stopped and looked up at him imploringly. 'I just can't, much as I want to. It wouldn't be right.'

Matteo's heart swelled with love for her, for her bravery, her honesty. He'd hoped for more time to win her over, win her back, but he needed to repay bravery with bravery, honesty with honesty. 'I know, Charlie. I remember.'

'What do you remember?' she half whispered.

'That we separated, started divorce proceedings, that I let you down. That I'm a fool who let you go. That I'm sorrier than you'll ever know.'

CHAPTER EIGHT

CHARLIE STARED UP at Matteo, shock and relief warring in her heart 'You remember? How…when?' The words could barely form themselves.

'Yesterday, when you told me that things have been difficult over the last year it struck a chord. All night I had vivid dreams. I don't know if they were memories but this morning everything just seemed a little bit clearer; that's why I went for a walk. I went through everything I knew and after I fell the clouds cleared and I remembered it all.'

'I see.' Charlie sat down heavily on the nearest lounger and stared at her hands. 'Then why did you ask me not to even mention the past…?' She began to feel a little bit sick as she remembered the earnest expression on his face as he'd asked her to give him some time. Was it some kind of game? But no, for all his faults, Matteo was straight as a die. He would never play with her like that; he wasn't dishonest.

'Charlie.' He knelt before her, taking her unresisting hands in his. 'I can't tell you what a shock it was to go from thinking that we were about to get married to remembering the mess I've made of everything. I needed

time to process it before talking to you about it. And...'
He took a deep breath.

'And?' she prompted him.

His grip tightened on her hands. 'Carlotta, *cara*, the car accident, the reason I was in that car was because I was coming down to see you.'

'You were? But why?'

'Oh, Charlie. When I got back from New York and you were gone I told myself it was for the best. I agreed to the divorce because I knew that's what you wanted. It felt like I should go along with your wishes, make the separation as easy as possible. I owed you that at least. But then I realised I would never forgive myself if I just let you walk away without telling you how I felt, trying to win you back. I needed to ask you to give me one more chance. I guess I was a little distracted, trying to figure out what to say, my attention wasn't properly on the road.'

'You were coming to see me?'

Matteo nodded. 'Maybe it was wrong of me not to tell you this morning, and wrong of me to ask for a little bit more time. I just wanted to bring you here, to show you that I don't always break my promises, that I can be spontaneous and put you first. I wanted to show you how our marriage could be, not how it was. I guess—' he smiled ruefully '—I wanted to win you back. I want to win you back.'

'I see,' she said slowly. 'You think I'm the kind of girl you can seduce with delicious pizza, ice cream and a luxury hotel suite with incredible views?' She twisted to look out at the lit-up city. 'Fair play. I guess I am exactly that kind of girl.'

He smiled then, slow and sensuous, and her heart jolted.

'Matteo, I want you to know that I didn't want to lie to you. I wanted to tell you about our marriage straight away, not bring you here and pretend everything was okay. But the doctor said not to give you any sudden shocks and she seemed so worried about you. When she said you might have died…' She could hear the tremble in her voice, felt her throat close with threatened tears. 'I never did stop loving you; I hope you know that. Hearing how close you came to dying just made me realise how much. But love was never the issue, was it? Our lives are just so different; what we want is too different for us to be together.'

'Maybe we're a little bit wiser now? Charlie, losing you, receiving those damn divorce papers and knowing I was just six weeks away from setting you free made me re-evaluate everything. And then fate stepped in, gave me the chance to reset the clock, to live as if we were still fresh and new, reminded me why you're the best thing that happened to me. It's been a wake-up call. What do you think, Charlie? Is there any way that we can start again?'

How she wanted to say yes. How she wanted to lean into him, to kiss him until neither of them could think any more, to stagger through to one of the bedrooms entwined around him, kissing every step of the way, and to allow him to make love to her while she made love right back as if this really was the honeymoon he'd promised.

'I don't know, Matteo. I don't want to allow myself

to hope and then for nothing to change. I don't know if I can go through being let down again.'

'I can't make you promises about what won't happen; I can't see into the future. But I can promise that I'll do my best, Carlotta, *cara*.'

There was so much else to say, so much else to think about, but Charlie was tired. She was tired of grieving, she was tired of hurting, she was tired of lying. All she wanted to do was to feel and to love and be loved, for tonight, at least. Slowly she rose to her feet, drawing him up with her and stepping in close so their bodies touched and she fitted right in against him, just like she always had, as if they were made for each other.

'I'm tired of talking, Matteo,' she said. The expression in his hazel eyes was unfathomable as she reached up to cup his cheek. 'I'm tired of talking and I'm tired of thinking. I don't know what tomorrow will bring, I don't know if we have a future, but there's now. We can live for now. Help me forget, Matteo.'

He didn't move for a long moment, just stared at her with that unreadable expression. 'Are you sure?'

'I've never been more sure of anything in my life.' Charlie raised herself onto her tiptoes and pressed her mouth to his. It wasn't the most seductive, the most practised kiss, but her heart was in her lips and with it she expressed everything she didn't have the words for. How much she wanted him, how much she desired him, how much she wished things had been different. How glad she was that he was here, standing next to her in this beautiful place, how all she wanted was for him to take her inside, strip her clothes from her and make her forget.

Matteo stayed stock-still for a second longer and then, with a muttered curse, he returned the kiss hard, covering her mouth with darkly sensuous intent and sweeping her up in his arms as if she were the petite dancer she'd wanted to be, not a five foot eight, long-legged woman. Still kissing her, he strode through the penthouse suite and into the master bedroom, where he laid her carefully on the bed as if she was the most precious thing he'd ever seen and stood back, looking at her in a slow appraising manner that sent ripples of need shuddering through her.

Slowly, intently, Matteo removed first one of her sandals then the other before running his hands up her bare legs, and she shivered beneath his touch.

'Sit up,' he commanded, his voice low and guttural, and slowly she obeyed, allowing him to unzip her dress, wriggling to help him slip it off her, until she sat there in just her bra and pants. Matteo stood back, surveying her again, silent as he swept his gaze down her body. She could feel the track of his eyes as if he were touching her, her flesh tingling where his gaze fell.

Nearly two months had passed since she'd left him; it had been two weeks before that when they'd last made love and that had been a sad, farewell lovemaking as if they'd known what lay ahead, slow and sweet, not like this dark, simmering passion igniting between them.

'Your turn,' she said, holding his gaze, challenging him.

Slowly, intently, Matteo unbuttoned his shirt, one button at a time with slow, strong fingers until at long last he slipped it off and began to unbuckle his belt. Now it was her turn to look at him, to glory in the play of muscles on his shoulders, the deep olive skin, the smattering of hair on his chest, tapering into a line on his stomach. For ten days she'd lain on her sun lounger next to this magnificent body, desperate to touch it, and now here was her chance. She waited until he stepped out of his trousers, then reached out and ran one finger down his chest slowly, a light caress. Matteo stood still, only the faintest quiver showing how much her touch affected him as his eyes darkened with passion. They stayed there for another long moment until she reached one hand out towards him.

'Come here.'

Matteo needed no further invitation. In an instant he was beside her, around her, enveloping her, kissing her, touching her in all those sweet, secret places that belonged to him. Charlie returned the kisses and caresses, biting softly into the skin on his shoulder, running a hand up his arm, glorying in the muscles of his stomach, reaching down to cup him until he moaned, stilling her hand.

'Damn, Charlie. Not yet.' And then it was her turn to moan as his mouth moved down her throat, dropping light teasing kisses on the tops of her breasts as his hand slid down her body to find the very core of her. She moved under him with little half cries as he stroked her expertly until she pulled him to her, sighing in sweet relief as he completed her. He was hers, and she was his. And nothing could change that. For tonight at least.

Charlie had no idea what time it was, but as she stirred and opened her eyes she noticed how the moon streamed in through the windows. Matteo slumbered next to her, his arm slung possessively around her, and for a moment all she wanted to do was to nuzzle in against him, breathe in his sharp, spicy scent, luxuriate in his hard, toned length and go back to sleep. But her brain had cranked into gear with the opening of her eyes and so, after a moment, she slid carefully out of the covers and padded over to the window. Leaning against the sill, she stared out at the now sleeping city, only a few lights dotted here and there showing she wasn't the only person awake. Despite the clear sky, the stars were faint, thanks to the streetlights, but the full moon hung low and bright.

The night was warm, so warm she didn't need her nightgown or robe, safe in the knowledge that as no windows faced her nobody could see her as she stood at the window wearing nothing but the light of the moon. Charlie had never minded nudity, always happy for a quick skinny-dip or to sunbathe in some secluded spot. It was one of the many things about her that she knew Matteo found simultaneously amusing, arousing and frustrating. He was far more of an always keep a bag with a swimsuit and a towel in the car just in case instead of a shed your clothes and take a chance kind of guy. And that had been part of the charm, coaxing him into taking a chance, letting caution fly. She'd loved the fact that opposites really did attract.

She couldn't help but smile, slow and secretively, as she relived the previous couple of hours. They were living proof that opposites attracted, were still attracted. But was that attraction enough? With that thought any last trace of sleepiness fled. Instead her mind was filled with all the thoughts she'd been trying to suppress ever since she'd made the decision to bring Matteo to Italy. After all, she could have deposited him safely in Kensington with a paid nurse and an excuse for her absence, sent him to a secluded luxury hotel. But she'd wanted to come here, wanted to look after him, to snatch a last few days with him.

Had wanted to make love with him again.

What was she *doing*? When would she learn to think before she acted? Surely, surely she'd learned her lesson over the last few days. Her chest constricted until she yearned for air, space. Creeping to the bathroom, she extracted her silk robe from the back of the door and wrapped it firmly around her then, with a last glance at the still peacefully sleeping Matteo, she slipped out of the bedroom and into the living room.

Charlie hadn't had a chance to explore the well-stocked bar before, but luckily there was enough light for her to find and open a bottle of mineral water and put some ice into a glass. She poured herself a large drink, collected her book from the table and a soft throw from the sofa and slid open the door to the terrace, breathing in the cooler night air. Was it still night-time or was it very early morning? At what point did it tip from up too late to up too early?

Wrapping the throw around her, Charlie lay down on one of the loungers and stared up at the night sky, her book unopened in her hand.

'Can't sleep?' She started, looking up to see Matteo leaning against the door, clad in just a pair of boxers slung low on his hips. Desire trembled through her, despite all their exertions to quench it earlier that night.

'It seemed a shame to waste this gorgeous terrace when the moon is so beautiful,' she said, smiling at him. But he didn't smile back, his brows drawn together in query.

'Having regrets?'

'No, no, not at all. I was just...' she hesitated '...I was just wondering what happens next.' She laughed a little shakily. 'I know—most unlike me. That's your job, isn't it?'

'Then you tell me not to worry about the future, that it usually takes care of itself. Let's just live in the moment.'

Charlie shivered as she heard her words parroted back to her, echoing the thoughts preoccupying her mind. 'Maybe that's not always the best philosophy after all. I guess I've been thinking a lot over the last few weeks. Thinking about where we went wrong, about the part I played.'

Matteo pushed himself off the door frame and, hooking a chair, placed it next to her, sitting down and taking her hand. 'Your part? I don't want to be some kind of martyr here, but I thought we both know what went wrong. I wasn't around, physically or emotionally. I expected you to accommodate me and didn't stop to think about what you wanted. There's a list of my unreasonable behaviour in those divorce papers. Very chastening. I told my lawyer to work with yours to make it as speedy and as easy as possible so you could get the divorce straight away but I didn't expect it to be such hard reading.'

Charlie winced, drawing her knees into her chest and wrapping her arms protectively around them. 'It's a horrid process. I'll be honest; that list was cathartic. I genuinely felt that you didn't compromise at all and I compromised too much. But it's not that simple, is it? We both had a role to play in what went wrong and I need to acknowledge my part in that. And we both know that the truth is we didn't really know each other when we got married. If we had been sensible, if we'd waited then either we would have ironed out those problems earlier or we would have separated long before we got to that point. Which would still be hard, but not as hard as a divorce. And that's on me.'

Matteo stilled. He had thought that nothing would be as hard as returning home to realise Charlie had gone and he'd not lifted a finger to stop her, that nothing could be as hard as reading the list of behaviours deemed unacceptable and realising he couldn't argue with any single one. But seeing Charlie curled up, her expression unusually serious, eyes clouded and voice full of heartbreak was possibly the hardest thing he'd ever had to do.

'Hey,' he said, deliberately keeping his voice light. 'What do you mean? I proposed to you, remember? If anyone was to blame for the speed of our marriage it was me.'

But she shook her head vehemently, dark blonde, honey, copper and bronze tendrils trembling as she did so. 'Come on, Matteo. We both know that I pretty much goaded you into it,' she said, and although her voice was still serious and her eyes darkened to navy her mouth trembled with the beginning of a smile.

'You most certainly did not.' His outrage wasn't entirely feigned.

She uncurled then, turning to look at him, and he couldn't stop himself reaching out to run a finger down the curve of her cheek. She leaned into his touch, eyes half closed.

'I was completely in control of every moment of that proposal,' he told her and she regarded him provocatively from under heavy lids.

'We had gone to the beach and I was telling you about a friend of mine who had just been blindsided by a ridiculous proposal.'

'Not everyone would think that someone organising a flash mob outside her favourite café was ridiculous,' he interjected and she raised an eyebrow.

'Anyone with any sense would. You said to me that you thought flash mobs and big events would be completely up my street and I said that actually I thought nothing was worse than a public proposal. I told you how much I hated planned proposals full stop and the worst way to propose to me would be with a carefully chosen ring already bought and hidden and waiting for the perfect moment in a perfect restaurant in a perfect city. I told you...'

'You told me,' he said softly, 'that your perfect proposal would come out of nowhere. The moment would just be so perfect that one of you would just know that this was it, that you were meant to be, that they would just ask. Right there, right then with no ring and no preplanned words. Just in the moment. And we walked a little longer and then we paddled and you fell in and as I pulled you up I asked you to spend the rest of your life with me. Because I knew.' He could never have forgotten, no matter what happened, that moment of perfect clarity.

'Yes, but you wouldn't have if we hadn't just had that conversation. I put the thought there. Oh, not on purpose, but I did all the same. You wouldn't have even dreamt of it otherwise.'

'Maybe not that exact moment,' he admitted. 'But Charlie, I would have proposed to you sooner, much sooner rather than later. Only I would have offended you by booking an expensive restaurant and buying a ring I thought you'd like and waiting for the perfect moment.' He smiled wryly. 'I might have even committed the cardinal sin of hiding it in your dessert or in a glass of champagne. And then you would have said, *No way*, and then where would I have been? Much better that it was then and I wasn't left humiliated in a restaurant.'

She laughed at that. 'I have total faith that you'd have done better than that. But let's not forget that I was the one who said, *Why wait?* If it hadn't been for having to wait three weeks for the banns to be read I'd have married you the next day. I suggested Vegas, remember?'

'I had no doubts, no hesitation. I didn't need a project plan or a Gantt chart or a SWOT analysis to figure out if it was the right move. I was just as keen to rush it through with you. None of the blame for that is yours alone, Charlie. I was right there with you.'

'You were with me because I was already there. Because I'm the person who everyone knows will do something crazy and then they'll just say, *Oh, that's so Charlie*. None of my friends or family were even slightly surprised when we announced our engagement and wedding date, whereas yours were appalled, even those that tried to hide it.'

'But that's what I loved about that time, not knowing where we were going next. You were such a breath of fresh air. I had no idea how dull and stale my life had got until you blew into it and turned it upside down.'

'Until you realised you quite liked things a little less windblown. Like I said, I was furious. I changed my hair for you, the way I dressed, gave up my job. Turned into the little wife waiting at home with your dinner drying out in the oven and was all self-righteously angry. I told myself I made all the compromises. But I didn't, not in my heart. I should have accepted that if you are in the middle of a big business deal you probably can't take a long lunch break to come picnic with me. I should have known that buying a dress from an experimental designer just out of art college is a privilege, but that doesn't mean I should wear it to a fundraising ball full of clients you're trying to impress. I told myself that you married me for me and I shouldn't have to change for you. But I wanted you to change for me. How is that fair?'

Matteo sat back and stared up at the moon as he took in her words, took in the truth of them. He loved everything about Charlie, her vibrancy and her warmth and the way she lived every moment to the full. But the asymmetrical orange and yellow and lime-green dress, although probably very stylish in the end-of-year degree show where she had bought it, would have looked outlandish at the fundraising ball thrown by the philanthropic client he was trying to attract. But should he have asked her to tone it down next time, suggested she shop somewhere more conventional? Should he have told her that her hair was all very well for a primary school teacher but it was out of place in the royal box at Ascot?

He knew the answer.

Just as he knew that, much as he'd wanted to spend long lunches with her, to knock off early, to take long weekends, he simply hadn't been able to bring himself to make the time. Those golden weeks after they'd met, his concentration had been on her, not work, and part of him couldn't help thinking that lapse in concentration had contributed to his grandfather's stroke, no matter what the doctor said. The problem hadn't been his lack of time, just as the problem hadn't been Charlie's taste in clothes; it had been his reaction. He'd been so curt, so cutting by the end, knowing he was hurting her and taking out the guilt he felt about both her loneliness and hurt and about his grandfather's stroke and slow recovery on Charlie. Maybe he had subconsciously blamed her after all. He knew that was what she suspected. But no; he had blamed himself. For taking his eye off work, for letting his grandfather shoulder so much while he was off staring at the stars on a beach with Charlie.

'If you'd crashed a week later,' Charlie said, 'I wouldn't be here. I'd have been in Vietnam.'

Matteo turned back to her, surprised by the apparent change in conversation. 'Vietnam?'

'Yes, because obviously I wasn't going to just mope around and feel sorry for myself; I had to do something impulsive. Because that's what I do. I don't like to feel sorry for myself or look back. I like to move on to a new adventure and hope I get over whatever's upset me soon. So I got in touch with a friend who I knew was travelling and arranged to meet her in Vietnam. I told her that I was going to party my divorce away, even though all I really wanted to do was to hide away and lick my wounds. I married you on impulse, walked out on you on impulse and was going to leave the country and put it all behind me on an impulse—only I impulsively decided to nurse you through concussion and lie to you instead.' She gave a bitter little laugh that tore at his heart. 'I live my life on a whim. What kind of person does that make me?'

'Going on holiday doesn't make you a bad person, Charlie.'

But she didn't listen, half talking over him. 'I've been taking a hard look at myself since we split up, trying to figure out why I reacted so badly to your suggestions.'

'You have every right to dress how you want. And every right to be furious with me for speaking to you the way I did.'

'I did and I do. But why is it so important to me to be so different? I was always an extrovert, the kind of kid who loves putting on plays and meeting people; embassies can be pretty boring places, full of protocols—where we went, who we went with, even friends had to be vetted. I felt so confined all the time, apart from two things. One was when I danced and the other was when my parents would say, *Let's just have fun today*, and we'd head out without an embassy driver and just be normal tourists.'

'That makes sense.'

She reached out and took his hand, her fingers laced through his, her smile tender as she looked at him. 'I know it was worse for you, raised by nannies and boarding school. Now I know how lucky I really was to have parents who loved me, the chance to live in such amazing places. But back then I felt very hard done by. When I found out Phoebe was going to live with our grandmother I just decided then and there that I was going to as well. My parents tried to persuade me to come to Singapore with them but I talked them round, and it felt so liberating to make my own decision, to have some control of my own destiny, to do what I wanted when I wanted. I decided I always wanted to live like that, on my terms. My friends always said that there was no Keep Out sign that didn't entice me to go in, that I considered all rules optional, a *no* a green light.'

'And you get away with it. I couldn't believe the way you talked that security guard round that time you climbed into the locked yard.'

'I wanted to see the statues,' she protested, 'not wait until the next morning and queue up. But the funny thing is that, for once, coming here to Italy, I had a proper plan. I was going to wait until you were better, and then I was going to find a reason to go back to London. I was going to be mature and stay distant from you. Make sure you were okay but no more. But I couldn't even follow that plan, could I? Tonight wasn't supposed to happen.'

'Do you regret it? Because I don't, Charlie. Even if you told me that it was the last time, even if you walked away, grabbed a bag and headed off to Vietnam, Australia or Timbuktu. I wouldn't regret it. I'd regret what happened to us, and I'd regret that we hadn't managed to make it work. I would regret that in the end I couldn't convince you to give me another chance, but I don't regret being with you again. Not a single moment of it.'

She closed her eyes. 'Neither do I,' she whispered.

'Why overthink it, Charlie? We made some mistakes, I know that, but we were good together in so many ways. We are good together. This holiday, concussion and all, has been incredible. We are incredible. We can be incredible.' He paused, looking for the right words.

Less than two weeks ago he'd been driving down to Kent to persuade Charlie to give him another chance, to apologise, to try to persuade her to come home. He'd never know if he'd have succeeded or if she'd have turned him away and flown off to Vietnam, determined to party their divorce away. But that was before. Before they'd spent all this time together, before tonight. Surely she could see that it made sense for them to try again with so many regrets—and so much passion— between them.

'We both know better now. We know what we have to get right next time. Learning is a painful process, Charlie. It would be a shame to waste all that progress on the same outcome.'

'I want to say yes.' Charlie's gaze locked onto his. 'You don't know how much I want to say yes. To not look back and to throw myself into a new start, the way I always throw myself into something exciting. But Matteo, we are on holiday, nothing is as normal. We always worked well when we were living apart from our responsibilities. We were good together when we were dating, living for weekends and evenings in the headiness of falling in love. We are working now because you're not actually *at* work, and I'm not embarrassing you and you're not frustrating me. We know that when things are good we are very good, but is that enough?'

Matteo could almost see her slipping out of his reach with every word. 'We don't have to make any decisions now; let's see how it goes. Take it a day at a time.' He was aware of the irony as he spoke. Charlie was urging caution for possibly the first time in her life and here he was, telling her not to plan for tomorrow, to take each day as it came. If they'd both learned these lessons a little earlier they might not be in this position now.

He tried again, his voice low and coaxing, not letting her gaze slip from his. 'You said yourself, we're good on holiday. So let's have a holiday, let's have a second honeymoon, let me help you put on the gala. Let's work together to make it the best ballet gala Ravello has ever seen. In the end, we can take stock and either we can part knowing we gave it our best try, or maybe we'll know that this is where we are meant to be. Together. What have we got to lose from two more weeks?'

She didn't answer at once, a whole myriad of expressions passing over her mobile face. Indecision, hope, wariness, interest and a flicker of the old impulsive excitement that he didn't realise he'd missed until he saw it flash into her eyes.

'No promises?'

'Not one.'

'We just live each day and enjoy ourselves? No plans?'

'Not even for the next day. We'll see where our whims take us.'

She paused for one eternal second and then nodded. 'It sounds to me suspiciously like you're daring me and you know that I can't resist a dare. Okay, I'm in. Two weeks, no promises, no decisions until the end. Besides, I've committed to the gala now and it will be a lot easier with you by my side.'

Matteo sent up a silent prayer of thanks to whatever Roman deities were keeping an eye on them—hopefully Venus and not one of the more mischievous gods. He'd acted badly over the last few months. Being given a chance to try and make things right was more than he probably deserved but he wasn't going to let the opportunity slip away.

'It won't be the only thing that's easier,' he said, moving to sit beside her and slipping an arm around her shoulders, drawing her in so that she nestled into him. 'I've been pretty lonely at night in that huge bed all by myself.'

She drew back and smiled up at him, her mouth a sweetly provocative tilt. 'Is that so?'

'Absolutely.'

'And you're hoping I might be able to do something about it?' Her eyes were laughing at him now.

'I was counting on it.' And with that he kissed her, hot and hard, need and passion and all those weeks of pent-up frustration erupting through him with an undercurrent of relief. He'd bought himself some time. He had two weeks in which to convince this wilful, impulsive creature that living with him didn't mean losing everything that made her special. And two weeks to teach himself to let go, to put Charlie first.

This time he wasn't going to let her down.

CHAPTER NINE

'MATTEO, WE'RE GOING to be late!' Charlie called for probably the third time in as many minutes. 'Come on, you haven't seen intimidating until you have faced an entire room of dance parents. It's bad enough that I am turning up as the unknown English girl; I don't want to be late as well.'

This week was full of irony. It was usually Matteo who was strictly punctual and Charlie who had a more fluid attitude towards time. But not where her work was concerned. Maybe that was part of her problem. She didn't like to be too serious so maybe Matteo had just never realised how important her work was to her, how very much she had invested her time and emotions in the Kensington gala.

'I'm sorry, I'm sorry.' He exited the study and her heart gave the same painful yet pleasurable jolt it always did upon seeing him. You'd think that a year and a bit after meeting him she'd have got used to seeing him, but somehow her body always seemed to turn into an overeager puppy at the very sight of him.

And, to be fair, he was looking particularly delectable today, still holiday casual, but slightly smarter than

he'd been all week in a white linen shirt and grey tailored trousers. She could always tell that Matteo was
half Italian by the way he dressed, with a certain flair
that most Englishmen lacked. His dark hair was a little
longer than usual and freshly slicked back and he had
decided against shaving that morning. She reached up
to rub the stubble on his chin affectionately.

'How did it go?' she asked. After they'd returned to
Ravello she'd handed over all Matteo's electronic de-
vices with an apology for the subterfuge. She'd waited
for him to lose himself in work despite Jo's promises
to filter emails but, to her surprise, he'd managed to
keep his work down to a couple of hours over the last
two days. But today he'd called his grandfather and had
been closeted in the study since breakfast.

He groaned. 'It was fine. I think, underneath it all,
he is glad that I'm alive and well and recovered. But he
is clearly frustrated that I'm not going straight back to
work.' He smiled at her. 'I told him that I was owed this
time and everything is in good hands.' But, although
the words were positive, she could see the very real ex-
asperation beneath the smile. His grandfather always
knew exactly which buttons to press and liked to push
down on them hard.

'And he sounds fine?' She knew how much he worried about his grandfather's health.

'He talked at me nonstop for ninety minutes so I'll
say so.' He pulled back and gave her a full once-over,
whistling long and low. 'You look very professional.'

'The ballet world is very particular,' she said slightly
defensively, reaching up to touch the loose bun she'd
piled her hair into. Maybe the leggings, short wrap skirt

and cut-off cardigan were a little bit of a costume, but Charlie always felt better in a costume. 'I need to look the part.'

'I do believe you're nervous,' he said in obvious surprise and she could feel her cheeks flush.

'If it was drama or jazz or musical theatre I'd be fine. I know it's silly. I've been teaching ballet up to Grade Four for years and most of these kids won't be anywhere near there yet, but you can't cover up a bad *port de bras* with personality the way you can a jazz square, and these kids have been taught by the best.'

'I have no idea what you just said but it sounds terrifying.'

'Welcome to my world,' she said darkly, grabbing her bag and tablet containing the videos Natalia had sent her and her favourite music to teach to.

Maria was in residence so they didn't have to lock up, setting off up the driveway in a companionable silence as they trod the now familiar path to the village below. Charlie's mind was whirling as she went over all her preparation. She'd start with a warm-up of course, some barre work and then centre exercises before the actual rehearsal. Natalia had combined several grades together into larger groups, so thankfully she only needed to deal with three classes. The rest of the gala would be composed of demonstrations by a handful of professionals Natalia had studied or danced with and some of her older students who'd gone on to study at specialist institutions. None of that was any of Charlie's concern, to her great relief. Lucia and a couple of her friends were responsible for the venue, programme and ensuring all the guest dancers were met and looked after. No, Charlie's responsibilities were limited to looking after and preparing the fifty local children who would be taking part in the gala. Easy.

'It seems like a lot of work,' Matteo mused as they finally exited the villa gates and made their way towards the footpath that cut out the need to use the longer and less sheltered road down to Ravello.

'What does?' Charlie asked, jolted out of her thoughts.

'The gala. I agree it's a really good cause but it seems such an inefficient way of raising money. Many of the people around here have more than enough money to help dozens of charities. I don't understand why they don't just hold a benefit, serve some drinks and food, get this famous dancer to perform, bid on some nice items and write some cheques. It'd be a hell of a lot easier than trying to organise so many children. Rehearsals and costumes and fifty kids aged under fifteen? Seems like a recipe for disaster to me.'

'Someone still has to actually organise a benefit,' Charlie pointed out. 'Book a venue, sell the tickets, organise the caterers, find those auction items. It's a lot of work as well, just for a different audience and with a different vibe. This will be a lot more fun. Besides, benefits have their place, of course they do, but I've been to a lot over the last year and although some have been brilliant and come from a genuine desire to change things, others are a little more about being seen to do the right thing, don't you think?' Her chest squeezed with painful hope as she posed the question. Because, of course, benefits and being seen to do the right thing was exactly how Matteo operated. Not because he was unthinking or uncaring, but because he was representing

Harrington Industries and every cheque was as much a PR exercise as a donation.

'In what way?'

'I just found some of those dinners and concerts and balls we attended a bit hypocritical,' she said carefully. 'There were people wearing outfits that cost more than the money they donated, sipping fine champagne and doing business deals while ostentatiously writing huge cheques. Don't get me wrong, I know this is how much of the world works and the money raised can be life-changing. It's just not my style. Meanwhile, these children will have a wonderful experience and learn the value of thinking about others. What's wrong with that?'

Matteo held up his hands as if in mock surrender. 'Wrong? Nothing at all. It's just as I said, it's an awful lot of work.'

'In this case, work you volunteered me for,' she pointed out, and he laughed.

'Point taken.'

They were nearing the village now and the path thinned so they were forced into single file. Charlie fell behind Matteo, her mind still tumbling with thoughts stemming from their brief conversation.

The truth was that Matteo's careless suggestion that she step in to help his goddaughter had stirred up the still unresolved hurt and anger from the night of the Kensington gala. The night when they hadn't even argued, just stared at each other in mutual inability to empathise with the other. The night that had led her to tell Matteo she couldn't see a way their marriage would work and maybe she should leave. The night he had said that maybe that would be best. She didn't know if he had expected her to go through with it but while he was in New York she'd packed her things and returned to her grandmother's.

He still didn't know how much he'd hurt her—no, he knew how much but had no real idea why. He understood that he'd closed down emotionally, been physically as well as mentally absent, but didn't realise that his lack of interest in her activities, in her life had been equally hurtful. But was it fair to dredge up that argument again? After all, he was committed to trying to put things right. And, truthfully, she couldn't deny that the last two weeks had been among the best of her life.

But if she didn't say anything then how could they solve all the problems that had led to the breakdown of their marriage in the first place? If she wanted to just enjoy these weeks in Italy and then head off in their separate ways then brushing the past under the carpet was the best policy—and that option was available to her; Matteo had made that very clear. But, with every day, Charlie knew that she didn't want that outcome. That this marriage, this man were worth fighting for—and that meant that, sooner rather than later, she needed to be completely honest.

At that moment they reached the hall where Natalia taught dancing and the rehearsals were to take place. The gala itself would be held in the gorgeous surroundings of the Villa Rufolo on an evening when it wasn't holding one of its famous concerts, the audience for once made up primarily of locals, not well-heeled visitors—although the illustrious line-up of stars had led to tickets selling to plenty of outsiders.

Charlie inhaled. The parents would think their children perfect no matter what they did on stage, but knowledgeable outsiders raised the stakes and the children had lost well over a week of rehearsals already. She only had ten days until the dress rehearsal, which meant she had just ten days to make sure each dance was perfect and every one of the children knew every step, cue and mark. It was down to her.

No more delaying, she told herself. Straightening her shoulders, she pushed open the door and walked confidently into the hall as if she did this every day.

Which in her old life she had.

She could hear an excited buzz as she walked in, the high-pitched squeals of children playing, the low confidential hum of gossiping parents, all undercut with anticipation for the strange new teacher that only Lucia had met. She was aware of every head swivelling to look at her and Matteo, what felt like hundreds of pairs of eyes sweeping up and down her, judging her posture, her walk, her outfit and bearing as silence descended so suddenly it was as if someone had switched the volume down.

Still displaying an utmost confidence externally, despite her inner trepidation, Charlie walked up to the front of the room and turned to face the parents seated in rows at the back, the children sitting cross-legged and expectant on the wooden floor. Matteo stood just a step away.

'Buon giorno,' she said calmly, projecting her voice with every bit of stage training she possessed, ensuring that her words reached every corner of the room despite not raising her voice. 'I'm sorry to say my Italian is not

up to the job of teaching you in your own language,' she said, and waited for Matteo to translate. 'I know some of you can understand English, and I will speak slowly for those of you that do and my husband, Matteo, will translate for the rest of you. It's not ideal, I know, but luckily much of the language of dance is universal. I'm sure we will muddle through.'

Charlie was relieved to see some answering nods as she went on to explain that she'd met Natalia and had all her notes and thoughts, noting the ripple of relief that ran around the room at those words, before giving a brief introduction of her own training and experience.

'I know you are all excited,' she concluded, addressing her words to the seated children. 'So am I. This is a great opportunity and should be a wonderful experience for all of you. It's my job to make sure you're all in the best place that you can be and I am sure you know that means we have some hard work ahead of us. We will start with a warm-up and then some barre work before we head into rehearsal. I want you all to skip around the room to start off with. Like butterflies, please. Ready? Go?'

Matteo leaned back against the wall, arms folded, and watched his wife. He'd never seen her in her natural habitat before, never seen her teach a class, although he'd picked her up from them, seen her bid farewell to excited children who would bob little curtseys and call her Miss Charlie. He'd found it charming, cute—and told her so. Which, he was realising, had been pretty damn condescending of him, as if her dance teaching was just a hobby.

In fact, the more he thought about it, the more he realised he'd regarded her whole life as some kind of quirky hobby, easy for her to put aside when they married, barely listening when she'd suggested they live in Kent and he mix commuting with working from home. She'd love London when she was used to it, he'd told her, as if she hadn't grown up in several capital cities all over the world. As if her existing life was inferior to his.

In reality, she'd been as busy as him. Teaching primary school was exhausting; he knew he couldn't do it. And yet she'd finished a busy day of teaching maths and English and science and music and PE to over thirty children still of an age to find sitting still a chore, before heading to her second job and another two or three hours of teaching several dance styles to pupils aged as young as two all the way to her senior citizens' beginners ballet. No wonder she'd been bored at home all day. Charity committees, entertaining and shopping were never going to satisfy her. And yet he'd been the one who had persuaded her out of applying for jobs. He'd liked knowing that Charlie was available when he needed her to accompany him to a function or on a business trip and knew that the demands of the school term would have made her presence impossible.

He'd known then that his decision had been selfish, quietened his conscience with the reminder that it wasn't unusual in his social group and that once they had children she'd find more to occupy her. As if he were some fifties businessman, lord and master of his home. As if he were his grandfather. He could only now recognise the influence his grandfather's comments had had.

It was painful watching her because she was so clearly in her element, despite the language barrier. One minute she was demonstrating a step, the next gently straightening a small hip or curling an arm, nodding approval or smiling a word of praise. How could anyone miss how quickly the children had taken to her? How their faces lit up with happiness at every word of praise and how diligently they copied her when she gave a correction. The parents seemed impressed too, sitting watching with narrowed eyes, nodding in agreement when Charlie made a suggestion.

Matteo's fists curled. He had taken her at face value, his mercurial, impulsive wife, but there was a depth to her that, although he'd known it was there, he'd never bothered to explore. A depth obvious in this room, with every dedicated moment she spent on the tiniest detail, the genuine laughter and happiness when a series of steps were executed perfectly.

It was a long morning, with three classes and three rehearsals before everybody came together to rehearse the finale. The afternoon sun was high overhead when they were finally over.

'I am so sorry,' Matteo said as Charlie stopped to stretch her arms out, oblivious to the curious looks of passers-by. 'I had no idea what I was signing you up for. You must be exhausted.'

But, to his surprise, she laughed. 'Oh, no, I could teach all day. I love it.'

'So I'm forgiven for volunteering you?'

Putting an arm through his, she kissed his cheek, warm and sweet and undeserved. 'I think you're punishing yourself enough. That was a lot of translating today and there's far more to come. But it was fun to hear the children make fun of your attempts at ballet terms.'

'Funny for you, maybe,' he half grumbled, although he suspected that she knew that by the end he'd been hamming up his misinterpretation, charmed by the peals of giggles every time he'd said *jeté* or *plié*. 'I loved watching you teach; it's like a dance in itself. And you notice everything. How are you correcting a wrong leg in one corner and a misstep the other side of the room?'

'I don't know. Practice, I guess.'

Their route took them through the main square and he nodded at a table in a shady corner. 'I don't know about you but I could do with a drink and something to eat after that.'

'That would be lovely, thank you,' Charlie agreed and they took a seat, ordering small beers, water and some antipasti.

'I'm sorry,' Matteo said once their drinks had been delivered, along with a bowl of olives and some piping-hot arancini. 'I didn't realise how much teaching means to you, not until today. You came alive in there. Is it the same in the classroom?'

'Different in the classroom in some ways. I have them for much longer, of course, and there's no diversity in age. I do like the difference between tots and teens; it's a lot of fun. But I get the same buzz of connection. When a child gets something you've been trying to convey, that moment of clarity is really special. My first primary school class are all in secondary school now but they come back and visit sometimes, and knowing I had a small role in shaping these curious almost-adults is inspiring.'

'And your classes in Kensington? Were they more like today? You were working towards a gala there as well, weren't you?'

Charlie took an arancini ball and pulled it apart on her plate, the hot mozzarella stringy between her fingers. 'I wish you'd come to see the Kensington Community Dance project; it had an incredible vibe. Classes are classes; they all have a similar feel, although I didn't teach ballet there, just jazz and musical theatre, but our gala was very different. No guest artists, very few proud ballet mums making sure their budding prima ballerina was suitably recognised. Not every child had the right clothes or shoes.'

Putting the remains of her arancini down, Charlie took a gulp of water. 'I know it's hard to see, living like you do with your beautiful house in your beautiful square, a driver to take you to work, reservations for all the best restaurants, but there is so much poverty almost right on your doorstep.'

'I know,' he said, stung. He might not volunteer, might not have time to actively participate in the community the way Charlie had, but he donated enough. He was very generous with local initiatives. 'I'm not oblivious, Charlie.'

'The community centre where the project is based tries to reduce some of that inequality. There are so many children living in the same borough and yet they might as well be on different planets. Some, the privileged children of embassy staff, our neighbours, go to private schools with every kind of activity you could imagine, from musical instruments to learning Mandarin to fencing. In their spare time they play tennis in the park at exclusive clubs, they go horse-riding, they learn ballet with the top companies. Whereas the children who come to the community centre, many of their parents don't even speak English, their schools are too strapped for cash to offer any activities, they've never picked up a tennis racket or ridden a horse. We try and plug some of that gap but it's not always easy. Cultural differences, family expectations, even having somebody who is free to bring you to the centre for your class: when your parents are working three jobs, getting you to tap class on time each week just isn't a priority. But the gala, that was their chance to shine. It was about showing off their achievements, celebrating them as much as about funding the next year's activities. They all put in so much work. I just wish you had been there to see it.'

Her voice was filled with sorrow, with hurt and an undercurrent of the anger that had flared up the day of the gala when he had come home, not to escort her there, but to pack for an unexpected trip to New York.

'I'm really sorry that I was called away at the last minute. I did offer to donate whatever it was you needed to raise that night...'

Charlie looked up at that, her gaze holding his, cold and proud. 'And that's just it. All that work was to give the children a chance to show a world which writes so many of them off before they have even left school just what they could do, about showing that they were important, that they mattered. But they didn't matter to you, and the work I did meant nothing to you. You thought a cheque would make up for your lack of interest. We did need the money, but just writing a huge cheque bigger than everything else we raised that night didn't make you some kind of hero. It made you someone who devalued every carefully donated prize, every saved-up-for ticket, every home-made costume.'

'That's not true,' he protested, but the words rang hollow and he knew it. He hadn't been interested in spending an evening in a local hall watching children he didn't know dance and sing.

'You didn't listen when I talked about it,' Charlie continued. 'You thought it was a cute way of keeping me occupied, that because it was unpaid it had no intrinsic value. And that was a problem, that *is* a problem. I'm not just your wife; I'm a person in my own right and what I do matters. It should matter to both of us, not just to me. But you think what I do is worthless and until you recognise that, until that changes, we have no chance of a lasting future, Matteo.'

Matteo stared at Charlie, devastated by the truth in her words, by the cold, proud hurt in her eyes, in her voice. He was responsible for this. He had made his beautiful, vibrant wife feel worthless, let her think that he thought her worthless, that she was nothing more than his consort. He'd made her feel that her actions and passions didn't matter. Of course, *of course* that had never been his intention, had never ever been his meaning and yet in this case he couldn't deny that his actions definitely spoke louder than words.

He inhaled, low and deep, trying to find the right words. 'You're right.'

Charlie looked up from a plate where she had been examining the remains of the arancini intently as if they held the secrets to the universe. 'Pardon?'

Sitting back, he kept his gaze on hers, tried to make sure his expression was as open and honest as possible, even though emotions had never been easy for him to show. 'You're right. I was an absolute idiot and it's a miracle you are here, that you didn't leave me in the hospital. Of course what you do has value and just because I might not always recognise that value is no excuse for not seeing that. What's important to you should be important to me as well because *you're* important.'

'I...' It wasn't often that Charlie was at a total loss for words but she didn't finish the sentence, just shaking her head in disbelief. 'A bit of an idiot, maybe. I know things were difficult.'

Typical Charlie. One moment furious at him, the next minute giving him a get-out clause. Not this time. If they were to have any chance then he had to be totally honest, painful as that was. 'I put myself first, my company first, expected you to fit into my life, and there is no excuse for that. All I can say is that I didn't plan it that way. I had no intention of marrying you and then trying to change everything that makes you so special. It wasn't planned. It wasn't intentional—and the crazy thing is it's definitely not even what I wanted. It's not what I want. The truth is, the time I spent with you before we married, and those too brief days of our honeymoon, were the happiest days of my life. It was like stepping out of my confined reality full of expectations I never quite lived up to into a world I hadn't imagined possible. Everything seemed brighter, sounds were more musical, even the smells were fresher...'

He laughed, slightly embarrassed. 'I'm not sure what's worse, that I sound like a terrible poet or that I mean every word. That's the way it was. For the first time ever I questioned everything I thought real. I questioned my decision not to live with my mother. My decision to put work before everything, to try and live up to my grandfather's standards even though I knew full well he would just keep moving the goalposts, that I would never quite be good enough. Even though I knew that somehow it was my job to atone for the sins of my father and to accept that role willingly. With you, all that melted away. I dared to be happy, really happy. But then Grandfather had his stroke…'

Charlie reached out and covered his hand with hers. 'I know this,' she said softly. 'I do know this, Matteo. I am so sorry to have made you feel that I'm blaming you for everything. To think that I consider you a bad person in any way. I don't; I wouldn't be here if I did. I know that actually the opposite is true. That you spend your life trying to do what's right. That you might never have put me first but you were never putting yourself first either. I know you have huge commitments, bigger than the two of us. But, selfishly, I wanted to be first for a little longer.'

'That wasn't selfish, Charlie. That's just the way it should be. The way I wanted it to be. But when I got back to London and I saw my grandfather looking vulnerable for maybe the first time in his life, knowing he needed me for the first time, I couldn't let him down.'

'Forgetting all the very qualified and very well paid people you employ to actually help you run Harrington Industries? You have to trust in them.'

He smiled wryly. 'I know that, my grandfather knows that, but he made it clear that he could only relax, only heal knowing I was taking care of everything. Part of me knew that he was playing me even then. He can't help it. But at the same time he was the one constant, Charlie. I may not like the way I was raised. I might have cried myself to sleep those first years at boarding school, resented him when he made me choose between the company and spending the summer here with my family, but he was there, and there was no one else I could say that about.'

He took a sip of his tart beer and stared out at the square, filled with tourists and locals, couples and families, chattering, happy people, secure and together. 'It might have hurt every time he made digs about my parentage, the expectations he put on me. It might have been infuriating, knowing that no matter what I did, what deal I landed, the profits I made, he would expect me to do better. That doesn't stop me wanting to make him proud. And he needed me then, for the first time. How could I have let him down? Even though I knew at some level that he was using the situation to drive a wedge between us. Part of me will always yearn for his approval, Charlie, even though I know it will never come. Even now, sitting here, doing my best to convince you that you are the most important thing in my life, there's a bit of me replaying the conversation I had with him earlier and hearing the disapproval in his voice, the dig underlying every single word. But I choose to stay here with you. I choose you if you'll have me. I've learned my lesson.'

Charlie blinked, her eyelashes damp. 'Let's not make any decisions now,' she said, lacing her fingers through his, her thumb circling the back of his hand. 'Not today, not when the sun is shining, we have cold delicious drinks and even more delicious snacks and beer and we are sitting in one of the most beautiful villages in the world.' She smiled at him, the gesture a little wobbly. 'I don't need to forgive you, Matteo. I just need to know that if we do try again things will be different. That I can be me, faults and all, a little impulsive, sometimes reckless. Of course you can tell me if you're not comfortable, but don't try and curb me. And in return I'll be respectful of your work and the hours you put in and I'll make sure I am appropriately dressed for work situations, just as long as you never ever suggest a dress that can only be described as mushroom colour ever again.'

Matteo stared at her, his mind tumbling. 'Wait there.' He pushed his chair back, leaving Charlie looking after him in confusion as he strode across the square and around the corner where he knew there was a small pharmacy. It was so small and so localised he wasn't sure it would have what he needed, but a quick perusal of the shelves yielded results and he chose a box almost at random, paid for it hurriedly and within seconds was back at the table where Charlie was sitting still, staring at him in confusion.

'What on earth...?' she began.

'Here.' He handed her the box. 'I should have done this a long time ago.'

Charlie took the box and stared down at it, tears falling freely now. 'Hair dye? Oh, Matteo, that is a gorgeous purple.'

'It'll suit you.' He reached over to tilt her chin, wiping a tear from her soft cheek. 'I mean it, Charlie. I do like your hair this way, but I miss the flash of colour.' He grinned. 'It makes you easy to find when we're out.'

She swatted his hand away, but was laughing as she did so. 'Whereas you need a tracking device. I never knew a man so likely to stop and not tell me. I've lost count of how many times I've said something to you, only to realise you're actually half a mile behind me replying to yet another email.' She glared at his watch. 'Curses to whoever invented smartwatches.'

Matteo unbuckled it and handed it to her. 'Here.'

'What? Seriously?'

'I was quite happy for the two weeks I didn't have it, not checking emails every minute, and I even survived without knowing my step count. Go on. Give it away, sell it, whatever you want. I'm free.'

'You'll be begging me for it back within twenty-four hours,' she said, sliding it into her bag and standing up. 'Okay, let's go. I've already paid.'

'What's the hurry?'

She winked. 'I have to dye my hair—and then I intend to thank you very, very thoroughly.'

'In that case,' he said, grabbing her hand and towing her away from the table, 'what are you dawdling for?'

And as she slipped her hand through his arm, laughing, Matteo dared to hope that maybe they would be all right after all.

CHAPTER TEN

CHARLIE ROLLED OVER onto her back and half opened one eye, only to instantly close it again against the bright morning sun filtering in through the curtains. But, although she tried to regulate her breathing and slide back into sleep, she knew it was a waste of time; she was wide awake.

She lay there for a moment, trying to figure out why she felt a little peculiar, touching at her emotions gingerly as if testing a sore tooth. But there was no twinge, just a blanket calm. Contentment. *Contentment?* That was it, why she felt so odd. She had often been happy, exhilarated, full of joy and, just as often, could find herself despairing, covering it with her usual insouciant brand of get-up-and-go and mixing things up. But she rarely felt this calm contentment.

Squinting against the morning light, she reached out a toe and rubbed it lightly against the hard muscles of Matteo's calf. She waited a moment but he didn't stir, not even when she ran her hand suggestively along his arm. Rolling back onto her side, she looked at him, learning him by heart all over again. He was naked, half covered by a sheet, his expression surprisingly relaxed in sleep, a marked improvement on the habitually pinched look he'd worn the last few months of their marriage. But then he'd rarely slept, working all hours.

But that was then and this was now. Charlie drank in the sharp, haughty slant of his cheeks, accentuated by high cheekbones, the strong, straight nose, not quite large enough to be called Roman, and the full sensual mouth, now relaxed, but so often severely set.

To those who didn't know him, Matteo could seem remote, serious, even curt and yet that façade hid so much more depth than she had realised possible when she'd first met him. When he'd first introduced himself she'd been desperate to impress him, wanting him to think her worthy of a grant. But, for those first few minutes, she had thought him little more than a suit with power. A handsome suit, admittedly, one who made her pulse beat a little bit faster and her throat dry up with every glance from under those straight brows. But a suit nonetheless and Charlie wasn't interested in suits. But he'd whisked her out for dinner and by the time her first course had arrived she'd seen that behind the tailored handmade clothing was a man who seemed genuinely interested in her project—more, interested in her. A man who asked probing questions, drew her out and listened intently to every answer. Whose hardwon smile gave her a sense of satisfaction, of fulfilment.

If Matteo thought that she had brought light and laughter into his life then she needed to acknowledge that he had brought depth to hers. He validated her and all she was. Had seen through the costume and colour to the heart of her.

Reaching up, Charlie pulled at a lock of her hair and looked at the purple-tipped ends, that same new contentment warming her through as she stretched out luxuriously, feeling aches in all her secret places, a reminder of just how much she had thanked Matteo the night before and why. Impatient, she nudged him.

'Wake up, sleepyhead,' she said, and it was his turn to roll, stretching out with a yawn. She watched the movement appreciatively as he looked sleepily at her.

'What time is it?'

'No idea. You got rid of your watch, remember, and we agreed phones had no place in the bedroom.' She couldn't help a smile curving her mouth as she spoke, remembering how they'd rushed up the stairs the evening before, barely making it to the bedroom, phones left on the coffee table, unneeded and unwanted.

His own smile was suggestive, a deliberate sensual curve that sent her stomach tumbling in desire. 'So, did you wake me for anything in particular, Mrs Harrington?'

She nestled closer, running a hand across his arm again, and this time felt him quiver ever so slightly under her touch. 'Well,' she breathed, 'I thought we might finish what we started last night...'

His eyebrows shot up. 'Finish? Oh, I thought we finished all right. You're telling me that you want more?'

She allowed her gaze to travel slowly over him, deliberately lingering on every inch of his torso. 'If you're up to it, that is.'

'Up to it?' In one fluid movement he turned over and pinned her to the bed, and she wriggled under the delicious weight of him. 'Do you want me to show you how up to it I am?'

'Oh, yes, please.' She wound her arms around his neck. 'I thought you'd never ask.'

Matteo didn't move for one eternally torturous moment, just looked steadily into her eyes, his own gaze full of heat and desire. And then, when she thought she couldn't wait any longer, he dipped his head and kissed her.

She'd been expecting his kiss to be hard. Their lovemaking over the last few days had been frantic, passionate, as if they were both trying to make up for lost time, almost punishing themselves for the time apart. But this kiss was different, sweet, slow and so sensual she could feel her toes literally curl.

Matteo took his time, muttering to her in a mixture of Italian and English as he trailed kisses along her throat, pausing at the pulse in the hollow of her neck, his knowing hands sliding along her body, making her gasp against him. Desperate to speed things up, to take some control, she reached out for him and he captured her hands in one of his, holding her lightly but purposefully.

'No, you don't,' he told her. 'I believe you threw down a challenge, my lady, and I'm never one to back away from a challenge.' Anticipation rippled through her at his words and she submitted. It was a most delicious torture, to lie and wait as he leisurely explored her body with his clever, clever hands and teasing kisses. She closed her eyes, giving herself up to sensation, to the feel of him, his touch. This was where she belonged. They fitted together. He and she. For now at least.

'Capri at last!' Charlie said rapturously as Matteo expertly steered the small boat towards the harbour. She watched him do something complicated-looking with the tiller and grinned. 'I had no idea you were such an accomplished sailor. It's bringing out all my pirate fantasies.'

'Later,' he promised her, and her body weakened at the look in his eyes. A look just for her.

They moored at the main harbour and as she disembarked Charlie looked around excitedly. She'd heard a lot about this fabled isle, home to emperors and sirens. But, although the harbour was undeniably pretty, it wasn't noticeably fancier than Amalfi, where they had sailed from, or Positano, yesterday's post-rehearsal destination. Matteo was delivering on his tour guide promise and she was loving every sun-drenched second.

There were boats everywhere, clustered around jetties and moored out at sea, every conceivable style from small rowing boats and dinghies to fancy cruisers. A larger jetty served the ferries and hovercrafts and groups of tour guides waited at the end for the day trippers to disembark, offering them trips to the fabled Blue Grotto. A row of painted houses lined the bottom of the tall peaked cliff, many of them home to shops, cafés and hotels.

'This way,' Matteo said, gesturing towards a little building that resembled a station at the foot of the high cliff. Charlie gave him a questioning look and he laughed. 'We can take the funicular up or if you prefer we can walk, but I warn you, it's pretty steep.'

'Funicular every time,' Charlie said emphatically, and he took her hand as they dodged amongst the tour groups and large family groups in order to join the queue for the steep ascent to the top of the cliff.

They waited in line, hand in hand, just two lovers amongst the many couples day-tripping over from the Amalfi coast and she revelled in the sheer ordinariness of it. As Matteo bought the tickets Charlie adjusted her huge sunglasses and smoothed down her trousers. She'd opted for cut-off capris today, in honour of the island for which they were named. Lime-green, she'd teamed them with a white tank top patterned with tropical fruit. A matching scarf held back her hair and offered some relief from the sun and she'd opted for the large white hoop earrings again. The only thing that didn't match were her sensible white trainers. Matteo had warned her they would be doing some climbing and so she'd left her heeled sandals behind although she had packed some sparkly flip-flops for later.

It didn't take the funicular long to ascend to the top of the hill. Charlie looked down at the steep drop and shivered. 'I always find these things unnatural,' she murmured to Matteo and he squeezed her hand reassuringly. But she was relieved when the doors opened and she was back on solid ground. Within seconds she found herself in the main square of Capri town and she took in every detail eagerly. The square wasn't large and most of the space was filled with tables, waiters bustling around, little alleyways and wide paved streets leading enticingly off, all thronging with tourists.

'What do you want to do first?' Matteo asked. 'There's a really lovely walk up through Capri town to the tip of the cliff and to Tiberius' villa, then back through some beautiful woods right by the sea. The views are incredible; best not to think about the poor slaves that he threw off those cliffs though. Or we could go across to Anacapri and get the chairlift. It's up to you.'

'I've had quite enough of being held up in the air by machinery for now,' Charlie said. 'I vote for the walk, gory history or not. But first, did you say something about coffee being an essential experience here?'

'I believe I did. How about that café there?' He gestured towards the tables and they took a seat at a recently vacated one in a shady corner spot with excellent views all around the square. He leaned forward confidentially. 'Just remember how horrified you were by the price of those drinks we had overlooking the Pantheon in Rome.'

'We could have bought an entire meal for the price of two small beers,' she protested and he laughed.

'Well, those beers may seem quite reasonable compared to what we are about to pay. Consider yourself forewarned.'

'Then why don't we go somewhere else; we don't need to sit here.' She half rose but Matteo laid a hand on her arm, staying her.

'It's a tradition. You're paying for the view, the location. Besides, it's not as if we can't afford it.'

She shook her head at him. 'Not all of us are accustomed to such wealth, you know; there's no harm in being a little frugal.'

'I like to treat my wife; is that such a crime?' he asked, and she smiled.

'I guess not.'

The coffee *was* ludicrously expensive, but luckily it was also delicious. They took their time, people watching, Charlie making up as outrageous a story as she could about many of the people they saw walking by, challenging herself to make Matteo laugh, to coax a smile out of him. It wasn't hard; his memory might have returned but he was still like the Matteo of old, easy company, interested in everything she had to say, his mind on her and where they were, not on his phone or his tablet. As promised, his watch had been locked away in a drawer back at the villa and he had barely checked his phone since they'd left the villa earlier.

When she finally felt as if she'd got as much value out of the coffee as she could, they started to explore the small town, Charlie treating Matteo and herself to ice creams, watching the cones made fresh as they stood there, the hot batter expertly shaped and immediately hardening and cooling ready to receive her raspberry and lemon and his dark chocolate and liquorice *gelato*. Slowly, enjoying the intense flavours, they wandered along the route they'd chosen.

The road to Tiberius' villa was well signposted and obviously popular. Shops lined the street, well-known designer names to cater to the privileged clientele who came to this beautiful island, and soon they ended up in a residential area, gorgeous villas hidden behind high walls and locked gates. Charlie peeped through every chink she could find, seeing just enough to whet her imagination. 'Imagine living here,' she said every ten or so yards as they passed yet another beautiful villa.

'Ravello not good enough for you now?' Matteo asked mock indignantly and she nudged him.

'I have quite fallen in love with Ravello as you know, but this place is iconic; it was the playground of some of the biggest stars in the fifties and sixties. It's obviously my spiritual home.' She stopped to stare long-ingly at a white villa poised on the cliff, its infinity pool perfectly positioned as if a swimmer might dive straight into the sea far below. 'That must be the worst part of being rich,' she said. 'You see a glorious place like this and you could buy it if you wanted. Where's the fun in always getting what you like? While us more down-to-earth folk get to play *If only* and daydream. Much more fun.'

Matteo joined her at the gate. 'Okay then, let's play. How would you come to live there?'

She thought long and hard. 'I come to Capri to be a companion to an ageing English film star,' she said after a while.

'And does said ageing English star have a danger-ously sexy half-Italian nephew?' He dropped a kiss onto her neck and she leaned back against him.

'Maybe. He's a playboy disgrace who doesn't trust the companion as he thinks she's out to get his great-aunt's fortune. Oof, it's hot,' she said, abandoning make-believe to swig some water.

There were plenty of other people walking the same route but it didn't feel too crowded as they climbed up and up, the sun beating down upon them as it neared noon. Enjoyable as the walk was, Charlie was relieved when they passed a tree-lined glade and Mat-teo agreed to her suggestion that they take the oppor-tunity to stand in the shade and cool down. It wasn't a long walk but steep, made harder by the temperature.

Taking a much-needed breath and more water, Char-lie swivelled slowly to take in the view. Looking up, she could see the Villa Jovis perched at the very top of

the cliff and shivered as she remembered some of the
history detailed in her guidebook.

'How could they have imagined back then that two
thousand years later we would be coming to gawp at the
villa when people were murdered and tortured there—
just like the Colosseum? It seemed so surreal to be
walking around surrounded by tour groups and running
children, listening to spine-chilling tales of slaughter,
unable to imagine how much blood was spilled there.
And we're shocked and say it's barbaric but are we
any different? There's no respect for those thousands
of lives lost there; it's just another tick on the tourist
list. Two thousand years make the horrors just seem
inconceivable.'

She turned to Matteo but his mind was clearly elsewhere as he fished his phone out of his pocket. 'I'm
sorry,' he said. 'It's been vibrating. I know I promised,
but...'

'No, go ahead.' She knew he wouldn't be able to relax
until he knew who was calling him and why. 'It's fine.'

She wandered over to the edge of the shaded terrace
and peered down at the sea below, an intoxicating turquoise that made her want to dive right in, at least she
would if she wasn't several hundred feet up. Where were
the swimming spots on this island? Matteo would know.

She turned, a question on her lips, then stopped as
she took in the rigid look on his face.

He barely seemed to know she was there. 'Good
God! When? I see.'

'What's happened?' she said, swimming forgotten,
but he didn't acknowledge her question, still engrossed
in the call.

'Yes. Yes. Of course. Right. Agreed.'

He ended the call but made no move towards her and her stomach dropped as she noted his compressed mouth, his brows drawn together, every trace of the holiday-maker gone. Even in shorts and a T-shirt, he was suddenly every inch the deputy CEO of Harrington Industries.

'What's happened?' she repeated as he pocketed his phone, his face even grimmer if that was possible.

'I'm sorry. I have to go.' He rummaged in his pocket and held out the return ticket for the funicular and a handful of notes. 'You stay here, go up to the villa as we arranged, get yourself some lunch. I need to take the boat back for speed, but there are plenty of ferries across to the mainland; you'll be fine. Don't let this stop you enjoying your day.'

'Of course you need to take the boat back; I can't sail,' she said, realising as she said it that who took the boat was so not the point she needed to be making. 'Anyway, I'm not staying here without you... Matteo, *what happened*?'

He ran his hand distractedly through his hair and for a moment she saw a flicker of fear behind his set expression, then it was gone, as if it had never been. He was shutting down, she realised wearily. Just like before.

'It's my father.'

In a moment she was by his side, her hand clasping his arm. 'Is he okay? Has there been an accident?' Of course she'd go back with him; he'd need her support. She knew he wasn't close to his father, resenting his party-filled lifestyle and the way he had so easily left

Matteo to be brought up by his grandfather. From what Matteo had said, his father had kept custody of him legally but hadn't seemed to care whether his small son was at boarding school, in Italy or alone in his grandfather's austere Richmond mansion with a series of nannies—his grandfather just as absent, only in his case through workaholism. Moderation, it seemed, was not a Harrington gene.

Matteo shook his head. 'No, no, he's just been caught bribing.' He closed his eyes. 'Just! The fool. As inept at illegal business as he is at any other kind of work.'

'Bribing? Who?'

'I don't know; he was over in Chile. He's a director of Harrington Industries, not that he's ever done a day's work in his life. I don't even know why he was in Chile; last I heard he was on his yacht in Nice. But he's been arrested on suspicion of bribery. This could be an absolute disaster for us PR-wise. I need to get back to London and talk to our Head of Security before he heads out to Chile. He'd better take our Comms VP as well to handle the story at that end. I should be in the UK handling any PR fallout. Damn him. What was he thinking?'

It wasn't his father he was so concerned about, more the potential reputational damage to Harrington Industries.

'But what about your father; is he okay?'

'He's been bailed.' The hard line of his mouth curved into a humourless smile. 'He'll be fine; he always slides out of these things. But an allegation like this could go very badly against us. Open up all kinds of investigations. We are clean, of course, but we can't afford to have any mud sticking, not with the delicate negotiations we have coming up in China.'

'You can't go back to the UK alone. I'll come with you.'

But his head shake was decisive. 'You have the gala, Charlie.'

The gala. Of course. A feeling of déjà vu swept through her. Once again she was on the cusp of doing something that showcased the best of her talents and once again her husband wouldn't be there to see it. Not to mention that he'd promised to be by her side the whole time, that she needed him to translate.

'You'll be fine,' he said, as if reading her thoughts. 'Lucia can translate for you, and you know the children now and they know you. You don't need me.'

If only that was true. 'How long will you be?'

'I don't know. But I promise I'll be back, Charlie. Back for the gala.'

She looked at him levelly. 'Don't make promises you can't keep, Matteo. Don't put either of us through that. Not this time.'

In two steps he was over to her, cupping her face with his hands, kissing her, quick and desperate. Taken aback by the fierce need in his embrace, she clung to him, only to find herself put firmly to one side.

'I won't let you down, Charlie. Trust me.'

Charlie watched him stride away until he was out of sight; he didn't look back once, as if she was already forgotten. For a moment she thought about giving up, returning to Capri town, heading back to the harbour and getting the first ferry back to Amalfi. But nothing would be served by her giving up her day out, even if it wasn't the day she'd planned. With a heavy heart and slow steps, she returned to the path and made her way up towards the Villa Jovis, thinking she'd gladly throw the whole of Harrington Industries off the cliff.

She did her best to enjoy the rest of the afternoon, combining sightseeing with a little bit of shopping and a plate of excellent pasta in a restaurant on a quaint side street, but her spirits were low, no matter how much she told herself to buck up. Charlie had never minded being alone before; she was quite used to it, even in strange places, thanks to some solo backpacking and day trips out alone when staying with her parents. She didn't *do* lonely, just like she didn't do sad or regrets, but today she couldn't deny that she *was* lonely and sad and full of regrets for both the day they hadn't shared and what that meant in the long term.

Of course Matteo had to go back, she told herself. But at the same time she couldn't help thinking that he had his phone and his laptop back at the villa, that Harrington Industries had an experienced Head of Security who could sort out the bribery issue, and plenty of PR professionals to sort out any negative press. What would standing in the London office actually achieve that he couldn't do just as well in Ravello? But of course his grandfather had summoned him back and Matteo had obeyed. His grandfather was probably glad of the opportunity. He'd taken to calling Matteo every morning and she knew that every single one of those conversations began with, *When are you coming back?*

Now it was her turn to ask that question. And to prepare for the likely answer to be, *Not now, not yet.* Then, *Not at all.*

CHAPTER ELEVEN

MATTEO DREW A weary hand through his hair and blinked a couple of times, his eyes dry and sore. He had no idea how long he'd been sitting at his desk, no idea what time it was: hell, he barely knew what day it was.

From the moment he'd landed at Heathrow it was as if his time away had never been. The second he'd set foot back in this office, work had descended on him like some kind of eternal punishment from a Greek myth. As soon as he thought he'd finished one thing, another twenty landed in his inbox and that was without even considering the mess his father's actions had got them into. Thanks to the time difference, he was in constant communication both late at night and early in the morning to Chile, liaising with Harrington Industries' Heads of PR and Security, who had gone out to try and salvage the business deal his father had so clumsily been trying to arrange and to ensure the arrest didn't make it into the papers.

Alongside all this was an underlying niggle of worry about his grandfather's health. He had seemed fully recovered from the stroke, but the last few days had clearly taken their toll; his face was tinged with grey, his mind less sharp than usual. Although the same could not be said for his tongue. That was as on point as ever.

All of this meant that Matteo had barely had a chance to speak to Charlie, let alone make plans to return to her. She assured him that she was fine, that she understood his absence, but he had made promises to her that right now it was looking increasingly unlikely he could keep. What that meant he could barely think about, partly because his mind was so consumed with work and partly because he knew he wouldn't like the answer.

The buzzer on his desk vibrated and a second later Jo, his PA, popped her head around the door. If he felt exhausted she looked it, immaculate as always, not a hair out of place, not a crease in her suit, but she had deep hollows under her eyes. 'For goodness' sake, Jo, go home.' He tried a smile to soften his words. 'When did you last sleep?'

'I could ask you the same question.' She nodded significantly at the sofa bed in the corner of the office. 'Have you actually been to your own house since you got back? Or have you been here every night?'

There was no point lying to her. 'It seemed silly opening up the house just for me,' he said. They both knew that wasn't the reason he hadn't gone home. It didn't feel like home any more, not without Charlie.

'You grandfather wants to see you. Are you free, or shall I put him off?'

He sighed. 'There's no point delaying the inevitable. I'd like to persuade him to go home and get some rest as well. Look, Jo, I'm serious. Go home. It's an order. I don't want to see you back here for at least twenty-four hours.'

'I hate to ignore a direct order, but I think you might need me for a few hours more yet. I promise I'll go home this evening, and if nothing else has happened to take the rest of the week off. Deal?'

'Okay, but at least take an hour. Go for a walk or something. Get yourself a sandwich.'

She nodded and closed the door softly behind her. Matteo sat back and stretched.

Ten minutes later he was ascending in the lift to his grandfather's penthouse office suite. Matteo could have had the rooms alongside as deputy CEO but preferred to be a couple of floors below, next to some of the other executive board and decision-makers. The lift opened into the opulently carpeted lobby and Matteo strode straight through, past the open-plan office where his grandfather's PA guarded the entrance to his lair. He greeted her cordially as he rapped on the heavy oak door, not waiting for an invitation before opening it and stepping into the large corner office with views out over Kensington Gardens.

He had expected his grandfather to be exactly where he was, seated behind his huge antique desk, but Matteo hadn't expected to see the man lounging on the leather sofa on his right. Head bowed, brows drawn together, he exuded exhaustion. His father looked nothing like his usual urbane playboy self.

'Dad?'

His father looked up and managed a faint smile. 'Matteo, good to see you.'

'When did you get back?'

'A couple of hours ago,' he said. 'Your grandfather wanted me to come straight here and explain myself.'

His tone was mildly sarcastic, but his smile softened the words.

'As you can see, Matteo, the prodigal son has returned.' His grandfather's voice was dry.

'But without the fatted calf,' his father said.

The resulting thump of a fist onto the desk reverberated around the room. 'That's right, make jokes. You put the company name into disrepute and now you're trying to make it a laughing matter. But what else could I expect from you? You've always been a wastrel!'

Matteo held his hands up to stem the flow of angry words. His father looked completely unlike himself. It wasn't just that he was tired and obviously visibly shaken by his experiences during the last few days; there was almost an air of humility about him that was more disconcerting than his usual insouciance. Meanwhile, his grandfather was greyer than ever, shaking with anger.

'Why don't I take it from here, Grandfather? Go home. Get some rest. Everything is completely under control now. I should have Barry's report in the next couple of hours, but verbally he's reassured me that this has all been kept under wraps. Go and get some sleep. I'll see you back here in the morning.'

It wasn't often that Matteo issued orders to his grandfather, let alone saw them obeyed by the proud old man, but to his surprise his grandfather didn't even protest, getting up and making for the door on shaky feet, almost hunchbacked with weariness. This time last year Matteo had been made aware of just how fragile his grandfather was getting—he was nearly eighty after all. Just because he carried himself with the arrogance of someone indestructible, it didn't mean that he was.

'Sleep?' his grandfather managed to scoff. 'When I start taking naps it'll be time to put me down.'

'There's no harm in naps and you shouldn't be putting in these kinds of hours,' Matteo said gently as his grandfather reached the door. 'The doctor was very clear.'

He had refrained from ever uttering the word *retirement*. He knew exactly how his grandfather would respond to that, but maybe it was time to start having some conversations about semi-retirement. Maybe his grandfather should take on a chairman role and let Matteo step up to CEO. He was more than ready, but he didn't want to mount some kind of coup. It had to be done with his grandfather's blessing, if such a thing was even possible. But it had to be possible. His grandfather couldn't carry on like this—and Matteo couldn't allow him.

'Don't fuss over me, boy,' his grandfather snapped and then he was gone.

Silence fell until Matteo's father laughed a little shakily. 'Still his charming self, I see.'

Matteo's protective instinct surged. 'What did you expect? He's not been well, and you haven't exactly helped. Bribery? What were you thinking? Why were you in Chile?'

His father regarded him coolly. 'I am a director of this company. Whether you like it or not.'

'In name, maybe.' He crossed to the window and stared out at the London landscape beyond. 'When have you ever done a full day's work?'

His father didn't answer for a long while, and when he turned Matteo was surprised to see a look of infinite sadness on his face.

'I need a shower, a shave and to change. And then, son, maybe you and I should go out and have a proper talk.'

Matteo sat back in the comfortable leather armchair and fought to keep his eyes open. The delicious three-course dinner and the glasses of wine which had accompanied it had made him realise just how weary he was. His father had taken him to his club, the kind of panelled walls, leather fittings and macho atmosphere that Matteo would usually avoid, but today it seemed right for this unexpected meeting between father and son.

During the dinner they hadn't talked about anything too personal, his father asking a few questions about how Charlie was and Matteo's accident, but mostly they had kept to neutral topics: sport, mutual friends, the chat of casual acquaintances, not father and son. Now his father too sat back and regarded him. He looked much more like himself, shaved, his hair immaculately slicked back, dressed in a linen suit, every inch the ageing playboy.

'I was in Chile because I knew there was an opportunity there with mining rights.'

Matteo raised an eyebrow. 'You are interested in mining rights?' He tried to keep the incredulity from his voice.

'As I said before, I'm still a director. I'm certain my father would quite happily have struck me off the board if he could, but that's the beauty of a family-owned business. He has no power to do so.'

'And so you decided to get these rights by any means possible. Damn the consequences?'

'It was a misunderstanding.' His father looked pained. 'I was involved in some exploratory talks; I had no idea the official was corrupt and under investigation. I offered to have a talk with my old college about opportunities for his son—I had no idea how it would be construed. I'll know better next time.'

Next time? 'Does that mean you are planning to get further involved?' He stilled. Surely his father didn't think he could just roll in and become CEO after a lifetime of not doing anything?

His father shook his head, humour glimmering in the hazel eyes so like Matteo's own. 'I've no intention of starting a nine-to-five at my age, coming into the office every day. But I do want to have more purpose to my life.'

Matteo couldn't have been more staggered if his father had announced that he had superpowers and was saving the world in his spare time. 'Purpose?'

'I'm barely past fifty,' his father pointed out. 'Maybe it's time to grow up a little. I've met someone...'

Here we go again. Matteo fought to keep the sardonic sneer off his face. Any revelations his father had were usually because he'd met someone. How many times had he been married now? Five or was it six? To say nothing of the series of uniformly lovely girlfriends who seemed to accompany him between marital adventures.

'I see.'

'I don't think you do, not this time, Matteo. Claudine is different. She's nearly my age with children of her own and a thriving business. She likes me, she may even love me, but she doesn't respect me. And maybe she has good reason not to. It's made me take a good long hard look at myself, realise I need to make some changes.'

'By getting arrested for bribery?'

His father laughed. 'As I said, that was an unfortunate misunderstanding. It's all been cleared up now. Look. We need to figure out the best place for me to be. I'm not quite ready for nine-to-five, but surely I could be of use. I have a lot of connections; people do seem to think I'm charming, you know. Besides, my brain may be a bit rusty but every school report I ever had said I had a lot of potential, I just chose not to use it. Maybe it's time I did use it. What do you think, Matteo? Could we be a team?'

Matteo picked up his coffee and took a sip. He was wary where his father was concerned, wary of his whims and his passions. Could this time really be different? Was he really ready to start again—and if so was Matteo ready to give him a chance? Give them a chance?

'We'll see. Let's talk once we know this arrest business has really been cleared up and things aren't quite so fraught.' He managed to resist adding, *See if you're still interested in a few weeks' time.*

Silence descended for a while, unusual for his father, who was usually a fount of small talk. Finally his father sighed. 'I know it's up to me to apologise, it's up to me to make things up to you. I let you down badly when you were a child—and just because I was barely more than a child myself then that doesn't make it okay.'

Taken completely aback, Matteo had no idea how to respond. While he was still figuring out a reply his father spoke again. 'Have you seen your mother at all while you've been in Italy?'

Matteo knew that his parents spoke more to each other than they did to him and had always found that disconcerting. 'I haven't had time.'

'You blame her more than you blame me, don't you?'

This was such an unexpectedly insightful thing for his father to say that again Matteo could only sit and stare. 'I don't blame either of you for anything. Things are what they are.'

'We weren't good parents to you, I know that. We were just so young and wild, our lifestyles so excessive. We lived for the moment, which is fine at twenty-one, but not when you have a year-old child needing you to grow up. It seemed easier—and admittedly more fun—to leave you with your nanny, and at your grandfather's, to ignore our responsibilities, but it wasn't right. Matteo, you should know that when we split up your mother did want you. Your grandfather...' He hesitated. 'I don't know if I am doing the right thing telling you this. I promised your mother long ago I wouldn't, but you have a right to know. Your mother wanted you, but your grandfather persuaded her to give me custody, which meant giving him custody. He said he'd take her to court, that he had evidence that she was unfit to care for you and he would make that public and she would never see you again. Or she could give in and have you for a few weeks during the summer. It took a long time for her to recover from that; she went off the rails badly for a while, as you know, which, of course, justified your grandfather's point of view as far as he was concerned. But he wasn't worried about your well-being; he was just determined to hang on to his Harrington heir.'

Suddenly half-remembered memories began to make some kind of sense. His mother's silences and tears, overheard snippets of conversation, his grandfather's jeers. And with that sense came the beginnings of a peace of mind he hadn't even realised he craved.

'But why?' Matteo managed.

'I suppose you were his chance to try again. I was never good enough for him; he made that clear my whole life. He'd washed his hands of me totally by the time I was eighteen. But with you he got to try again—and I allowed him, despite knowing that he wasn't exactly paternal. I should never have let that happen. I'm sorry.'

Matteo stared at his father in disbelief. His mother had wanted him all along? His grandfather had kept him from her. This changed everything he thought he knew about his life, about who he thought he was.

'Why did no one ever tell me this before?'

His father shrugged. 'I wanted to, but your mother didn't want to come between you and your grandfather. She said you'd made your choice when she remarried and she tried to get you back. She was stronger then, prepared to go to court, no matter what was thrown at her—it helped, of course, that her husband was influential. But you didn't want to live with her; you made it clear that you blamed her for leaving you and that you were bonded with your grandfather. She said it would break your heart if you knew what your grandfather had done; she put your happiness first. But you're no longer a child and you need to know the truth. So call her, Matteo. Go back to that lovely wife of yours, spend some time in Italy and call your mother.'

Matteo didn't ask how his father knew that he had been in Italy; his father always knew more than he expected.

'Your mother was sorry not to have been invited to your wedding,' his father added, 'not to have met your wife. I think it's opened up some of those old wounds. That's why I wanted to say something. It's not too late to right some of those wrongs. I'm realising that myself.'

'Nobody was invited to the wedding,' Matteo said. 'Charlie's parents couldn't get away and so I promised her that we would have a big party, renew our vows in front of everybody who loved us. But somehow I never found the time and then it was too late.'

'Too late?'

'She left me,' Matteo said, and as he said the words he realised that maybe he had been waiting for that ending all along. He'd always thought Charlie loving him was too good to be true. Part of him had known he was never enough for her, the boy whose mother didn't want him, whose father didn't want him. The boy not good enough for his only parental figure, always trying to live up to expectations. The boy condemned to boarding school, an ever-changing series of nannies, abandoned by all who knew him. How could that person be worthy of anyone, especially someone like Charlie? At some level, Matteo had been waiting for Charlie to realise she had made a mistake since the day they'd met.

The question was, had he been pushing her away, not willing to live waiting for her to realise she'd made a mistake any longer? Was that what had happened? Because when she'd left he felt almost vindicated, alongside the devastation. She'd proved him right.

But this time he had decided to fight. He'd put his grandfather's expectations first as a teenager and nobody knew what it had cost him to turn his mother away. He'd never even admitted it to himself. This time he'd realised that he had to risk himself, to make himself vulnerable, to ask for another chance. And fate had given him that chance. So why was he here in a gentlemen's club in Mayfair with his father, not back in Italy? Charlie had a gala in just two days' time and he had promised to be there. Just this morning it had seemed impossible that he'd ever be able to keep that promise; now he knew it was impossible not to.

He had to prove to her that he meant it, meant that she was the most important thing in his life and that if his life didn't have space in it for her then he needed to make changes and find that space. He needed to prove to himself that he wasn't scared. That he could be all in, publicly, privately, emotionally and for ever.

He had to be vulnerable. Matteo took a deep breath and looked up at his father. 'I need your help,' he said.

'Charlie, don't look so worried.' Lucia patted Charlie reassuringly on the arm. 'I'm sure it will all come together tomorrow.'

Charlie groaned. 'I have put on literally countless shows,' she said. 'And I do not recall a single dress rehearsal that has gone as badly as that. I hope you are right; I don't know what else I can do...'

Everything that could have gone wrong during the dress rehearsal had. The sound system had broken and Charlie had ended up playing the music from her phone, which barely made enough sound to reach the stage. Three girls had tripped over their costumes, four had cried because they didn't like the colour they were wearing, countless had forgotten their cues, their spots and which way to turn.

She'd hoped for a straightforward run-through; instead she had endured four hours of tears, tantrums and children threatening to quit. Mentally, she'd also indulged in all three, but her job was to try and stay calm, unflappable and keep everything together.

Why was she doing this again? This wasn't her home, she didn't really know these children, this wasn't even her family. It was Matteo's family, and he wasn't here. Again.

She summoned up a weary smile. 'It'll be fine,' she said, not knowing who she was trying to convince most. 'I'll see you tomorrow.'

The walk back up the hill towards the villa seemed to take for ever. The footpath seemed long and lonely and deserted when it was just her, steeper than she remembered when she had thoughts weighing her down, not conversation distracting her. Things didn't improve when she got back. Maria was popping in to clean, but Charlie had reassured her that she didn't really need her services when she was out most of the time rehearsing. This meant she came back to an empty building and what felt like an endless lonely evening to dwell on everything that might go wrong the next day.

Some salad was waiting for her in the fridge, along with a chilled bottle of wine, but she wasn't really hungry, nor did she want a drink; she just knew it would make her thoughts churn even more.

It had been four days since Matteo had left. He'd managed a few quick texts and just one hurried, distracted call. She'd known taking care of the bribery business would be time-consuming, but his very presence back in London seemed to have unleashed a storm of unrelated and equally urgent work and he had been inundated. He'd mentioned that his grandfather seemed ill and he needed to clear some of his workload before he could return.

Charlie didn't want to dwell on what had happened before and be pessimistic about the future but history seemed to be repeating itself in a pattern she was already familiar with and she didn't know how to handle it any better this time than she had last time.

Maybe they were kidding themselves that this marriage could work. They were too different, wanted different things, had different values. Love and desire could only get a marriage so far; there also had to be shared goals, communication—and actually spending time together couldn't hurt either. She hadn't made a fuss when he'd returned to London, nor had she made it some kind of test, but it was turning into a test anyway. And one they were failing. He was absent and she was becoming increasingly resentful. They were turning full circle.

She stared bleakly out of the window, no longer seeing the glorious view. The gala was tomorrow and he was going to miss it. Again.

Last time she'd left him out of anger, to make a point, to show him she wasn't going to sit at home and wait for him to let her in. She wasn't angry this time, just bone-weary and tired. Because this time they had tried, they had talked and confided and learned and grown and it still wasn't enough. There didn't seem to be a compromise, a middle way. They worked here in Italy, in courtship, but the whole thing collapsed as soon as reality intruded. It would be better for them both to make a clean break. To keep the last couple of weeks as the idyll it was, a sweet memory, not taint it with a long-drawn-out withering.

Charlie slowly climbed the stairs. She'd moved her belongings from the cosy room she'd first occupied into Matteo's spacious suite after they'd returned from Rome. The bed seemed far too big for one, every empty corner full of ghosts. She opened her wardrobe and her gaze fell onto her suitcase. The divorce papers were in the front pocket. All she needed to do was instruct her solicitor to submit them and in six weeks they would both be free.

It would be the right thing to do. The mature thing to do.

It would be the hardest, the most painful thing she had ever done. Because this time she wasn't fuelled by anger or self-righteousness. It would break her heart—literally, it felt like—and, worse, she knew it would break Matteo's. But they had to move on from this stalemate. She had to be the bigger person, whatever the cost.

Charlie swayed, and for one moment she felt the weight of her decision almost overwhelm her. She summoned every ounce of courage she possessed, swallowing back the regret and devastation and pain. That could come later. Slowly, methodically, she changed into her swimsuit and, pulling a wrap around her, she collected her book and phone and headed back downstairs and outside, plonking herself down on a sun lounger, determined to try and relax.

But as she opened her book her phone rang, disturbing her attempts to calm her thoughts. Her heart jolted, hope shooting through her, only to disappear when she saw Lexi's name on her screen.

Picking up the phone and pressing the Accept Call button, she tried to figure out what time it was over in Vietnam. 'Hey, how's it going?'

Her friend sounded her usual exuberant self. 'It's good—you should see this place, Charlie. It's paradise.'

'Still paradise with a bronzed New Zealand surfer?' she managed to tease. Some part of her marvelled at her ability to hide her feelings.

Lexi laughed. 'Oh, yes, it's going well. Most of his friends have moved on, there's just a small group left so it's a much more chilled vibe. You will love it. When are you coming out? You said a week or so and it's been more than three. We'll be moving inland soon and I'd hate for you to miss this place. The snorkelling and diving are amazing.'

Charlie lay back and stared out at the horizon. Backpacking, sightseeing, sea and surf and partying. She'd met Lexi a few years ago through mutual friends, a teacher like herself wanting a travelling companion for the summer holidays. The two of them had hit it off, both enjoying a balance between sight-seeing and partying, tourist places and exploring off the beaten track.

Lexi was obviously having a great time and Charlie could be out there with her. What was she doing ago-nising about someone who would always have priori-ties other than her?

She'd always followed every opportunity offered to her in the past—and now here was an opportunity star-ing her in the face. Maybe she should just do what she always did and head off.

'It does sound amazing…' She couldn't hide the longing in her voice.

'Then come,' Lexi said. 'I'll send you the details of where we are. We'll be here for at least two more weeks. Get a flight and join us. Look, I have to go; there's a cocktail with my name on it. But don't overthink it, book a ticket and let me know when your plane gets in, okay?'

'I'm not quite promising anything,' Charlie warned. 'But I will let you know either way.'

'You do that. Hope I see you soon.'

Charlie put the phone down, then shucked off her wrap and dived into the cold, clear water, surfacing with a splutter and striking out across the pool. With each stroke her mind spun faster and faster, replaying the short conversation with Lexi and her decision to leave Matteo. She couldn't deny how much part of her wanted to cut her losses and run. But what would that achieve? She was no longer a teenage girl with no con-trol of her own destiny. She couldn't spend her whole life jumping into the next thing, could she? At some point she would need to put down some roots.

If what she and Matteo had was worth fighting for, then maybe instead of giving up she should fight.

She'd married a man with commitments. She had married a man who was responsible for thousands of jobs and she had married him knowing both of those things. She wanted him to recognise her own achievements, of course she did, but there had to be some kind of give and take. She wanted him to change? Well, maybe she needed to change as well, maybe she needed to grow up and support him the way she wanted to be supported.

Did it really matter if he was standing by her side for this gala? Did it really matter if he had to disappear off with no notice? It wasn't all about his actions; it was also about her reactions. She sped up, welcoming the burn in her muscles. The problem was she had never allowed herself to need anyone before. She'd always been so proud of her independence, of doing her own thing, and then, in true Charlie style, she'd thrown herself wholesale into marriage in an all-or-nothing kind of way, with the result that she'd felt hard done by playing the role of the barely noticed little wife at home.

But what if she did things differently? Stood up for herself, made sure Matteo knew her boundaries, got a job, her own friends, as she should have done from the start. But if she did stay, did try again, then she needed to mean it. No more impulsive walking out when things got tough.

Charlie grabbed the side of the pool, her chest heaving with the exertion, her stomach roiling with guilt.

She knew that Matteo found it hard to trust, that at some level he didn't feel worth loving at all. She knew this and had still walked out on him. She couldn't play at marriage again, not with him. She had to recognise that he was a work in progress, not the finished article, and so was she. She had to decide whether she was in, all the way in, no matter what the future held, or else she should walk out and go to Vietnam right now.

Love wasn't enough. Commitment had to be part of the package too. Give and take and forgiveness and tolerance. He deserved it all.

And so did she.

The only question was, could they get there or was it already too late?

CHAPTER TWELVE

IT WAS TIME. Every child was miraculously in the right costume, all hair had been styled, sprayed and glittered, stage make-up applied, and they were lined up in the correct groups. Every single guest dancer had been collected from various bus stops, train stations and airports, entertained, fed and watered to their preshow requirements and shown to their dressing rooms. The audience was sitting expectantly in their seats, an eclectic mix of proud families, from great-grandmothers down to tiny siblings, seasoned ballet-goers who'd come to see Violeta and her partner and some of the rising stars from Italy and Europe's best academies, and a handful of tourists who had bought tickets simply because they wanted to see a show.

Charlie stood in the wings peeping out at the audience and inhaled, trying to steady her nerves. She had done all she could. It was down to the kids now. Down to the kids, Lucia's fierce organisational skills and Natalia's excellent choreography. She knew that Natalia had managed to get here to watch her students and was sitting somewhere in the audience, but the children hadn't been told so as to not get them even more overexcited or nervous than they already were. She moved her gaze to a reserved and empty seat near the front and tried to suppress her disappointed sigh. The other person she'd hoped to see was nowhere in sight. Matteo had, as predicted, not made it. And this time not even a word of apology, a curt offer to donate towards the cause or a casual promise to make his absence up to her.

Folding her hands, she breathed in long and deep, trying to steady the myriad emotions tumbling through her. The disappointment at Matteo's absence, the nerves for the gala itself, the fear for her future. Pulling out her phone, she reread the message Lexi had sent earlier that day with details of flights from Rome and London over the next few days. She had her passport, her summer wardrobe and her jabs were up-to-date. There was nothing to stop her heading out the very next day if she wanted. Charlie waited for the usual hit of adrenaline the thought of an adventure gave her but she felt nothing but sadness.

The truth was that going to Vietnam would be a line drawn under her marriage for ever. Oh, she could justify it as a holiday; there was no way Matteo was in any position to quibble if she told him she'd decided she deserved some time away. She could tell herself that going to Vietnam was a sign that things were different now, that if they got back together she was no longer walking the martyr's path of waiting for him whilst feeling sorry for herself. But she would be running away, no matter how she spun it, and there was no coming back from that.

The sound of applause woke her from her endlessly whirling thoughts as the programme director for the

Villa Rufolo took to the stage to start the evening. Resolutely pushing all thoughts of Matteo from her mind, Charlie plastered on a smile and turned to the first group as they filed to the side of the stage. The youngest group were opening the gala, a huge task, but luckily, unlike the older girls and boys, who were fully aware of what a momentous occasion this was and had the nerves to match, her smallest dancers were just looking forward to getting out on stage and performing. Four assistants were stationed in the wings to dance alongside them in case anyone forgot the steps and Charlie herself was ready to dive on stage to rescue any child who might freeze or melt down.

But she needn't have worried. The music began, the children tiptoed out to their spaces and the gala began, every child performing as if they had been born to it. And a couple of them had been, she thought, including Rosa, who danced her solo beautifully without a trace of nerves.

The evening went by in a blur. Charlie was responsible for about half an hour of the hour and a half programme, and even though she had stepped in late, every second was as spine-tingling, nerve-racking and exciting as every other show she had put on. This was what she loved, she realised, seeing the children that she had coached, coaxed and brought out of their shells performing to their best ability. She enjoyed her classroom teaching but it was the Christmas plays, the carol concerts, the Easter parades and all her various dance productions that really made her job so satisfying. This might not be her choreography, they might not be her students, but they were on stage because of her and the buzz was incredible. No matter what her future held, teaching dance had to be part of it.

Luckily, there was enough assistance in the dressing rooms for Charlie to stay watching in the wings all evening and she was right there when Violeta Costa and her partner performed their duet, the balcony scene from *Romeo and Juliet*. Charlie's eyes filled, her chest tight as she watched the perfectly executed steps, the emotion conveyed through music and movement, experiencing the poignant joy of seeing someone at the absolute top of their profession perform. Alone in her spot, it felt as if she was experiencing a private performance just for her and it was almost a shock when the applause rang out, the audience on their feet. But then, this audience had also been on their feet for every one of the small children's performances, generous with their love and applause.

As the lights dimmed ready for the next dancer she relived the *pas de deux* in her mind, feeling the passion in every step and gesture. Was this how she'd always thought love would be, sudden and fiery and all-consuming and potentially doomed? Had she always been influenced by the drama of love rather than reality, expecting it to flare hot and passionate until the flames went out? She'd never had any particular longevity in her previous relationships, although they'd always been full-on from the start. She loved falling in love, she loved that first touch, the getting to know them part, the butterflies in her stomach and the way her whole body would quiver with anticipation for a word, a glance, a kiss. But that kind of attraction and excitement, the fun of falling in love, was only part of a marriage. A long-term relationship needed something steadier alongside flirtation and heady desire. And being steady was something Charlie had run from since the day she'd finally quit her life as an embassy child.

Matteo didn't need flutters and flames; he needed steady. He needed supportive. He needed someone to remind him that life wasn't all work, to remind him that he didn't bear the responsibility for the whole world on his shoulders, that his grandfather's expectations were ridiculous, that he was allowed to cut loose sometimes.

She hugged herself, suddenly cold and shamed. Matteo needed someone who wouldn't impulsively suggest marriage and impulsively walk away from it, somebody who wouldn't think heading off to Vietnam was the best way to escape a difficult situation. He needed someone on his side. Not a martyr who allowed him to get away with putting his marriage second, but a partner, someone who would weigh up a difficult situation and calmly decide what she would do with that information. His childhood had been cold and lonely. He needed help to see he deserved love and happiness, that putting his happiness before his duty was allowed.

The question was, could she be that person? Not only that, but could she maintain all that made *her* happy within that marriage? Not play the perfect wife until she was bored and resentful. Could she find balance? It was ironic; she was a dancer and yet balance was something that had eluded her for her entire life.

But she already knew the answer to the biggest question of all. Did she want to spend her life without him? She could fill it with travel and adventures and excitement, but something would always be missing. She knew that now. She just had to find a way to let him know.

Finally, the gala was over and all Charlie needed to do was ensure that every child was changed and left with the right parent or guardian. Thanks to her helpers it wasn't too long before she'd seen them all run into the arms of proud parents and grandparents, ready to be whisked off to celebratory meals. Tonight the village squares would be full of proud local families. A party had been planned for all the guest dancers and some of the region's more illustrious residents to raise some more money whilst thanking the guest artists for their support. Charlie had an invitation but she wasn't really sure whether she was up to smiling and playing nice. Not when she needed to speak to Matteo. To tell him she was coming home. To him.

'Charlie, thank you so much.' Lucia rushed up, a smiling Natalia by her side. 'You've made Rosa's year—I'm so glad you're part of my family.'

'It was nothing,' Charlie said, slightly embarrassed as she thought about how close she'd been to leaving the family. 'It was all Natalia's doing. I just supervised really.'

But Natalia shook her head emphatically. 'You were on your holiday, Charlie, and yet you gave up all this time to help my children, and to make their dreams come true. I hope to see you next time you're in Ravello; you must allow me to take you out and thank you. It's a shame you won't be living here permanently; I could do with an assistant teacher, especially one who can teach so many alternative disciplines. Is there any way I can persuade you?'

Charlie laughed as Lucia exclaimed how wonderful that would be, but inside she felt a wisp of sadness that they couldn't really stay in Ravello, live in Matteo's villa. She was at peace here in a way she'd never really been before, the combination of the sun and the scenery and the sea certainly helped, but it was more than that. It was as if she'd finally found her home.

'Have you seen Matteo yet?' Lucia asked and Charlie was just trying to find the right way to say that he hadn't been able to make it after all when Lucia added casually, 'He was looking for you—oh, there he is, over there with my aunt. It's lovely to see them talking so warmly. The rift between them has always upset the family. She made some mistakes when she was younger, we all know that, and poor Matteo did pay the price. But she loves him very much, and his siblings have always been desperate to get to know their big brother better. Maybe this is a new start for them—for Matteo. It would be lovely if you visited more often and we could get to know each other properly.'

Matteo? Here? Charlie stared at Lucia in surprise, her whole body frozen.

'Where was he during the gala; his seat was empty?' she asked as calmly as she could, as if this news wasn't a huge surprise to her.

'In that corner over there. They arrived a little bit late, typical Matteo, and of course he had brought a larger group than expected so they had to have some extra seats at the back. But they didn't mind; they said how much they enjoyed it.'

Charlie was aware that her legs shook and her whole body ached with anticipation as she made her way over to the part of the famous botanical gardens Lucia had indicated. She stopped when she saw a small group of people, drinks in hand, chattering animatedly in a little palm-tree-lined glade. She instantly recognised Matteo's tall lines and the woman next to him must surely be his mother. She had the same profile, the same haughty cheekbones and determined nose and chin. But was that Matteo's father next to her—what was he doing here? And his grandfather? She'd never expected to see the four of them in the same place, especially on seemingly cordial if not intimate terms.

Her gaze travelled further, to the edges of the group. She gave a little gasp. 'Gran? Phoebe? What on earth are you doing here?'

Matteo turned at the sound of Charlie's voice and saw her face light up, surprise and happiness mingling in her joyful expression. He felt himself relax just a little. It had all been worth it, all the corralling and coaxing, and using every bit of his charm to try and persuade everybody to be here for the gala. Getting his father and his grandfather onto the same plane had been an adventure by itself, even the luxurious private jet too small to house the pair of them. Luckily, Phoebe and Charlie's grandmother's presence had diluted the toxic atmosphere, and Charlie's grandmother had chatted animatedly throughout the short flight, keeping the topics light-hearted and ensuring there was no chance for his grandfather to start muttering about bribery or his father to get defensive.

It had been a lot easier getting his mother to attend; she'd said yes before he'd even finished asking the question, her joy at hearing his invitation both warming and shaming. He'd asked her to use her usual rooms at the villa, but she'd elected instead to stay with Lucia, saying that he and Charlie needed some time alone. Lucia had agreed, organising hotel rooms for his father and grandfather, Phoebe and Charlie's grandmother, a miracle at such short notice during the busy summer season.

Two other very important guests were due to arrive in the morning, flight times and work commitments meaning they couldn't make the twenty-hour turnaround needed to get to Ravello in time for the gala. But tomorrow was the important day, if Charlie would just say yes.

Matteo inhaled. He was putting everything on the line here—his hopes, his dreams and his pride—and this time his pride was the least important thing of all.

'Matteo phoned and insisted we came over. He can be stubborn, can't he? But how could we turn down chauffeurs, private jets and posh hotel suites? By the way, private jets are everything, Charlie. I can't believe you even tried to claim they weren't.' Phoebe rushed over to give her cousin a hug. 'You're looking well,' she added, and Charlie beamed, enfolding her cousin in a close hug before doing the same to her grandmother.

Matteo's heart lifted at the unadulterated happiness on her face. 'How?' she asked, looking around the group in bewilderment.

'I decided to be a little bit impulsive,' Matteo said with a grin and she smiled up at him, her heart in her eyes.

'You're a good pupil,' she said, and he dropped a kiss on the top of her head.

'I had a good teacher,' he murmured in her ear as

he introduced her to his mother, who immediately embraced her warmly.

'I've been dying to meet you. I'm so happy this day has come,' his mother said.

'Me too,' Charlie told her.

There was a lot to talk about and Matteo stood back, watching Charlie make the rounds of their blended families, Lucia and her husband and children joining them. Charlie made an effort to single out his grandfather who, although he'd given her elegantly styled purple-tipped hair a suspicious glance, surely had to approve of her vintage blue calf-length ballgown teamed with a silk wrap. She looked elegant, cool, like some kind of fifties film star gracing the gala with her presence, and he noted people looking over at her, clearly asking each other who she was, pride filling him. *That's my wife*, he wanted to shout.

Matteo himself was doing his best to charm Charlie's grandmother and Phoebe, both of whom he knew still regarded him with some suspicion, but the glamour of the evening mixed with Charlie's evident happiness thawed them somewhat. But all he wanted was Charlie to himself. It seemed an age before he could take her arm and discreetly steer her away from the rest of the group, walking through the gardens until they reached the railings at the top of the cliff and pausing there, looking out over the view beyond. It was dark now but they could see the Amalfi coast lit up below, and the lights of the ships further out at sea.

'That was quite a surprise,' Charlie said at last, turning to him, her hand on his arm.

'A good surprise?'

'The best.'

'Good, because I have another surprise for you.' He took a deep breath and held her hands. 'If I was a different man and if you were a different woman maybe I would have asked this earlier, got on stage at the end of the gala when you were receiving your flowers from the children, done it in front of all your family and friends.' He stopped and grinned although his heart was hammering so hard he could feel it vibrating in his chest. 'Or maybe I would have whisked you to some elegant little restaurant and slipped this into your wine glass.' He released her hands and pulled a small box out of his pocket, holding it out. 'I know better than that, however. I hope you forgive me for buying this in advance and planning to give it to you tonight.'

Charlie took the box but didn't open it, looking up at him, eyes wide. 'I've already got an engagement ring,' she said. 'I may not have worn it for a while, but I have it. It's in my case; I take it everywhere.'

'I know. This isn't an engagement ring or a wedding ring. You have those and I hope you feel you can wear them again. This is a please stay married to me ring; it's an eternity ring.' He flicked the box open and she gasped as she took in the gorgeous art deco eternity ring, emeralds and sapphires and amethysts side by side on the platinum band.

'Oh, Matteo.'

'I bought this for you in New York. It was an apology and a promise to do better and a pledge all in one. Only when I got back you were gone. I told myself it was for the best but I kept the ring; I couldn't bear to sell it. I meant it then and I mean it now. This is a let's be together for eternity ring. This is a let's do better next time no matter what ring. What do you think?'

Charlie didn't answer for a long moment, but when she finally took it from him her eyes shone. 'I say yes, Matteo. I've been doing a lot of thinking, about what kind of person I am, the kind of person I want to be. How to maintain my independence and be happy and yet be the kind of wife you can rely on. I've been thinking that if I come back I have to be all in, no matter how hard it gets. But I know that being with you is worth every bump in the road, you're worth it, Matteo.'

It was his turn to pause, overcome by her words. 'I almost got buried again in responsibilities,' he confessed. 'I was so close to not fulfilling my promise to you. But I also had to figure out what I want from life. My role, the legacy my grandfather wants to give me is important, but so are you. I need to make some changes, persuade my grandfather to take a step back, bring in people I can trust so I don't feel the need to manage everything myself, give my father a chance now he claims to be a reformed character, get to know my mother...' He laughed shakily. 'It's quite a list but I can only do it with you by my side. You asked me a few days ago what kind of person you were. The kind of person who gives up her holiday to make a child's dream come true, the kind of person who tries to solve every problem she sees, the kind of person who embraces life. The person I want by my side every step I take, the person I want to support in everything that makes her happy.'

'Oh, Matteo. That's where I want to be too. Wherever that is, London, here, Kent, it doesn't matter.' She laughed then. 'Although let's make sure it's here often. Natalia offered me a job, well, half offered, and I was so tempted to say yes. I love it here.'

'Who knows?' he said. 'I am planning to work from home a lot more so we could have a home in Kent, or maybe here. I am willing to see where the adventure takes us.'

She softly pinched his cheek. 'Is this really you? I don't think I have ever been happier.'

'Maybe save some of that happiness for tomorrow because I have one more surprise for you. Tomorrow we're coming back to these gardens for a small party, one where we get to say our vows in front of our families. I promised you we would have a proper celebration with our parents and it's shameful I never found the time. Your parents arrive in the morning.' He paused, trying to read the slightly stunned look on her face. 'I hope that's okay. It will be pretty embarrassing if you think it's too soon to make that kind of commitment. I have just realised how stressful being impulsive can be.'

Charlie just stared at him. 'My parents are coming here?'

'They wanted to be here tonight but it wasn't possible, but they arrive in Rome tomorrow morning and should be here mid-afternoon.'

'You organised all this for me?' She stepped closer, running her hand softly down his cheek.

'For us,' he said, dipping his head and kissing her at last, the way he'd wanted to do since he'd seen her. She kissed him back ardently and sweetly, her body entwined around his. He pulled back to study her face. 'I love you, Charlie. I don't think I've ever said that enough. I certainly haven't shown it enough, but I do. I love you. My heart is yours always.'

'And I love you, Matteo. I'd much rather be with you and see what adventures life brings us than anything else in the world.' She reached for him again and he swept her into his arms. His wife once again. This time, he vowed, he would do everything to make sure she stayed that way. For ever.

* * * * *

AN UNEXPECTED FATHER

MARIE FERRARELLA

To All the Target and Grocery Store Clerks Who Came
In During the Coronavirus Pandemic So We Could
Shop and Buy Food You Kept Me Sane Thank You!

Prologue

This had to be a dream, Brady Fortune told himself. A really bad dream.

No, not a dream, he amended.

A nightmare.

And any second now, he was going to wake up and everything would be just the way it was supposed to be. Life would be back to normal.

But it wasn't back to normal. It would never be back to normal again.

Brady felt completely numb, from his stunned, frozen heart, right down to his very toes.

It took him a moment to realize that he was clutching his outdated cell phone so hard, it was perilously close to being snapped in half.

Breathe, damn it, Brady. Breathe!

The simple directive throbbed over and over again in his head. He drew in a deep breath, then let it out. His heart continued racing at an uncontrollable pace. He drew in another deep breath, but that didn't help either.

His heart was still pounding like a bass drum.

"Mr. Fortune? Mr. Fortune, are you still there?" Brady heard a faraway voice on his cell phone asking him. The deep voice corkscrewed its way deep into his consciousness.

It was the voice of Allen Mayfair, Gord and Gina's lawyer. The man who had just sent his entire world reeling before it burst into flames.

"Yes, I'm still here." Brady heard a voice that sounded a lot like his own answering the lawyer's question. It took him another couple of moments to realize that the hollow, stunned voice he heard actually belonged to him. Brady tried again. "Yes, I'm still here," he repeated more firmly.

"I realize that this must be such a shock to you. I am really sorry to be the bearer of such terrible news, Mr. Fortune," the lawyer was saying.

Five minutes ago everything had been fine. And then his phone rang. Mayfair was calling to break the worst possible news to him: that his best friend, Gordon, and Gord's wife, Gina, had been killed in a horrific motorcycle accident.

He refused to believe it.

He had to believe it.

Brady was realistic enough to know that life was about terrible things happening, terrible things that were hiding in the shadows, ready to just jump out at you at the worst possible time.

As if there was *ever* a good time for something like this to happen.

"No," the voice on the other end of the call assured him. "They didn't suffer. It was instantaneous."

He knew he should have been comforted by that, but he wasn't. Wasn't because he knew he wouldn't ever hear Gord's deep voice calling him up to *get off your duff because we've got things to do and places to see*. Never hear his best friend's oddly high-pitched laugh again when something struck him as being weirdly funny.

Never see Gord again or do any of the things they had made plans to do ever since they were kids.

"Mr. Fortune? Did you hear my question?"

No, he hadn't. His mind had gone elsewhere. "Wh-what?"

Brady realized that he had gotten lost in his thoughts again, silently railing at Gord for being such a thoughtless fool as to go riding on a motorcycle like that when he had little kids to think of.

Little kids who were all alone now.

"No, I'm sorry. I didn't," Brady apologized.

"Could you repeat what you just said?" He hadn't a clue as to what the lawyer had just said and he wasn't up to trying to pretend that he knew.

Mayfair patiently repeated his question. "I asked how soon you think that you could come by to pick up the twins?"

"The twins?" Brady repeated numbly, his brain incapable of processing the question or making any sense of it.

Nothing was making any sense to him anymore.

"Yes, the twins," the lawyer repeated, then added in the boys' names as if that would clear everything up. "Toby and Tyler. Gordon and Gina's children."

"Why would I be picking them up?" Brady wanted to know, confused.

He wasn't all that good with kids. Had Gord thought he could somehow comfort the twins if something awful were to happen to him and his wife—which it had, Brady thought angrily. Brady's eyes stung as he blinked back tears. Gord knew him better than that.

"Wouldn't they be better off with one of Gina's relatives? Or Gord's parents?" Anyone but him, Brady thought. He was in need of comforting himself. He wasn't in any position to offer it.

"Apparently they didn't think so. As I told you, Mr. and Mrs. Jefferson named you as their twins' legal guardian in their will."

"Legal guardian," Brady repeated. Obviously, he'd missed that part of the conversation.

"Yes. That means that you are now completely responsible for Toby and Tyler," the lawyer patiently explained.

"You mean for now?" Brady asked, trying to get his bearings. This had to be some kind of temporary arrangement until the actual guardian or guardians for the twins could come for them.

This was all so surreal. His head was still swirling as fragments of thoughts continued to chase one another through his brain.

"No, permanently," Mayfair told him. His voice indicated that he was rather confused as to why the man he was speaking to would have thought the arrangement for the twins' guardianship was only temporary.

And just like that, with those words, Brady's whole life was completely and indelibly changed forever.

Chapter One

Six months later...

Looking back, it seemed rather incredible how much time had somehow managed to go by since his friends' deaths. Six months since he had become an instant father. Six long, grueling, painful months and if anything, Brady felt more lost than ever in this new role he had assumed.

He hadn't even had time to properly grieve over the loss of his best friend. The moment he walked in the door from work during the week, not to mention the whole of the entire weekend, Brady was too busy chasing after two overly-energized four-year-olds. Four-year-olds whose batteries never seemed to run down or need even a minimum of recharging.

From the moment Toby and Tyler opened their eyes—and they opened them *really* early—until they finally shut them at what seemed like way too late at night, the twins were engaged in non-stop movement.

Six months ago, at the beginning of this whole exhausting adventure, Brady had thought that someone from either Gord's family or Gina's would challenge him for custody of the twins. But it turned out that long before her demise, Gina had become estranged from her family. And while Gord's parents did care about their twin grandsons, they were an older couple, which was why they ultimately had to pass when it came to assuming custody of the boys. Gord's mother and father just didn't have the stamina or the energy to keep up with preschoolers who, Brady had no doubt, were first cousins to that cartoon Road Runner that dashed from one place to another, sometimes in midair.

Brady couldn't really blame Gord's parents. If he could have somehow, in good conscience, found a way to get out of this unexpected guardianship that had been thrust upon him, he definitely would have.

But with no one left to take in the twins—they would have had to go into foster care, which

Brady couldn't allow—he felt that he owed it to his friend to honor his wishes and keep the boys. Owed it to Gord even though the selfless act might very well ultimately wind up being the death of him.

He could swear that his hair was turning gray even though he was only twenty-nine.

If he had to make some sort of a comparison between what he was going through and life in general, he'd have to say that it was like walking into the middle of a war without a weapon *or* a handbook. Quite honestly, Brady felt that he didn't have a single clue as to what the rules were when it came to child rearing.

He didn't even know which side he was actually supposed to be on.

Did he side with the kids or did he take a stand? Or was it a little bit of both and if so, how would he know how little and how much?

He felt totally lost, not to mention outnumbered.

Until he had begun to spend more time with Toby and Tyler on a regular, far more personal level, Brady had actually believed that most children under the age of seven or eight were innocent and pretty much just mischievous.

As it turned out, he was the clueless one.

It took Brady a while, but he finally realized that he was dealing with two adorable, devious little con artists who were out to get away with as much as they possibly could at any given time.

He was ashamed to acknowledge it now, but because Toby and Tyler had such innocent-looking little faces, they actually had him believing that their parents allowed them to stay up late *every single night*. Not only that, but they claimed—"innocently" again—that they were allowed to eat whatever they wanted to whenever they wanted.

What they *didn't* want to eat were vegetables or anything that could be viewed as even remotely healthy. Because he had grown up with Gord, who had been just as carefree, wild and unpredictable as his twin sons were now, Brady believed all these wild allegation that the twins were solemnly telling him at first.

But then it slowly began to dawn on him that even Gord would have put his foot down at some point. And even if his friend hadn't, Brady became convinced that his friend's wife, Gina, would have.

It was around that time of his awakening that Brady realized that he couldn't allow things to slide like this any longer. He needed to do something about the situation—and fast—because it was all coming apart at the seams right before his very eyes.

The beginning of the end happened when his

exceedingly patient mother, Catherine, cornered him when he came home from work one night, admittedly late, from the sporting goods store that he managed.

He knew something was up by the expression on his mother's face before he even had a chance to close the door behind him.

"Come here, Brady," his mother called to him, patting the seat next to her on the sofa.

Tired from his long day, he crossed to Catherine on leaden feet as an urgent voice in his system cried *May-day*!

"You know I love you, don't you, Brady?" Catherine Fortune asked her son.

Brady's heart continued sinking. Opening statements like that didn't bode well. They only went downhill from there. Still, he tried to console himself, this was his mother he was dealing with.

He hoped for the best.

"Y-e-s?" Brady responded, drawing out the word as if doing that could somehow squash any negative message prefaced by that kind of opening statement.

Brady mentally crossed his fingers.

"And I wouldn't hurt you for the world," the tall, still-quite-handsome woman continued.

He could feel his heart sinking down even further in his chest.

"Go on," Brady said, bracing himself for the worst while desperately praying for the best—or at least not so "worst" if that was at all possible.

"But I quit," Catherine declared, informing her son with finality.

At first, the word—one he had never associated with his mother before now—wouldn't process.

"Quit?" he asked.

"Yes, quit," Catherine repeated, emphatically. "I can't babysit these little—heaven forgive me—*hellions* any longer."

His mother had never resorted to name calling or damning labels before. This had to be *really* bad.

"What happened, Mom?" Brady asked with a soul-weary sigh.

"They just won't listen to me," his mother complained. The whole situation was obviously a source of great pain for her. She didn't like leaving her son in a lurch like this, but the twins were just too much for her to handle. "And frankly, I'm getting too old for this."

"You're not old, Mom," Brady protested.

Catherine immediately cut him short before he could get any further. "Flattery isn't going to get you anywhere, darling."

Brady's mouth felt dry as he cast about for

some sort of a solution that would convince his mother to continue helping out with the twins.

"How about if I try to get them to promise that they'll behave?" he asked.

It was a desperate question asked by a desperate man because he hadn't a clue how to begin to get either of the twins to behave. If he had, he wouldn't have needed the help he was asking for.

Catherine pinned him with a look and summed up the situation neatly. "The only way you could get them to even remotely do that is by nailing the door to their room permanently shut. No, Brady, I'm sorry. It pains me greatly to say this, but my mind is made up." Rising, Catherine cupped her son's cheek with sorrowful affection. "I really hate to do this, darling, but I have no choice. Those boys have worn out my soul and you and I know that it's not going to get any better."

Brady felt as if his back was up against the proverbial wall and he had nowhere to turn. "What am I supposed to do, Mom?"

"Have you thought of sending them to military school?" Catherine Fortune suggested to her son in all seriousness.

"They're four, Mom," Brady pointed out. Because they were such whirlwinds of activity, it was a fact that had a habit of getting lost. "I don't think a military school would accept them. Besides, I don't really want their spirits broken—just contained. A lot," he added with feeling.

Catherine laughed softly under her breath as she shook her head. "Well, good luck with that," she told Brady.

He was going to need more than luck, Brady thought as he watched his mother leave.

For a time, after his mother had withdrawn from her baby-sitting duties, he went through a small army of nannies. Vetted by an agency, they came—and went—with a fair amount of regularity. Some of the nannies lasted for a couple of weeks, others lasted only for a couple of days.

But they all had one thing in common. None of them lasted for long. Some left cryptic comments in their wake, others left in icy, stony silence.

Like the other nannies who had left before her, the short, squat woman looked like the very epitome of the perfect nanny, but even Mildred McGinty felt as if she was outmatched.

"I've been a professional nanny for twenty-seven years, Mr. Fortune, and I have never, *never* encountered such insufferable, rude, disrespectful children in all that time." Mrs. McGinty drew herself up to appear taller than her actual 5'1" height. "I believed I could put up with anything, but today was the absolute *last* straw.

I caught those two demons—" she pointed a trembling finger in the general direction of the twins "—trying to toast marshmallows *in the middle of the living room floor*! Somehow, they found matches. If I hadn't been there, your whole house could have burned down—and most likely would have!" she declared angrily just before she slammed the front door behind her, permanently storming out of Brady's house.

Well, that would explain the soot marks, Brady thought wearily, looking down at the telltale marks in the middle of the throw rug.

Tyler was pulling on the edge of Brady's jacket. "We're sorry, Unca Brady," the twin said, looking contrite—at least for the moment.

"Yeah, we didn't mean to set the rug on fire," Toby piped up. Of the two overactive dynamos, Toby was the unofficial ringleader. "It just got in the way."

At least they knew enough to apologize, Brady thought. He knew he was grasping at straws, but straws, or pieces of them, were all he had.

They weren't malicious kids, he told himself, just really, really mischievous. Somehow, some way, that mischief needed to be tamed and contained, Brady decided in desperation.

But how?

He had been through an army of nannies, as well as sitters, and that clearly wasn't working.

Damn, but he needed help, Brady thought wearily. Big-time.

And soon.

And then suddenly, as if in a prophesy-like vision, he thought of Rambling Rose, the small Texas town he'd taken the twins to in January. At the time it was for his nephew's first birthday celebration. His older brothers Adam and Kane had resettled there, and they couldn't stop talking about how great the place was. They kept stressing how very family-oriented the town was.

He had resisted buying into the idea of living there, although his brothers did their best to talk him into it. At the time he was happy living near their folks in Upstate New York, happy with his job and his lifestyle—but all that was quickly changing and truthfully, it wasn't even his lifestyle any longer. Abject chaos had replaced what had once been his carefree existence, wiping out weekends spent with friends, watching sports and playing cards, not to mention dating. Nothing serious, but something he had looked forward to. Now there was no time for any of that.

Now all he wanted, heaven help him, was some sort of peace and quiet—or at the very least the *promise* of peace and quiet. As a matter of fact, given everything that was currently going on, he had begun to feel that he was willing to sell his soul for that.

Funny how things had a way of changing, Brady thought. His requirements had been a great deal different six months ago.

All right, onward and upward, he told himself.

Brady wondered just how surprised his family would be if he suddenly turned up with the twins in tow in the middle of the night.

Chapter Two

A month later and life in Texas still hadn't gotten any easier, Brady thought, trying hard not to let it all get to him.

Knowing he had to do something, Brady had uprooted the twins as well as himself from what was swiftly shaping up to be a hopelessly chaotic life and brought them to Rambling Rose. He felt that making the move during winter break from preschool was the best time to make the change. That way, everyone would be in downtime and the twins would have a chance to meet and get to know some of the kids in the area.

There was only one problem with that. There was no "winter break" in Rambling Rose. That meant although he had promised the boys there would be kids for them to play with in this new town, at the moment, there weren't any around. All the kids in town were attending school.

"There's no one to play with, Unca Brady," Tyler lamented for what seemed like at least the tenth time that day.

"Yeah, you said there were gonna be kids to play with. But there aren't any," Toby said in what could only be construed as an indignant manner.

After being around the twins for these last six-plus months now, Brady had learned that this sort of whining could only get worse, not better. Not only that, but it was liable to continue for *hours*.

Brady looked around at all the towering boxes that were lined up in almost every room. He had planned to make at least a decent dent in unpacking them today and putting some of the things away.

But his sanity took precedent over neatness— and he was fighting to preserve the former.

Knowing that all the kids were in school, desperate, he made a spur-of-the-moment decision.

"Well, if the kids aren't going to come to you, you're going to go to the kids," Brady declared. He could tell by the looks on their faces that the twins had no idea what he was talking about. It didn't matter. He knew what he had to do.

"Okay, boys, get ready. As soon as I find what I need to take with me, we're leaving," he told Toby and Tyler, thinking of the papers he needed to properly register the twins in school.

In the scheme of things, this was far more important than finding the right cupboard to house the dishes or where to put the pots and pans.

But it seemed that the twins apparently needed some convincing.

"Where are we going, Unca Brady? Huh? Where?" Toby wanted to know, shifting from foot to foot as Brady plowed through several boxes, searching for the custody papers he knew the preschool would want.

The papers wound up being housed in a red folder at the bottom of the third box. He had deliberately placed the custody papers in a red folder to make locating them easier. The only problem was that he'd forgotten which box he had placed the folder in.

He supposed that he should be grateful that he hadn't left the box back in New York, he told himself.

"Where, where, where?" Toby continued to ask, reciting the single word over and over again like some sort of a mantra.

"Preschool," Brady answered. "I'm registering the two of you at preschool."

"But we already went to preschool," Tyler told

him. He drew himself up as if that was the end of the discussion. "We're done."

"Oh no, you're not. Not by a long shot," Brady told the boys. "This is a new preschool."

Toby tilted his head, studying his guardian. "Is it like the old one?" he wanted to know.

This could go either way, Brady thought, so mentally, he flipped a coin, took a chance and said, "Yes."

"Then we don't wanna go," Toby informed his beleaguered guardian.

Brady pressed his lips together to suppress a few choice words he knew he could no longer utter in the company of children. Venting, even though it might make him feel better, was no longer permitted.

"That's where the kids are," he told the twins. "Oh."

Momentarily stumped, Toby looked at his brother, then motioned for Tyler to follow him to the corner and confer over this newest development.

Reaching the private "conference" area, the twins lowered their voices, something that Brady wasn't used to, considering their usual pitch was much higher. Glancing in his direction, the twins conferred with one another about the situation.

Brady wanted to prod them along but something in his gut told him this was a necessary process to help cement the still-very-new tenuous relationship between the twins and him. So he waited.

Finally, Toby raised his head and both boys looked up at their guardian. "Okay," Toby declared. "We'll go to preschool."

"Good choice," Brady told them, silently adding, *It's also your only choice.*

He had no desire to strong-arm the twins, but he would if he had to. Toby and Tyler were definitely going to preschool whether they liked it or not. He preferred them liking it, but if worse came to worse, he knew what he had to do.

"So, boys, what do you think?" Brady asked the twins less than an hour later as they stood on the preschool grounds. He thought that this process might be made a little easier if the boys felt that they had some sort of say in the matter.

"It's big," Tyler finally said as he looked around, his eyes huge with wonder.

Brady picked up on the one twin's awe. He didn't want the boy to feel overwhelmed. "It won't look so big once you get used to it."

Toby looked as if he was ready to begin exploring right then and there. He yanked on Brady's hand. "Can we get used to it now, Unca Brady?" he wanted to know, pulling again, harder this time. "Can we, huh, can we?"

Brady tightened his grip on both boys' hands because he knew that Tyler would follow his twin's lead and would begin pulling him in a minute. They weren't strong, but their enthusiasm made them very difficult to manage.

"Not yet," Brady responded. "First we need to sign you up."

Toby's face puckered up as he tried to understand. "What's that?" he wanted to know.

"That's when they put your name on a sign," Tyler explained.

Uncertain, Toby turned toward Brady. "Is that what they do?"

"Close enough," Brady answered. He wasn't about to waste any more time standing outside the preschool. He wanted to get the boys *inside* the building.

Still holding onto each twin, he found himself grateful that Gord and Gina had only had twins and not triplets because he'd be out of hands.

Mindful over every step he had to take, Brady carefully guided the boys, who were behaving more like squirming puppies than flesh-and-blood children, into the school's registration office.

The moment he walked in, Brady became instantly aware of the short, dour-looking woman seated at the registration desk.

Harriet Ferguson, according to the nameplate

on her desk, continued watching him as made his way over to her as he held on to each of the twins.

"Ms. Ferguson?" he asked, knowing it was a needless question. The woman nodded. Taking a breath, Brady pushed on. "I'm Brady Fortune. I called earlier about registering Toby and Tyler here at your preschool." He nodded toward the twins.

There appeared to be no sign of any sort of recognition on the woman's part.

Instead, Ms. Ferguson shifted razor-sharp eyes to appraise the barely restrained twins. "I take it you don't put much store in disciplining these two." She pressed her lips together in disapproval. "I'm afraid that your sons might fare better someplace else—"

There wasn't so much as a touch of warmth in her voice, Brady realized. But he needed the boys to be accepted here. This was the only way he'd be able to work, to take care of all those errands that never seemed to end, to be sure he could provide all of the things the boys needed to grow up safe and healthy. And he really wanted the boys to make some friends their own age, too.

Having nothing to lose, Brady decided to plunge in.

"They're not my sons," he told the woman.

Ms. Ferguson looked a little taken aback by

that. "I don't understand." It was obvious that hadn't been discussed. "Then why—"

"I'm their guardian," he told her, anticipating the woman's question. "I'm afraid that their parents were rather lax when it came to discipline and instituting any sort of structure. Actually, until just recently," Brady confessed, "Toby and Tyler had never even been inside a nursery school, much less attended one. Boys, stop it," Brady cried, trying to get the twins to settle down until he could at least finish getting them registered.

"Humph, I can readily believe that," Ms. Ferguson said in a dismissive tone. "But as I started to say earlier—"

Anticipating getting torpedoed out of the water, Brady quickly interjected, "It's not just that these boys aren't used to having a structured day—I'm afraid that they're dealing with something far more serious." Seeing that he had caught the woman's attention, he pushed on. "Six months ago, they lost both their parents in a motorcycle accident. *That's* why I have custody of them.

"I'm not ashamed to say that this is all really new to me." He laughed almost self-deprecatingly. "Six months ago I was living in upstate New York, managing a sporting goods store and dealing with adults practically on an exclusive basis. Now—"

He raised his hands in a hapless fashion as he looked at the squirming boys.

"I'm clearly out of my depth here, but I am trying," he stressed. Brady looked at the woman, giving it his all as he exuded charm. "Will you help me, Ms. Ferguson? Will you register Toby and Tyler at your school so I can begin the process of getting these two boys to settle down a little?"

"It's *Mrs.* Ferguson," the woman pointedly corrected him. "And yes, I will register them— provided you have all the necessary paperwork with you, of course," she qualified.

Brady pulled out the red folder he had brought with him. "I have everything all right here," he assured the woman, placing the folder in front of Mrs. Ferguson on her desk.

With short, almost regal movement, Mrs. Ferguson opened the folder and glanced through the pages that were contained there. She raised her hazel eyes to look at him when she was done.

"Well, you're organized. That's a good first step," she told him.

Because Brady had brought everything he could possibly think of that might be even remotely be required, the process, mercifully, went rather quickly.

Finished inputting all the information into the

computer, Mrs. Ferguson rested her fingers on the keyboard and raised her eyes to look at his.

"All right, Mr. Fortune, I need one last thing from you." Her voice was almost pregnant with meaning.

At this point Brady felt exhilarated and almost giddy. He had actually managed to get the twins registered—well, almost registered—and he was willing to do anything to reach the finish line.

"What do you need?" he asked, then, still riding the wave of exhilaration, answered his own question. "A kidney? Because if you require a kidney, you've got it! Just name the hospital," he told her.

Mrs. Ferguson almost smiled, Brady observed. "That's very generous of you, Mr. Fortune, but no, a kidney won't be necessary. But I will need a list of people who are authorized to pick up your twins if you're not able to come."

That caught him off guard. He thought of his mother and the fact that she had thrown up her hands in the end. He didn't want to put any undue burdens on his family. But in the end, he knew he had to comply with Mrs. Ferguson's request, especially since, logically, if he was going to be working, he'd certainly need to ask his siblings for help.

So he gave her the names of his brothers, Adam and Kane, who were living here in Rambling Rose, and whose children were enrolled at the same school. Adam's one-year-old son, Larkin, was in the day care program, and Kane had recently gotten engaged to Layla McCarthy whose two-year-old daughter, Erin, was in one of the older groups. Kane couldn't wait to become Erin's official dad, although he had obviously already taken the little girl into his heart.

Maybe I should be asking Kane for parenting advice, Brady mused.

Tired of being patient, not to mention quiet, Toby spoke up. "I wanna go play now," he cried, tugging hard on Brady's hand. "Are you done yet? Huh? Are you?" the boy wanted to know, all but ready to jump out of his skin if he didn't do something soon.

This was nothing new, Brady thought. But what was new was what Tyler said just as Toby pulled free.

"I want to stay here with you," the other twin told him.

Tyler had caught him totally by surprise. Brady wasn't prepared for that.

Neither was he prepared to have the boy all but wrap himself around his leg, holding on for dear life as if he was hermetically sealed to it.

Brady put a comforting hand on the boy's head. "Hey, Ty, what's up?"

Tyler looked up at him wearing the most serious expression Brady could recall ever seeing on the twin's face.

"I don't wanna leave you," Tyler cried.

In an instant, Toby was on his twin's other side, tugging at his brother's arm. "Yeah, you do," he told Tyler. "We're here to play!" he declared as if it was a battle cry.

Torn, feeling suddenly helpless, Brady looked toward the unsmiling gatekeeper, silently asking Mrs. Ferguson for help.

Mrs. Ferguson appeared to visibly soften right before his eyes.

"The boys will be fine," she assured him. "But in my opinion, *you* could definitely use some help."

Uh-oh, here it came. He knew that look, Brady thought. Mrs. Ferguson was about to recommend either a psychiatrist or a psychologist to help sort out this messy situation. Either way, he wasn't interested. He didn't need therapy. He needed help managing the twins. He needed help with his kids.

His kids. God. Would he ever get used to those words?

Meanwhile Mrs. Ferguson was apparently searching for something in her desk drawer.

"Ah, here it is," she said triumphantly, holding up the business card she had just found and passing it to him. "There you go."

Nodding his head, Brady forced himself to smile as he took the card from her. He glanced at the name imprinted on it. It read H. Radcliffe and included a phone number on it.

Without comment, Brady shoved the card into his pocket. He had no intention of calling whoever this was. In fact, he planned to toss it away the moment he left the building.

But for now, he played the game.

"Thank you," he said, nodding his head at the older woman.

"You're most welcome," Mrs. Ferguson responded. She gave him a penetrating look, as if she could read his thoughts. "I would call that number if I were you," she emphasized.

The next moment, the woman was on her phone, making a call.

Brady took that as his cue to leave, but when he started to, one hand around each twin's hand, Mrs. Ferguson held up her forefinger, keeping the harried guardian in his place.

"Jenny?" she said to whoever picked up the phone on the other end, "I have two new students who need to be brought to Mrs. Nelson's room."

"Who's Mrs. Nelson?" Toby wanted to know, not bothering to keep his voice down.

"I don't want to go to her room," Tyler cried, once again wrapping himself around Brady's leg.

Mrs. Ferguson had no sooner hung up than

the young woman she had called—Jenny, looking as if she had been one of the students here
a short while ago—stepped inside the registration office.

"You called, Mrs. Ferguson?" the lively-looking
young blonde asked.

"Yes, I did." The administrator gestured toward the twins. "Toby and Tyler need to be taken
to their new classroom," she told Jenny, then
turned toward Brady. "You're free to go now, Mr.
Fortune. Don't forget to get a more complete list
back to me," she reminded him.

Brady watched as the twins left with the
young woman who was escorting them to their
new classroom. Tyler looked back at him and
waved tearfully. Nervous for the first time about
leaving them, Brady waved back.

"Don't worry," Mrs. Ferguson told him, noting the concerned look on his face. "I promise
that they will be fine. And you should call that
number," Mrs. Ferguson reminded Brady. There
was a finality in her voice that all but sent him
on his way.

"Yeah, right," Brady murmured, watching
until Toby and Tyler disappeared from his line
of sight.

Time for him to go, too, he thought. He realized he still hadn't eaten anything, even though
he'd made breakfast for the twins before taking

them to school. Maybe he would stop at the Hotel Fortune for that breakfast and some really strong coffee, emphasis on the latter.

The sooner, the better, he thought.

The thought sustained Brady as he drove away from the preschool.

He forgot all about the business card in his pocket.

Chapter Three

"Hi, Cowboy. What brings you by to my neck of the woods?"

The question, asked in a melodious voice, had Brady abandoning his thoughts and looking up to see his cousin Nicole Fortune. The executive chef of Roja was standing beside his small table holding a pot of coffee in her hand. There was a wide, welcoming smile on her lips.

"So, can I interest you in another cup of coffee since you seemed to have drained that one?" she asked, nodding at the empty cup sitting right in front of him.

"You twisted my arm," Brady told her, then

asked, "Would it look bad if I just drank that coffee straight out of the pot?"

Nicole laughed as she poured her cousin a second cup. Then, setting the pot down on the table, she slid into the booth opposite Brady. "That bad, huh?" she asked sympathetically.

Brady took an extra-long gulp of the inky black coffee, letting it wind all through him before he put the cup down and addressed her question.

"You have no idea," he replied with a sigh.

"You're right, I probably don't," Nicole readily admitted. "Talk to me, cousin," she urged. "That's what I'm here for."

Brady smiled at her. "Not that I don't appreciate the offer, Nicole, but don't you have enough work to do?" He glanced around the restaurant. "I mean, it can't be easy, running the kitchen and keeping everything flowing smoothly."

"You're absolutely right, it's not," Nicole agreed. "But I've got good people working for me and right now, the morning rush is over and the afternoon insanity hasn't started yet, so I'm free for a few minutes." She leaned forward over the table for two, putting her hand over his, silently urging her cousin to open up to her.

"C'mon, Brady. Two ears, no waiting. Talk," she coaxed. When he didn't begin to bare his soul to her, she made her best guess at what was bothering Brady. "Is the move getting you down? I know that Rambling Rose has to be a huge change from New York for you, but—"

"Oh, it is," Brady assured her. "But it's actually a nice change." He thought how accommodating all of his cousins had been from the moment he had let them know he was coming to Texas with the twins. Busy though they were, they had even taken the time to help him find a cozy three-bedroom home in a very reasonable price range. He couldn't have asked for anything more. "I know I could definitely get used to the peace and quiet—if I could find some peace and quiet," he qualified wistfully with another sigh.

Nicole arched a well-shaped eyebrow, slightly confused by Brady's comment. "You're going to have to explain that," she told him. "My brain is currently in slow gear."

"Fair enough." He readily admitted that his previous statement might have sounded cryptic and confusing. "Let me put it another way. Six months ago my biggest decision was which bar to hit on a Saturday night. Now I'm constantly putting out small fires—" he thought of the aborted marshmallow roast the twins had once planned to hold on the living room floor back in New York "—sometimes literally." His laugh was self-deprecating. It helped him cope. "I tell you, I have newfound respect for my parents. Those two people managed to raise eight kids—two of whom were twins—without losing their minds. Looking back now, I realize that had to be one hell of a juggling act on their part." He shook his head. "Honestly, I'm surprised that they didn't both drink themselves into a stupor every night."

Nicole smiled knowingly, having gleaned the one significant kernel out of her cousin's rambling narrative. "So we're talking about the twins."

Brady nodded vigorously. "Oh yes, we're definitely talking about the twins," he confirmed. "Do you know that with all her experience and all her knowledge, my mother actually threw in the towel after trying to look after Toby and Tyler? That woman raised *six* active kids and yet those two four-year-olds turned out to be too much for her."

Her cousin looked really worn out, Nicole thought. If anyone was ever sorely in need of a pep talk, it was Brady.

"You're overlooking one important thing, Brady," she told him.

"And that's what?" he asked. "That Toby and Tyler are really space aliens?"

"No, silly," Nicole laughed. "When Aunt Catherine was 'effortlessly' raising all of you little critters, she was younger than she is now.

A *lot* younger," his cousin emphasized. "And age makes a huge difference, trust me." She smiled at Brady encouragingly as she watched him consume more coffee. "Give Rambling Rose a little time to work its magic on those kids. They'll settle down a bit before you know it. Probably not a whole lot, mind you, but enough for you to survive the exhausting process of raising them.

"Right now, from what I hear," Nicole continued, feeling that he needed a bit more support, "you're holding your own and doing a damn fine job—especially for a 'clueless bachelor,'" she told him with another wide, encouraging smile.

"I *do* think I've done a damned good job," Brady agreed with his cousin, "considering the situation and my total lack of experience."

Nicole's eyes crinkled with humor. "Well, I see that your ego hasn't been damaged any in the process."

Rather than laughing, a dubious look came over Brady's face. He was taking this conversation seriously, she realized.

"Well, by all rights it should have been," he told Nicole.

Her brow furrowed. "Again, you're going to have to explain that, Brady. I'm afraid I don't follow you."

His thoughts were coming into his head in daunting snippets. He really did need to get hold of himself before someone decided he actually *did* need a shrink.

"I just registered the twins for preschool today," Brady told his cousin.

The fact that Brady was here at Roja by himself had just hit her. "I should have asked you where you managed to stash those little wild mustangs."

"They're at the preschool where I registered them." He felt he was repeating himself, but then, maybe he hadn't been all that clear earlier. But then, he was still frustrated at Mrs. Ferguson's less-than-veiled suggestion that he get psychiatric help.

Incensed all over again, Brady said, "Do you know what that woman who runs the school had the gall to imply?" He didn't wait for Nicole to ask him "What?" but went straight to the answer. "That I needed a shrink. She doesn't even know me. Where does she get off saying that to me?"

"Maybe from years of running the nursery school?" Nicole suggested, doing her best to keep the smile out of her voice. It wasn't funny, but his anger made him look adorable.

However, Brady wasn't buying the excuse Nicole made for Mrs. Ferguson. He dismissed the very thought.

"Well, I don't need therapy or someone telling me that all my problems stem from episodes of traumatic toilet training."

"Well, maybe not all your problems..." Nicole said, an amused smile playing on her lips.

"Very funny," Brady said. He knew he was overreacting and told himself to calm down. "If you didn't brew the best damn coffee I've ever had," he informed his cousin, "I'd take my business elsewhere."

"What business?" Nicole asked her cousin drolly. "Were you planning on paying for the breakfast you just had?"

Brady was about to answer that he hadn't come here to mooch off a member of his family when the words froze on his tongue, immobilized there by the sight of what had to be one of the most beautiful women he had ever seen. She had just walked into the restaurant, clutching a single sheet of paper in her hand.

Gorgeous though she was, the expression on her face made him think of a frightened deer that had wandered out of the forest and was desperately looking for a way back before she ran into a hunter.

Nicole's back was to the restaurant's doorway, but she saw the expression on her cousin's face. "What are you looking at, Brady?" She turned around to look in the same direction that her cousin was gazing in. Able to spot a job applicant a mile away, Nicole was instantly alert. "Uh-oh, unless I miss my guess, duty calls," she told Brady, then explained, "I put out the word that we were hiring.

"If you'll excuse me for a few minutes, this shouldn't take long," she predicted.

Nicole rose and made her way over to the woman, flashing a smile as she went.

When the young woman noticed her approaching, in Nicole's opinion she looked both relieved and apprehensive at the same time.

Very mysterious, Nicole thought.

Reaching the other woman, Nicole put out her hand. "Hi, I'm Nicole Fortune, executive chef of Roja," she said by way of an introduction. "May I be of some service?"

In response, the young woman nervously all but thrust the paper she was holding into Nicole's outstretched hand. "Hello." The woman said the word almost as if it was an afterthought. "Um, I heard that Roja might be looking for help and well—" she flushed a little "—I'm looking for a job."

Nicole looked down at the paper and realized that it was a résumé. However, it wasn't exactly in keeping with the kind of resume she was looking for.

While Nicole focused on the menu, she had made certain that she was familiar with all the various aspects of running a restaurant, from the kitchen staff to the waitstaff. Though hiring the latter was usually the job of the general manager, she was filling in today.

Judging by the résumé the applicant had just given her, none of these things were even remotely familiar to the woman who was standing before her.

Nicole raised her eyes to look at the young woman. "I don't see any references on here to you having any cooking or experience waiting tables," Nicole pointed out.

"That's because I don't have any—but I'm a quick study," the woman added in a hasty postscript.

Nicole looked the woman over with a discerning eye. Though she was well-dressed, the petite woman with the long brown hair and warm chocolate-brown eyes seemed to have a slightly desperate air about her.

This wasn't going to work out, Nicole thought. She tried to let the hopeful applicant down gently. "While it is true that we are looking to hire a few people, the hotel, and so by extension, the restaurant, is only looking to hire locals at the moment."

"Oh, but I am a local," the young woman assured Nicole quickly. Then, in the interest of honesty, she corrected herself. "That is, I've been living in Rambling Rose for the last three months. But that counts, doesn't it?" she asked hopefully.

The chef frowned a little. "I'm not sure if that actually qualifies." In response to the disappointment she saw on the young woman's face, Nicole had a slight change of heart. "Tell you what, I'll talk to our hotel manager and then I'll get back to you," she promised. "As soon as possible." Nicole smiled kindly, then excused herself and headed back into the kitchen.

The lightly tanned young woman's cheeks turned a shade of pink. She knew when she was being dismissed. Mustering what dignity she could, she murmured, "Well, thank you for your time," as she turned away.

From his vantage point at the table, Brady had been privy to this little minidrama and he found himself utterly intrigued by the woman applying for a job. Having just been in the same position himself recently, looking for work, he could totally sympathize with what she had to be going through, He, of course, had family to turn to and for that he was eternally grateful. Every single one of them had been warm and welcoming. Without their warm welcome and their help, settling in with the twins would have been so much more challenging.

For some reason, he got the feeling that this woman didn't have someone to turn to.

What was her story, he couldn't help wondering.

From the way she moved, not to mention the way she was dressed, Brady had already been able to tell that she wasn't someone who was accustomed to waitressing. There was just something about her body language, the way she carried herself, that told him she wasn't the type who balanced plates on a tray for a living.

So why was she here, looking to apply for a job as a waitress? Could she be down on her luck? He could feel another wave of sympathy swelling up within him.

Half rising in the booth, Brady attempted to get the woman's attention.

"Excuse me," he began, watching her face for a response. When she shifted her brown eyes to look in his direction, he saw that she looked a little leery. "I couldn't help overhearing," he began, then realized that might not be the best approach. He tried again. "Look, can I buy you a cup of coffee? Maybe you'd like to talk," he suggested. He nodded at the empty seat facing his.

She looked somewhat apprehensively at the stranger. While he did sound sympathetic, she knew she couldn't just open up to him. For one thing, she didn't know this man from Adam—

and she was well-aware of how misconstrued things could be.

The young woman gathered her shoulder bag to her. "Look, I really should be going," she told him. With that, she began to put space between them and headed toward the exit.

Maybe she misunderstood his offer, Brady thought. Raising his voice, he told her, "I wasn't trying to hit on you," before she had a chance to open the door. "I've got my hands filled with my kids."

The woman stopped then and slowly, almost reluctantly, turned around to face him.

Brady took it as a good sign. But he remained where he was, using the sound of his voice to draw her back. "I was just looking for someone to talk to, nothing else, I promise," he told her, raising his hands as a sign of innocence.

There was something about the stranger's voice that broke through the barriers that she had newly erected around herself. And, even though she told herself this could all be just a lie to draw her in, the young woman scrutinized the friendly stranger for a long moment.

"What is it that you want to talk about?" she finally asked him.

Brady nodded toward his table. "Then you'll have coffee with me?"

She pressed her lips together, debating accepting the invitation.

"Well, I guess that I could use the coffee…" she began rather hesitantly.

"Great," Brady enthused. "Then I won't feel so bad about bending your ear," he said with a warm laugh that seemed to corkscrew right into her chest.

Looking around the restaurant, Brady raised his hand and managed to catch the eye of the lone waitress who was on duty at the moment.

Seeing him, the waitress came over to their table. "What can I get you?" she asked, looking from one occupant to the other.

"Could you bring a cup of coffee for the lady?" Brady requested.

The waitress nodded. "Sure thing," she responded obligingly. And then she promised to "be right back," as she quickly left to get the coffee.

"Okay, now that that's taken care of, take a seat," Brady said, then added, "Please," when the woman still looked as if she was undecided about staying.

Brady noticed that when the stranger did sit down, she perched on the edge of the seat, like someone who was prepared to make a quick getaway if it came down to that.

Again, he couldn't help wondering just what

this person's story was. A woman who looked the way she did shouldn't have a care in the world, but it was apparent that she did.

Big-time if he didn't miss his guess.

Maybe he could draw her out if he told her a little about himself, Brady thought just as the waitress returned with the coffee.

"Will there be anything else?" the waitress asked, looking from Brady to his new coffee companion.

Brady, in turn, looked at the woman sitting opposite him, raising an eyebrow as he asked her, "Would you like anything else? Maybe a croissant?" he suggested.

But the young woman shook her head. "No, thank you. The coffee will do just fine. Really," she stressed.

The waitress nodded. "Well, if you change your minds, just let me know," she told them cheerfully. "My shift doesn't end for another couple of hours," she added just before she withdrew, leaving the two of them alone to share whatever stories they had to tell.

The woman was barely out of sight before the awkwardness set in and for the moment, all conversation faded.

Chapter Four

Harper had to admit that she felt just a little awkward sitting here like this opposite a complete stranger.

"So tell me about these kids who you said were filling your hands," Harper, the woman sitting opposite Brady, said after taking a sip of her coffee.

"Toby and Tyler," Brady said, giving his coffee companion their names. "They're twins," he added as if that should explain everything, including why he was so frazzled. "I just finished registering them at the preschool." The experience vividly brought back the feelings of resentment that had been raised. "Do you know what the woman at the registration office had the nerve to imply?" He didn't wait to be asked to elaborate. Instead, Brady told her, "That I needed a psychologist."

Though she was trying to be sympathetic, Harper didn't see the problem. Was she missing something? "Why would that annoy you so much?" she asked, reading between the lines and interpreting his reaction to what she viewed as a well-meaning suggestion. "Everyone needs a little help sometimes." She could see by the look in his eyes that the man was distancing himself from both her and her suggestion. Harper decided to attempt another approach. "If you don't mind my asking, where's the twins' mother?"

Brady drew himself up, his body language telling her that she had just crossed a line and to back off. "She's dead," he answered.

Harper had no idea the man was a widower. And at such a young age. Her heart instantly went out to him. "Oh, I am so sorry," she told him, not wanting to scratch what could possibly be a fresh wound. "Maybe the three of you—you and your boys—could benefit from some counseling. This has to be a very difficult time for all of you," she told him compassionately.

As she watched, the stranger's face clouded over.

"It is extremely hard," Brady informed her

coldly. This was a mistake, he thought. "And having a total stranger sitting in judgment over my actions doesn't help."

Did he mean her? Just in case he did, Harper backed away from the topic. "I'm sorry—I didn't mean to offend you," she began.

But Brady was already on his feet. "No," he told her. "The fault is mine. I was the one who engaged you in conversation when I shouldn't have." His tone left no room for any further exchange. His nerves felt raw.

Taking out a twenty, he left it on the table between her cup of coffee and his. "That should cover everything. Have a nice day," he told the woman crisply.

And then he walked away.

That settled it, Harper thought, getting up from the table herself. All men were crazy.

At least he had done something positive, Brady thought, attempting to comfort himself when he went to pick up the twins a few hours later. If nothing else, he had managed to get the boys registered for preschool. One thing down, four million to go.

After parking his car in the school lot, he was unsure just where to go to pick up the boys. Deciding to take a chance, he followed the gaggle of parents who gathered at one of the gate entrances on the far side of the schoolyard.

He kept his eyes peeled, afraid he might miss connecting with the twins. But he needn't have worried. When the preschoolers and kindergarteners came pouring out of the building, he spotted his two immediately.

And then his heart sank.

Tyler was crying. The boy made a beeline for him the instant Tyler saw him.

Toby was a couple of steps behind his brother and the moment he saw the boy, Brady could tell that Tyler's twin had been in a fight.

Tyler threw his arms around him while Toby, looking guilty, hung back.

"Okay," Brady began, bracing himself. "What happened?"

The question was for both of the twins, but only Tyler answered him. His voice trembled and it was obvious that he was either on the verge of tears, or had just *stopped* crying.

"I didn't think you were coming back, Unca Brady. I was so scared," he added after a beat.

That really got to him. Brady put his arm around the boys, hugging them both. "You know I'd never leave you, boys. I brought you here so you could play with the other kids. You were supposed to have fun," he reminded the twins, "not worry about me coming back—because I'll always come back for you," he assured Tyler. "For both of you," he stressed, looking over at Toby. "Okay, what's your story?" he asked the other twin.

Toby turned to him, then looking a little too innocent, and replied, "No story."

Brady raised a skeptical eyebrow. "Then why do you look like you were in a fight?" he wanted to know.

It was Tyler who piped up with an answer. "'Cause he was in a fight."

"Toby, is this true?" Brady asked the disheveled twin, placing his hand on the boy's shoulders.

Toby shrugged his small shoulders and looked off into the distance. "Maybe," he finally admitted.

"Okay, and why were you fighting?" Brady wanted to know.

Tyler shrugged again, but this time he followed the action up with an answer. "'Cause that kid made fun of Tyler." Toby vaguely pointed off into the distance. There were still a number of children in that area. "He called Tyler a baby for crying. I made him take it back," he added proudly.

"Look, Toby," Brady told the twin wearily, "while I think it's great that you stood up for

your brother, you can't settle things by pummel-
ing people who annoy you."

Toby's brow furrowed. "What's pum-pum—
that word?" he finally asked.

"It means beating up the other guy," Brady
explained to Toby, then stressed, "You can't do
that."

"How come?" Toby asked, confused. And
then he proudly declared, "I won."

"Because eventually, someone might wind up
beating *you* up when you come out swinging and
I'd rather that didn't happen." Feeling as if his
lecture was going nowhere, Brady decided it was
time to wind it up. "C'mon, guys, let's go home."

Taking each twin by the hand, Brady brought
them to his vehicle.

After securing the twins into their separate
car seats in the rear, Brady set out for home.

Maybe that woman in the registration office,
Mrs. Ferguson, was right, he thought as he drove.
Maybe he did need help.

One thing was for sure—this certainly wasn't
going the way he had hoped it would. If it was,
by now his own life should have been settling
down into some kind of orderly routine. Instead,
it felt as if the chaos was only growing, absorbing him.

If it got any worse, he was fairly certain that it
would wind up swallowing him up whole.

Trying to smother the desperate feeling he felt bubbling up inside him, Brady thought of the card that Mrs. Ferguson had given him. He hadn't had time to throw it away yet, the way he had planned.

Slipping his hand into his pocket to make sure it was still there, he came in contact with the business card. Okay, that settled it.

He decided to make the call.

What harm would it do? And who knew, maybe talking to this H. Radcliffe guy might even help him. It certainly couldn't make it any worse.

He realized that Toby was asking him a question. "We going back tomorrow?"

"Yes," Brady answered, bracing himself for a fight. "You are."

Toby totally surprised him by saying "Cool."

It was Tyler, the more quiet of the pair, who protested, "I don't wanna go!"

"It'll get better," Brady promised automatically. "Besides, you don't want to be known as a quitter, do you?" he asked, thinking that would convince the twin to go back.

But again, Brady discovered he was wrong.

"Why not?" Toby challenged him.

Everything was always a debate, Brady thought wearily. "Just give it another shot, okay?" he asked, then added, "For me," for good measure.

But it was Toby who shocked him by telling his twin, "I'll be there to take care of you, Ty."

Brady looked up in the rearview mirror to see Tyler's reaction. The boy still looked somewhat unconvinced, but he didn't protest any further.

When they got home, Brady made sandwiches for the boys and put out two servings of grapes as dessert. While the twins were busy eating— and using the grapes to lob at each other—Brady went to place a call to H. Radcliffe.

He was more than ready to admit that he needed help—but instead he found himself leaving a voice mail.

According to the message, H. Radcliffe was out of the office.

Most likely saving someone else's sanity, Brady thought. The next moment, he found himself talking quickly in hopes that H. Radcliffe would get back to him sometime today. Right now, it was the only thing Brady had to cling to.

"Hello, this is Brady Fortune. You don't know me, but Mrs. Ferguson at the Rambling Rose preschool suggested I get in contact with you. She's the one who gave me your card," he added, thinking that might help tip the scale in his favor. "I've recently become the guardian for four-year-old twins and I realize that I'm *really* out of my depth here. I could really use any help I can get. Please give me a call back as soon as possible. I'll be waiting for your call," he added for good measure. And then he left his number.

Brady was aware that the polite way to go would have been to say *at your earliest convenience,* but at this point, he felt the situation was way beyond anyone's convenience. Certainly beyond his. His life felt as if it was in a state of constant emergency and he desperately needed help dealing with it *now.*

Brady ended the call just as he heard a crash coming from the other room.

Brady went to investigate this latest threat to his peace and quiet, fervently hoping that H. Radcliffe would listen to his messages before going to bed tonight and give him a call.

Harper saw the blinking light on the landline in her studio apartment the moment she walked in. Crossing her fingers and hoping that this was about a possible job, she didn't even bother taking her jacket off. Instead, she went straight to the phone on the nightstand and hit the green arrow marked Play.

She listened to the message twice.

There was no doubt about it. Someone was calling about a possible position.

Someone wanted to hire her, Harper thought,

her heart leaping up in her chest. Finally, just when she had begun to give up all hope, there was suddenly a light at the end of this extremely long, dark tunnel.

What that meant, she thought, was that she didn't have to convince that chef at Roja that she had what it took to be a waitress—because truthfully, she really didn't.

Now, with any luck, she could actually get back to what she was good at—being a nanny.

Harper played the message for a third time to make sure she wasn't getting ahead of herself.

No, she wasn't wrong, she thought. The man who had placed the call definitely sounded as if he was looking for a nanny, no doubt about it.

It also occurred to her that the voice on the phone sounded somewhat familiar, but even though she concentrated, she couldn't place the voice.

Maybe, she decided, it was her imagination.

It didn't matter, though. All that mattered was getting back to what she loved doing—working with children. If she got this job, that could wind up being the answer to all her problems. She didn't even care about the salary.

Harper smiled to herself.

Just when she was ready to give up, the sun had broken through the clouds. Apparently moving to Rambling Rose hadn't been the beginning of the end for her. It had wound up being only an excruciatingly long, but ultimately temporary pause.

In truth, she had never wanted to come out here in the first place. A few months ago, she had been working in Dallas as a nanny. But when Justine Wheeler, the woman she had been working for, had been transferred to Rambling Rose by her employer, she had begged Harper to come with the family.

Harper had really wanted to say no, but she had trouble asserting herself, so she had agreed to the woman's pleas and wound up moving here even though her common sense told her not to.

It wasn't actually the location she had a problem with, it was the fact that the woman's husband had slowly become progressively more and more flirtatious.

She did her best to keep the man, Edward, at a distance, but apparently Justine's husband didn't accept any of her rebuffs as genuine. The situation between Harper and Edward had been a very touchy one at that point and the move to Rambling Rose only seemed to make things worse.

Harper loved the children she was taking care of, but more and more she found herself trying to politely avoid the woman's husband. While Edward Wheeler had always been nice to her, after they had made the move, he became a little *too* nice.

He grew even more flirtatious, a lot more than she was comfortable with.

When he made an outright, undeniable pass at her, Harper decided that she had no choice but to quit. But when she told Justine she was leaving, without citing the reason *why*, Justine once again begged her to remain, playing on her sympathies and her love for the children.

The woman did everything in her power to make her stay. She said that they were new in town, lamenting that they would never be able to replace her on such short notice.

So once again against her better judgment, Harper agreed to stay on. But, predictably, things only got worse. The Wheelers' marriage was coming apart at the seams. So when Justine saw her husband flirting with Harper, she got the totally wrong idea. She viciously blamed Harper for all her marital woes and fired her on the spot. She never gave her a chance to defend herself.

Harper had never once mentioned to Justine the uncomfortable situation she had endured all this time. At that point she knew that whatever she said wouldn't be believed anyway.

With that in mind, Harper packed up and left immediately.

Her only regret about leaving was the couple's

two little girls. The girls were heartbroken and cried when she left.

That was how she had wound up being job-less in a town where she didn't know anyone. She had no funds and with her parents gone, she had no one to go back to. Her only family was a brother who was currently in the army over-seas. She was not about to ask him for any help. She had always taken pride in earning her own way. They did correspond, but not all that often. She refused to be the one in their relationship who just complained and unloaded, especially given the pressures he was under. So she kept her emails short and upbeat.

However, to make matters worse, Justine Wheeler had quickly begun spreading vicious lies about her so all of her potential nanny jobs quickly dried up. If she had any doubts that was happening, having the phone go dead in her ear quickly convinced her that this was true.

No one called the number on the cards that she had made up.

With her back against the wall and very little money in her pocket, Harper had started look-ing for any sort of work at all. That was how she had wound up interviewing for a waitressing job.

Quickly exhausting her meager savings, she needed money and she needed it fast.

Truthfully, she had given up all hope of getting any sort of a position as a nanny. But someone had obviously decided to give her a try and they had called the number on one of the numerous cards that she had left scattered about the town in her wake.

Harper's hand was trembling as she called the number that was left on her voice mail. As she listened to the phone on the other end ring, she prayed that the person who had called was home—and that he hadn't found a nanny yet.

Mentally, she counted off the number of rings.

Her heart had started to sink when the phone rang six times.

The person wasn't home.

And then she heard the receiver being picked up.

She could feel her pulse going into overdrive. Her mouth was dry, but even so, she forced herself to start talking.

Quickly.

Chapter Five

Harper had no idea why she felt so nervous. After all, it wasn't as if she was new to this whole thing. She had been a nanny for a number of years now. That meant that she had placed calls and made appointments for interviews before.

The problem right now was that she felt at the end of her rope and this could very well be the lifeline she had been hoping for—if she didn't somehow wind up messing everything up.

The deep voice echoed in her ear as she heard the man say, "Hello?"

Her heart lodged itself in her throat.

Here goes everything, Harper thought.

"Hello, Mr. Fortune? This is Harper Radcliffe.

You called me earlier today about needing my services," she said, trying to sound as cheerful as she could. She waited for his response. When there wasn't one immediately, Harper thought that his cell reception might have possibly gone down. "Hello, Mr. Fortune? Are you still there? Did you hear me?"

Brady had heard her—and there was something strangely familiar in her voice, but he couldn't quite figure out what it was. He shook his head and dismissed the sensation.

Realizing that the woman was still waiting for some sort of response, he answered, "Sorry. Yes, I heard you. Um, about the reason that I called," he began.

"Yes, of course." *Push on, Harper, push on*, she silently ordered. "Why don't I meet you at Provisions tomorrow, say about eleven o'clock, to discuss the matter? If that fits in with your schedule, of course," she quickly tacked on.

"Provisions," Brady repeated. Was that how these shrinks did things? Get you eating and then get you talking? Curious, he couldn't help asking, "Isn't that a little unusual?"

If this potential client had turned out to be a woman, she would have readily gone to their house. Harper thought. But this was a man and after her last experience with her employer's husband, she wanted to meet this man somewhere out in the open.

But she couldn't very well tell him that because he might take offense, so she said, "I prefer our first meeting to take place in a neutral location."

Neutral location. The woman on the other end of the call made it sound as if they were about to negotiate some sort of a peace treaty, not discuss a problem he might be having with suddenly finding himself raising two rambunctious little boys.

But then, what did he know? Maybe this was the new approach to psychology. He was game for anything.

"Sure. Why not," Brady sportingly agreed. "Eleven o'clock tomorrow at Provisions," he repeated. "I'll be the harried-looking man on his way to having his hair turn prematurely gray."

Thinking he was trying to lighten the mood by joking, Harper laughed. She actually understood how he probably felt. Some of the fathers she had worked for in the past acted as if fatherhood was the hardest job in the world instead of the absolute joy it could be. To her way of thinking, it was her job, in part, to show them the way.

"All right, then, Mr. Fortune. I'll see you tomorrow at eleven," Harper said just before she hung up the receiver.

This was it, Harper thought, looking down at the phone. This could very well be the job she had been hoping for.

The long, frustrating dry spell might *finally* be over!

Her heart racing, Harper hurried over to the closet where she had hung up her small wardrobe to pick out just the right outfit for the meeting tomorrow. Aware that first impressions were everything, she needed to look her most competent for the interview.

The next day, Brady was surprised that he was nervous. He hadn't thought he would be, but he actually was.

It didn't matter, really. Even if the idea of talking to someone about his feelings made him uncomfortable, he reminded himself that this wasn't about him. He was doing it for the boys, to get a better handle on how he could give them the best life possible.

Maybe, he admitted, just maybe he was doing it for himself, too. So that he could manage to keep them all together, so that he could see the boys grow up to become young men.

Damn, Brady thought as he straightened his tie, life had become much too complicated in these last six months. But then, he thought, if things weren't complicated and confounding, he wouldn't have to be meeting with this Harper Radcliffe and the woman would probably be out of a job.

Brady sighed. He was overthinking this, he told himself. And overdressing as well, he decided, taking another look at himself in the full-length mirror. He looked as if he was dressed to meet some high-class dignitary—not a therapist.

He glanced at his watch. It was too late to change, he thought—unless he wanted to be late. And he knew if he was, Ms. Radcliffe would probably make some sort of a big deal out of that, claiming it was an unconscious attempt to demonstrate his superiority over her or some such nonsense.

No, he wasn't going to waste time changing into something more casual. Besides, maybe this woman would be impressed—or intimidated—by what he was wearing. Either way, it might wind up working in his favor.

And so would being on time for this meeting, Brady told himself as he left the house.

Right now, Brady was really grateful that he had gotten the twins registered yesterday. Because dragging the boys to this meeting might have proven to be difficult at best.

He didn't want to consider what it might have wound up being at its worst.

Brady did his best to bolster his confidence.

Maybe he'd even learn something, he thought as he drove to the restaurant.

What he needed to do was keep an open mind, Brady told himself. After all, that was why he had made the phone call to begin with, right? To learn something that he could actually use when it came to dealing with the twins—or possibly even learn what it was that he was doing wrong with them.

Because, to his way of thinking, by all rights, Toby and Tyler should have been calming down by now—shouldn't they? He had to be doing something wrong, he thought. Possibly even failing them. But how?

The question continued gnawing at him—and his gut—as he got out in the restaurant parking lot.

It suddenly occurred to him, as he walked toward the restaurant's entrance, that he should have asked for this woman's description. Otherwise, how was he going to recognize this person that Mrs. Ferguson had recommended to him? He didn't have a clue what this woman looked like. Until she had called him back, he hadn't even known that she *was* a woman.

Walking in through the restaurant's double doors, Brady stood in the entrance and looked around the restaurant.

How was he—?

Brady abruptly stopped as he stared into the dining area.

Wasn't that…?

The knockout he'd had coffee with at Roja yesterday—or had begun to have coffee with, he amended, recognizing the woman he had met.

What was she doing here, he wondered. This had to qualify as one hell of a coincidence, Brady couldn't help thinking. Unless…

And then it hit him like a ton of bricks.

Oh wow!

The knockout and the woman he was meeting were one and the same.

Harper saw him from across the room. The man who had bought her coffee yesterday because, according to him, he had needed to talk to someone. Then, as she proceeded to do just that, attempting to give him a little advice as well, the man had abruptly pulled back and walked out of the restaurant.

And then it suddenly hit her. *That* was why the man on the answering machine had sounded so familiar to her. It was *him*. The widower with the twins, she recalled.

He was the one she was meeting?

Wow, talk about it being a small world, Harper thought. They just couldn't make this kind of stuff up, she silently marveled, watching as the man from yesterday's abbreviated encounter at Roja began to walk toward her.

"Harper Radcliffe, I presume?" Brady asked as he came up to the table where she was seated.

For Harper's part, she smiled at him as she inclined her head.

"Brady Fortune," she said. Because it was the polite thing to do, she put out her hand to him. "Nice to formally make your acquaintance."

Brady took her hand in his. He couldn't help thinking how delicate it felt to him.

"Same here," he responded.

And then something in his head suddenly yelled *May-day*! He couldn't go through with this, Brady decided. "Although, I've thought it over," he told her, "and I've changed my mind."

Harper wasn't sure that she was following what he was saying to her, although part of her did have a very uneasy feeling that she knew. The man was dumping her before he even gave her a chance.

Why?

She pressed on, feigning ignorance.

"Changed your mind about what?" she asked him.

Brady was straightforward in his answer— or at least he thought he was. "About retaining your services."

Another person would have taken that as their

cue to leave. They would have stood up and just walked away with their dignity intact.

But another person wasn't as desperate as she was to be gainfully employed again. Employed in not just any field, but the field of her choice. As a nanny.

So rather than just pick up and leave, Harper decided to press the matter. "May I ask why?"

"Because I don't believe in them," he told her point-blank.

"You don't believe in *them*?" she repeated, utterly confused. What was that supposed to mean? And just what did he mean by *them*?

"Are you going to question and take apart everything I say?" Brady asked, not knowing whether he was offended or just confused.

"Sorry," she responded crisply. "I'm just trying to wrap my head around why a grown man is telling me that he doesn't believe in nannies."

Brady blinked, totally confused now. What was this woman talking about? "What?"

Okay, Harper thought, now this extremely handsome, infuriating idiot was just trying to bait her for some unknown reason. "Why you don't believe in nannies?" she repeated, enunciating every word slowly and clearly.

"I didn't say that," Brady insisted.

Harper took a deep breath, digging deep for the patience that served her well when she worked with children. This man was a real challenge, she thought.

"You just said you don't believe in what I do for a living. You referred to them as my *services*." Her eyes pinned him against the wall. "Are you with me so far?"

He stared at her, his confusion only growing. "What sort of a mind game is this?" he wanted to know. "Because if this is your way of trying to get me to spill my guts to you, well, it's failing. I'm just not about to do that."

Harper did a mental double take. He must have had a hell of a childhood, she couldn't help thinking. "Why would you want to do that anyway?" she questioned. She had absolutely no desire to be privy to this man's spilled "guts."

"Well, isn't that what you people want?" he challenged. "To get your would-be patient to share their so-called deepest, darkest secrets with you?"

"Okay, back up here," Harper told him, holding up her hands as if that would somehow physically make him stop talking. "What exactly do you mean by 'you people'?" she wanted to know.

"You," he said, gesturing at her. Then elaborated by adding, "Shrinks."

"Shrinks?" she repeated, staring at him. "The only thing I ever 'shrank,'" she informed the man sitting opposite her, "was a load of laundry when I wasn't accustomed to the washing machine."

And then she realized that it was all starting to make sense now. The man's hostility as well as his confusion, it all made sense.

"Are you telling me that you think I'm a psychologist—or a psychiatrist?" She wasn't sure which he was accusing her of being. The only thing she knew was that while she respected the vocations, she was neither of those professions.

"Aren't you?" he asked, beginning to feel just the slightest bit foolish. If this was a colossal mix-up, how did he fix it?

"Oh lord, no," Harper answered with a laugh. "If I were one, I'd probably be a little more together than I am now. Maybe a lot more together," she amended with a genial shrug.

Wow, talk about making a mistake, Brady thought, totally embarrassed now. He had just made a huge mistake by inserting not just his foot in his mouth, but both of them.

All the way in.

At the same time.

"Then what are you?" he asked, thinking back to the card that Mrs. Ferguson had pressed into his hand. The card with this woman's phone number on it. He'd thought that Mrs. Ferguson had believed he needed help and had mistakenly thought she was giving him the name of a psychiatrist to help him find his way out of this emotional maze.

"I'm a nanny," Harper told him. "I thought you knew that."

Brady shook his head. "There was nothing about you being a nanny on the card I was given. It had your name on it and the slogan 'Help when you need it.'" His eyes met hers. "That's not exactly crystal clear," Brady complained.

Harper closed her eyes. *Damn*, she thought.

When she opened them again, she said, "You're absolutely right. That was my fault. I should have been clearer." She made a mental note to redo her business cards.

Since she was being so nice about it, Brady was willing to share in the blame. "I guess I just read into it," he admitted.

Harper brightened. "Let's start all over again." She put out her hand to him. "Hello, I'm Harper Radcliffe and I'm a nanny currently between jobs. Would you have any interest in making use of my services?" she asked him.

For a second, he just stared at her. And then he smiled. Broadly. "You have no idea how much I would *love* to make use of your services, Ms. Radcliffe," he told her.

Maybe it was the fact that he had used the word *love* or maybe her last experience with her boss's husband had completely colored her reaction to men in general and she would have reacted this way no matter what he said. In any case, Harper suddenly felt a cold wave washing over her, warning her that this had turned out to be a really bad idea.

To make matters worse, this man was just too damn handsome for either one of their own good. Besides, she had learned to be very wary of gorgeous men, predominantly because they were accustomed to getting their way whenever they wanted.

Taking a job with this man was just asking for trouble and she had had enough trouble, as far as she was concerned, to last her a lifetime.

"On second thought," Harper told the man before her, "I've decided that maybe we're not such a good match after all." She rose to her feet before the stunned Brady was able say anything in response. "Thank you, but no thank you."

And with that, Harper turned on her heel to walk out of the restaurant.

Chapter Six

"Wait, Harper—Ms. Radcliffe," Brady corrected himself, calling to the woman he had begun to think of as his potential lifesaver. "You're leaving?"

The way he said it, he sounded stunned, like someone surprised to find themselves being abandoned. Against her better judgment, Harper turned around and decided to give the man an extra minute before retreating.

"I'm afraid this isn't going to work out," she told him.

Brady continued to stare at her, totally at a loss. "But why are you turning this job down before you even meet Toby and Tyler?" he asked her. "Isn't that against the rules in the Nanny Handbook?"

He knew she needed the work. Why else would someone who was a professional nanny by trade have been looking into getting a waitressing job at Roja? It certainly couldn't have been the enticement of being on her feet for eight hours a day or more, carrying heavy trays and putting up with irate, irrational customers' complaints.

He waited for her to make him understand— or to change her mind about her decision.

Before Harper could frame any sort of a response to Brady's question, two young, pretty blondes who had obviously heard the exchange between her and Brady approached their booth.

And from the look on Brady's face, he recognized them.

Were they ganging up on her, Harper wondered.

"Brady, I thought I heard your voice," one of the women declared. She was obviously pleased to see him, but she appeared to also be concerned at the same time. "Is there something wrong?" she wanted to know, looking from him to Harper.

She looked down at the table. "It can't be the food. There's nothing here. Is it my waitress? Is she taking too long to bring you your order?" the woman asked.

Not waiting for an answer, her eyes shifted to Harper. She smiled and extended her hand. "Hello, I'm Ashley Fortune and this lovely creature next to me is my sister, Megan. We're Brady's cousins and the owners of this restaurant. And you are...?"

"Harper Radcliffe," Harper replied, feeling just a little awkward about the way the two women were regarding her.

Megan only had enough time to say, "Hi," To Harper before Ashley returned to what she viewed as the problem. "Is there anything I can do to make this a better dining experience for you?" she asked, looking at her cousin.

He knew that his cousin was referring to the food at the restaurant, but all Brady could think of was that he was losing his shot at getting a nanny—one that had come recommended by Mrs. Ferguson. And he still hadn't the slightest idea why that was happening.

Desperate, Brady glanced at both his cousins and said, "You can use those charms of yours to talk Ms. Radcliffe here into being the twins' nanny. Maybe if she came over to the house to meet them, she might change her mind about turning the job down."

It was a long shot, but it was the only one he had left, Brady thought.

Megan's face instantly lit up. "Oh my lord,

yes. Those sweet boys could definitely benefit from a woman's steady presence in their lives. You would be a virtual lifesaver, Ms....Radcliffe, is it?" Megan asked her, obviously uncertain if she had heard the last name correctly.

"Harper," the young woman being laid siege to said, feeling that using her last name in this case was a little too formal. "My first name is Harper."

"Well, Harper, how would you like to feel like the cavalry and ride to our cousin's rescue?" Ashley wanted to know. Not waiting for an answer, Ashley wiggled into the booth, sitting on Harper's left side.

Not waiting for an invitation, Megan immediately sat down on Harper's other side, immobilizing her in case she had any thoughts about making an escape before they convinced her to take the job their cousin was offering her.

Looking on, Brady decided that the young nanny probably didn't stand a chance against these two—at least he hoped she didn't because he *really* needed her. He had the good sense not to smile too broadly as he watched his cousins go to work.

"He's a really good guy," Ashley was telling the nanny. "He relocated here all the way from upstate New York because he needed help with

his twins—well, they're not really *his* twins—"
she corrected herself.

"They are in the eyes of the law," Megan
pointed out. "Brady got legal custody of them
when his friends—the twins' parents—died in
that awful motorcycle accident," she quickly explained to Harper.

This was the first she was hearing about this.
The fact that the man wasn't the twins' blood
relative but was still taking on the task of raising them raised his stock in her eyes by a hun-
dredfold. Maybe she had been too hasty, turning
him down, she thought.

"But our confirmed bachelor here," Ashley told her as she gestured toward her cousin,
"didn't have a clue how to get a puppy to listen
to him, much less two overenergized four-year-
olds. He thought family might help, but we're
all busy trying to make a living, so we haven't
had the time to be of much help with the twins,"
Ashley confessed with obvious genuine regret.

"Which brings us to you," Megan said. "Nannies are supposed to be able to get kids to jump
through hoops and be on their best behavior,
right?" she asked Harper, pinning her with a
look.

Harper felt as if she was on the receiving end
of a one-two punch. She laughed at the last thing
Megan had said to her. The woman was being

highly optimistic in her assessment of what a nanny could actually do, she thought.

"You have obviously either read or seen *Mary Poppins* one too many times," Harper told the two sisters.

Ashley looked genuinely disappointed. "So that's it?" she asked. "You're turning the job down without even meeting the kids?"

Megan jumped in then. "Oh, but you've got to meet the boys and give them a chance to steal your heart," she insisted, then added, "For all our sakes."

Okay, Brady thought, seeing his cousins do their act. They were laying it on thick. Too thick. This really wasn't fair.

"Ashley, Megan, you're ganging up on Ms. Radcliffe. Give her a chance to breathe," he told them. And then he turned what Harper could only describe as his beautiful, heartwarming brown eyes on her. She could feel herself melting. "All I ask is that, in all fairness, you come and meet Tyler and Toby before you decide to turn this job down."

Harper looked from one side to the other, taking in the three faces that were literally pleading with her to do the right thing.

To do the *only* thing that she was born to do, she reminded herself.

Ordinarily, she would have immediately jumped

at the chance. But she wasn't and she knew what was stopping her. Justine Wheeler's husband—or at least the memory of Justine Wheeler's husband—was what was causing her to second-guess this whole situation and actually shy away from it.

She was afraid of history repeating itself.

But this man who had met with her—according to her terms—was in dire need of someone to help him manage the twins he had unexpectedly gotten custody of. She couldn't allow that awful experience she had gone through with her boss's husband to keep her from what she had once regarded as her life's calling.

She was good at her job, damn it, and she needed to feel that way again. Needed it as much as apparently Brady Fortune appeared to need her.

Harper could feel herself coming around ever so slowly.

"Well, I'm still not sure I'm the right person for this job, but I'm not accustomed to being unfair," she told Brady. "So I will reserve judgment until I meet Toby and Tyler—"

She got no further. Megan threw her arms round her, hugging Harper hard.

"You won't regret this," Megan promised fiercely.

"Well, one thing's for sure," Brady told Harper. "I know that *I* won't regret this."

He would have hugged the person he considered to be the potential answer to all his prayers just the way that Megan had, but he had a feeling that doing so might just spook her enough to make her change her mind, so he remained where he was, sitting opposite Harper as well as his cousins in the booth.

Megan put it into words for all of them. "You're the answer to a prayer, Harper. Three prayers."

"Most likely even more than that if we could take an accurate head count. Everyone in Rambling Rose wants to help Brady with his newly acquired family," Ashley confessed. "But truthfully, in this situation, you're probably the only one who knows what she's doing."

Too much flattery had always embarrassed Harper. She was only doing what came naturally to her. "I wouldn't go that far," Harper told the three cousins, deflecting words of praise she felt she hadn't earned yet.

"I would," Brady freely admitted. "If you can get them to listen to you, you'll be doing better than I have in six months," he told her.

Harper cleared her throat. "All right then, you want to take me to meet your boys?" she asked, ready to leave the restaurant.

"More than anything in the world," Brady told her. As she began to rise, he caught hold of her wrist, anchoring her in place. "But they're in pre-school right now and the last thing I want to do is disrupt their day." He smiled at the phrase he had inadvertently used. "They're perfectly capable of doing that all by themselves. But, like I said, they're in school right now. That gives us at least a couple of hours before I wind up bringing you before the firing squad."

"You're really not selling this, cousin," Ashley told him with a laugh.

Brady looked as if he knew he had made a mistake and wasn't sure just how to backtrack from it. His shrug was innocent. "I guess I was just being honest."

Harper found herself coming to his rescue. "Honesty is a very admirable quality." There was approval in her voice that she didn't have to feign.

"I will be as honest as you can bear as long as you promise to give the twins a chance," Brady told her in all sincerity.

She looked at him for a long moment, then nodded. He'd sold her. "Fair enough."

Ashley looked at her sister, relieved. "Well, our work here is done," she declared, beaming as she rose from the booth. Megan slid out from the other side. "Thank you," she repeated, looking at Harper. "Well, enjoy your lunch, you two—and oh, by the way," she added, squeezing Harper's hand, "Lunch is on me. Order anything you like. The sky's the limit," Ashley emphasized.

Taken aback, Harper said, "That's very generous of you."

"I just want to make you feel welcome here at our restaurant. You'll find that it's a very warm place," Ashley told her with a wink.

"Well, you certainly have made me feel welcomed," Harper told her. "Or guilty if I decide to turn the job down," she added, viewing the situation from the flip side.

Sitting back in the booth as his cousins took their leave, Brady observed, "You know, that's very astute of you."

He watched in fascination as an almost beatific smile slipped over her lips.

"I deal with children," Harper reminded him. "And children, bless 'em, can be positively the most manipulative little creatures on the face of the earth."

Tickled, Brady laughed, finding himself appreciating her view on the situation. "Something tells me you are most definitely the right woman for the job," he told her.

She wanted to stop him right now. "Let's not get ahead of ourselves," Harper warned. "We'll take this one step at a time."

"Right," Brady agreed. He proceeded cautiously. He didn't want to blow this now that it was finally happening. "Step one is ordering lunch," he reminded her. "And my cousin did say the sky's the limit."

"That was very generous of her," Harper told him as she scanned the menu she had just picked up.

"Well, we try to take care of each other in Rambling Rose," he told her.

"Apparently," she murmured, attempting to make a selection between the choices she had narrowed down to. "It must be nice to have such a big family."

"I never really thought about it," he admitted to Harper. "I mean, I didn't grow up with my Texas relatives, but I had five siblings—including a twin brother. So it was just something that was always a part of my life, but now that you mention it, I guess it is nice. Although," he told her, "there were times I really did want to be alone—and that's when life seemed to be the most crowded."

Spoken like a real bachelor, Harper thought. A bachelor, she was willing to bet, who wasn't through planting his wild oats. And, if she took this job being nanny to his newly acquired twins, that would leave him free to go on planting to his heart's content, she thought.

The next moment she told herself that wasn't her concern one way or the other. What *was* her concern, if she decided to take this job, was whether she and the boys meshed. Could she be a plus in their lives or would this turn out to be just a way for her to earn a salary?

If it turned out to be the latter, then she wouldn't take the job, Harper decided. Even though she needed it, it had never been about the money for her. Instead, it was what she could bring to the table and add to the lives of the children she took care of.

That was what was important to her.

"So, what will it be?" Brady asked, his voice breaking into her thoughts.

Rousing herself, Harper realized that she hadn't really heard him. "Excuse me?"

Brady held up the menu, drawing her attention to it. "Lunch," he prompted, tapping the dark green cover. "What did you finally decide to have?"

Her mind wasn't on food. At the moment, she was too preoccupied thinking about meeting the twins. But she didn't want to keep him waiting while she made up her mind about something as trivial as lunch.

"I can't make up my mind," Harper told him, not going into why she couldn't. "Why don't you choose for me?" she suggested.

Though she looked delicate, Harper Radcliffe didn't strike him as someone who abdicated her choices, even when it came to something as simple as ordering lunch.

"Are you sure?" he asked her. When she looked at him quizzically, he explained, "One of us could be a vegan, or have a food allergy, which means that the other person shouldn't be the one making the choices for lunch."

That was a really odd thing to say, Harper thought. "Well, I'm not a vegan," she told him. "As a matter of fact, I happen to really like eating meat."

"No kidding?" he asked, his face lighting up. One of the last few women he had gone out with—pretwins—had been a devout vegan. "So do I. I'm very partial to steak." Brady grinned. "Guess what, Ms. Radcliffe? I think that I just found something that we have in common."

Harper laughed. "I'm sure there are probably other things."

"I look forward to finding them out," he told her in all sincerity.

Uh-oh, Harper thought. There were red lights flickering inside her head.

"Tell you what, why don't we use this time to get to know a little about each other?" Brady suggested. "Over lunch," he elaborated, then added, "So I can get to know just what sort of a person I'm handing the care of my best friend's kids over to."

"That's why you want to get to know me better?" she asked, still not certain.

"It'll do for starters," he replied, his eyes meeting hers.

Harper felt something warm shimmying up and down her spine. Was that a sign of things to come? Or had her bad experience with Edward Wheeler managed to color the way she saw even the most harmless of comments? She didn't know. But for now, she decided to give Brady the benefit of the doubt.

She lowered her eyes to look at the menu. "I think I'm ready to order now," she told him.

He smiled and nodded. He'd figured she would be better off making her own choice.

Chapter Seven

As he drove home from the restaurant, Brady kept raising his eyes to look in the rearview mirror every few seconds.

He was relieved to see that Harper was still there, still following him in her unimpressive, fifteen-year-old four-door car just as she had told him she would.

Even so, Brady half expected to see the car make a U-turn and head back to wherever it was that Harper was currently living.

But mercifully, the woman he had wound up pinning all of his hopes on in the last couple of hours was still there. Still following him.

He was happy that she was actually willing to keep her word and meet with his kids.

Brady suddenly gripped the steering wheel harder as he realized the import of the thought that had just gone through his head.

His kids.

When exactly had that happened? Brady asked himself, clearly stunned.

When had he started thinking of Toby and Tyler as "his" kids instead of Gord's kids? Or even "the" kids? He had no answer for that, only that the term had somehow snuck up on him.

To give Harper's meeting with the twins a better chance of going well, he'd decided it should take place on his own home territory. Brady had asked his brother Kane to pick up the boys at the preschool when he went there to pick up his fiancée's daughter. Since Kane already had a set of his own keys to the house, Brady had asked Kane to bring the boys home and stay with them until he himself could get there with Harper.

He knew that his brother had to sympathize with what he was going through to some degree. Kane was soon to become an instant father himself when he married Layla, who came with a precious little girl in the bargain.

Nothing seemed to daunt Kane, Brady thought, checking in the mirror again to make sure that Harper's car was still behind him.

It was.

But then, Brady thought, both of his older brothers probably thought the same thing about him. That nothing daunted him.

He had certainly thought that about himself until six months ago. These days it was just a struggle to try to take everything in stride and not let things like cuts and scrapes, and broken glasses and plates, get to him. Lord knew it wasn't easy. Trying to get the twins to actually pay attention and listen to him when he told them to do something had shown Brady a whole new side of himself. A side that had turned out to be a great deal more flappable than he would have ever thought possible.

But after today, with any luck, things should be a lot calmer, he promised himself. All he had to do was convince a perfectly sane, rational woman that she'd actually enjoy living in a circus-like atmosphere where three-foot clowns ran the show.

No big deal, right?

As he drew closer to the new house he had recently purchased, again with the boys in mind, he saw Kane's car parked in his driveway. His brother had managed to get here ahead of him, he thought, even though he had been closer to it than Kane was.

Part of Brady had hoped to bring this nanny

into his house before all hell had a chance of breaking loose.

Brady wondered if this was the kind of situation where the term *trial by fire* had initially originated.

Instead of parking his car in the garage which was overloaded with boxes, both his and the boys', Brady decided it was simpler to just choose a spot in the driveway. He parked over to one side, making sure he left plenty of room for Harper's vehicle. It wasn't that her car was big, but it gave the impression that it was close to being on its last legs, which meant that it could very well die soon. When it did, it would need a lot of room to allow other vehicles to come and go easily.

After getting out of his car, he turned his attention toward helping guide Harper into a space away from both his car and Kane's.

It went a great deal better than he would have predicted.

Until his would-be nanny got out of her car. She didn't exactly look happy, he thought.

"Was all that gesturing you were doing your way of telling me that you don't think I'm capable of parking my car without damaging yours, or damaging whoever belongs to that one?" she asked, nodding toward Kane's truck.

He hadn't meant to insult her, Brady thought.

He supposed there was such a thing as over-thinking a situation.

Brady launched into damage control. "No, I guess I was just afraid that you were going to change your mind and tear out of here at the first sign of a problem."

"What kind of a problem?" she wanted to know, not following him. "Parking a car?" she asked, saying the first thing that came to her mind. "I've been driving since I was sixteen," Harper told him. "And the reason this car looks as if it's been driven in a demolition derby for the last ten years is because I bought it—very used—from a friend of mine after my car caught fire because of a defective fuel pump. Andrew was always hard on his cars," she said, mentioning the vehicle's previous owner by name.

Harper regarded the vehicle parked away from the other two vehicles. She had to admit that hers looked very much like a pariah. "It was all I could afford."

"You don't have to explain anything to me," Brady told her.

"I beg to differ. The look on your face says I do," Harper contradicted.

He was about to make another disclaimer about the situation when his front door suddenly flew open and both of the twins came racing out.

Toby and Tyler made a direct beeline for

Brady till they spotted the person standing next to him and abruptly stopped short.

"Who's this?" Toby wanted to know. He looked Harper up and down and apparently tried to size up the situation. Putting his little hands on his hips, Toby turned toward Brady and demanded, "Did you get married?"

"Is that why you had Unca Kane pick us up?" Tyler asked, not to be left out. "'Cause you were getting married?"

Kane came out, one hand wrapped around the hand of the brand-new addition in his life, a sweet little girl named Erin. "They heard the sound of your voice and got away from me before I could stop them," his brother admitted, slightly embarrassed.

"You don't have to apologize," Brady told him. "I appreciate you picking them up for me." Aware that everyone was looking at the woman with him, he quickly made the introductions. "Harper, this is my brother, Kane, and Erin. Kane, this is Harper Radcliffe."

While Erin hid behind Kane's legs, Kane leaned over and extended his hand to the young woman with his brother.

"Nice to meet you, Harper. I take it you're the one Brady thinks is going to bring order back to his chaotic life. Bless you for that," he added with a wide smile that Harper thought made him look a great deal like the man she had followed here.

"And these are the twins, Toby and Tyler," Brady told Harper, pointing at each of them in turn. "Boys, this might be your new nanny."

For just a moment, the twins were almost well behaved—and then they started firing questions at her, their young, high-pitched voices blending into a cacophony of dissonance.

Not wanting Harper to feel as if she was being hemmed in, not to mention overwhelmed, Brady said, "She hasn't made up her mind about the job yet, boys."

He was secretly pinning part of his hopes on the twins being able to tug at her heartstrings, and part on his own charm wearing her down. Although, he was ready to admit, that charm was beginning to wane somewhat. He just hoped that it was still strong enough to convince Harper to take on something she had supposedly professed to love doing.

Mentally crossing his fingers, Brady looked at her and asked, "Right?"

"Right," Harper answered, her expression giving nothing away.

Tyler still appeared to be stuck in first gear. Tugging on the bottom of Harper's blouse, he asked, "If you marry Unca Brady, does that mean you're our mommy?"

Toby frowned, taking on a superior air. "No, stupid, that makes her our aunt, right?" He looked up at Harper to back him up.

As Brady watched her, he felt as if he was observing Harper diving into the deep end of the pool. Squatting down to be on the same eye level as the twins, she addressed Toby. "Well, number one, I'm not marrying your Uncle Brady, and number two, you should never call your brother stupid."

"Why not?" Toby wanted to know. It was clear that the boy didn't like being given any sort of restrictions, even when it came to using words.

"What's number three?" Tyler piped up so as not to be ignored.

These boys were clearly going to be a test to her abilities, Harper thought. She could feel it. They were bright. Very bright.

Well, she did enjoy a good challenge, Harper mused philosophically. It made the whole experience that much more interesting.

Rising to her feet, Harper placed a hand on each small shoulder. "There is no number three," she told Tyler, then qualified, "—for now. But I'm sure there will be. Eventually. And you shouldn't call anyone stupid," she told Toby, "because everyone is smart in their own way."

Toby's frown deepened. "Stevie Jordan isn't smart," he told this new nanny.

"Oh, I think you're being too hard on this Stevie, Toby," Harper told him. "I think if you try, you can find something that Stevie is smart about or good at. You just have to think about it."

"Naw," Toby said, shaking his head as he waved a dismissive hand at the idea.

"Would you try?" Harper coaxed, looking into the boy's eyes. "For me?" she added, lowering her voice, one friend to the other.

And as Brady looked on, the twin he considered to be the more rambunctious one of the duo seemed to puff up his chest as he pretended to consider the pretty lady's request.

Brady realized that Toby was almost blushing as he replied, "Well, okay. For you."

Dumbfounded as well as very impressed, Brady looked at Harper. "Wow, I think I just witnessed a miracle." Unabashed admiration filled his eyes. "Anything you want, I'll pay it!" he promised the woman with heartfelt enthusiasm. "You have to take this job. Anything," he repeated. "Just name your price."

"I think he means it," Kane said as he began to make his way toward the truck, still holding on to Erin's hand. "I'd hold out for top dollar if I were you," he told Harper with a wink. "If Brady here can't pay it, the family will take up a collection.

"*Really* nice meeting you, Ms. Radcliffe,"

Kane told her again, shaking Harper's hand before he opened the rear door of his truck. "I hope I'll be seeing you here again," he said as he hoisted Erin up in his arms, then placed her in her car seat. He carefully made sure all the belts were secured. "Good luck, Brady," Kane called out to his brother before getting in behind the truck's steering wheel.

Nodding, Brady said, "Thanks again."

The next moment, his brother forgotten, Brady was looking at the woman he was trying to hire. Counseling himself to put one foot in front of the other, he crossed his fingers and looked at Harper.

"Why don't we go inside and you can get to know Toby and Tyler a little better?" he suggested. Everything was riding on this and so far, the twins hadn't blown it. He was hoping for another miracle.

Brady pushed the front door open a little wider. It was a not-too-subtle invitation to the woman who he was hoping would come around to seeing things his way.

"I'll go in," Harper agreed, "but I don't think I really need to get to know Toby and Tyler a little better," she told Brady.

What did that mean? Brady wondered, getting a sinking feeling in his stomach.

Oh damn, the twins have managed to some-

how torpedo this in record time, he thought. Back in New York, it had taken at least a day, and sometimes even more time, before the twins succeeded in doing something to make a babysitter or a nanny go running for the hills. But this, this had happened before Toby and Tyler even gave the woman any time to walk in the door.

"Are you sure?" Brady asked her, struggling to tamp down a desperate feeling. There had to be *something* he could say or do, he thought.

"Yes, I think so," she replied.

He could feel his heart sinking down to his toes. "Isn't there anything I could do or say to make you change your mind?" he wanted to know.

She looked at Brady, clearly confused. "Why would you want me to change my mind?"

Brady went for broke, feeling that at this point, he had nothing to lose. "Because, frankly, I need you, Ms. Radcliffe." Then realizing she might get the wrong idea—even though he did find himself attracted to her—he gestured toward the twins. "*They* need you," he said with emphasis.

"And?" she questioned.

"And?" Brady echoed quizzically, at a loss as to what was going on. "There is no *and,*" he told her. "We *all* need you," he stressed. "It's as plain and simple as that."

Harper nodded her head. "I understand that."

"And you're still not going to take the job?" he asked, desperation gnawing at his insides.

Harper stared at him. "When did I say that?" she wanted to know.

He felt like someone who was doomed to go around in circles. "When you said that you didn't need to get to know them better," he pointed out.

"I *don't* need to get to know them better," Harper insisted, "because I've made up my mind."

The way she said it gave him a glimmer of hope, but he wasn't going to jump to any conclusion because it might be the wrong one in the end. It might wind up jeopardizing any chance he had left to get her to agree to work with the twins and turn them into little people. Little people who he had a prayer of ultimately helping nurture—safely—into adulthood.

So he asked, "To—?" and waited for Harper Radcliffe to say the right words. Words that would put his life back on track.

"—to accept your offer to become their nanny," Harper concluded.

"You have no idea what that means to me," he cried. Then, thinking that what he had just said might scare her, he quickly backtracked on his enthusiasm.

Or at least tried to. "I mean—"

Harper took pity on him and stopped Brady

before he could continue. "That's all right, I think I know what you mean and you're right, I do think that I can do some good here." She made eye contact with Toby and then Tyler in turn. "If you boys will let me," Harper told them sincerely.

It was obvious that Toby and Tyler weren't sure exactly what this new lady with the bright smile wanted them to do. But Harper could tell by the expression on their small, animated faces that they were willing to go along with almost anything—which was why she felt fairly confident that this would all go well once she and the boys became used to one another.

Brady knew that he was risking having this all fall apart on him, but he needed to make sure that this woman who had the power to turn everything around in his life understood exactly what was involved.

"You do realize that this is supposed to be a live-in position, right?" he asked her.

"It is?" He hadn't mentioned that earlier. Her last position had been a live-in one and that had ended badly. She didn't want a repetition of that.

"Is that a deal breaker?" he wanted to know, then started talking fast. "Because if it is, we can come to some sort of an arrangement for the time being," he said, desperate not to have her change her mind.

Harper looked at the twins' upturned faces, thinking over what Brady had just said. He was willing to be flexible. She could be the same.

"Why don't we do that?" Harper suggested. "We'll play this by ear to begin with. I'll come in every morning and stay until the twins are in bed and asleep," Harper told her new boss, smiling at the twins as she cupped each of their faces with one of her hands. "After that, we'll see how it goes."

"Is something going somewhere?" Tyler asked, perplexed.

"My sanity if your new nanny changes her mind," Brady said, looking at Harper with unabashed gratitude in his eyes.

"You're gonna stay?" the boys asked in unison.

"I'm going to stay," Harper confirmed.

The twins cheered, warming both her heart as well as Brady's.

Chapter Eight

"**Y**ou wanna see my room?" Toby asked, although as far as he was concerned, it was a foregone conclusion that this new nanny did.

Not waiting for an answer, Toby wrapped his small and surprisingly strong fingers around Harper's hand and enthusiastically began pulling her toward the winding staircase.

"It's *our* room," Tyler told Harper indignantly, making a face at Toby as he corrected his twin. His small eyebrows drew together in an irritated V.

"He only sleeps there 'cause he's afraid of sleeping alone," Toby told Harper.

It was obvious that Toby didn't want this new

mother figure in his life to think that he was the baby of the pair.

"Am not!" Tyler insisted, clearly upset that Harper might believe Toby.

Rather than distance herself from this brewing argument, the way he would have—and had on occasion—as Brady watched the events unfold, Harper got into the middle of this scuffle quickly. And then managed to quell it.

"I'm sure your uncle Brady put you both in the same room so that you could keep each other company," Harper told the twins. "Trust me—it's really nice to have a brother around you can talk to when you have something you want to share."

Tyler slipped his hand into Harper's other hand, not wanting to be left out. He wanted to lead her up the stairs just like his twin.

"Do you have a brother?" he asked her eagerly. The more sensitive twin clearly wanted to learn everything there was about this new, special nanny his "unca" Brady had brought into their lives.

"I do. He's a soldier and halfway around the world right now," Harper replied. "But when we were kids, growing up, we would share secrets together." She smiled nostalgically. "You two are very lucky to have each other," she told the duo as she allowed them to take her up to their room.

"How come you think that's so special?" Toby wanted to know, making a face at Tyler. "I don't."

"Oh, you don't mean that," Harper told Toby. "And you're particularly lucky because you were each born with your best friend right there by your side. I think that's really special," she said.

Toby's lower lip curled. "Yeah, well, maybe," he was willing to guardedly admit.

For his part, Tyler shrugged a little too carelessly. "Toby's okay, I guess," he said.

Standing at the bottom of the stairs, watching this unfold, Brady could only marvel at his good luck. After what felt like an endless parade of countless nannies who had passed through his life, it looked as if he had finally, *finally* struck gold.

This woman was nothing if not the answer to a prayer, he thought.

Very honestly, part of him was afraid that he was dreaming. Brady was even tempted to pinch himself just to make sure he wasn't.

But then, if he was dreaming, he really didn't want to wake up.

The next moment, Brady thought of going upstairs just in case Harper ran into any trouble.

But then, he told himself that maybe it was better this way.

Barring any screams or cries for help, Brady decided to keep out of this, at least for the first couple of minutes or so. As much as he wanted this woman to stay—she gave off a competent air, the twins seemed to take to her instantly and added to that, Harper Radcliffe was extremely easy on the eyes—Harper needed to know what she was up against.

In all fairness, Toby and Tyler didn't mean to do half the things they did. He'd learned that about them. They were just being...boys, he thought with a resigned sigh. Then again, when he thought about some of the escapades he and his twin brother Brian had gotten into as kids, he supposed he should consider himself lucky.

It was up to him to make sure they didn't kill themselves while they were doing it. And an important part of that involved having him find the right person to be their nanny. He couldn't be with them 24/7. He needed to earn a living so that he was able to pay expenses for the three of them.

Brady glanced at his watch. It had only been five minutes, but it was way too quiet up there. Quiet made him even more nervous than the sound of screaming and the loud, jarring noises of things falling or being thrown.

Okay, he told himself. They had had enough time together. It was time to rescue Harper while there was hopefully still someone left to rescue.

Brady took the stairs two at a time, a sense of urgency mounting inside him with every step.

By the time he reached the landing, Brady was braced for the worst. He had once walked in on the twins tying up one of their nannies. The furious words that came flowing out of that woman's mouth were very far from PG rated.

The moment he managed to free her, the woman had stormed out of the apartment, threatening him with a lawsuit.

The lawsuit never materialized and he could only think that angry nanny wasn't able to find a lawyer who would stop laughing at her long enough to take on the woman's case.

He'd lucked out then, Brady thought. But there were only so many miracles allotted to a person and he couldn't separate himself from the idea that he had already exhausted his supply.

Still, it didn't keep him from hoping.

The door to the twins' room was open.

As he drew closer, Brady heard the sound of Harper's voice. She wasn't yelling or even telling the twins that they had to stop doing something.

She was reading, he realized. Reading a story to the twins. And for once, neither of the boys was offering a running commentary or their own version of what was being read to them.

The twins were actually being quiet—without being gagged, he thought in amazement.

Brady reached their room and saw that the twins were sitting on their beds, looking totally enthralled with the story that Harper was reading to them.

Gina had bought that book for them, Brady suddenly recalled. It was one of the last things the twins' mother had done before she had ridden off on the back of Gord's motorcycle, along with her husband, into eternity.

Brady remembered attempting to read the book to the twins just once, only to be stopped by Toby who refused to be quiet long enough for the story to be read.

Even Tyler had piped up, crying out, *That's mommy's book. You can't read it. Nobody can read it. Just Mommy,* he had tearfully insisted.

Brady had left the book on the shelf then, thinking that when the boys were older, maybe one of them would want to read it, even though it was clearly a fairy tale written for children and they, by then he assumed, might be a good deal older.

Suddenly he heard Tyler asking, "Why would that guy give Jack some old beans for his mommy's cow?"

Toby, ever practical in his own way, had a more immediate question. "Why didn't the beans squish in his pocket?"

"That's a very good question," Harper told

Toby. "Why do you think they didn't squish in his pocket?"

No doubt wanting to have Harper praise him too, Tyler raised his hand to get her attention. "'Cause they were magic beans, right? That's why they didn't squish, 'cause they were magic. Right?"

Harper smiled at Tyler. "You're absolutely right, Tyler. You boys are both very, very smart. I see that I'm going to have to work super hard to keep up with you two guys."

Tyler immediately took her words to heart. "Don't worry, I'll slow down for you," he promised.

Not to be outdone, Toby joined in. "Yeah, me, too. I'll go slow. Real slow," he emphasized.

Harper looked from one twin to the other, her hand on her chest in a show of how touched she was by their "sacrifice."

"You would do that for me?" she asked.

"Uh-huh!" Toby told her, nodding his shaggy head up and down.

"We sure would!" Tyler told her. Then, seeing Brady in the mirror over their bureau, Tyler swung around to look at his guardian standing in the doorway. "Can she be our nanny, Unca Brady?"

"Yeah, can she? We like this one," Toby added. "She's nice."

Harper had already agreed to be their nanny, but obviously the twins wanted to verbalize their approval. Brady laughed as his eyes met Harper's. "You have no idea how high that praise really is," he told the woman. "These two 'angelic' looking boys have sent so many nannies running for the hills that I've completely lost count. I can't tell you how happy I am that you decided to take this job."

"Me, too," Tyler told her, beaming up at Harper.

"Me, three," Toby cried, not to be outdone.

"Well, I do love a challenge." Harper affectionately tousled each boys' hair. "Have you boys eaten yet?" she asked them.

"Uh-uh," Tyler answered, shaking his head, sending soft brown hair flying back and forth around his sweet cheeks.

"Nope," Toby said with emphasis.

"Why don't you boys show me to the kitchen so I can look in the refrigerator and see what we can whip up together for dinner?" Harper suggested.

"You're beating up food?" Toby asked excitedly.

Harper struggled not to laugh. She didn't want to hurt anyone's feelings. "*Whip up* in this case means *cook*," she explained.

Toby cocked his head, as if that would help

him understand things better. "We're going to *cook* dinner?" he asked skeptically.

"Yes, we are. It's never too early to learn," Harper assured the boy.

"I wanna learn," Tyler told her, hoping not to be left behind.

"That's good because I'm going to need your help. *Both* of you," she said to the twins.

As she spoke, Harper was keenly aware that Brady was slowly circling around her, giving her an elaborate once-over. One she knew she wasn't meant to ignore. "Can I help you with something, Mr. Fortune?" she asked, turning to face him.

"No. I'm fine," he told her. "I'm just looking for wings."

Harper blinked. "Wings?"

"She's not a bird, Unca Brady," Tyler told him. "She's our nanny."

"I know she's not a bird," Brady said, not looking away from Harper. "But angels have wings, too. I was just looking for Ms. Radcliffe's wings."

"Who's Ms. Radcl—radcl—Ms. Rad?" Toby finally asked, settling on the only part of the name he could manage.

"She is," Brady told the twin, nodding toward Harper.

"No, she's not. She's Harper," Toby said. "She

said so." Big blue eyes turned toward the woman for confirmation. "Right?"

"You can't call her by her first name, Toby," Brady told the boy.

"I can't?" Toby asked, surprised and confused. "Why not?"

"No, it's okay, really," Harper assured her new employer. "*Radcliffe* is just too much of a mouthful for a four-year-old."

Toby drew himself up to look taller. "I'm almost five," he told her.

"Oh, my mistake," Harper apologized. "For an 'almost' five-year-old," she told Brady, restating her comment. "So unless it really makes you uncomfortable," she told Brady, "the boys can call me Harper. I'm fine with that."

No, he wasn't uncomfortable with it, but he wasn't the one who mattered here. This was between Harper and the twins. A soldier knew when to retreat—and Brady considered himself a good soldier.

"If it's okay with you, it's fine with me," Brady told her.

"Okay, now that that's settled," Harper said, turning back to the twins, "why don't we go see about making dinner?"

Tyler's eyes were shining in anticipation of what lay ahead. "Yeah, why don't we go see about making dinner!" he cried, echoing Harper's words.

Feeling like she was almost surrounded by the twins who were shifting around her and moving from side to side, Harper went to the kitchen.

Crossing to the refrigerator, she opened both doors at the same time. Considering its size, it had very little to offer on the inside.

She found a small block of sharp cheddar cheese, less than half a package of sliced ham, a few eggs and two peppers, one red, one green. Both were one day away from being on their way out.

Harper was studying the contents a moment too long, causing Toby to make a suggestion. "Maybe we can call 'takes out.'"

Still holding the doors open, she glanced down at the pint-sized assistant who had spoken last. "Takes out?" she questioned.

"Yeah," Toby told her, happy to be able to offer his help. "Unca Brady calls a place and then he takes it out when they come here with it. Takes out," he repeated for emphasis.

Harper pressed her lips together to keep from laughing. She had the feeling she was going to be doing that a lot.

She glanced over toward Brady, who spread his hands wide for her benefit, indicating that the process Toby had just told her about was a pretty frequent one for them.

"I see," she told the boys. "Well, I don't think we need to call for 'takes out' yet."

"We're going to eat that?" Tyler asked doubtfully, scowling into the refrigerator.

"You're going to eat frittatas," Harper informed the twins.

"Fer-what-as?" Toby wanted to know, his tone indicating that he didn't like the sound of that.

"I think I can show you better than I can explain it," Harper said, "But the idea behind it is to take a bunch of things you find in the refrigerator, put them all together and mix them up with eggs to make one big tasty meal," she concluded, simplifying the process for the twins as much as possible.

Toby still made a face. "Doesn't sound very good," he complained.

"It tastes better than it sounds," Harper assured the boy.

Toby continued to show his disapproval. "It'll have to," he said.

"Toby." There was a warning note in Brady's voice.

"No, no, that's okay," Harper told Brady, coming to Toby's defense. "He's entitled to his opinion. Just as I'm entitled to try to get him to change his opinion. And tomorrow," she informed Brady, "while the boys are in preschool, I'm going to go shopping to get this to look like an actual refrigerator instead of a holding zone for things about to go bad. And you boys are going to help me make this—" she gestured into the refrigerator "—into a good meal."

While Toby and Tyler vied for position so each one could exclusively offer his willing hands to the new nanny, the look on Brady's face told her that she was going to live to regret what she had just said.

In fact, she had two challenges, Harper thought. The first was getting the twins involved without becoming a danger to themselves, and the second challenge came in the form of getting Brady to retract that smug, sexy smile of his.

Harper was fairly certain that she was up to both challenges.

"Okay, boys, let's get to this," she said in a voice that all but declared, *Let the games begin.*

Chapter Nine

The moment Harper set out all the ingredients she intended to use to make this very first family meal, she could see Toby eyeing the knife lying on the table beside the scarred cutting board. She had been a nanny long enough to know an accident that was waiting to happen.

Moving quickly, her hand covered the knife handle before Toby could grab it.

Looking at him, she judged that his small face must have fallen at least half a foot. But it was also obvious to Harper that the more active twin didn't intend to give up easily.

"You said you wanted me to help," Toby whined, pouting.

"And you will," Harper assured him. Her eyes swept over the little people on either side of her. "Both of you," she stressed, then looked down at the boys' hands. "But I think you and your brother are pretty set on keeping all your fingers just the way they are and that's a really sharp knife." Harper lowered her voice and added conspiratorially, "I'm cautious about using that knife myself."

"What's caw-caw—that word?" Stymied, Toby surrendered his efforts to pronounce the word he had heard her use correctly.

"It means being super careful," Harper told the twin. "See this?" She held up her left hand and pointed out what looked like an old, curved scar right at the base of her thumb.

"Yeah?" Toby answered as Tyler all but moved into his shadow to take his own look at the scar. Both boys appeared fascinated.

"I did that when I was ten years old," Harper told them. "I was trying to cut a small piece of ham for a snack when the knife slipped and I wound up cutting my thumb."

"Did it hurt?" Tyler asked her. The look on his small face was the very picture of sympathy.

"Oh, it hurt like crazy," Harper told the more sensitive of the twins.

"And did you bleed?" Toby wanted to know, his eyes wide with anticipation.

The truth was that there had been a lot of blood. She still remembered being queasy, but that wasn't something she felt she should go into for a number of reasons. So all she said was, "Uh-huh," then changed direction. "Now, if we're going to make this dinner" she continued, "this is going to be a team effort—but I head the team." She let her words sink in. "Agreed?"

Two shaggy heads bobbed up and down, slightly out of sync.

"Agreed," the boys all but eagerly proclaimed in unison.

While this minidrama was unfolding, Brady was standing off to the side in the doorway, observing everything as it happened. He found himself in awe at how deftly Harper handled all this.

Harper Radcliffe, where have you been all my life? he silently asked in unadulterated admiration.

Feeling that this nanny-miracle worker might want her space to continue to weave her magic in peace, Brady withdrew from the kitchen entrance altogether. He crossed his fingers that whatever was happening at the moment would continue to go on happening.

"Can I get you anything?" Brady asked the twins' new nanny much later that evening, after

Toby and Tyler had finally settled down and gone to sleep. Dinner had been a huge success and far tastier than he had anticipated. Harper had just now finished cleaning up the mess left over from preparing dinner. Brady looked around the kitchen, clearly impressed with how neat everything appeared.

The woman was a wizard, he decided. She was definitely a pleasant change from some of the nannies who had been there before her. "Coffee? Tea? A life-long contract?"

Harper laughed, taking one last look around the kitchen to make sure she hadn't overlooked anything. "No, I'm good," she told Brady.

"You certainly are," he agreed with no small enthusiasm. He said it with such feeling that Harper looked at him in surprise. He realized that he needed to clarify himself before she misunderstood. "You have no idea what a breath of fresh air you are after the army of less-than-satisfying babysitters and nannies who have trooped through the twins' lives."

Not wanting to say anything negative about the women her employer had previously hired—especially without being privy to more information—Harper speculated, "They probably just had their own take on how things should be managed."

Recalling certain incidents, Brady frowned,

but decided it was best not to rehash bad times. Moving forward was far more advisable.

"To be honest, I didn't know what to expect. I just knew what didn't work. Until I witnessed you in action. Just so you know, you have a position here for as long as you want it." He laughed softly to himself, thinking of the twins. "For life if it comes to that."

It was Harper's turn to laugh. "I doubt very much that those boys are going to want a nanny hanging around when they turn eighteen, but it's nice to know that I've found steady employment—at least for the time being."

Brady nodded, although he couldn't help wondering why this petite miracle worker was being so cautious in her response.

He nodded toward the sofa. "You know, given the day you just put in, you're welcomed to put your feet up and unwind," Brady told her. He wanted her to feel comfortable here.

"If you don't mind, I'll take a rain check," she told her new employer. Hoping he wouldn't take offense, she explained, "It's been a long day. I'd just like to go home and get some sleep."

Brady felt an unexpected twinge of disappointment, which surprised him. But he managed to respond well. "Whatever you say," he told her. "You're the boss," he added with a smile.

Looking at him, Harper could literally feel her

heart skip a beat. *Get a grip, Harper. Remember Justine Wheeler's husband...*

Stop it, she chided herself. *Brady's nothing like that man,* Harper silently insisted, remembering the man who had caused her all that grief. But comparing the new with the old, she reminded herself, did a disservice to both Brady and the new job she had taken on.

A job she knew she was lucky to find after the depressing spate of time she had just gone through, searching for employment in both her field—and then out of it.

Don't blow this just because you're afraid of history repeating itself, Harper warned herself. *Yes, Brady Fortune is good-looking and charming. That doesn't mean that he's a reptile, eager to jump your bones the first chance he gets. You can't allow Wheeler to spook you that way,* Harper reprimanded herself.

She knew she was being logical and making sense, but that didn't make this any easier for her. Harper still couldn't help feeling nervous and uneasy being around Brady. She was hoping that once she got into some sort of a daily routine with the twins, this uneasiness would eventually fade away.

At least she could hope for the best, Harper thought as she left his house and drove to her very small studio apartment.

It took her an incredible amount of time to wind down. Every time she finally managed to doze off, visions of her new employer's sexy smile would make her eyes fly open as her heart pounded wildly.

She barely managed to get any rest at all.

"Did you sleep well?" Brady asked the following morning. He was coming into the kitchen to grab a cup of coffee before he got started with his day. He was surprised to find Harper was already there, preparing breakfast.

Harper looked over her shoulder. She noticed that instead of casual clothes, Brady was wearing a suit. He looked very dashing, as if he was ready to take off somewhere. She bit her tongue not to say anything about his appearance. She didn't want to do anything to create the wrong impression.

Which also meant not mentioning what had turned out to be a relatively sleepless night, a detail best kept to herself rather than risking having Brady read something into that, too.

"Yes, thank you," Harper responded cheerfully to his inquiry. Nodding at the frying pan, she said, "I'm making breakfast."

"I can tell," Brady teased. Assuming she was making it for the twins, he told her, "The boys'll be hungry when they get up."

"And you?" she asked pointedly. "What can I make for you?"

He indicating the coffee machine and the full pot. "Coffee'll do fine."

She gave him a reproving look. "Can't start a day on just coffee."

Brady responded with a laugh. "Well, with these guys, I haven't had the time to think of extra things like making myself breakfast. Getting Toby and Tyler fed was enough of a challenge for me to face first thing in the morning."

She couldn't help thinking that he cut an impressive figure in that suit he was wearing. "So, now that I'm here, you thought you'd go formal?" she asked, doing her best to sound serious.

"Oh, this?" he said, looking down at his attire. He'd forgotten all about the suit he'd put on. "Since you're here, I don't have to look for a sitter for the kids and I can finally go and get up to speed at the hotel," he explained, then added a footnote for her edification. "The Hotel Fortune is run by my cousins and they're putting me to work at the concierge desk."

"Not on an empty stomach they're not," she informed him decisively.

Harper's response surprised him. "You sound like my mother," Brady told her.

"I'll take that as a compliment," she said, adding, "Call it a by-product of being a nanny all these years. Now sit." Harper pointed to the chair at the head of the table. "Since I started making breakfast before you came down, it's ready," she told him, anticipating what he was about to say. "You can't complain that you don't have time to wait because you don't *have* to wait. Voilà," Harper declared, placing the plate of scrambled eggs, toast and bacon in front of him. "And yes, the coffee is ready, too," Harper told him, quickly pouring a cup for him and placing that next to the plate.

She might have anticipated what he wanted to say, but not what came afterward.

"Join me?" Brady asked, nodding at the chair opposite his.

Harper glanced at the mug of coffee she had poured for herself earlier. She had kept taking small sips of the brew while she worked.

"Okay," she agreed, bringing the mug over to the table, "but just for coffee. I've got two small tornadoes to beat to the punch."

Brady laughed.

"I probably shouldn't say that," she amended. "Let me rephrase. I want to be upstairs and getting the boys up before they have a chance to come bounding out of bed and get rolling on their own," she told him instead.

The idea of actually waking the twins up voluntarily seemed totally foreign to him. "I always thought it was criminal to wake them up. I was confident that they'd be up and creating havoc soon enough."

Harper smiled at his honesty. In his defense, she could see where he was coming from. "I guess we have different approaches. Mine works for me."

Brady could only shake his head. "More power to you, Ms. Radcliffe." He saw her wrinkling her nose. "What is it?" he asked, waiting for her response.

It wasn't what he anticipated.

"Given the close proximity that we'll be working in, I think you should call me Harper. It's less formal," she told him.

Brady had always found that he was usually able to read people—at least he could before this bombshell had exploded in his life. After all, he'd had no clue that his late best friend had made him the guardian of his twins—certainly not until all of this had engulfed him, blotting out his old life.

In Harper's case, he had thought that calling her by her first name was a liberty that would spook her and cause her to step back. Obviously he was wrong there, too.

"I didn't want to take any liberties that might make you feel uncomfortable," he explained.

Maybe she had misjudged him. For that matter, maybe he was more sensitive than she had given him credit for.

"I appreciate that," she told him, her eyes smiling at him. "But *Harper* will do just fine. Calling me Ms. Radcliffe makes me feel like an old schoolmarm out of the 1890s."

"Can't have that," Brady agreed. And then what he was putting in his mouth registered belatedly with his brain. He looked at his fork in wonder, as if he hadn't really been paying attention to what Harper had prepared for him. "Damn but this is good. I know it's only scrambled eggs, but this doesn't taste like any scrambled eggs I've ever had before. What did you do to them? And moreover, have you ever thought of opening up your own restaurant?" he asked as he took another big bite of his serving.

Brady watched as the smile on her lips seemed to take over every inch of Harper's face. "And call it what?" she asked, amused. "Eggs Galore? No. That's a very nice compliment," she responded, "but I'm very happy being a nanny. As a matter of fact, when I had to stop being a nanny, those were the longest, emptiest three months of my life." Although she had always longed for a family with all the trimmings, she had learned that wanting and having were two different things. Much to her dismay, love had never found her. That was the main reason she had initially decided to fill the emptiness by becoming a nanny.

Brady realized that he had no idea what had transpired to bring that hiatus about.

He knew that he thought of Harper as a great nanny because he had witnessed her with the twins and was impressed with both her creativity and her ability to all but pull a rabbit out of a hat. She didn't seem to get flustered by anything that the dynamic duo came up with. As a matter of fact, she was utterly unflappable.

But he still wanted to know what had happened to separate her from the vocation she professed to love since she *did* clearly love it.

"Just what happened to your last position?" he wanted to know. "You didn't mention it."

She took a breath. Incidents and details crowded her mind, jockeying for position. She wasn't up to putting them in order, nor did she want to remember them—not yet.

"Long story," Harper told him evasively, then reminded Brady, "and you did say that you were in a hurry."

Brady knew evasion when he encountered it and grinned at Harper.

"Yes, I did, didn't I?" And he really was. Finished eating, he rose from his chair. "But this isn't over," he informed her. "You've aroused my curiosity, Harper Radcliffe," he told her. "When

I get home tonight, you'll have to tell me what went down that wound up separating you from a job you obviously love."

Harper was not about to be honest with him and tell him about the obnoxious octopus that had been her employer's husband—a little fact that didn't keep him from making more and more uninvited advances on her.

Instead, she forced a smile to her lips. She had the next eight hours to come up with a believable story, she thought as she watched her new employer walk out the front door.

With any luck, that would be enough time.

Either that, or maybe he would even forget about asking her about it by then.

Chapter Ten

Callum Fortune stood back and covertly observed his cousin go through his paces at the Hotel Fortune concierge desk for the good part of an hour.

Finally stepping forward, Callum came up to the desk and openly complimented Brady. "From the moment I first laid eyes on you, I just had this feeling that you were going to work out."

The Hotel Fortune had been Callum's latest project. Something he had undertaken with the hope of bringing even more tourism to Rambling Rose.

A real estate developer and contractor by trade, Callum and his siblings involved in Fortune Brothers Construction had been experiencing a great deal of success in their efforts to build up the small Texas town of Rambling Rose a section at a time. Their pediatric center, veterinary clinic, upscale retail stores, wellness spa, and farm-to-table restaurant had all been well-received by the locals and were doing quite well.

Which was why the pushback against the luxury hotel Callum had wanted to proceed with next had been such an unexpected, unpleasant surprise. But it turned out that the down-to-earth locals resented such a large-scale project being forced down their throats—or at least that was how the residents of Rambling Rose viewed the idea of an unwanted "monstrosity" being built in their midst.

After much negotiating, a level of understanding between the two sides was finally reached, thanks in no small part to the intervention of Callum's cousin—and Brady's older brother—Kane, as well as Rodrigo Mendoza, the restaurant consultant for Provisions who had ultimately contributed his expertise to the hotel, too. Rodrigo was also engaged to Callum's sister Ashley, the general manager of Provisions. Thanks to his experience, Rodrigo had a little more insight into the locals' reactions to the original building plans—and had been able to convince Callum to scale back.

After all the protests were aired and reviewed, Callum and his siblings wound up designing a more welcoming and homey, albeit upscale, boutique hotel than they'd originally planned. But it was well worth their efforts.

After its official opening last month on Valentine's Day, the Hotel Fortune was a certified success. Though Callum had hired a general manager, he still made it his business to check in on the operation of his pet project. Today that meant observing their new concierge.

Granted, Brady had no experience in that area, but he had managed a sporting goods store, so he was no stranger to management and thinking on his feet. In addition he had good business sense.

The best part of all, in Callum's opinion, was that Brady had more than a little charisma. And that, he knew, was something that couldn't be taught. A person either had it or he didn't and that came in quite handy when dealing with guests.

After watching his cousin in action after a hotel guest came down to register a complaint about her accommodations and then left with a smile on her face, Callum knew that he had hired the right person for the job.

"You're a natural, Brady," Callum told his cousin, well pleased.

"Just grateful for a chance to prove myself—

and earn a living," Brady replied modestly. "I've got mouths to feed now."

He had learned not to allow compliments to go to his head. The last six months had taught him that fate was mercurial. He was determined to keep one eye on the prize and one eye on the future. It wasn't just about him anymore. He had the twins depending on him and he couldn't lose sight of that.

Wrapped up in getting Hotel Fortune off the ground and up and running, Callum had gone off track about that. "Right," he said with a nod. "How are the twins doing these days? I've heard some pretty hair-raising stories," Callum added with a hearty, amused laugh.

Brady leaned in a little closer, not wanting his voice to carry. "Quite frankly, it's one big balancing act," he admitted.

"I can give you the name of a babysitter if you need one," Callum offered.

He was fairly certain that he and his wife could share a contact or two that they trusted to watch their two-year-old girls. After all, he didn't want to risk losing Brady since his cousin seemed to fit so well into this new position.

"Thanks," Brady demurred, "but it looks like I won't be needing a sitter."

Callum grinned. He was really feeling good about the hotel. Things were finally all coming together and he could afford to relax just a little. Even laugh a little if the situation called for it.

"I didn't know you dabbled in black magic," he said to his new concierge.

Brady picked up on Callum's inference and got a kick out of it. "No black magic. I lucked out and hired this fantastic nanny."

"Fantastic, eh?" Callum raised his brow, instantly picking up on his cousin's enthusiasm.

"She is absolutely incredible with the twins," Brady said with gusto. "She had them both eating out of her hand within minutes. I never saw anything like it. I don't know how she does it," he said quite honestly, "but I am definitely going to make sure I hold on to her."

"As long as you don't wind up *actually* holding her," Callum warned.

Brady looked at his cousin, puzzled. "I'm not sure I follow you."

"I've learned that business and pleasure don't always mix," Callum cautioned. "If this nanny is an answer to a prayer, as you seem to indicate, I'd make damn sure I didn't do anything to rock that boat—or you risk this nanny handing in her notice. These are very tense times, cousin. Even the most innocent of moves run the risk of being misunderstood and since you've indicated that you're very pleased with what this nanny brings to the table and manages to do to keep your world running well, I'd make sure that your positions of employer and employee don't wind up getting blurred."

Funny that his cousin should mention that, Brady thought. Because if he was being strictly honest about it, he would have to admit that he was attracted to his boys' nanny.

Very attracted.

But Callum was right. The last thing he wanted to do was throw a monkey wrench into the works and risk losing someone whom the twins responded to and obviously liked. No possible, fleeting romantic tryst was worth that. Not when Harper Radcliffe could afford him the peace of mind that the dynamic duo were being looked after and well taken care of.

Brady flashed a smile at his cousin and employer. "Message received. Loud and clear," he assured Callum. "Besides, I wouldn't want to wind up confusing those energetic little rug rats about where Harper and I stand."

"Harper?" Callum questioned.

"That's the nanny's name. Harper Radcliffe," Brady told his cousin. "I actually find myself daydreaming about being able to look forward to some sort of a routine in the coming days— other than here at the hotel," he qualified.

Callum laughed. "I see that your requirements are really low—not including the hotel," he added with an amused smile.

"Oh, on the contrary, Callum. My requirements are very high. You weren't there for these last six months," Brady told his cousin. "My entire life went from carefree to chaos." He stifled a shiver as he recalled certain instances. "Make no mistake about it, this woman is worth her weight in pure gold—maybe even platinum."

Callum sympathized with his cousin. He didn't know if he would have had the stamina that Brady did. And once again, he had to give credit to his wife, who was herself a single parent to young twins when they met. Still, he couldn't resist poking fun at Brady. "Don't take this the wrong way, Brady, but whatever you do, don't let this Harper person suspect that you feel that way or you'll wind up turning your whole paycheck over to her every week."

Despite the humorous tone, Brady found himself getting defensive for Harper's sake, although, quite honestly, he wasn't sure what that was all about. "I don't think she's the type to take advantage."

"Well, for your sake, I really hope you're right," Callum told him. "But be careful. You don't know her all that well."

"I've entrusted that woman with the lives of two little boys. *My* two little boys. I know her well enough," he told his cousin, then added, "Call it a gut feeling."

Callum nodded and held up his hands. "Okay, cuz. Good enough for me."

Brady wasn't fooled by his cousin's tone for a moment. Because they were still at work, though, Brady felt it prudent not to comment on Callum's words of caution.

Instead, he went back to work.

Because he was still engaged in learning all the preliminary details involved in running the concierge desk, Brady wound up putting in an extra-long day.

He wasn't able to get back home until almost nine thirty.

As he let himself in, Brady couldn't help thinking back to when nine thirty was just the beginning of the evening for him, not the tail end of the day.

Now it felt like he had put in an eternity and a half since this morning. All he could think of was crawling into bed—fully dressed—and falling asleep.

As Brady turned the key in the lock, opening the front door, he fervently prayed that his human jumping beans had been put to bed. Even so, he had visions of them standing on the other side of the door, ready to jump up at him.

Ready to play.

With this unsettling image in mind, Brady slowly eased open the front door, looking around twice before finally stepping inside the house.

As he did so, he released the breath he was holding. It didn't seem possible, but the twins had to be asleep. Otherwise, he *knew* they would have come bounding out of nowhere to greet him.

Listening, Brady embraced what were clearly the sounds of silence, praying they would last until he could reach the sanctuary of his bedroom and shut the doors.

"Don't you want to eat?"

Surprised by the voice that seemed to come out of nowhere, Brady swung around and saw Harper standing a few feet away.

Once she saw Brady pull up outside, Harper had debated keeping silent and just letting him go up to his room before going home herself. Not only did she know he had to be tired, but that way they wouldn't have to finish the conversation they'd started that morning. She could put off having to explain why she hadn't been able to work as a nanny for months.

But doing that would mean allowing Brady to go to his room without having anything to eat. Of course, he might have very well gotten something to eat before he left the Hotel Fortune, but in good conscience, she didn't want to just assume things.

So, she put her own comfort aside and asked her question the moment he entered.

Brady didn't answer the question immediately. He just stared at Harper as her question finally registered.

Finally finding his tongue, Brady answered her. "Thanks, but after getting Team Chaos bedded down for the night, you probably just want to go home and get some well-earned rest yourself."

She had to admit that his answer caught her off guard. But then, she didn't think that way.

"I know I'm just the nanny, but I don't see my job ending when those little dynamite sticks defuse and close their big blue eyes," she informed him. "Besides, when you called earlier to say you'd be working late, I decided to make you a light dinner. I figured that anything heavy wouldn't sit well and might wind up keeping you awake." Harper gestured toward the kitchen. "Come," she invited. "Sit."

The tone was one he guessed that she used on the twins. "I'm not a little boy," he pointed out.

"No, you're not," she agreed. "But you don't have to be a little boy to need a little accommodating yourself. I'm just doing my part," she told him with a smile. "And the sooner you stop arguing with me and eat, the sooner we can both go to bed."

No sooner had she said that than the words replayed themselves in her head.

Appalled at how that had to have sounded, she turned a bright shade of red from her cheeks all the way to the tips of her ears.

Her eyes darted toward his face. "I mean—"

At another time, Brady might have gotten a kick out of watching Harper try to talk her way out of what she had inadvertently said. But he was tired and besides, he actually felt bad for her. After all, he reminded himself, the young woman was just being kind and thoughtful, going out of her way for him. Making her feel uncomfortable was no way to pay her back.

"I know what you mean, Harper, and you're right. I should just shut my mouth and stop giving you a hard time for being so thoughtful." He sat down at the table, all but collapsing in the chair. "Just know that if the meal involves a lot of chewing," Brady warned, "I'm not really up to it. I know my day was nothing like what you probably went through," he allowed, "but I feel as if someone used my body as a dust mop to clean everything up throughout the entire hotel."

Harper looked at him, genuinely concerned and sympathetic.

"I did not have a day anything like that," she

told him. "Actually, the boys and I had a great deal of fun today. I admit that they do require a lot of energy to keep up with," she qualified. "But they *did* listen to me, which I consider an extremely important part of the whole."

Brady couldn't help thinking of all the other nannies who had come, and then gone, through his doors. The ones who threw their hands up just before they walked out and the ones who had rather sharp, painful things to say about the twins' attitude before they, too, left.

For the umpteenth time, Brady thought of how very lucky he was to have stumbled across this saint of a woman.

Which brought him back to the question he had had for her this morning. What had made her leave her last place of employment without having another place waiting as backup?

But just as he was about to ask, Harper placed a large, steaming bowl of chicken noodle soup on the table before him.

The aroma was exceedingly tempting.

So much so that it succeeded in enticing him and suddenly, Brady realized that he was incredibly hungry and could most definitely eat.

But before he did, he raised a quizzical eyebrow in Harper's direction.

Harper put her own interpretation to the expression on his face. He wanted to know why she was serving him this rather than a sandwich or a piece of chicken.

"I figured that you might welcome some comfort food at this point," she explained. "The most comforting thing I could think of was chicken soup."

Brady laughed softly as he picked up his spoon. "So now you're a mind reader."

"It comes with the territory. It's a basic requirement when you're a nanny." She said that with such a straight face, for a moment he thought Harper was serious.

Brady waited for the first spoonful to wind its way through his body. She was right. It *was* comforting. "Well, in my book, you're an angel."

She shook her head. "Uh-uh."

She was rejecting something he clearly meant as a compliment. Curious, he asked, "Why not?"

"The wings would make it really hard to get through doorways," she explained. "It would also make it hard to chase after mischievous little boys."

"I am way too tired to argue," Brady told her. Although not too tired, he thought, to respond to the smile that curved her lips.

"Good," she declared.

Yes, it was, Brady thought. But the assessment really had nothing to do with her being an angel.

Chapter Eleven

There was no doubt about it. Brady found himself torn when it came to Harper.

Part of him was utterly thrilled that he had, through no real efforts of his own, found her and hired her to be the twins' nanny. The woman was clearly perfect for the job.

But at the same time, there was a part of him that regretted hiring her because being her employer tied his hands. He couldn't make any sort of a romantic move on her because that would ruin everything. Not to mention that it would put both of them in an awkward position.

But despite that, something told him that Harper Radcliffe could very possibly be "the one." The one who could, quite simply, complete him.

They hadn't even kissed and yet he felt that there were some definite vibes there. Vibes that told him, given half a chance, he and Harper could have something very special.

Get a grip, man, Brady ordered himself, his mind straying from his work. *Look at what you have and not what you "might" have.*

As the boys' nanny, Harper brought him incredible peace of mind and as far as Brady was concerned, peace of mind was worth more than gold.

He needed to keep his thoughts from drifting and daydreaming. Right now he had a real problem to deal with. One that, as the days went by and he got more and more of a handle on his job at the hotel, grew more serious in nature. His family had told him that two months ago, there had been an incident at the hotel—a serious one.

According to what Callum had said, the balcony had seemed to suddenly give way. The whole thing could have turned out to be a lot worse than it was, but bad enough that there had been even one person on that balcony when it had given out. He supposed they'd gotten lucky, considering that the so-called accident had occurred during a Fortune family gathering. Grace Williams, the first hospitality trainee to be hired at the hotel, was the person who was injured. She had hurt her ankle and was on the mend, thankfully. She was now working as the hotel's manager and was also engaged to Brady's cousin Wiley.

Still, any way Brady looked at it, it was an injury that should not have happened. Closer inspection of the balcony had uncovered that the incident might not have been an accident. It seemed possible that the balcony beams had been tampered with.

If that was true, it would mean someone was attempting to sabotage what Callum and his brothers were trying to build.

So far, Callum told Brady when he first filled him in about the incident, the police hadn't been able to find proof one way or another. But Kane had reviewed the damage—and his inspection certificates received prior to the accident—and he was almost positive that the break had been caused deliberately. Which meant that until that culprit was found and brought to justice, the general feeling among the Fortunes was that they had to keep an eye out around the hotel.

Brady kept it low-key and never spoke about it in front of the guests, but he encountered one of the management interns in the back office days later.

"So how's the investigation progressing?" he

asked Jay Cross point-blank one afternoon when he ran into the trainee. It struck him that Jay had that cowboy look about him, as if he had just come in from riding his favorite horse, instead of conducting business at the hotel.

The dark-haired man knew immediately what Brady was referring to. "No hard and fast suspects yet," Jay responded. "At least, no suspicions that panned out yet," he amended, "but everyone here has been on the lookout for any unusual behavior that might point us toward the right suspect. Or at least in the right direction," he qualified. "Eventually, though, the perpetrator will make some sort of a misstep that'll give him or her away. Whoever did this can't get away with it forever," Jay maintained with conviction.

But Brady didn't feel as confident as Jay did. "You really believe that?"

"Absolutely," Jay replied without any hesitation. "Everyone makes mistakes and that's what eventually gives them away. If he or she is sloppy, it'll be soon. If they turn out *not* to be sloppy, it'll probably take longer to find them. But it *will* happen," Jay said with certainty. "It's just a matter of time. Until then, take heart in the fact that we'll *all* be on the lookout."

Brady merely nodded and wound up paying lip service to what had been meant as words of comfort.

Well, Brady thought as he drove home that evening, the job was definitely not without its challenges. And heaven knew it certainly wasn't dull. But he was not about to complain. He got to work with a lot of different people and focus on keeping the hotel running smoothly. Plus, of course there was that mystery to solve.

Brady was well aware of how the public's mind worked. If the Hotel Fortune suddenly attained the reputation that it wasn't safe, no one would want to stay or dine there, and business would go from a growing enterprise to a nonexistent one.

They needed to catch whoever had done this. And soon.

A thought suddenly hit Brady. Maybe it was someone with a vendetta against the Fortune family in general, or perhaps just one Fortune family member in particular.

What they needed, he thought, was to take a closer look at just who might profit if the hotel was suddenly failing.

He had a great deal to occupy his mind, Brady thought as he pulled up to his house.

Including Harper.

Her world revolved around Toby and Tyler now. But that definitely didn't mean that her work was any less challenging than his. It was just on an entirely different level.

And, Brady thought, Harper didn't even have any adults to talk to during the day in order to help maintain her sanity. That had to be more than a little challenging for her.

The least he could do, he decided, was to attempt to bolster her.

Standing on his doorstep, Brady pulled back his shoulders and pasted a smile on his lips before opening the door and walking in.

The first thing that registered was the toys scattered everywhere. Toys he had initially bought for the twins in an effort to keep them occupied. That never succeeded for more than a few minutes. Maybe a couple of hours, tops. But in the end, the toys just contributed to the overall feeling of chaos.

Right now it felt as if he had just walked in on the aftermath of a war.

"Who won?" he heard himself asking Harper, who was on the floor, tossing toys into a huge box meant to house them and keep them from being underfoot.

Surprised, she looked up at Brady. Doing her best to tidy up, or at least gather up as many toys as she could, Harper had managed to lose track of time. She hadn't thought that Brady would be home yet.

Obviously she had miscalculated.

"That hasn't been determined yet," Harper

admitted. "But I was ultimately hoping it would turn out to be a draw."

"You're too modest. My money's on you," Brady told her, picking up a toy truck that had managed to lose one of its rear wheels. He tossed the truck into the large collection box.

"Optimist," she said with a laugh. Harper nodded at the remaining toys—they still comprised a large heap. "Why don't you just leave all that?" she suggested. "You've put in a long day. You shouldn't have to come home and spend more time cleaning up after the twins."

She was referring to his work at the hotel, Brady thought, trying to remember if he had shared anything with her or if that was just her natural ability to intuit things.

"The way I see it, Harper," he told her, continuing to gather the toys off the floor, "you put in a long day, too."

Rather than grumbling, the way some of the other nannies before her had done in situations far less trying, Brady watched as a smile blossomed over Harper's appealing face.

"Yes, but my day consisted of playing games and teaching Toby and Tyler how to be patient while the other twin had his turn at one of those games. By the way, Tyler has a real aptitude at board games while Toby has excellent hand-eye coordination when it comes to video games," she told him.

Brady remembered the last time he had played a video game with them. He had wound up breaking the twins apart when the game went up to a higher level.

Laughing, he shook his head. "No doubt about it. I don't care what you say—you're clearly a saint."

He was embarrassing her. "You're exaggerating way too much."

But he had another perspective. "If anything, I'm understating things," Brady told her.

She made her way over on her knees to another pile of toys. "You know, you don't have to flatter me. I've already told you that I'm staying."

Brady grinned as he followed her, picking up toys along with her. "Call it insurance. And I really did mean what I said. No flattery intended," he told her. "Until you came along, I saw grown women break down in tears or go running out the door, threatening me with bills from their psychiatrists as they ran."

Harper shook her head. "If a woman is that fragile, she has no business trying to help raise overactive children."

Trying his best to be fair, Brady emphasized the full picture. "Hey, there's two of them to do the damage. Sometimes the nanny felt outnumbered." He found himself moving closer toward Harper as the pile of toys grew smaller and more manageable. "So, what wonderful things did they do today? Or am I safer not knowing?" he asked.

Harper got a kick out of the way Brady had worded his question—and the way out he had given her. Her grin widened. "Let's just say that what you don't know won't hurt you."

There seemed something almost ominous about the way she put that, Brady thought. She had piqued his curiosity.

"Does that ever end well?" he wanted to know, rolling her words over in his mind.

"It's just better if we leave it at that. Trust me," she added as she bent down to pick up yet another toy that had seen better days.

"Guess I'll just have to," Brady agreed as he bent down to pick up the same toy.

They managed to bump foreheads and as they raised their heads up at the same time, they wound up having their faces almost perfectly aligned.

Which also meant that their lips were inches apart.

All the pep talks he had given himself, all the reasons he had laid out as to why he couldn't allow his feelings to get the better of him, all that went up in smoke.

Before he knew it, he let his instincts take

over and the next moment, Brady found himself kissing her.

The fallen toy was completely forgotten as it toppled back down to the floor. Instead of a broken truck, Brady was holding on to Harper's shoulders. Rising to his feet, his lips on hers, he brought her up with him.

The kiss continued and as it did, it generated a lot of warm, vibrant feelings that went coursing through Harper, taking her very breath away.

More than anything, she was tempted to go with it, to follow this feeling wherever it might take her.

But she knew she couldn't.

The twins were what was important here, not her feelings or her very strong attraction to Brady. She had already been forewarned that this road would lead to nowhere.

Reluctantly she drew her head back just an inch. "Um, I've got dinner on the stove warming for you," she said.

That wasn't the only thing she had warming, Brady couldn't help thinking, more than a little tempted to steal just another second longer with this incredibly arousing woman.

"Does Unca Brady have a boo-boo?"

They all but jumped apart at the sound of the small voice asking the question. Brady and Harper turned toward the voice, almost in unison, to see Tyler standing in the living room doorway. He appeared to be rubbing sleep from his eye.

Harper, Brady noted, turned out to be extremely quick on her feet. Recovering her composure, she asked the little boy, "What makes you ask that, Tyler?"

"'Cause when I fell and hurt my knee, you kissed my boo-boo to make it all better," Tyler reminded Harper. "Did you fall on your face, Unca Brady?" the little boy wanted to know. His voice echoed with sympathy.

Relieved to have an answer for him, Brady went with the excuse the little boy had all but handed him on a silver platter. "Yes, that's it, Tyler. I tripped and fell on my face."

Tyler looked Brady over very carefully. Brady waited for the twin to point out that there were no marks anywhere on his face. Instead, the boy merely nodded.

"Harper made it all better, didn't she?" he asked his guardian. "Just like my mama used to," the little boy added wistfully.

Brady's heart filled up, and he found himself at a loss for words. Instead, he put his hand on the boy's shoulder, giving it a quick squeeze.

Tyler's words definitely tugged on Harper's heart as well. Whatever might have happened between her and Brady was pushed into the background, officially bringing that part of the evening to a close as far as she was concerned.

"Tyler, would you like to help me get your uncle Brady's dinner for him?" she asked the boy.

Tyler surprised both of them by asking, "Will that help his boo-boo go away?"

"Oh definitely," Harper assured the boy, glancing in Brady's direction for backup.

"Nothing would make me feel better faster than getting something to eat," Brady said, playing along with the game.

The boy's small head bobbed up and down, the question of helping out obviously settled.

"Sure I'll help," he told Harper, then added solemnly, "I want him to feel better. I don't want anything to happen to Unca Brady." He turned around to look at Brady, his small face extremely serious. "Be careful, Unca Brady. Don't hurt your face," the little boy warned him.

"I'll be careful," Brady assured the twin.

But Tyler still looked very skeptical. "Do you promise?" he asked his guardian.

Surprised that Tyler cared that much, Brady told him, "I promise."

But Tyler still wouldn't let him off the hook. "Cross your heart?"

Harper could see that Brady was struggling

not to laugh. Mentally, she kept her fingers crossed.

"My heart, my eyes, and anything else you want crossed," Brady told the boy.

Getting the answer he wanted, Tyler burst into giggles, his solemn expression a thing of the past. "Okay!"

"Well, if the negotiations are over," Harper told the twin, "then I'm still going to need your help in the kitchen, Tyler."

Determined to please, Tyler's small brow furrowed up. "What's nego-nego—that word?" he wanted to know.

Tyler definitely was a sponge when it came to soaking up knowledge, Harper thought. "Negotiations," she repeated. "Why don't I explain it while you help me?" She took his hand and led him into the kitchen, patiently answering his questions on the way.

As he went to help his nanny warm up dinner, Tyler looked as if he could levitate right where he walked.

Looking at Harper, Brady knew the feeling.

Chapter Twelve

The more he saw her in action, the more Brady found himself to be totally in awe of Harper. She was nothing short of phenomenal when it came to handling the twins.

As much as Brady hated to admit it—because he had once seen himself as being able to master any and every situation he came across —when it came to parenting and disciplining two rambunctious little boys, Brady was totally out of his league.

Even after putting in six grueling months on the job, he still didn't have the vaguest idea what to do when it came to managing the twins.

He just wasn't cut out for parenting, Brady thought, resigned. While Harper seemed to be a natural. Somehow, she just instinctively knew what to do, how to get the lively twins to back off. And, more important, how to get them to behave.

Moreover, she could get them to *want* to behave.

It seemed to Brady that the two hellions who had come roaring into his life on an express train were in competition with one another as to who could be the more well-behaved around Harper. And, he'd noticed, in competition as to who could manage to earn her first smile of the day.

"You don't drug them, do you?"

Harper looked at Brady, stunned by his question and certain she had to have misheard what he had just said. "Excuse me?"

"I'm joking." He held up his hands and grinned. "But I am curious. They're…well, not exactly calm," he said tactfully, "but less wild around you than they are around me. Why is that?"

She smiled at him. The man certainly needed to be educated in the ways of children and their instincts. "Because they sense they can have their way with you while they're not that sure how far they can push me. And, I'm happy to say, I get the feeling that they don't want to do something that might make me leave."

It was the tail end of another excruciatingly long day. Brady had come home early—and had come very close to regretting it. His intention had been to attempt to bond with the boys, but that just wasn't happening. After much bargaining—and with Harper coming in to back him up—he had succeeded in getting the twins to bed.

When he had followed her out of the boys' room and made his way downstairs, he was completely wiped out. "Let's face it," Brady told Harper when she had asked him if there was anything wrong, "I'm just not cut out for this."

"This?" Harper questioned, clearing away the last of the mess that the twins had managed to create as they played today.

"Being a parent," Brady answered, then specified, "Child-rearing." He took in a disheartened, shaky breath as he added, "While you, you're a natural. I'm surprised that you don't have kids of your own," he told her.

"It takes the right man for that," she answered. Their eyes met for a long moment, communicating things neither was free to say out loud yet. But it was still there.

Clearing her throat, she turned her attention to what Brady had said previously. Sitting down on the sofa, she patted the place beside her, silently urging Brady to take a seat.

"That's a very nice compliment you gave me earlier," she told him as he sat down beside her. "But not a very realistic one. Nobody starts out knowing what to do when it comes to kids. I've been working as a nanny for several years now because I love kids, but I certainly didn't come on the scene knowing what to do. I had to learn that just the way that everyone else did. Just like you," she emphasized, deliberately looking into his eyes as she made her point.

"I haven't learned anything and it's been over six months," Brady protested.

He was selling himself short, Harper thought. "Six months of you adjusting to the situation you found yourself thrown into, headfirst," she declared. "Six months of you adjusting to the needs of two mischievous, overactive, demanding little boys while learning how to put your own needs a distant second." Didn't he realize that, she wondered.

"If you ask me, all things considered, I think that you're doing very well, Brady. Give yourself a break and a little credit here," she urged him, placing her hand over his.

Then suddenly realizing what she was doing, Harper pulled back her hand. But she didn't withdraw her seal of approval, which was evident in what she said to him. "If you ask me, Brady, you're being much too hard on yourself."

Brady frowned, shaking his head. "I don't know about that," he said.

"Well, I do," she informed him with certainty. "The thing that you have to remember is the most important requirement of being a parent—or a guardian," she emphasized. "A heart."

He laughed dryly. "I'm pretty sure my doctor said I had one on my last checkup."

"I'm serious, wise guy," Harper chided with a laugh. "If you truly care about them—and trust me, kids have a way of sensing if you do or don't—then everything else will just fall into place. And, the way I see it, you have enough love for both of us." Harper's words played themselves back in her head the moment she said them. She instantly turned crimson. "I mean—"

The woman had just spent several minutes trying to make him feel better about himself as a surrogate parent. He wasn't about to have her struggling to walk back something she'd had no intention of saying in the first place.

"I know what you mean," Brady assured her. "And I do appreciate it."

For a moment, he debated asking the question that had resurfaced in his mind, the one he had asked her days ago. Ordinarily, he would just let it go. But the more he got to know her, the more curious he found himself about the details of her life.

"You know," he said, approaching the question cautiously, "you never did tell me why you decided to leave your last position."

As he watched, the confident, outgoing young woman, who was such a natural when it came to handling the two free-spirited boys he had taken into his home, suddenly became introverted and reticent.

After a long beat, Harper finally said, "My last job didn't end well," growing more uncomfortable with each word she uttered.

But she could see that Brady was waiting for more information. She forced herself to say something, while still keeping it as vague as possible. Because although she liked him and was coming to think of Brady as a fair man, ultimately she didn't know how he would react to the reason she had been fired. After all, it was just her word against her former employer's. What if he didn't believe her? At the very least, that would bother her. At its worst, it might cause Brady to fire her. She decided not to go into it.

Since it happened, she had done her best not to think about the circumstances at all. But it wasn't easy. "Let's just say that the situation became… complicated," she finally told him.

"Complicated?" Brady questioned.

"Complicated," she repeated, saying the word with such finality that he knew the subject was closed until further notice.

Possibly permanently.

In any event, Brady knew when to back away and not push the situation.

Switching directions, Brady didn't entirely drop the subject, just decided to approach it from another angle.

"I think the reason you're so good at what you do is because you become emotionally involved with your charges and their families." He sighed. That wasn't anything that he could have been able to deal with. "It comes naturally to you," he said. "Me, not so much," he admitted. "As a matter of fact, I can't say that I'm really any good at something like that."

Something like that.

Was he telling her that he wasn't one to get emotionally involved—or worse, was he warning her off? She didn't know, but in any case, she wasn't about to buy any trouble. It might do her good to keep a distance between herself and this sexy, good-looking man.

A man she had already kissed and would have gone on kissing—or more—had Tyler not had a bad dream and come downstairs looking for her and interrupted them.

The fact that Brady had also kissed her back—

and maybe had even been the one to initiate the kiss—wasn't really that important. What was important was that they *had* kissed and that kiss could have very well blossomed into something a great deal more if not for Tyler's untimely entrance.

She was going to have to keep her guard up against that sort of thing ever repeating itself.

That would bring a whole new meaning to the word *complicated*, she thought.

It was definitely time to retreat, she thought. Gathering herself together, Harper suddenly rose to her feet. "Let me get you dinner," she told him with forced cheerfulness.

Brady caught hold of her hand to stop her. Abruptly realizing what he was doing, he released her hand. When she looked at him quizzically, he told her, "I didn't hire you to serve me meals, Harper. I hired you to be Toby and Tyler's nanny."

"I know that," she answered crisply. "But it doesn't hurt to go the extra mile and make an extra serving when cooking for the boys and myself. Unless you don't like my cooking," she suddenly realized. Was that why he was saying no? Because he didn't like what she made?

"Anything I don't have to cook myself tastes great," he told her, then assured her with feeling,

"But so far, everything you've made has been really exceptionally delicious."

Harper grinned. "Nice save," she congratulated Brady.

"Not bad for a man who's half asleep," Brady conceded with a tired smile.

Harper laughed warmly at his comment, her revived sense of humor bringing her old self back to the foreground. With a wink, she told Brady, "Not even bad for a man who's wide awake. Come, follow me," she urged, leading the way.

Brady's stomach grumbled as he followed Harper to the kitchen. The grumbling reminded him that he had completely lost track of the last time that he had actually eaten today.

Harper was more than happy to turn her attention toward doing something productive instead of wrestling with her growing feelings and digging up situations that made her feel very uncomfortable. Her last job was in the past and she fully intended to keep it there rather than to draw it out and expose it to the light of day.

Heaven knew it wasn't because she had ever harbored even the slightest feelings for her last employer's husband. On the contrary, by the time she had been given her walking papers, Edward Wheeler had made her skin crawl with his very presence. The idea of anything happening between them was enough to make her physically ill. The man had turned out to be a notorious player and it galled Harper that his wife actually believed that she would do anything so reprehensible as to have a romantic affair with the father of the children she was being paid to watch over and take care of.

That would have been a terrible breach of trust on her part and she just wasn't that type of person. It hurt her that the woman would even *think* that was possible.

Water under the bridge, Harper silently insisted.

No, the subject was better left closed and under wraps, Harper thought. If she said anything about it to Brady, gave him any sort of details, then at some point, she was certain the subject would resurface again and haunt her.

That was the last thing she wanted, Harper thought. She had a new job, back doing what she loved, and she wasn't about to risk that because of something that never happened.

Harper roused herself, bringing her mind back to the present. Placing a serving of pork chops, mashed potatoes and green beans in front of Brady, she told him, "If there's nothing else, I think I'll be going home now. The boys were particularly active today and to be honest, my batteries are drained and need recharging," she confessed.

"You didn't even have to do this," Brady reminded her. "All I need from you is to take care of the boys. That was what we had agreed on at the outset," he reminded her. "I could have found something to eat."

"And mess up the kitchen while you were doing it?" she asked. She had seen Brady when he was searching for something. The man was definitely *not* neat. He was more like a tornado that had been let loose. "No, this way's better," Harper assured him. "Less to clean up in the long run."

Unable to resist, he cut a piece of pork chop and slipped it into his mouth. For a second, the expression on his face looked like that of a man who had unexpectedly found his way into heaven. "This is really good," he told her with feeling.

Pleased, Harper smiled with satisfaction. "Toby and Tyler thought so, too."

Moved, he couldn't let this pass without telling her how valuable she had become to his life in such a short amount of time. "I am so glad you're here, Harper."

That caught her off guard. *He didn't mean that the way it sounded*, she warned herself. He was just talking about her cooking and how she managed the boys.

Not wanting him to think she was rude,

Harper told him, "I'm glad to be here, too," as she began to make her way out of the kitchen.

"No, you don't understand," Brady said. "Until you got here, dinner used to consist of hot dogs, hamburgers and the occasional pizza." He knew there was no excuse for that, but sometimes easy was better than nothing at all. "Until you came into their lives, Toby and Tyler didn't realize that vegetables could actually be a tasty part of an evening meal."

He had such an adorable expression on his face, Harper couldn't help laughing. "Then I'm glad I came along," she told him. "I guess that would explain why the twins thought soda pop was one of the essential food groups," she teased.

"Like I said," Brady told her after taking another healthy-sized bite of the seasoned pork chop, "I make a terrible parent."

She was not about to stand for him putting himself down. "The most important part of being a parent is wanting to be there—and you were. You *are*," Harper emphasized, her eyes meeting his. "Now, if there's nothing else," she told him, "I'll be leaving."

There *was* something else. He wanted to ask her just to stay at the table and keep him company. Nothing more than that.

But at the same time, he knew that was being selfish. Harper had certainly earned her rest and the least he could do was let her go home and get to bed.

The word *bed* instantly conjured up images in his mind that had absolutely no business being there. Images of Harper sprawled across his king-size bed, her arms stretched out to him as he lowered himself over her.

All the more reason to send her on her way, he thought. Heaven knew that if he had her stay, that would tempt him to want to progress to something more than just conversation, and if he went that route, he risked having her leave.

Permanently.

He had already risked losing her with that juvenile stunt he had pulled that day while she had been picking up toys and he had gone to help her—and wound up doing something completely out of character, Brady upbraided himself. If it hadn't been for Tyler and his nightmare, who knew what might have happened?

He couldn't allow that to happen a second time no matter how attractive he found Harper, Brady thought. Without knowing it, that little boy had managed to rescue the situation—and him. Because, if Harper hadn't miraculously come into his life, who knew where he and the boys would be right now? Or, for that matter, if he could even manage to juggle work and this situation he had somehow found himself in.

"Sorry. I didn't mean to keep you," Brady apologized. "Go home, get some well-deserved rest so that you can put your track shoes on in the morning and keep up with those little whirling dervishes."

His words created an image in her head and Harper couldn't help but laugh.

"That is a very colorful way to describe them," Harper told him with approval.

"Really? I thought I was actually understating the situation. Heaven knew that until you came along, I felt like someone trapped inside of a never-ending cartoon program."

Harper smiled as she made it to the front door and opened it. "Glad I could change that for you," she told Brady.

Brady watched as she walked out of the house.

"Yeah," he murmured under his breath to her back. "Me, too."

Chapter Thirteen

Things were progressing well at the Hotel Fortune and even his home life had seemed to fall into some sort of a heartening routine, Brady thought. While he couldn't exactly say that things had become peaceful, at least they were no longer in a state of constant turmoil.

If there was a fly in the ointment, it was that the search for the person who was behind that balcony collapse had not been fruitful. The investigation was ongoing and while some of the suspects had been cleared, there were still a lot of people who needed to be investigated.

Brady found that really frustrating and disturbing.

In an effort to keep moving forward and re-main productive, Brady forced himself to focus on the positive things and not obsess over the negative.

Easier said than done, he thought late one eve-ning after Harper had gone home and he was in bed. He found his thoughts turning toward her and that really didn't help him, either. During the day, when his time was filled to the brim with hotel concerns, it was easy not to think about Harper. And even when he came home and the twins were still bouncing around, all he could concentrate on was how much his life had changed.

But once they had been put to bed, Harper left and the house grew quiet, it was really hard for him not to think about her and how she had brought such incredible order and peace of mind into his life.

And by the same token—even after she went home for the night—how she also managed to fire up his imagination and stir his longing.

Really stir his longing.

No woman had ever been front and center in his life. That wasn't to say that he didn't enjoy their company whenever he could, but he had never been singularly focused on any of these women.

However, it seemed that lately, totally unbidden, Harper kept popping up in his thoughts as well as occasionally in his dreams. He kept telling himself he shouldn't—couldn't—allow any of these mental meanderings to bear fruit. And yet, no matter what he did, he couldn't seem to eliminate the really powerful longing he felt for her.

Any way he looked at it, it was an explosion waiting to happen.

Brady had shared a particularly nice evening meal with her tonight as well as an extended conversation centering around the twins'—mainly Toby's—exploits at preschool. But when he and Harper parted company, it was her smile, not the conversation or even the really tasty meal she had prepared, that insisted on lingering on his mind.

And was now keeping him awake.

He couldn't keep doing this to himself, Brady silently insisted, turning on his other side and punching his pillow in an attempt to get it into a comfortable, more welcoming shape.

He wasn't succeeding.

So when the phone rang after ten o'clock that night, he was still awake and up to answering it. Hoping this didn't involve some sort of an unforeseen hotel emergency, Brady mentally crossed his fingers and picked up his cell.

Braced for anything, he said, "Hello?"

"Hi, Big Brother, how's it going?"

At the sound of the cheerful, soprano voice in his ear, Brady immediately bolted upright in bed and propped himself up against the headboard.

"Arabella?" he asked although he was certain that it had to be her.

He hadn't heard from his only sister in a while now. Because it was Arabella, he just assumed that she was too busy having fun to bother calling. She had a zest for life he almost envied now. The next moment, he realized that he wouldn't change anything about the way his life had evolved, chaos and all. He admitted to himself that he had grown to care about the twins. When had that happened, he marveled.

"You have any other sisters I don't know about?" Arabella asked him, amused.

"No, in your case one is definitely enough," he assured her. And then he grew a little more serious. "Is anything wrong? Are Mom and Dad okay?" he wanted to know.

Brady was aware that his sister, four years his junior and incredibly independent in her dealings, kept unorthodox hours. However, since he had become the twins' guardian, he looked at things in a far different light than he had back when his days had been carefree and life hadn't been nearly as structured as it was now.

Now he was more aware of the darker things

in life and the consequences they could bring
with them.

"They're fine, Brady. Does something have to
be wrong for me to call my favorite big brother?"
his sister asked.

Uh-oh, he thought, the phrase *favorite big
brother* setting off alarms.

"No," Brady answered, "but you have to
admit, Belle, you don't usually call. So what's
up?" he wanted to know.

"Maybe I've just decided that it's time for me
to grow up a little," Arabella answered—a bit
too loftily in his opinion.

"Are you sure there's nothing wrong?" Brady
asked again. Because of the chaos the twins had
initially brought into his life, he wasn't about to
take things at face value anymore and coast. He
liked being prepared for possible disasters *before* they happened.

"Yes, I'm sure," Arabella answered. "Relax,
Brady. I just wanted to see how you and your
little wild bunch were doing—although I have
to admit, until you turned this into an interroga-
tion, you did sound as if you're more relaxed than
you were the last time we talked." She laughed
as an image came to mind. "For instance, you
don't sound as if you're in the middle of fighting
an out-of-control five-alarm fire."

"That's because I'm not," he told her. Since

she had expressed an interest, he decided to fill her in. "Things are going pretty well with my new job—and as for the *wild bunch* as you called them, they're actually beginning to calm down—at least enough for me to be able to catch my breath."

"What happened?" she wanted to know. "Did you find a doctor to write a prescription for junior-sized tranquilizers?" Arabella teased.

He was more than happy to give credit where credit was due. "Even better. I found a nanny who's absolutely incredible. Her name's Harper Radcliffe," he told his sister before she could ask. "And she's really fantastic with the twins," he added with wholehearted enthusiasm.

His passionate tone was not lost on his sister. "Is that all she's great with?" Arabella asked, amusement evident in her voice.

Alarms went off in Brady's head. "Hey, you're reading much too much into this, Belle." He laughed shortly. "I see you're still a hopeless romantic."

"Not hopeless," Arabella protested, wanting to set her brother straight.

He noticed that she hadn't vetoed his entire statement. "But you are a romantic," he countered.

Arabella sniffed. "Not everything has to be labeled, Big Brother," she told him. Before he could argue the point, she got back to the reason she had called. "So then you feel that everything is going well in Rambling Rose?" she pressed. "You don't have any regrets about moving there?"

"No, not for one minute," Brady readily assured his sister.

"Well, that's good to hear." She paused for a moment, then decided to release her bombshell. Like ripping off a Band-Aid, she decided to do it quickly. "Especially since I've been thinking of making the move to your fair town myself."

The thought of seeing his sister again pleased him. In his estimation, it had already been far too long. The last time they had seen one another, he was still living in upstate New York. "Really?"

"Really," Arabella replied, pleasure throbbing in her voice.

And then she hesitated, just for a moment, as she gathered her courage together. If he said no to this, it would turn out to be very awkward.

"If I did come out, would you be able to put me up until I found a place of my own? Or would I be in the way?" she quickly asked.

Arabella wanted everything out in the open and if her brother, despite his protest, had something going with this "fantastic" nanny of his, the last thing she wanted to do was interfere with that. She didn't want him resenting her presence.

Brady knew exactly what his sister was driving at and he immediately put an end to that line of thinking.

"No, you wouldn't be in the way," he told Arabella. "But for your own sake, you might want to rethink staying here."

She didn't understand. If he didn't think she would be getting in the way, why would she want to rethink staying with him? It didn't make any sense to her.

Arabella put the question to him. "Why?"

Brady didn't mince any words. "Do you think you're up to putting up with the boys twenty-four/seven?" he wanted to know.

She didn't hesitate. "Sure. I haven't seen them since before you moved to Rambling Rose. They've probably grown at least six inches. Maybe even a foot," she teased.

"Not quite," he answered. "Okay, then consider yourself invited to stay," he told her. "Just let me know when you're going to be coming out."

"Will do," Arabella promised. And then she circled around to the *real* reason that she had called him. "So, things are going well for you at the hotel?" she asked again, searching for a way to broach the question that was foremost on her mind.

"For the most part, yes," he answered. He was becoming suspicious now. "Why do you ask?"

"Oh, no reason," she said quickly. "I just want to know if you're happy. Oh, by the way," Arabella began a little too innocently, "did you happen to run into Jay Cross anywhere while you've been working at the hotel?"

At the mention of the man's name, Brady's mind went back to the discussion he'd had with Jay regarding the ongoing investigation into the balcony incident.

"I think I talked to him about a week ago," he told his sister. Then, because he had a feeling that this was what she was ultimately getting at, he told Arabella, "He's doing well there."

Pausing, Brady didn't hear his sister say anything in response, so he decided to press her. "Why do you want to know?"

"No reason, really," she answered a little too quickly and too innocently. Realizing that her brother probably wasn't fooled and wasn't about to let the matter drop unless she gave him some sort of an actual reason for her question, Arabella cast about and managed to come up with something. "Jay was nice to me when we met at Larkin's birthday party back in January," she said, mentioning their little nephew, "and I was just wondering if he was still in town, that's all."

She wasn't fooling him for a second. Arabella

was displaying too much interest in Jay Cross. But for the time being, Brady decided to play along. "Yes, he's still there."

Hearing his tone, Arabella frowned. "Get rid of that smirk in your voice, Big Brother."

"I don't know what you're talking about," he said a bit too quickly.

"Yeah, right." She laughed at him. "You never did learn how to lie well."

"We can't all be as convincing when it comes to fabricating things as you are, Belle," he told her. And then he dropped his bantering tone. "It'll be great to see you again, Belle."

"You sure you don't mind fitting me in?" she questioned, somewhat serious now. "Between your job and your nanny, you must be awfully busy."

Brady heard only one thing in the question she posed. She was making assumptions and he intended to set his sister straight immediately.

"She's not 'my' nanny, Belle," he told her seriously. "She's Toby and Tyler's nanny."

"Right." Arabella couldn't keep the smile from her face. "I'll try to remember that. Okay, I'll let you get back to your beauty sleep. And I'll give you a call just before I'm ready to move to your neck of the woods," she told him.

Brady laughed, getting a kick out of his sister's phraseology. "Oh, you're going to fit right in here," he teased.

"I'll have you know that I fit in anywhere I set my mind to," Arabella informed him.

"I never doubted that," Brady replied. Lack of confidence had never been Arabella's problem.

He was still smiling to himself as he hung up. It seemed that little by little, his family was all relocating to this not-quite-so-dusty little town.

And he, for one, was really looking forward to seeing Belle here.

"C'mon, let's go!" Toby cried, eager to get Harper and his "unca" Brady out of the house. He was all set to make a mad dash for the car. "You're too slow," Toby complained, looking accusingly at his twin who was hanging back. Toby was shifting from foot to foot.

"I'm waiting for Unca Brady," Tyler told his twin, looking at his uncle loyally.

Harper had come in early carrying a packed picnic basket. She had promised the twins they would all go on a picnic on Saturday if they managed to be good for three days running.

As far as the twins were concerned, they had fulfilled their part of the bargain. As an added bonus, the twins had gotten Brady to agree to come along with them on this venture.

Harper looked at Brady dubiously now. "Are

you sure you want to come?" she asked as she allowed Toby to pull her out the front door.

"Are you trying to talk me out of it?" Brady asked, amused.

"No, heaven forbid. It's just that with all the hours you put in working at the hotel, it occurred to me that you don't get much time to rest," Harper explained.

Humor curved Brady's mouth as Tyler pulled on his arm, getting him closer to Harper's car. "Are you trying to say this little excursion won't be restful?" Brady asked innocently.

"Only if you compare this to being a lion tamer," Harper pointed out.

"That sounds intriguing," Brady said with a laugh.

Spurred on and inspired, Toby immediately began to make lion noises—or what the little boy thought passed for lion noises.

With the picnic basket already in the trunk, Harper placed a hand on either boy's shoulder and herded them both into the backseat of her vehicle where their car seats were waiting.

"Down, Simba," she told Toby.

Toby's brow furrowed as she secured the car seat straps. "Who's Simba?" he wanted to know.

She turned her attention to Tyler's straps. "That's a lion in a story," she told Toby.

"Do you know him?" both boys asked almost simultaneously.

"Not personally," she told the boys with a straight face.

"Nobody knows lions," Toby declared knowingly as he spoke up.

Tyler, however, would have believed Harper if she had told him she could walk on water. Backward.

"Harper does," he told his twin, then turned toward her for confirmation. "Right, Harper?"

"Not this time," she told Tyler. It was all she could do not to hug the boy. His innocence touched her heart. "Now let's go. My guess is that you don't want to miss this picnic, so we need to hurry."

The forecast was for rain later in the day and she'd already warned the boys that once the raindrops began to fall, they were out of there, no arguments. The twins had reluctantly agreed.

"You sure you don't want me to drive?" Brady asked her as she crawled out of the backseat and opened the driver's-side door.

"I'm sure." Her tone left no room for arguing. "This is your day off, remember?" she reminded him.

"When do you get a day off?" Brady wanted to know. So far, she seemed to have come in every day without fail.

She flashed him a wide grin. "What makes you think I'm working?" she deadpanned.

"Just kind of looked that way, that's all," Brady answered with a smile.

"When you love what you do, it's not work. You just sit back and relax," she told him, getting in and buckling up. "I'll handle the driving."

He looked a little dubious about the whole venture and then shrugged. "Sure, why not? My insurance is all paid up," he said as he got into the passenger seat, then buckled up.

She gave him a look that might or might not have been meant to put him in his place. "I'll ignore that," she said, starting up her car.

Brady braced himself against the dashboard. He'd never liked not being in control of the vehicle he was in.

As it turned out, though, he had nothing to worry about. But then, he told himself as they reached their destination, he should have known that.

Not for the first time, he thought that being with Harper was an on-going learning experience.

Chapter Fourteen

As it turned out, the rain that was projected never materialized. Consequently, what was supposed to be only a short picnic wound up being an all-day, exhausting affair. Because of that, the twins ran themselves totally ragged. They certainly outlasted a number of other children whose parents and families had also thought that a short spring picnic was a really good idea.

"You have a really lovely family, my dear," one sweet-faced grandmother warmly commented to Harper as she and Brady were carrying the exhausted twins to the car.

Harper opened her mouth to protest that neither the twins nor Brady were hers, but then she decided that the situation was too complicated to explain quickly. Besides, the older woman appeared to be taking such satisfaction in the picture they made. The woman was literally beaming at them.

So, in response to that, Harper merely told the woman "Thank you," and proceeded with the sleeping Tyler to the car.

"You know," Harper said quietly as she carefully eased Tyler into his car seat and then securely fastened his seat belt around his small body, "I don't think I've *ever* seen either one of the twins so quiet. I think that running around in the open like this really drained them—a lot."

"I think we might have stumbled onto something," Brady joked. Toby murmured something against his shoulder as Brady put the twin into his car seat. He stood back and regarded the sleeping boys. "They look like angels, don't they?" he asked Harper. "Nobody would ever guess what little devils these guys can actually be." He smoothed Toby's hair back from his forehead. His smile faded as he paused and looked at the twin thoughtfully. "Hey, Harper?"

"Yes?" she asked, preoccupied as she checked the seat belts a second time to be absolutely sure they were secure.

Brady was still looking dubiously at Toby. "Is Toby supposed to be this warm?"

The concern in Brady's voice caught her attention. She did what she could to reassure him. "Well, he has been running around all day so he's bound to be warm," she told Brady as she leaned over the boy to make sure everything was all right.

She fell back on the timeless, tried-and-true method to determine whether or not a child was running a fever. She kissed his forehead. However, the moment she did, Harper shook her head.

"But Toby shouldn't be *this* warm," she told Brady.

"So you think he has a fever?" Brady asked her, his stomach making itself into a knot as he anticipated her answer.

"I *know* he has a fever," Harper answered. There was no room for an argument in her tone. "Let's get these two guys home," she told Brady as she handed him her keys. "Here, you drive." Accepting the car keys, he looked at Harper quizzically. She knew what he was about to ask. "I want to be able to turn around in my seat and keep my eye on the twins in case they need something."

Twins. Plural. Alarms immediately went off in Brady's head.

"Does Tyler have a fever, too?" he asked apprehensively.

"Not that I can tell, but they did run around

together all day." She saw the apprehensive look wash over Brady's face. She did what she could to reassure him. "That doesn't necessarily mean that they're both going to get sick," she said as he started up the car.

Brady knew that he needed something to cling to, no matter how thin. "It doesn't?"

She realized what he was asking her—and why. Harper rose to the occasion. "No, I've known one kid to come down with the flu while his sibling, sleeping only a few feet away, didn't even get so much as a cough or a sore throat, much less come down with anything more serious."

Brady appreciated her effort. It hit him that he came from a large family. He had grown up surrounded by siblings. "How did I miss all this growing up?" he upbraided himself.

"Don't beat yourself up," Harper told him. "Kids are usually self-centered and don't really pay attention to anything around them. It's normal," she assured Brady. "And another thing you might not be aware of, a lot of kids run a temperature in the morning, then it's gone in the afternoon, only to reappear in the evening. It's all part of a pattern. For the most part, kids are really resilient." Harper's eyes met his as he came to a red light and turned around to look at her. "It's going to be okay," she promised Brady.

Toby suddenly stirred, moaned and then opened his eyes. Harper looked at the boy more closely. She could see that his eyes were watery.

"Harper," Toby said in a raspy voice that made it sound as if he was on the verge of crying. "I don't feel so good."

"We're taking you home, honey. You're going to be okay," she told the twin firmly. Harper twisted around in her seat so that she could hold the boy's hand.

It felt hot, just like the rest of him.

"Drive a little faster, Brady," she told him in a calm voice that belied the concern she was feeling.

"I'll take him up to his room," Harper volunteered when Brady pulled up in his driveway. "You bring up Tyler."

"Maybe they should be in separate rooms," Brady suggested. He felt totally at a loss as to how to handle any of this.

"I think that's kind of like closing the barn door after the horse got out," she replied. "They're always together so Tyler has been exposed already. If he's going to get sick, he will," she told Brady as she carried Toby to the front door.

Holding Tyler against his shoulder with one

hand, Brady quickly unlocked the front door for her with the other.

"I already checked out Tyler," she told Brady, "and he doesn't feel warm to me."

Walking into the house, she carried Toby up the stairs and into his room. She set him on the bed, then very carefully took off his clothes and put him into his pajamas. The boy slept through most of it, waking up for a moment only to fall back asleep.

Brady stood back, looking really concerned. "Maybe we should take him to the hospital," he said as he changed Tyler into his pajamas.

"It's probably just a cold or maybe the flu," she told Brady. "I'll go get the thermometer so we can see what we're up against."

Because Toby had fallen asleep, Harper took the boy's temperature under his armpit. She adjusted her reading because of the thermometer's location.

Despite how hot his head felt, Toby's temperature wasn't registering all that high.

But Brady still didn't feel better about the situation. "I can't stand to see him like this," he told Harper as he looked down at Toby. The twin looked incredibly small and vulnerable to him. "Look, I know you usually go home at the end of the day, but would you mind staying, you know, the night?"

Damn, he sounded like some awkward teenager, Brady thought, annoyed with himself. He decided to level with her and confessed, "I'm really out of my element here. I'll pay you overtime," he quickly offered.

"You don't have to pay me overtime," she told him, waving the suggestion away. This was not about the money. It never had been. "I'll be happy to stay with Toby."

"You will?" Brady looked visibly relieved. He needed someone here who knew what they were doing. "You have no idea how grateful I am."

Harper smiled at him. "Oh, I think I can guess. Why don't you go to bed and get some sleep?" she suggested, then told him, "I'll stay in here with the boys."

Brady looked around the room as if he hadn't seen it before. "But there's no bed for you," he pointed out.

"No, but there is a recliner," she said. It had been the first thing to catch her eye when she had initially seen the room. "Don't worry. I'll make do," Harper assured him. "Now go to bed. He'll probably wake up tomorrow morning with energy to spare."

He looked at the boy's tiny face, concern evident on his own. "I hope you're right," he told her.

"I'll remind you that you said that," she promised with a smile. "Now go, get some rest."

"Okay."

Exhausted and drained, Brady left the room, convinced he wasn't going to get a wink of sleep.

He was asleep a second after his head hit the pillow.

Brady woke up with a start.

It was morning.

How did that happen? he upbraided himself. Somehow, he had slept straight through the night. That hardly ever happened anymore. At least, not in the last six months.

Awake now, thoughts of Toby flooded his brain. Guilt was less than half a beat behind.

Looking down at himself, Brady realized that he had fallen asleep in his clothes. Since he had, there was no need to get dressed. He even had on his shoes.

Brady quickly made his way to the twins' room.

He found Harper there and she was already awake, looking uncommonly fresh, especially given the situation.

That only succeeded in making him feel twice as guilty as he already did.

Moving as quietly as possible, Brady came up behind Harper and asked her, "How is he?"

"Well, he still has a fever," she told him, not wanting to hide anything from Brady. "But the good news is Tyler seems fine. When Toby wakes up, I'm going to give him a sponge bath, try to lower his temperature."

"The hospital—"

"Will still be there if we decide to take him as another option later. But at the moment, I don't think there's a reason to panic. I'll make him drink a lot of liquids. I'll watch him and if his fever goes up or he gets worse, we can take him in then. But in my experience, that's a last resort."

He didn't know if he was up to this waiting game. "Why don't we just take him in now?" Brady wanted to know.

"Because we might not have to," Harper explained. "And I don't think you want to teach him to panic at the first sign that he might be coming down with something," she added.

"But—"

"You want to raise these boys to learn how to take things in stride," Harper advised, then asked, "Don't you?"

She was making sense, Brady thought, nodding his head. "You're right," he agreed, then looked down at Toby. "I guess this whole thing just made me lose my head."

She laughed softly and gave his hand a quick, warm squeeze. "Face it. You're a first-time parent and you got into the game late. Reacting the way you did is just a sign that you care," Harper told him. "And in case that fact managed to escape you, that's a good thing."

He blew out a long breath. Becoming the twins' guardian had made for a rough six months, but to date this was by far the roughest thing he had gone through. "I'd go to pieces if you weren't here, you know that, don't you?" he asked Harper.

To his surprise, she shook her head. "No, you'd get on the phone to one of your married cousins or siblings and you'd ask for their advice," she contradicted. "And then you'd get through this."

He wasn't buying it. She was an important part in his being able to handle this. "Don't sell yourself short. If you weren't here, I'd be a complete basket case by now," he told Harper.

"No, you wouldn't be," she insisted. "But instead of arguing with me, why don't you go down and make us some breakfast?" Harper suggested.

He laughed at the idea. She had to know better, he thought. In case she didn't, he asked her, "I take it you have your heart set on coming down with a case of ptomaine poisoning."

Harper smiled, taking him at his word. "That bad, huh?"

"Well, I can open a cereal box," Brady responded. "And the refrigerator to take out a carton of milk, but not much else."

She shook her head, totally amazed at his inability to do something she considered to be so simple. Scrambling eggs. But then, she had been the one to do the shopping, she recalled. Prior to her first trip to the grocery store, there hadn't been all that much in the refrigerator, she reminded herself.

"You stay with the boys. I'll go and grab a quick shower," she told him, beginning to leave the room.

"Um, Harper?"

She turned around and looked at Brady. He looked utterly lost again, she thought. "What do I do if he wakes up?"

She didn't understand his problem. "Same thing you've been doing when he wakes up."

"But he's sick now," Brady protested.

She still didn't understand. "Hasn't he ever been sick before?" Harper asked incredulously.

"Not really. He had a slight cold once, but that didn't slow him down. But now..." His voice trailed off as he looked at the boy. Suddenly, Toby looked almost terribly lost in his bed.

Brady couldn't remember ever feeling so helpless in his entire life.

"If he wakes up, you take hold of his hand and tell him that everything's going to be all right."

She looked at him with sympathy. She imagined this had to be hard on Brady. "Really sell it," she advised, then asked, "Anything else?"

"No," Brady answered. He was up to this, he told himself. Everything was going to be all right.

"Be back soon," Harper promised.

She wasn't gone five minutes when Toby moaned and opened his eyes. Brady's first instinct was to call for Harper.

Instead, he made his way over to Toby. "How are you feeling, soldier?" he asked the lethargic-looking little boy.

Huge puppy-dog eyes looked up at him. "Terrible," he complained.

"Well, you'll be back to your old self before you know it," Brady promised, trying to sound as positive as possible.

Tyler was up and he crawled up next to him as he asked, worried, "He's not going to die, is he?"

"No, he's not going to die, Tyler," he told the boy. "Whatever made you ask something like that?"

"You looked so worried," Tyler answered. "I thought that maybe...maybe..." He sniffled. "Well, you know."

Yes, he knew, Brady thought. The boy had let his imagination get the better of him. "Don't worry, Ty." He hugged the boy to him. "Toby will be back to his old self very soon."

Tyler rolled that over in his head. "Can it not be too soon?" he asked.

"Why would you say that?" he wanted to know.

Tyler tugged on the bottom of Brady's sweatshirt, beckoning him to bend down to his level. "He's nicer this way. Doesn't call me any funny names or anything," he whispered.

"Well, when your brother gets better, we'll have a talk with him about that," Brady promised. That seemed to placate Tyler. "All right, boys, what would you like for breakfast?" he asked, doing his best to pretend everything was going as usual.

Toby, who looked as if he was slipping in and out of consciousness, stared up at Brady. He shook his head. "I'm not hungry."

"Now there's a first," he said, trying to lighten the mood because Tyler looked apprehensive as he stared at his brother. Toby had always been an eating machine.

"Maybe we should take him to the hospital," Brady murmured, feeling uneasy about the situation. What if he got really bad?

"Hospital?" Tyler cried, his voice going up. The word hospital made him think of his parents. His grandmother had told him that his parents had been taken to the hospital and had died there. The facts had gotten muddled, but the effect remained. "Is he going to die?" the little boy cried, his eyes welling up immediately.

"No, he's not going to die," Brady said firmly, trying to reassure Tyler. "I'm just a little worried, but we're not going to the hospital yet. Let's wait a little and see if your brother can get better on his own," he told Tyler.

He fervently hoped he wasn't being too lax. By the same token, he didn't want Tyler to panic.

Brady looked toward the door, willing Harper to come back and take over. She had a way of making everything seem as if it was going to be all right.

He never needed to be reassured more than he did right at this moment.

Chapter Fifteen

All things considered, Toby's fever cleared up rather quickly. But it was obvious to Harper that the little boy wasn't back to his normal self. Whatever he had come down with was lingering in his system. The mischievous glint was gone from his eyes and his behavior was entirely subdued.

That was when she put in a call to the recently built Rambling Rose Pediatric Center and asked to speak to the boys' pediatrician, Wayne Patterson. She wanted to be sure she wasn't being too laid-back about the whole thing. The doctor himself came on the phone. He listened quietly to her narrative, then said something that put her mind at ease, indicating that he was on top of the situation.

"Sounds like Toby caught what's been making the rounds lately," Dr. Patterson told her. "You say that Toby's fever only lasted for the day and that it's gone now?"

"Yes, but he doesn't have any of his usual energy," she told the doctor.

"That's normal, too," the doctor confirmed. "Just keep him resting for as long as possible. Be sure to give him plenty of liquids and see that he eats well. No junk food," Dr. Patterson specified. "This should run its course in a few days, tops. If it doesn't, or he starts to regress, call my office immediately and bring him in. But between the two of us, I don't think you have anything to worry about," the doctor concluded.

That was a relief, Harper thought. She had begun to think that she was being too blasé. "Thank you, Doctor."

"My pleasure, Ms. Radcliffe," the pediatrician replied.

Though heartened by the pediatrician's prognosis, Harper still remained at the house for the duration of Toby's confinement. Tyler, too, stayed with his brother, no doubt still concerned. For the most part, rather than video games, she had all of them playing simple board games that the twins had brought with them when they moved to Rambling Rose.

When they grew tired of playing those, she read stories to them, holding Toby and Tyler captive by doing different voices for the various characters in the stories.

Since she was there, keeping the twins occupied, this allowed Brady to continue working at the hotel. But he made a point of trying to keep his hours reasonable so he could get home before either of the twins was asleep. He felt it only fair to provide Harper with at least temporary relief since she had agreed to stay at his house.

However, today Brady was unable to come home as early as he had the two previous days, although he did call to check on Toby's condition. When he finally did get home, no one was downstairs in the family room or the living room.

Growing apprehensive—had Toby gotten worse and been taken to the emergency room?—he went looking for her and the twins.

Taking the stairs, he experienced a sense of relief when he heard what sounded like a rollicking story being played out.

And then he heard the twins laughing.

Both of them, he realized.

That meant that Toby had to be getting better,

he thought, pleased. He hadn't heard Toby laugh since the boy had gotten sick.

Brady took the rest of the stairs two at a time. From the sound of it, he expected to find Harper and the boys gathered around the small TV he had brought into the twins' room.

When he reached the bedroom doorway, Brady was surprised to discover that there was no television program or Blu-ray Disc being played. All the different voices he had heard were coming from one source.

Harper.

Fascinated, he stood just shy of the doorway, listening to the story she told for several minutes—until Tyler looked up and became aware of his presence.

"Unca Brady, you're home!" the boy cried, running up and then throwing his arms around Brady's waist, hugging him as hard as he could.

Surprised as well as pleased, Brady smiled down at the boy, giving Tyler a hug back.

"It sure looks that way," Brady said to the boy. One arm around Tyler's shoulders, he guided the boy back to Toby's bed. "So how are you two feeling?" he asked the twins.

"Great!" Tyler cried with enthusiasm. He had never caught Toby's flu.

"I'm getting better all the time," Toby proudly

announced, then pouted, "But Harper won't let me get out of bed to play."

"Harper's a wise lady," Brady told the boy solemnly. "If I were you, I'd listen to what she has to say."

It was obvious that Toby clearly thought he was missing out on something. But instead of arguing with Brady—or Harper—he just sighed dramatically, a clear sign to Brady that the boy still wasn't operating at a hundred percent of his normal energy.

Well, he'd take what he could get, Brady thought. He glanced toward Harper, thinking that the woman had to have supernatural powers. There was no other explanation for Toby's behavior.

Harper took advantage of the slight lull. "Have you eaten yet?" she asked Brady.

He shook his head. "I came straight home so I could see these guys before you put them to bed," he confessed, smiling at the twins again. "Work ran long today," he said, explaining why he had arrived home later than he had the last few days.

Harper nodded. "Well, I left dinner on the stove, waiting for you. I'll go down and heat it up a little while you visit with the boys. Then, when I come upstairs, we'll trade places and you can go down and have dinner. How's that sound?" she wanted to know.

"Yes, ma'am, that sounds fine," Brady responded, saluting her.

The twins dissolved in a fit of giggles, as if they had been privy to a great joke.

Their response warmed Brady's heart. He realized how much he had missed the sound of their combined laughter these last few days.

He also realized, when he went back downstairs a little later after Harper had warmed up dinner, just how right all of this felt to him: coming home at night to find Harper there. Waking up in the morning to the sound of her moving around, usually in the kitchen, preparing breakfast for everyone.

It wasn't the meals—which were always uncommonly good—it was her presence in the house that made the difference. That made his house feel like a real home. He knew he really didn't want to go back to the way things were.

"Well, I think I finally got them to both fall asleep," Harper announced when she walked into the kitchen some thirty minutes later.

Brady had just finished eating the dinner she had warmed up for him. "Great. Sorry, I didn't mean to disrupt your nighttime routine," he apologized.

"You didn't disrupt it," she told him with a warm smile. "You coming in at that time was only a slight setback. Besides, this is your house," Harper reminded him. "You have a right to come in any time you want, you know."

He really wanted her to know what a difference she had made in all their lives. "You know that I appreciate you doing all this. I couldn't have managed any of this without you. I couldn't have *survived* all this without you," he amended with emphasis.

Her eyes crinkled as her smile grew wider. "Glad I could help."

"Yes, about that..." Brady began, searching for the right words to take advantage of the opening she had just given him.

Harper was about to pick up his empty plates. Something in his voice stopped her and she looked at Brady. "Yes?"

Here goes nothing, he thought. "Will you reconsider becoming a live-in nanny?"

She didn't answer immediately. Instead, Harper thought of all the complications that had arisen at her last job. Being a live-in nanny for the Wheelers had ended with unwanted advances, a terrible misunderstanding and an ultimate boot from her job.

Harper took a breath. "My immediate answer," she told him honestly, "would be no."

Brady realized that it would mean extra work and he thought that was what she was talking about. "I wouldn't expect you to say yes without offering you compensation for the extra time," he told her.

She shook her head. He didn't understand, she thought. "It's not about the money," Harper told him.

He stopped her right there. "I understand that. It's about the twins. But you have to know that they function so much better when you're around. You can make them do things that I just can't. In the few short weeks that you've been part of their lives, you've gotten Toby and Tyler to listen, to sit still and to, if not behave, then to *almost* behave." He laughed dryly. "I don't have to worry if the house will still be standing when I get home at night."

"Now you're exaggerating," she told him.

Brady's dark eyes met hers. "Am I?" he wanted to know.

"Well, at least a little," she allowed with that easy laugh of hers that always seemed to get to him.

He decided to lean on her good will. "It would really be helping me out," Brady told her. "And not only that, but it would also be great for the twins. C'mon," he coaxed. "What do you say? At least give it a trial run. You've got nothing to lose," Brady reasoned, "and the twins would be thrilled to have you around all the time."

She had never been good at saying no and she was having more and more trouble saying no to Brady. That in itself worried her, but for now she pushed that aside and into the background.

"Well," Harper said slowly, already beginning to relent, "I guess I can give it a try."

"Terrific! I promise you won't regret it," he told her enthusiastically.

Brady almost forgot himself and reached out to hug Harper, but he knew that would be totally unprofessional. Stepping over the line.

So he held himself in check. The last thing he wanted was to give her the wrong idea about him—even though it could, just possibly, be the right one. The truth of it was, he did find himself having feelings for her. But those feelings could very well destroy the best thing he had accidentally stumbled across.

A loving nanny for the twins.

So he restrained himself and merely offered Harper his hand.

"Here's to a really great working arrangement," Brady told her, the corners of his mouth curving.

"At least temporarily so," she qualified, shaking the hand he offered.

Brady laughed, finally rising from the table. He was holding his empty dinner dishes. "I'll tell you one thing. You do keep a man on his toes," he said.

She raised an eyebrow. "You mean off-balance?" she asked as she took the dishes from him. Harper brought them over to the sink.

"Yeah, that, too," he agreed, laughing.

Because it was true, he thought. She did keep him off-balance. But lately, especially after these four trying days, he was beginning to find himself leaning in a certain direction, a direction that no longer placed such emphasis on being a bachelor, carefree or otherwise. More important things were beginning to take front and center in his life. Namely the twins—and Harper.

Within another day, Toby's illness was a thing of the past. Very quickly, he was back at preschool and back to his former, very energized self.

"Guess what!" Toby cried, bouncing up and down one afternoon when Harper came to pick him and his twin up from preschool.

Two days had gone by since he had returned to school and it was as if he couldn't even remember ever being sick.

Harper pretended to concentrate in order to come up with an answer. "Your teacher was finally able to tell you and your brother apart?" she teased.

"No, she still can't do that," Toby told her. "But that's not exciting," he pointed out.

Yes, he was definitely back to his old self, Harper thought. She noticed that Tyler looked as if he was bursting with news, as well. Any second now, she knew the twins were going to start competing with one another and jockeying for position.

"All right, spill it. What's so exciting?" Harper asked the boys.

Toby and Tyler answered her in unison. "We're gonna be in the school pa-pa—in the school play," they finally said.

She'd heard that there was going to be a spring pageant, but she thought that was just something that they meant for parents and children to attend and she planned to join the boys and Brady. The thought of actually seeing Toby and Tyler on the stage, performing, had never occurred to her.

"Really?" she asked, mentally taking her hat off to the brave teacher who was going to be in charge of herding the little darlings onto the stage.

"Yeah, really. Guess what we're going to be," Toby said, dancing from foot to foot.

She shook her head. "I don't have a single idea. What?" she asked.

"I'll give you a hint," Toby told her magnanimously. And then he hopped.

"Rabbits?" Harper guessed.

"No!" they cried together. This time they both hopped, then Toby loudly cried, "Rib-bit!"

"We're green," Tyler hinted, lowering his voice.

"Frogs?" Harper guessed, playing along.

"Yeah!" Toby happily declared. "We're frogs. You gotta make our costumes," the twin added as if she should have already known that.

Terrific, Harper thought. She forced a smile to her lips, then said, "Great."

Tyler, ever the practical one, suddenly looked at her and asked, concerned, "You know how to make costumes, right?"

There was no doubt about it. The boy just warmed her heart, Harper thought. "Lucky for you, yes, I do." At least well enough to *pass* for a costume, she thought.

"Teacher says we've gotta learn our lies. Can you help us with that, too?" Toby wanted to know.

Lies? And then it hit her. "Lines, Toby. The word is *lines*. And yes I can," she told him.

He nodded, then looked a little mystified and asked, "What's lines, Harper?"

"Lines are the words you're supposed to say when you're on the stage."

"Learning lines sounds hard," Tyler decided.

She didn't want them getting disillusioned so

easily. "Not really," she told the twins. "It's like a game. It'll be fun," she promised them.

Tyler beamed at her. "Everything's fun with you, Harper."

"Thank you," Harper replied, giving the boys one huge hug. "I feel the same way about you."

"Do you think Unca Brady will want to come to see us be frogs?" Tyler asked.

"Oh, I know he will," Harper answered.

"But he's gonna be working," Tyler worried. "We gotta do it in the daytime."

"Oh, he'll find time for this," Harper promised the little boys. "He wouldn't dream of missing you guys."

"You really think so?" Toby asked, dubious.

"I know so," she assured the boys. She saw Toby and Tyler exchanging looks and grins.

When they grinned like that, it was usually a sign that they were up to something. But for the life of her, Harper hadn't a clue what that could be. For now, she put that sort of thing on the back burner.

"C'mon, boys. Let's go see your teacher so I can get a copy of the script and help you two memorize your lines."

"Yeah, let's!" Toby declared as he and Tyler both took one of her hands in theirs and went back to their classroom.

Chapter Sixteen

"Did ya see us? Did ya see?" Toby cried, all but flying off the stage after the class performance was over. The people in the audience were still applauding, but both the twins were excited and eager to find out how the two most important adults in their lives liked seeing them in the play.

"Yes, we certainly did see you," Brady answered, glancing at Harper. The latter was beaming her approval at the twins. "You were both fantastic!" he said.

"You were the most adorable, believable frogs I have ever seen," Harper said, adding her voice to Brady's. Turning her head so that only Brady could hear her, she whispered, "And their teacher did a brilliant job harnessing all that little-boy energy of theirs and putting it to good use."

"You can sure say that again," Brady agreed with a laugh.

"Say what again? Huh? Say what?" Toby asked, his head popping up in Brady's direction, all but whirling around, first going toward Brady, then to his nanny, finally back again.

"That you were both brilliant playing those frogs," Harper said, thinking fast.

Spotting their uncle Adam and his wife, Laurel, the twins waved at the pair. "There's Larkin's mommy and daddy," Tyler told Harper, pointing them out to her in case she didn't see the couple.

"Honey," Harper began, pretending to grow serious with the boy, "what did I say about pointing to people?"

For the space of a second, Tyler hung his head. "Not to," he answered solemnly. Still, to him pointing out their family seemed like something perfectly normal for him to do.

What Tyler said next caught both her and Brady totally by surprise.

"When you and Unca Brady get married, can we be a family like them?" Tyler wanted to know.

Harper felt all the air completely rush out of her lungs, leaving her somewhat dizzy and disoriented.

Brady saw the expression on Harper's face. She looked as if she had just seen a ghost. He hadn't a clue why she was reacting that way. Did she find the idea of being with him so terribly distasteful, he wondered.

He was going to have to ask her about that later. Right now he felt that he had to say something to keep the twins from asking Harper a lot of possibly uncomfortable questions.

Maybe it was his imagination, but he couldn't help thinking that she seemed as if she wanted to bolt.

"Hold it, boys. Nobody's getting married. Harper is your nanny, not my girlfriend," he reminded the twins pointedly.

Tyler looked at Harper, obviously disappointed. "Is that true?"

Harper nodded. *Nice save*, she thought, although at the same time, she felt a twinge of disappointment herself. "I'm afraid so," she answered out loud.

She needed this job and she knew that the kids needed her. And Brady, she thought, needed her to keep the kids reined in.

Even so, right now all she wanted to do was run away as fast as she could.

Harper closed her eyes for a second, doing her best to exercise control over her reaction. Otherwise, she was going to make herself crazy.

Because she didn't know what else to do, Harper found herself beginning to put up walls between herself and Brady.

But even doing that somehow didn't feel right to her.

For the next few days she did what she could to focus on the job as well as on the twins—and on nothing beyond that. Especially not on their handsome guardian.

But it wasn't easy, especially when circumstances kept throwing her and Brady together.

Circumstances like the upcoming Easter holiday and all that entailed.

As was to be expected, the twins had outgrown their nicer clothes, which meant that Harper needed to take them shopping for new outfits.

"Do we gotta go shopping?" Toby complained, fidgeting at the very thought of having to get new clothes.

"Tell me, do you want to get Easter baskets?" she asked the twins.

"Yeah!" the boys cried in unison.

"Well," Harper told the duo seriously, "the Easter Bunny told me that only good little girls and boys who wear their brand-new Easter outfits will be getting those Easter baskets."

The twins looked at each other, stunned. "For real?" they questioned.

She nodded her head solemnly. "For real," she told them.

Toby sighed as he looked at his brother. And then speaking for both of them, he said in a totally resigned voice, "Well, I guess if we gotta, we gotta."

Glancing over her shoulder, Harper flashed a smile at Brady. The latter looked very impressed. In his experience, even the twins' parents couldn't manage them the way that Harper could.

Since it was a Saturday, all four of them drove to the local shopping center to go shopping.

Once in the store, Harper swiftly made a number of selections for the twins to try on.

Tyler surprised them by keeping a positive outlook on this unwanted excursion. "And if we get new Easter clothes, does that mean we can go on the Easter egg hunt at Unca Brady's hotel?"

"It's not my hotel," Brady corrected the boy. "But yes, if you two get new Easter outfits, you can go on the Easter egg hunt." It seemed like the perfect trade-off, he thought.

Getting the go-ahead on that succeeded in firing up the twins' imagination. "Can we get a pet rabbit, too?" Tyler wanted to know.

Not waiting for his brother to get an answer,

Toby jumped in with a question of his own and, in typical twin fashion, he upped the stakes. "How about a pony? Can we get a pet pony?" he asked eagerly.

Not to be outdone, Tyler piped up with another request of his own. "I want a pet dinosaur."

Meanwhile, as these negotiations were going on, Harper was subtly getting the twins to try on the outfits she had chosen. She eased each boy into the clothes as she continued to distract them by getting them to talk about the pets they wanted Brady to get them.

"What kind of dinosaur?" she asked innocently, as if buying one was actually even a possibility.

"A big one!" Tyler cried.

"Yeah, a big one," Toby yelled enthusiastically. "And green! We want a green one!" he declared.

Damn but she was good, Brady thought, admiring the way Harper worked. She was stimulating their imaginations so that they didn't even realize that she was getting them to try on the various outfits.

The woman really had skills. Brady silently tipped his hat to her.

A passing saleswoman paused to watch this mini-performance with costume changes and nodded with approval. "Your wife is really very

good with your children," she told him. "Most
parents I see around here, especially around
the holidays, usually wind up losing their tem-
pers, screaming at their kids to behave and stop
squirming around while they're getting them to
try on new outfits."

The saleswoman smiled as she nodded at
Harper. "You've really got yourself a good one
here," she told him. Then she turned to the twins.
"You boys listen to your mama." The woman
eyed the outfits that Harper had draped on the
side of a chair. "Looks like she's found some
really nice clothes for you to wear for Easter."
Digging into her pocket, the older woman took
out two little plastic bags. Each was filled with
a rainbow of jellybeans. "Is it all right if I give
them these little bags of jellybeans?"

Harper saw the eager, pleading look on the
twins' faces. "Yes."

The twins practically cheered as the woman
said, "Here you go, boys," and handed each twin
a bag. "Happy Easter."

The title the saleswoman had bestowed on her
had Harper flustered. "I'm not their mother," she
told the woman. "I'm their nanny."

The woman took the correction in stride. "Oh.
My apologies," she said. "I meant no disrespect."
She looked at Harper and Brady. Her expres-
sion seemed to say that if they weren't a couple,

they should be. "It's just that you all made such a perfect picture."

"Pictures are just illusions," Harper told the woman a little too quickly.

"Of course." The saleswoman offered her an embarrassed smile and retreated.

Picking up the clothes that Harper had ultimately selected for the twins, Brady followed behind her and the twins, going to the register.

Harper's reaction to the saleswoman's assumption bothered him. "Just what is your problem?" he asked Harper under his breath, placing his credit card down beside the pile of clothing.

Afraid that this might wind up quickly escalating into something extremely awkward, Harper placed herself between Brady and the boys.

She seemed to almost be shielding them with her body, he thought.

"This is not the time or the place to talk about this," she informed Brady between gritted teeth.

"Fair enough," he agreed as he signed his name on the bottom of the sales receipt. "But this isn't over," Brady informed her. "We're going to talk about this again—and very soon."

A chill ran down her spine. Harper didn't answer him. Instead, placing a hand on each of their shoulders, she ushered the boys out of the store. That left Brady to follow behind, carrying the bags.

He brought the bags over to the car and put them into his trunk.

Because he didn't want to upset the twins—and he did want to be able to talk to Harper freely—Brady waited until he drove them all home.

The twins didn't even take any notice of the silence. They were too busy filling the car with their exuberant, high voices.

But Brady noticed the silence.

As did Harper.

The moment he pulled up in the driveway and the twins were freed from their car seat restraints, the duo bolted into the backyard.

Brady took out the shopping bags and carried them into the house, then left them in the living room. Once he was confident that the twins were playing and occupied, and he and Harper were alone, he cornered Harper, picking up their unfinished conversation.

"Okay, just what was all that about in the store?" Brady wanted to know. When she didn't answer him immediately, he pressed, "Why were you acting so weird?"

"I wasn't acting weird," Harper denied, her voice going up.

Avoiding his eyes, she moved about the kitchen, preparing everyone's lunch.

But Brady wasn't about to back down. As she went from counter to stove, then to the refrigerator, he continued to follow her around. He was determined to get a straight answer out of her.

When she still didn't say anything, he informed her, "Then you weren't in the same conversation as I was back in that store."

He was just going to keep following her until she gave him some sort of an answer, Harper thought, so she turned to him. "All right, maybe I was being a little erratic back there," she admitted. "But you have to understand, I just can't risk another fiasco."

"*Another* fiasco?" Brady echoed. "What was the first one?"

She really hadn't wanted to get into this. With no choice, she gave him an abbreviated version of what had transpired with her last position.

"The last family I worked for, the situation got a little…dicey," she concluded. "It finally got to the point where I decided that I had to leave—"

"What happened?" he wanted to know.

She wasn't ready to get into that. "It doesn't matter," she told him. "What matters is that leaving was very difficult. The little girls I was taking care of…they cried when I left." As she said it, she felt like she was reliving the whole ordeal.

It became almost difficult for her to breathe. "They had gotten too attached to me," she confided.

What she didn't add was that she was afraid that she was getting too attached to Brady and the twins—and that carried its own set of consequences with it.

"I see," Brady responded, thinking the situation over. "Okay," he decided, "maybe I let all this get out of hand." Although he really didn't believe that, it was obvious that Harper did. So, for now, until he could resolve this satisfactorily, Brady humored her. "I'll just remind the kids that it's your job to be with them and nothing more."

He saw that what he had just said had made her wince. Can't win for losing, he thought.

"Now what?" he asked out loud.

"Well, I'm afraid when you put it that way, it makes me sound so...mercenary," she finally complained.

At his wit's end, Brady threw up his hands in frustration. "Women can really be so damn confusing!" he cried.

"I'm not confusing," Harper all but snapped. "Don't you understand? I just don't want Tyler and Toby to get hurt." *Or me, either,* she added silently.

"Well, they wouldn't be if you didn't keep going up and then down and then up again about all of this. It's like trying to keep my eye on a yo-yo or a..."

His voice trailed off as he suddenly looked at her from a brand-new perspective. "Hey, I know what's going on here," he declared as things began coming together in his head.

"What?" she asked apprehensively, not knowing what to expect.

Brady grinned. "You like me." He said it as if it was the final answer to a puzzle.

"Well, of course I like you," she told him. And then it suddenly occurred to her what he meant by that. Harper quickly took back what she'd just said. "But I don't *like* you. Not like that," she cried.

She was scared. He could understand that. In a way, he had to admit that he was, too.

Brady pulled away, letting his hand fall to hers. "I'm sorry. I didn't mean to overstep."

Harper responded, "I know you didn't. Neither of us did. This is mutual. Brady—I just don't want to get carried away."

He met her gaze, and he could see that she was feeling the same conflicted emotions he was. Longing. Desire. Hesitation. It was in her eyes, and the way she had worded her protest.

"Neither do I." His voice was soft, coaxing. Skimming along her skin seductively. And then, just like that, almost against his will, he finally did what he had been dying to do for days now.

He kissed Harper.

As she felt his kiss's effects all but explode throughout her entire body, Harper tried to get a grip on both herself and the situation.

Pulling away from him, she put her hand on Brady's chest, keeping him at bay. "Brady, maybe we shouldn't be doing this," she told him breathlessly. But she knew her words were a lame attempt to put a wall up against the swell of need she felt—and wanted to give in to. Her fingers remained on Brady's chest, feeling him breathe.

Despite what she said, he could see that she wanted this as much as he did. It was in her eyes, and in the way she had worded her protest. But he didn't try to talk her out of pulling away. He just continued looking at her.

And just like that, they were back in each other's arms, kissing again.

Somehow, they had managed to get onto the sofa and the situation only grew hotter and more demanding from that point on.

Passion grew as he went on kissing her. The moment, the feeling, just continued to escalate until they found themselves tottering on the apex of the moment.

Breathing heavily, Brady drew back for a second, knowing that any second now, they would be crossing a line that he hadn't really considered crossing—until just now.

A line that, once crossed, would result in changing everything.

But as he leaned back in, ready to continue, ready to change the entire dynamic of their relationship, it was Harper who surprised him. She put her hands on his shoulders and pushed him back.

Confused, bewildered, Brady looked at her, an obvious question in his eyes.

"I can't," she told him again. "I just can't let this happen." She was crying now and seeing her like that, suffering like that, almost succeeded in breaking Brady's heart.

He tried his best to comfort her, but she shook her head, getting up from the sofa.

"I have to leave," she told him, her voice almost breaking.

Brady didn't understand what she was telling him. "The room?"

Harper shook her head. "No. Here. You, the kids. I have to leave," she repeated, tears sliding down her cheeks.

"But what *about* the kids?" he asked her, trying to make sense of what she was telling him. She kept pointing out how happy being a nanny made her. What was going on here? "They'll be devastated. Not to mention that they'll feel abandoned. And I have to work," he reminded her. "I need you to be here with the twins."

"I won't leave you in the lurch," she told him. "I'll look after them until you can find someone else to take care of them. But I can't live here anymore," she told him. "I'm going to move out," she said in case that wasn't clear.

And then she quickly left the room before she lost her nerve.

Chapter Seventeen

Harper went through the motions of preparing a full dinner for the family as if nothing had happened. For the most part, Brady stayed out of her way, but he did peek into the kitchen a couple of times to make sure that everything was going well—and that she hadn't abruptly left.

When he saw that she was still there, still cooking, he began to hope that maybe Harper had changed her mind about leaving after all. Maybe life might actually go back to what it had been before all this had gone down.

Brady mentally crossed his fingers. After all, if she actually left, he didn't know what he would do without her. He realized that he had grown to care for her a great deal.

However, at the dinner table, Brady noticed that the twins did almost all of the talking, going from one thing to another like bees that couldn't make up their minds which flower to land on.

For her part, Harper hardly said anything at all and that really worried him. He was at a loss as to how to make the situation right without making her feel that he was crowding her.

After dinner was over and Harper had cleared away all the dishes and washed them, instead of joining them in the living room where Brady was playing a game with Toby and Tyler the way she usually did, or taking them out for an evening walk, Harper quietly withdrew and disappeared into her room.

The twins were having an argument over the plot of a cartoon they had watched earlier, but seeing Harper leave the room had brought their "discussion" to a skidding halt.

Tyler looked at Brady, concern etched into his small face. "Is Harper sick?" he wanted to know.

"What makes you think that?" Brady asked, wanting to avoid discussing what was going on with the boys if he possibly could. He sought for a way to redirect the conversation.

"She *always* plays with us," Toby stressed,

speaking up. And then he pointed out the obvious. "She's not playing with us now."

Sensing that the boys needed to talk about it, Brady came as close to the truth as he could. "I think she just wants some time to herself." Mentally, he crossed his fingers that that was all there was to it.

"Did going shopping with us make her tired?" Tyler wanted to know, concern puckering his small face.

"Something like that," Brady answered vaguely.

"Well, I'm going to go and cheer her up," Toby announced. And before Brady could stop him, the twin took off.

The boy was quickly followed by Tyler. It was clear that the twin believed that if one of them could offer comfort, then two could offer twice as much.

Brady stood there for a moment, torn between letting them go and stopping them. He compromised by following the well-intentioned duo to Harper's room.

By the time he had reached it, the twins had already knocked on Harper's door and had gotten her to let them in.

Brady walked into Harper's room in time to see the sight of the nanny's opened suitcase stop the twins dead in their tracks. Something akin to shock registered on their expressive faces.

"Why are you packing up your things?" Tyler wanted to know.

"Are you going somewhere?" Toby asked, frowning at the suitcase.

A horror-stricken look came over Tyler's face as he asked, "Are you going away?"

Harper wasn't about to lie to the twins. "I'm going back to my apartment," she replied, placing a stack of blouses into the suitcase.

That just gave birth to a worse thought. "Are you leaving us?" Toby cried in disbelief.

Harper knew that Brady was watching her and it surprised her that he wasn't interfering or attempting to set the twins straight. Instead, he was leaving this all up to her.

She didn't know whether to feel grateful or feel abandoned.

For the time being, she decided to take the easy way out and just go along with the simplest explanation for her actions. To go into any explanation as to what she was really feeling was just too painful for her. She was afraid that she would start crying.

"Well, you're not sick anymore so you don't need me to be here every night, all night. I still have my apartment," she told them, which was true. Before she had accepted the position as their nanny, she had signed a short-term lease. It wasn't up yet and the landlord had refused to release her from the agreement—which now seemed like a good thing.

"Can't you get rid of it?" Toby wanted to know.

As she packed up the last of her things, she kept her answer simple. "Not really."

Toby's eyebrows knitted together in consternation. "Why?" he wanted to know.

This was harder than she had anticipated. "It's complicated," she answered.

Obviously that still didn't make any sense to the boy. "What does that mean?" he asked.

"It's what grown-ups say when they don't want to tell you something," Tyler, the more sensitive of the two, explained.

This was just going around in circles. It was time to wind the topic up. "I'll be back in the morning to make you breakfast," she promised the twins, zipping the suitcase and swinging it off the bed. "Probably before either one of you even wakes up."

Toby still looked skeptical. But Tyler just wanted something to hold on to. "You promise?" he asked her, looking up into her eyes.

"I promise," she answered without hesitation. "Now behave, both of you. And listen to your uncle Brady. I expect you to be good," she warned, adding, "I'll be back tomorrow for a full report," as she made her way down the stairs.

Setting the suitcase down, Harper extended the handle and pulled the luggage over to the door.

She wanted to pause and blow both boys a kiss, but she knew if she turned around to look at them, she wouldn't be able to make it out the front door. So she just kept going.

She was actually going through with it, Brady thought, watching Harper walk out. He really hadn't thought she would do it. He felt numb, like someone trapped in a bizarre dream, desperate to wake up.

"She left us," Toby cried, his voice vibrated in disbelief.

Tyler sighed heavily. "Everybody leaves us," he said sadly. "Mommy and Daddy left. Harper left and someday," he continued, turning to look at Brady before he said to Toby, "Unca Brady will leave us, too. 'Cause we're bad boys." His lower lip quivered. "Everybody says so."

That was when Brady realized that Tyler was crying and Toby was sniffling, doing his best *not* to cry.

The whole scene—and the declaration behind it—hit Brady like a powerful punch to the gut. He could remember his initial reaction when he found out that he had been appointed the twins' guardian. At the time all he had wanted to do was turn tail and run.

But at this moment, he realized that he didn't feel that way any longer. Somewhere along the line, without being aware of it, he had grown to love these two over-energized little boys. Love them fiercely with all his heart.

"Come here, guys," he said to them, sitting down on the sofa.

He drew the twins to him. For once, there was no jockeying for position, no fighting over who sat where. The twins just sank down on the sofa, one on either side of their "Unca" Brady.

Brady put one arm around each small boy and hugged the sad little soldiers to him.

"I'm not going to go anywhere," he told them. "And I will *always*, always be here to take care of you."

Tyler looked up at him. "You promise?"

"I promise," he told the twins, adding, "Even when you don't want me to."

"We'll always want you to," Tyler said solemnly, speaking for both himself and for Toby.

Though touched by the boy's serious expression, Brady could only laugh. "Remember saying that in ten or eleven years," he told the boy, knowing firsthand what teenage kids could be like.

"We'll remember," Tyler promised, nodding his head up and down.

"Yeah, we'll remember for a hundred years, not just eleven," Toby told Brady confidently.

The serious moment was lightened. *We'll see*, Brady thought, feeling his heart filling with love.

He continued sitting there with the twins, doing his best to offer them comfort and reassurance.

He also found himself thinking that maybe Harper had been right after all. The twins were getting too attached to her.

As for him, well, it was too late for him. He was attracted to Harper as well as attached and there was nothing he could do about it.

For whatever reason, she seemed to have some sort of emotional baggage weighing her down. She needed to deal with that before she could deal with anything else.

The way Brady saw it, it was in the best interests of everyone involved if he started to keep his distance from Harper. No matter how difficult that would be.

He believed her when she said she would be back in the morning and believed her when she said she intended to remain until he found someone to take her place. But even that wasn't going to be easy. He had been through interviews looking for a competent nanny before Harper ever came on the scene and *none* of the women he had spoken to even came *close* to holding a candle to her.

He had no reason to believe that things would be any different now than they had been when he had initially started his search. And after having Harper in their lives, he and the twins would just be settling for second best no matter who he hired.

Though he had low expectations, Brady made sure he put the word out that he would be interviewing nannies. If Harper was set on leaving, then it was best for all concerned if he ripped the Band-Aid off as soon as possible.

It was as arduous a task as he expected and his heart really wasn't in it, but he plowed through the interviews, talking to one woman after another. He finally settled on a middle-aged woman with two degrees in child psychology. Slightly heavyset, Sharon Overton had short, fluffy gray hair, thin lips and brown eyes. She seemed qualified and pleasant enough, but he felt she had no spark, no imagination.

Still, she was certainly better than the squadron of nannies he had already interviewed.

She just wasn't Harper, he silently admitted, but then, no one was.

The interview over, Mrs. Overton was set to

start as the twins' nanny at the beginning of April.

When it was finally decided, he told Harper. She received the news stoically.

He put his own interpretation to her behavior. "I know you didn't want to wait until then, but it's the soonest she can come on the job."

"I understand," Harper replied quietly. She could feel sadness flooding through her and did what she could to block the feeling. "In the interim," she continued, "we still have to get through Easter."

"You *are* coming with us to the big Easter egg hunt, right, Harper?" Tyler asked hopefully, watching her face.

"You said you would. You promised," Toby reminded her. "And we'll be on our best behavior," he declared, as if that would help to convince her.

"Well, I certainly can't resist an offer like that," Harper told the twins. "C'mon," she coaxed, "let's get the two of you dressed."

"And then can we help you get dressed?" Toby offered innocently.

"I can manage," she assured the boy with a wide smile. "But thank you. That was very thoughtful of you to offer." Moved, Harper kissed each of the boys on the top of his head.

Oh lord, she was going to miss them, she thought. Really miss them.

Harper felt a sadness fill her as she realized that this would probably be the last time the four of them would be together like this. April would be here in the blink of an eye and with April came the new nanny.

She told herself not to dwell on that.

Everything was going to work out for the best, she promised herself as they approached the Hotel Fortune.

"Oh boy, look at all these people!" Toby cried, his eyes growing wide as he glanced from one group to another. He didn't know where to look first. "Are they all gonna be hunting for Easter eggs?" he asked Harper. It was obvious that the idea worried him. "There won't be any eggs left," he lamented.

"Only the kids will be doing all the hunting for eggs," she told him with a wink. "Besides, you and your brother will probably outdo them all," she predicted with pride.

The twin puffed up his chest, as did his brother. "Yeah," he agreed gleefully.

The lobby of the hotel was crowded to overflowing and moving around was a challenge. There was even a long line of patrons waiting to be seated at Roja. It seemed like everyone at Rambling Rose wanted to have brunch at the hotel, Harper thought. She was about to say as much to Brady when she suddenly spotted a familiar face.

The *last* face she wanted to see.

It was her old boss, Justine Wheeler, the soon-to-be ex-wife of the man Justine had accused her of having an affair with. The woman who had also angrily accused her of trying to wreck her marriage, a marriage that was already beyond repair.

Realizing she had stopped moving, Brady turned around to look at her.

"Is something wrong?" he asked Harper. "You suddenly look awfully pale. Are you feeling all right?" he wanted to know, concerned.

She grasped at the way out he had just handed her. "As a matter of fact, I'm not. Excuse me, please," she said and without any further explanation or waiting for Brady to respond, Harper quickly ducked into the ladies' room.

Startled, Tyler watched his nanny take off. "Where's Harper going?" he asked Brady.

"She's going to the ladies' room, Tyler," Brady told the boy.

Toby asked the question he had always heard put to him whenever he said he needed to go to the bathroom himself. "Why didn't she go at home?"

"Maybe she didn't think of it when she was home." Brady was still looking toward the ladies' room, wondering if he should be concerned. "Don't worry. I'm sure she'll be right back," he said for the twins' benefit. "Meanwhile, why don't we look around?" he suggested, ushering the twins toward where the egg hunt was soon to be held.

She knew she was hiding, but what choice did she have, Harper thought.

She stayed in the ladies' room longer than she wanted to, trying to figure out what to do.

By the time Megan Fortune came in, looking for her, Harper had decided that she needed to go home.

"Harper, are you all right?" Megan asked her, looking concerned. "Brady sent me," she explained. "He told me that he was worried about you. Should he be?"

She didn't have time to worry about Brady. She had a feeling all hell was going to break loose any moment now. "I need to go home, Megan," Harper blurted out. She felt like a mouse, trapped in a maze with no way out. "Coming here was a big mistake."

Megan looked at her, totally confused and not a little puzzled. "I don't understand. Why would coming here be a mistake?"

Harper was searching for a rational way to

explain this to Brady's cousin when Justine Wheeler chose that moment to walk in.

The second that the tall, thin well-dressed woman saw Harper, a condescending, nasty expression slid over her sharp features. The look in her eyes bordered on hatred.

"Well, well, well, look what the cat dragged in. Apparently the rumors that I heard were true," she said smugly. "I see that you're here, trying to sink your hooks into another one."

Megan was instantly protective and indignant at the tone this woman was using, not to mention what she was saying. "Now just hold on, lady. You can't talk to Harper that way," Brady's cousin declared angrily.

Justine raised her chin, her eyes turning into angry slits. "I can and I will. I see she had you fooled, but allow me to set you straight about this she-devil.

"Pollyanna here is a gold digger looking for her next sugar daddy. Aren't you, honey?" Justine asked condescendingly, smirking at Harper. "She swooped into my life, all phony sweetness and light, mesmerizing my husband who she decided was going to be her next victim. But I saw right through her and put an end to it. I fired *her*," the woman declared proudly, "and threw *his* ass out. Make sure she doesn't get near your man," Justine warned, "unless you're ready to lose him."

Harper wanted to defend herself, to put Justine in her place, but what was the point? The more she would protest the picture the hateful woman painted, the more tangled up the whole situation would become. Justine had already made up her mind about her and from the looks of it, she wasn't about to hesitate spreading these terrible lies about her.

She obviously seemed to relish it.

Feeling like she was suddenly suffocating, Harper raced out of the ladies' room.

"That's right, run away," Justine stood in the ladies' room doorway, shouting after her. "But you can't outrun the truth!"

The taunt echoed through the hallway.

Chapter Eighteen

Despite all the other people and their children milling around the hotel lobby, Brady saw Harper coming toward him across the floor. It concerned him that she looked even worse now than she had when she had gone running into the ladies' room.

"Harper, did Megan find you?" he questioned, then realized that she must have. "Is everything all right?" The woman was as white as a sheet. "You look like you've seen a ghost."

Harper didn't bother commenting on his observation. All she told him was, "I have to leave now, Brady. I just came looking for you so I could tell you that I was going."

"Now?" he asked, perplexed. The whole point of coming here was for the twins to take part in the egg hunt. It had been Harper's idea in the first place. That was why they had gone shopping for new Easter clothes. He knew the boys would be really disappointed if they wound up missing the hunt.

"Now," Harper answered. "I'll get a cab. You stay with the boys. I'll call you later and explain everything."

He still couldn't believe that she was leaving. She hadn't been that ill when they left the house. How had she gotten so sick so fast? "But—"

"C'mon, Unca Brady. We gotta go!" Toby insisted. He pointed to the giant, six-foot white bunny that was crossing the lobby and heading toward the garden. "They're gonna start the egg hunt," the twin cried eagerly, pulling on Brady's leg as he tried to get "Unca" Brady to follow him.

Brady found himself torn between being a good guardian and being there for Harper, who was obviously in some sort of pain.

He hadn't counted on something like this happening. "I—" he began.

Harper shook her head. "That's okay," she assured Brady. All she wanted to do right now was to get away. "You should go," she urged him.

To keep Brady from arguing any further, she

quickly hurried away from him as well as from the twins and headed straight for the hotel's main exit.

"C'mon, Unca Brady, let's go," Toby cried. "The bunny's getting away!"

Grabbing Brady's hand, Toby wrapped his small, sturdy fingers around it and began yanking him out into the hotel garden.

The hotel staff in charge of decorations had been working all week to turn the garden setting into an Easter wonderland for what promised to be the first annual egg hunt.

Brady had already lost sight of Harper. Well, at least the egg hunt would divert the twins from the fact that Harper had just taken off like that, he thought. He was doing his best to look on the bright side—if there actually was a bright side to all this.

"All right, let's go," he agreed, picking up his pace as he tried to keep up with the twins.

Harper managed to get to her apartment in record time. The moment she unlocked the door and walked in, it felt small to her, even for a studio. Almost claustrophobic, she realized. She found herself feeling trapped.

But she was not about to venture out again.

Not until she mentally made peace with what she assumed was taking place beyond her front door.

She had no doubt that her former employer

was out for revenge. Justine's vicious take on what she believed had happened between her nanny and her husband was undoubtedly all over the Hotel Fortune by now.

The thought of having to face that wall of hatred was almost more than Harper could bear. It felt practically suffocating to her. And the awful thing about the whole situation was that she had never done *anything* to encourage Justine's husband. Not once.

The only thing she had ever been guilty of was being polite and not telling Edward Wheeler what he could do with all his unwanted attention.

Maybe she should have, Harper thought now. But it would have done no good.

Struggling to calm down, Harper took out her cell phone and placed it on the tiny coffee table in front of her so she could quickly pick it up when it rang.

It didn't ring.

Fifteen minutes went by. She decided that Brady *wasn't* going to call.

Well, she supposed that she couldn't really blame the man. When she had fled the hotel ladies' room, Justine's voice had been ringing in her ears. The woman had been extremely passionate in her diatribe. By now, everyone at the hotel's Easter festivities knew what Justine *believed* had happened.

Harper convinced herself that she was better off leaving.

No one should have to deal with those kind of lies.

"My lord, Brady, you should have heard that witch shrieking and carrying on," Megan told her cousin after she had finally found him. The moment she did, she quickly reported, in a nutshell, the reason she felt that Harper had taken off the way she had. "I would have left the shrew, too, if I were her husband." Just thinking about what had been said made Megan shiver. "That witch accused Harper of the most awful things! Things I *know* she couldn't have done," Megan said loyally. "Harper is just too good a person to have done any of those things."

It was all coming together now and making sense, Brady thought, listening to what his cousin was telling him. He understood now why Harper had been so distressed about her former employer—and why she wouldn't talk about it.

Harper had never struck him as a woman who spoke ill about someone, no matter how much they might deserve it. Still, he felt that she should have come to him about it. He would have listened to her and more important, he would have believed her and helped her deal with it.

As Megan said, Harper was just too nice. He,

on the other hand, knew how to handle vicious, mean-spirited people.

Momentarily turning away from the twins, Brady told his cousin that he appreciated having her go after Harper. "And thanks for telling me all this," he said, taking out his cell phone. There was no question in his mind that he needed to clear all this up and get Harper to come back. She needed to know that he didn't believe any of the lies the Wheeler woman was telling. "I have to call Harper and—"

The rest of what he was about to tell his cousin was cut short when they, as well as everyone around them, heard the awful scream.

Brady swung around to find that Toby, who had been running around the garden only a second ago, was flat on his back at the base of one of the trees.

He, Megan and Tyler, not to mention a number of other people, instantly ran over to the screaming boy.

"What happened?" Brady cried, stunned. How could this have happened? He had only looked away from Toby for a minute.

Maybe less.

Stunned, Toby could only cry in pain. Tyler quickly filled them all in. "Toby climbed up that tree." He pointed up to one of the higher branches. "He thought there were Easter eggs in that nest up there."

Tyler's explanation was drowned out by a fresh wave of Toby's screams. "My arm! It hurts, it hurts," the boy sobbed.

"I'll call an ambulance," Megan told her cousin. She looked sympathetically at Toby as she waited for her 9-1-1 call to go through. "Hang in there, Toby," she encouraged the boy.

Brady couldn't help it. He looked anxiously around the gathered crowd, hoping against hope that he'd see Harper making her way toward them. But he knew better. This was now the new normal, which meant that he was going to have to handle this situation without her.

He knelt down beside Toby and reassured him. But it was Tyler who shifted nervously from foot to foot. "Is he going to die?" he asked Brady, terrified.

Brady took the boy's hands in his. "Nobody's going to die, Tyler," Brady told him as calmly as he could, secretly relieved that he was able to say that to him. "Toby's going to be just fine."

As the sound of an approaching ambulance pierced the ongoing commotion, he wished he could say the same for himself.

"I'm afraid that the boy's arm is broken, Mr. Fortune," the young emergency-room physician told him after he had looked at the X-rays that had been taken of Toby's injuries. "Frankly, considering that Toby fell out of that tree, he's very lucky that his arm is the only thing he broke."

"I don't feel lucky," Toby complained. "It hurts!"

The physician, Dr. Neubert, looked sympathetically at the little boy. "I'm sure it does, but the good news is it's a clean break and considering how young Toby is," he told Brady, "it should heal fast." He smiled at Toby. "You'll be back to running around in no time," Dr. Neubert assured him.

Despite the positive news, Brady could see that Toby was doing his best not to cry.

The twin's lower lip quivered as he looked at him and said, "I want Harper, Unca Brady."

It killed him to have to tell the boy, "I'm afraid Harper's not here, Toby."

"Where is she?" Tyler piped up, ready to go looking for the nanny if it would make his brother feel better—because that would make him feel better, too.

Brady glanced at Megan, who had driven Tyler in his car to the hospital while he rode with Toby in the ambulance. He really didn't want to talk about this right now but Megan silently encouraged him. "Harper's home, Tyler."

"Home?" Tyler echoed, confused. "What's she

doing home?" he wanted to know. It didn't make sense to him. Toby needed her. She was always there when they needed her.

"She wasn't feeling well," Brady answered, sounding a little short. He saw Tyler's face fall and immediately felt bad as he apologized. "I'm worried about your brother, too, Ty. Why don't you keep him company for a minute? I want to talk to the doctor about something."

"About Harper not feeling well?" Tyler questioned.

Going on with life after Harper if he couldn't convince her to come back wasn't going to be easy, Brady thought. But that was something he would tackle later. The immediate thing was making sure that Toby received the proper care.

"No," he told the twin, "about Toby. I'll be right back," he promised as he stepped away. "Dr. Neubert," he called out to the ER physician, "I want to ask you a question." He stepped out into the hallway, the doctor following him.

Brady was in such a hurry to talk to the busy doctor, he didn't realize that he had left his cell phone on the chair next to Tyler.

But Tyler spotted it immediately.

Megan was in the small, curtained exam room with them. Right now she was talking to Toby. Taking advantage of her inattention, Tyler quickly put his hand over his uncle's cell phone and moved over to the furthest corner of the room. He turned his back to his brother and Megan.

Brady had left his cell phone unlocked. Tyler and his brother had cut their eyeteeth on cell phones, frequently playing games on their parents' and then Brady's phones when he let them. And he'd watched his uncle make enough calls that he knew exactly what to do. Tyler hit the folder icon for Contacts and scrolled through the names. Now he was grateful that Harper had worked with him and Toby to learn to write all their names. He recognized the name he was looking for.

Harper's.

Thinking that his "unca" would be back at any second, Tyler hit the little green arrow. He listened to the phone on the other end ring.

Harper saw Brady's name and number pop up. The second it did, her heart began pounding. She still had no idea what she was going to tell him, but right now, all that mattered to her was that Brady *was* calling.

"Hello?" she said uncertainly.

"Harper?"

That wasn't Brady.

For a second, the sound of the childish voice

on the other end threw her, not to mention that she was incredibly disappointed.

Brady wasn't calling her. One of the twins was. "Tyler?" she guessed because he was the more subdued one of the duo. "Honey, why are you calling me? Where's your uncle Brady?"

"We're in the hospital, Harper," Tyler told her, distress vibrating in his voice.

Harper's mind instantly began racing as all sorts of scenarios occurred to her. Her stomach tightened. "What are you doing in the hospital?"

"There was an accident, Harper," the boy blurted out. "Unca Brady needs you. Please come," he begged.

"Tyler? What kind of an accident?" Harper asked the boy. "Tyler?"

The only thing she heard in response to her questions was a dial tone.

Stunned, she stared at the cell phone.

An accident.

Harper's hand was trembling as she put her cell phone back in her pocket.

Her heart was pounding hard in her chest as she got her purse and found her car keys. Terrifying realizations filtered through her mind.

If one of the twins was calling her, that meant that Brady wasn't able to call himself.

Oh lord, had that horrible woman sought him out? Had Brady been so upset, so mad that he'd gotten into an accident after hearing Justine call her all those awful names?

What if he had been driving home with the kids and— A horrible chill went down her spine as she thought about Brady and the twins being hurt—or worse.

What if in Brady's case it *had* been worse?

He had to be unconscious because if he wasn't, why would Tyler be calling her instead of Brady?

What if it was worse than being unconscious, her mind posed.

What if—?

"Oh please don't let him die," she cried out loud as she raced to her car.

Harper didn't remember driving to the hospital. All she remembered was praying, as she flew through the lights, that she wasn't too late.

Nothing else mattered except that.

Brady couldn't die, Harper kept thinking over and over. He couldn't die.

She didn't remember parking her car. All she was aware of was running and praying.

Her heart in her throat, she asked the woman at the reception desk if a Brady Fortune had been brought into the hospital in the last few hours.

"Fortune, Fortune," the young brunette muttered under her breath as she scrolled through the list of names of the people who had been seen in the emergency room in the last few hours. "No, no Brady Fortune," she told Harper, looking up. "But there was a Toby Fortune brought in a while ago," she said. "They're still in the ER. I can—"

The receptionist didn't get a chance to finish. Harper was already running to the double doors that divided the ER from the rest of the first floor.

"You can't just go in there like that," the receptionist proclaimed, standing up so her voice would carry.

Harper only heard the woman as just so much background noise, barely paying attention to what she said.

He wasn't dead. Brady wasn't dead.

Those words beat like a refrain, over and over again, in her brain.

He wasn't dead.

But what was Toby doing in the ER?

All sorts of concerns crowded her brain.

She had no idea which exam room Toby and Brady was in, but she was prepared to go into each and every one until she either found them or they dragged her away.

But as it turned out, she didn't have to do either.

As soon as she stepped into the ER, she saw Brady standing in the hallway outside a room, talking to a nurse.

She didn't hear what they were saying. She

didn't *care* what they were saying. All that mattered was that Brady was there, standing up and talking.

He hadn't been hurt.

"Brady!" Harper cried half a beat before she threw herself, sobbing, into his arms. "You're not dead!"

He had no idea what to make of the emotional display or where she might have gotten the idea that he was dead. All he knew was that Harper was here, in his arms, and she had never felt so good to him as she did right at this moment.

He only realized that she was sobbing as he continued holding her.

Chapter Nineteen

Tyler threw his arms around her leg and wiggled in between Harper and Brady. "Harper, you came!" he cried excitedly.

"Hey, me, too!" Toby piped up, unable to reach Harper from his bed, but there was no way he wanted to be left out. "I'm the one who fell out of the tree!" the twin complained.

Wiping away her tears, she entered the room and embraced Toby, careful not to touch his cast. She knew that could wind up hurting the boy. "You don't have to tell me," she assured him. "I know that—and don't you ever do that to me again," she warned him. "I was worried sick."

"No, no more flying squirrel tricks for him,"

Brady declared, looking directly at the injured twin. "Right, Toby?"

"Don't worry, Unca Brady. I learned my lesson good," the boy told him solemnly.

Brady sighed as he rolled his eyes. "Oh, if only I could believe that."

"I really mean it, Unca Brady," Toby vowed, awkwardly crossing his heart with his left hand.

Twisting around to look up at Harper, who had stepped back and was leaning against Brady, Tyler hopefully asked, "Are you gonna go home with us, Harper?"

With all her heart, she really wanted to. But she had actually resigned from the position and Brady had hired someone else to take her place, so it was all out of her hands now.

"That's up to your uncle Brady," Harper said.

Tyler turned to face his guardian now. "Can she come home with us, Unca Brady?"

"Yeah, can she? Pleeeease?" Toby asked, adding his voice to the entreaty.

Brady was with the twins on this, but he didn't want to pressure Harper into agreeing to anything. "Sure. But only if she wants to."

"Do ya, Harper?" Tyler asked eagerly.

Toby gave her the most pathetic look as he echoed Tyler. "Do ya?"

Harper grinned broadly at the two boys. "Just try and stop me."

"Nobody's gonna stop you, Harper," Toby guaranteed. "Right, Unca Brady?"

Brady smiled as his eyes met Harper's. "Right," he agreed.

Brady brought his vehicle directly up to the hospital entrance as Harper stood to the side. She was holding on to Toby's wheelchair while Tyler waved madly at Brady just in case he didn't see them.

Toby was ready to break into a run and wasn't happy about being restrained in the wheelchair this way. "I broke my arm, not my leg. Why do I gotta sit in this stupid wheelchair?" he wanted to know.

"It's hospital policy, Toby," Harper told the boy. "You don't want to make anyone unhappy by breaking the rules now, do you?"

Toby hung his head and sighed. "No, ma'am."

She patted the arm that wasn't in a cast. "Good boy," she praised, just as Brady brought his vehicle to a stop before them.

"Ready?" he asked Toby, getting out.

"Oh, so ready," Toby declared with enthusiasm. "I just wanna go home with Harper."

Brady glanced in her direction and said, "Me, too."

Harper's heart warmed and swelled.

The next moment Harper secured Tyler into

his car seat while Brady did the same with Toby, lifting the injured twin because he was able to handle the heavy cast more easily than Harper. But when it came to securing the car-seat straps, Toby spoke up, asking that Harper do it. He even added "Please" to clinch his request.

"I'd be happy to," Harper told the twin.

Tyler leaned over, watching Harper as she finished securing his brother in the car seat. "I guess we're all back together again," Tyler announced happily.

"It certainly looks that way," Brady answered. "I can come by with one of my brothers and we can bring your car to the house later," he told Harper. Right now he knew it was important for Toby to be assured that Harper was coming home with them.

Getting into the front seat behind the steering wheel, Brady glanced at Harper as he started up the car. He couldn't begin to put into words how happy he was to have her here with them now.

After turning on the engine, he pulled out of the parking lot.

The words burned on her tongue. Harper couldn't keep this to herself any longer. She leaned in toward Brady so her voice wouldn't carry to the backseat as she told him, "I really tried to fight this, to stay away, but I just simply can't." She flushed, embarrassed, thinking of what had transpired earlier today. "I can only imagine what you might think of me."

He knew what she was talking about. "I only heard a little bit from Megan about what happened before Toby fell out of the tree." But then, he didn't need to hear everything. "Why on earth would you think that I would take that woman's word over yours?"

Harper shrugged. She couldn't really explain it. "I was just afraid, that's all. People tend to believe the worst."

"I don't," he told her simply.

She glanced over her shoulder at the duo behind them, but the twins, thanks to the extremely emotionally trying day they had both put in, were exhausted and had already fallen asleep.

Satisfied that the twins wouldn't overhear her, Harper turned around to face Brady. It was time that he heard the truth.

"I didn't realize what was going on at first but it turned out that Justine's husband began paying unwanted attention to me almost from the beginning. And he started complimenting me. First about the way I was handling his daughters, then about the way I looked and dressed.

"I thought maybe I was imagining things, but then he would find ways to corner me. I knew for a fact that he was seeing other women behind his wife's back and he tried more than once to add me to the pack. I needed the job—especially after Justine accepted a job transfer to Rambling Rose and talked me into coming with them. She said she couldn't take care of her children and handle the rigors of working on a new job. She made me feel that I would be abandoning her if I left, so I agreed to come with the family and didn't say anything about the way her husband was behaving."

Harper sighed, remembering. Wishing she didn't. "I just kept trying to avoid Edward—until Justine walked in on us and misunderstood my pushing Edward away as some sort of foreplay. She became livid, called me all sorts of names and fired me on the spot. She also said she was going to see to it that I would never work as a nanny again, here or anywhere else. Ever," Harper emphasized. "Justine had such an authoritative way about her, I was sure everyone would believe her."

Brady blew out a breath, shaking his head. "That's what bullies count on. That they can intimidate you. I'm sorry you had to go through that—and sorry that you *ever* thought I would take her side instead of yours," he concluded.

It all felt like a horrible nightmare now. "I never wanted you to find out and I *never* wanted you and the boys to suffer because of me," she told him.

Brady nodded. "I have to admit, when you first said that, that you needed space between us, I thought you were right." Glancing at her, he saw surprise flicker in her eyes. "That I needed to focus on the twins. I didn't feel that I had any business getting involved with you—or anyone right now—because of this whole situation with the twins. But it's too late. I love you," he told her. As she stared at him, dumbfounded, he went on to say, "The kids love you as well and to be honest, I believe that we're all better off together. You can see that, can't you?" he asked, searching her face.

Her mouth dropped open. She was utterly surprised at the depth of the feelings that Brady had just expressed. Feelings that were entirely mutual.

He had just poured out his heart to her and she hadn't made a single comment. He didn't know what to make of it. "Say something," he told her.

He had managed to take her breath away and she searched for the words to explain her silence and how she felt about what he had just said.

"I didn't think you were interested in a serious relationship," she confessed.

"I wasn't," he answered honestly. "I never expected *any* of this. It just happened. But when it's right," he went on, pulling up into his driveway and turning off the engine to look at her, "it's right. And this," he concluded, drawing her into his arms, "is so *very* right."

Glancing behind him, he saw that the twins were still asleep. So Brady kissed her.

Long and hard.

"I think," he said some moments later, "that should put an end to all the arguments."

She smiled up into his eyes. "At least for now."

There was a lightness within her. A lightness she hadn't thought she would ever be able to experience again, especially after everything that had happened recently.

It felt *wonderful*.

"Does this mean you're really gonna stay, Harper?" came a sleepy voice from the backseat.

Startled, they turned and looked at Tyler. "Hey, I thought you were supposed to be asleep, big guy," Brady said to the boy.

"I woke up," Tyler said, executing a yawn that was bigger than he was.

"So I see," Brady told the twin with a laugh.

Tyler turned to look at Harper. Nobody had answered his question yet. "So are you really gonna stay?" he asked Harper again, then before she could answer, he added, "Please say yes. If you do, it'll make Toby get better real fast," he promised.

"Well, I certainly can't argue with that," she

told the twin. Because he was still waiting, she answered, "Yes, Tyler, I'm going to stay."

But Tyler was still leery and he wasn't completely convinced. "For a long time?" he wanted to know.

"Yes, for a *very* long time," she answered.

"Yay," he cheered. At the same time, he was desperately fighting to keep his eyes open.

"I hope she plans on staying forever," Brady told the boy as he looked at Harper.

For her part, Harper was totally stunned to hear Brady say that. After everything that had happened, she hadn't expected that. "Do you mean it?" she asked him.

"I never meant anything more in my entire life," he replied. "There's a vacant position at the boys' school. I'm sure that the nanny I just hired to take your place—by the way, nobody can take your place—would be happy to transfer there.

"I realize that it might sound like I'm moving a little fast here," he allowed, "but I've already been dragging my feet too long and it's about time I started taking steps that were moving in the right direction—for everyone." He looked into her eyes, searching for a sign that she understood. "Am I making myself clear?" he asked her, afraid that his meaning was getting lost amid the myriad of words that had come spilling out of him just now.

Harper laughed helplessly. "Right now, my head is spinning around with all sorts of thoughts that are chasing each other," she confessed.

"Tell you what. Why don't we take these guys inside and I can try to make myself clearer after we put the twins to bed?" he told her hopefully.

Her eyes smiled at him. "Sounds good to me," she replied.

After getting out of the vehicle, they each took a twin. Harper carried Tyler while Brady had Toby in his arms and brought the boy into the house, careful not to jostle his cast. The last thing he wanted was to cause Toby pain and wake him up.

Harper realized that she still had the keys to Brady's house on her. Tucking Tyler against her shoulder, she reached into her pocket and got the keys out, then unlocked the front door. Holding it open with her back, she allowed Brady to come in and carry Toby slowly up to the room he shared with Tyler.

Harper was right behind them, moving almost in slow motion even though every fiber in her body was urging her to bring the boy into his room as quickly as possible so that she would be free to finally be alone with Brady. She wanted to be able to clear the rest of the air as soon as possible.

But that all involved her own needs, and her

needs, no matter what they were, did not take precedence over the twins' needs. She had lost sight of that for a little bit, Harper now realized, and that sort of thing could never be allowed to happen again.

Tyler moaned a little when she gently placed him down on his bed.

"Shhh, Tyler," she whispered to him. "Go back to sleep. You need your rest so that you can be there to help your brother tomorrow."

Tyler made a noise in response and it sounded as if he thought he was answering her.

Harper smiled down at him. "That's my boy," she coaxed. "Go back to sleep. I'm just going to take these clothes off so you can curl up under your blanket, okay, little man?" She was saying everything in a singsong voice meant to lull Tyler back to sleep.

He cooperated.

Harper finally managed to get Tyler undressed and comfortably lying back in his bed. She covered him with the blanket.

Raising her eyes to Brady's, she nodded toward Tyler and murmured, "Okay, one down, one to go."

Brady looked a little uncertainly at Toby. With his cast, he looked so terribly vulnerable to him right now. "Are you sure you want to undress Toby?" he asked her.

"You want to put him to bed in his clothes?" Harper asked, surprised.

"Well, given the circumstances, I'd rather do that than risk waking him up so that we get him into his pajamas. In this case, I think it's more important to let him sleep than to get him out of his Easter outfit." Having stated his case, Brady looked at her quizzically. "How about you?"

Smiling, she nodded her head. "My kid brother who would totally agree with you. As a matter of fact, he would be on your side even if you said that Toby should get to fall asleep in his street clothes every night."

"You don't talk about him often," Brady observed. He took her filling in the blanks as a sign that she was finally beginning to trust him. "You said he's in the army. Do you miss him?"

She was intent on carefully taking off Toby's shoes and socks. Finished, she placed them both neatly on the floor.

"Absolutely," she said with feeling, "My brother was kind of wild when he was a kid. The complete opposite of me. He was always getting into things, exploring." She smiled, remembering. "Jack took off right after high school and wound up enlisting in the army. Right now, he's going from one base to another, seeing the world and being as happy as the proverbial clam." Her smile widened as fond memories crowded in her head. "He's living life the way he always dreamed," she told Brady.

"And you?" Brady asked. "What is it that you always wanted?"

She secured Toby's blanket, making sure he remained covered. "To be exactly where I am," she told him. "Being the boys' nanny."

"Like I said when you first came to work here, taking care of the twins, I don't know how I got so lucky, but I know better than to question my good fortune—and theirs." The corners of his mouth quirked in an amused smile as the word replayed itself in his head. "You should only pardon the pun."

Her eyes crinkled as she stepped back, away from the boy's beds, and moved closer to the door. "I will if you will," she told him.

"Do you want to go into your room and have that talk now?" he asked Harper.

Harper looked over her shoulder. The twins were both asleep. With any luck, they would continue sleeping until morning.

"I think it's safe to leave them now," she whispered to Brady.

"Okay, then," Brady replied, gesturing toward the doorway. "Lead the way."

Chapter Twenty

The moment she walked into the room and heard the door close behind her, something told Harper that this time, it was going to be different.

A warm shiver shimmied down her spine and then her skin heated as she turned around to face Brady.

Her breath caught in her throat as he cupped her face in his hands.

"I don't need any explanations, Harper," he told her quietly.

Her mouth felt dry as she tried to talk. "Are you sure? Because I feel like I owe you one," Harper told Brady.

The space between them had managed to

grow smaller. "You don't owe me anything," he assured her. "Just always know that I'll have your back, no matter what," he said just before he brought his mouth down on hers.

The moment he did, Harper could feel it. She could feel a tidal wave suddenly swelling up and then washing over her with incredible power until every single part of her was drenched.

Her heart pounding like a giant timpani, Harper threw her arms around his neck, totally submerging herself in his kiss.

She didn't attempt to fight it. There was no point to even trying. No point in pretending that this wasn't what she had been wanting all along, right from the very first moment she had met him.

She gloried in the feel of his lips against hers, the oh-so-tantalizing feel of his hands as they moved slowly along her skin, claiming her.

His touch aroused her to such heights that she could hardly breathe, growing more and more dizzy.

Within moments, they were no longer standing next to the locked door in her room. Somehow, they had moved over and were now on her bed, urgently pressed against one another, desperately absorbing the feel of their bodies as heat radiated from each of them, merging into a giant flame that was only growing in size and scope.

Each kiss just fed on the next, creating an urgent desire for more. The passion between them mounted, increasing with each passing second.

The urgency of the desire between them grew more demanding.

All she could think of was splaying her hands and running her palms along his hard chest. But his shirt was in the way, fighting her. Harper almost ripped off two of his buttons in her desire to get the barrier out of her way.

Intent on getting them undone as fast as possible, she began to tug at the placket.

"Wait," Brady urged, then quickly unbuttoned the rest of his shirt. He stripped it from his torso and tossed the shirt aside without even glancing in its direction.

All that mattered was Harper, nothing else.

The moment the shirt was gone, Harper slid her hands over his chest. It was smooth and hard beneath her fingers.

Her breathing grew shorter, faster.

She began to tug off her own blouse. His hands moved hers away, then finished what she had started.

His eyes skimmed over her, touching her everywhere.

After that, who did what to whom became a blur. All she knew was that the rest of their clothing wound up flying off and then mingling on the floor when they finally landed.

And then their activity grew even hotter and more passionate, as well as more urgent.

Harper felt as if he was worshipping her with his hands. The second Brady began touching her, she just found herself wanting more and more.

There was no end to her desire, no satiation looming on the horizon.

She just wanted *more*.

Brady hadn't expected the sweet young woman to turn into such a wildcat, although there was a part of him that secretly suspected that this was bubbling, brewing just beneath the surface.

With each kiss they shared, his desire grew more demanding. Even with all the women he had known in his life, Harper had turned out to be a revelation.

The more he familiarized himself with her, the more he wanted to.

Their bodies completely nude and heated now, Brady reveled and feasted on each tempting curve before him, feeling as if he would never be able to satisfy his hunger for her.

But he gave it his best shot.

His mouth forged a network of hot, moist kisses up and down her supple, heaving body.

To his surprise, just as he was about to culminate his sensual journey and take her, Harper suddenly flipped around and began doing the very same thing to him, causing Brady's pulse to quicken erotically. His desire grew to such incredible heights, he didn't think he could hold himself in check too much longer.

In fact, he was certain of it.

So when she feathered her fingertips along his thighs, he caught her by the wrist and then drew her hand to his lips.

Why a kiss pressed to the palm of her hand could feel so sensually erotic was beyond her— but it did. So much so that she found that she was having trouble keeping her hands off him, trouble keeping her desire from exploding and drenching both of them.

Their bodies came together like two halves of a powerful magnet. They moved urgently against one another, heating until they all but incinerated.

And still the dance continued.

His mouth urgently slanting over hers, Brady finally took her.

He entered her slowly despite the urgency he could feel burning in his body. It was all he could do to prolong the ecstasy that hovered just beyond the perimeter, waiting to seize him.

The final moment hovered, about to explode. Her breath lodged within her throat.

And then she began to move, duplicating the ever-growing rhythm she felt throbbing within her.

They went faster and faster, moving to a tune that only they could hear beating and pulsing within them, growing ever louder until it completely claimed them. Taking them to the highest peak and then, finally, propelling them over the edge.

The heated vortex was waiting to seize them, making them one.

The sensation that had been created vibrated all through Harper, holding her in its grip until it finally began to fade. It slipped further and further into the distance.

And then it became part of the air.

Harper took in a deep breath, trying to steady her pulse, her quivering body. Finally it began to settle down and she nestled against him.

"That was some 'talk,'" she murmured.

Brady laughed, his arm tightening around her. "Remind me to have those talks with you more often."

She felt her smile spreading out to every part of her, completely lighting her up. "Oh, I'll remind you," she promised.

Brady had every intention of slipping out of her room once their lovemaking was over.

Harper needed her rest and he didn't want the boys to accidentally find them together this way.

Even so, he wanted to linger.

Just a little longer, he promised himself, holding her to him. All he wanted was just a little while longer, and then he would go.

The night somehow was able to get away from him. Neither one of them seemed to actually mind.

He made it out and to his own room just before the twins woke up.

This became the recurring theme defining their nights together from then on.

They didn't plan on it; it just seemed to happen. And Brady and Harper accepted it without any need for further discussion.

Each morning that Brady woke up next to Harper, he counted himself as one of the luckiest men on the face of the earth.

The more it happened, the more he knew that he never wanted that to change.

As Dr. Neubert, the ER physician, had predicted, Toby's arm healed without any incident and before long, the hyperactive twin was back to being his former self.

Added to that, Brady had filed papers to formally adopt the twins, officially making them a family.

Life was good. Very good.

Brady and Harper continued to end their nights in each other's arms, but Harper was determined that the twins wouldn't accidentally walk in on them together, so she made certain that Brady would go back to his bedroom before the twins were up.

But then, one morning, Brady seemed to slip up. He was still lying next to a drowsy Harper when she heard a knock on her door.

Before she could scramble up and get out of bed, the twins came barging in. Harper found herself wildly grateful that she and Brady were at least wearing their pajamas.

That wasn't always the case.

Gathering herself together as best she could, she realized that Tyler was carrying in a breakfast tray, one that looked precariously close to having its contents tumble to the floor.

"What are you guys doing here?" she asked. Glancing at Brady, she caught herself thinking that he was a better actor than she'd given him credit for. He looked as if he was taking the twins' unexpected appearance in stride. "Is everything okay?" she asked the boys. She was never too complacent when it came to the twins' behavior.

"Yeah! We brought you breakfast in bed," Toby

announced, looking at Brady with a wide smile. He had just recently gotten rid of his hated cast.

"So I see," Harper said. At least they weren't asking questions about finding Brady in her bed, she thought, taking solace in that. "What's the occasion?" she wanted to know.

"No occasion," Tyler answered in a higher voice than usual—and then he started to giggle.

Brady grabbed the tray before it could wind up on the bed or the floor.

Harper focused on what was actually *on* the tray. "Are those Pop-Tarts?" she asked Tyler.

"Uh-huh. I put jelly on them," Tyler proudly told her.

"And I brought the jelly beans and put them on the plates," Toby said, not to be excluded.

She had no idea what they were up to, but nonetheless she was delighted to take part in this unique family scenario.

"Well, it all looks delicious," she told the twins, forcing a smile to her lips. "I can't wait to dig in."

"Did you guys remember to bring the dessert?" Brady asked them.

"Dessert, too?" Harper repeated, amazed. "I'll be surprised if we don't go into some sort of a sugar coma," she told Brady.

Brady didn't comment on her observation. He

was watching Tyler, the more reliable twin, run out of the room.

The boy was back in a flash carrying a small bakery box. He brought it over to Harper and placed it on her lap.

"Open it, Harper," he urged.

"Yeah, open it," Toby cried, his eyes dancing.

"I will," she promised. "After I have the Pop-Tarts and the jelly beans."

"I think they want you to open it now," Brady told her.

That was odd. She looked at him quizzically. What was going on here?

"You know what they say," Brady told her. "You never know what could happen, so eat dessert first."

Since having her eat what was inside the box seemed to mean so much to all three of them, Harper gamely said, "Okay" and then opened the box.

There was no dessert in the pastry box.

Instead, Harper stared, stunned, at the small white box that was nestled in the center. Taking it out, she opened the white box to find a velvet box inside it.

As she opened that, she saw the most beautiful diamond ring she had ever seen sparkling inside it.

She looked up at Brady surrounded by the boys, their grins huge.

"Will you marry us?" Brady and the twins cried in unison.

Tears slid down her cheeks. It took her a moment to find her voice and then reply, with wholehearted enthusiasm, "Yes, oh yes, I will marry you. All three of you!" she declared, beaming at them.

The next moment, she found herself hugged by the twins, just before their "unca" Brady kissed her, amid their enthusiastic applause, to seal the deal.

The twins applauded for a long time.

* * * * *

MILLS & BOON

Coming next month

FROM BRIDAL DESIGNER TO BRIDE
Kandy Shepherd

"I'm thinking of the questions people might ask us at the wedding."

"Where did we meet?"

"Perhaps we met in LA. At a party."

"To which, sadly, I was not invited," he said with a mock mournful expression.

"Shame. There was a party at a waterfront venue in Santa Monica. I went outside for a breath of fresh air. You were outside—"

"Taking a break from a particularly boring business dinner." He paused. "And I saw this dark haired girl leaning against a palm tree. I was struck by her beauty."

Eloise giggled. "I like that. So what happened?

"I opened a conversation with a witty remark."

"I responded with something equally witty."

"We struck up a conversation. You hung onto my every word."

"Huh! How about I made you laugh?"

"You do that in real life, so that could work. Then you said you had to get back to the party."

"No! I'm sure I would have wanted to stay with you."

"Would you?" he said.

"Yes." Her gaze connected again with his in that surprisingly intimate way.

"I got your number. And I called you straight away to check I got it right."

"So when did you call me?"

"I asked you to call me when the party was finished. You did. Then I took you back to your hotel room."

"And…?"

"We talked all night until the sun came up," he said a smile dancing around the corners of his sexy mouth. "I was a gentleman."

"And I was wishing you weren't." She slapped her hand over her mouth. "Scratch that!"

He laughed. "So I wasn't such a gentleman the next night."

"Really," she said trying to sound prim instead of turned on.

It took a real effort not to focus on imagining the exciting details of his fictional ungentlemanly behaviour and her fictional response. Since that first kiss she had spent too much time fantasying over the prospect of making love with Josh. Now he sat so near to her in the privacy of her home, it was impossible not to acknowledge that intense physical pull. "And we spent as much time as we could together before you had to go back to Boston."

"We did. In fact, we hardly left your hotel bedroom." His tone was so exaggerated in its lasciviousness it made her laugh.

"If you say so," she said.

"I wished so," he said with a grin.

She was glad she had decided not to sit next to him on the sofa. It would be only too easy to let this game get out of hand and practice for real.

Continue reading
FROM BRIDAL DESIGNER TO BRIDE
Kandy Shepherd

Available next month
www.millsandboon.co.uk

COMING SOON!

We really hope you enjoyed reading this book.
If you're looking for more romance, be sure to
head to the shops when new books are
available on

Thursday 4th March

LET'S TALK
Romance

For exclusive extracts, competitions
and special offers, find us online:

MILLS & BOON

THE HEART OF ROMANCE

A ROMANCE FOR EVERY KIND OF READER

MODERN

Prepare to be swept off your feet by sophisticated, sexy and seductive heroes, in some of the world's most glamourous and romantic locations, where power and passion collide.
8 stories per month.

HISTORICAL

Escape with historical heroes from time gone by. Whether your passion is for wicked Regency Rakes, muscled Vikings or rugged Highlanders, awaken the romance of the past.
6 stories per month.

MEDICAL

Set your pulse racing with dedicated, delectable doctors in the high-pressure world of medicine, where emotions run high and passion, comfort and love are the best medicine.
6 stories per month.

True Love

Celebrate true love with tender stories of heartfelt romance, from the rush of falling in love to the joy a new baby can bring, and a focus on the emotional heart of a relationship.
8 stories per month.

Desire

Indulge in secrets and scandal, intense drama and plenty of sizzling hot action with powerful and passionate heroes who have it all: wealth, status, good looks…everything but the right woman.
6 stories per month.

HEROES

Experience all the excitement of a gripping thriller, with an intense romance at its heart. Resourceful, true-to-life women and strong, fearless men face danger and desire - a killer combination!
8 stories per month.

DARE

Sensual love stories featuring smart, sassy heroines you'd want as a best friend, and compelling intense heroes who are worthy of them.
4 stories per month.

To see which titles are coming soon, please visit

millsandboon.co.uk/nextmonth

MILLS & BOON

HISTORICAL

Awaken the romance of the past

Escape with historical heroes from time gone by. Whether your passion is for wicked Regency Rakes, muscled Viking warriors or rugged Highlanders, indulge your fantasies and awaken the romance of the past.

MILLS & BOON
MEDICAL
Pulse-Racing Passion

Set your pulse racing with dedicated, delectable doctors in the high-pressure world of medicine, where emotions run high and passion, comfort and love are the best medicine.